THE GODS OF
DARK SWELL

THE GODS OF DARK SWELL

THE RUINED FOREST

BOOK 3

DAVID DOWELL

Library of Congress Control Number:		2019906077
ISBN:	Hardcover	978-1-7960-0294-2
	Softcover	978-1-7960-0293-5
	eBook	978-1-7960-0292-8

Print information available on the last page.

Rev. date: 10/28/2019

To order additional copies of this book, contact:
Xlibris
1-800-455-039
www.Xlibris.com.au
Orders@Xlibris.com.au
794495

CONTENTS

PROLOGUE

How Did We Get Here?

MORTINAN STARED INTENTLY into his *eye*, as the dragon sent forth a burst of liquid fire out over the burnt forest and into the trees beyond it.

Glancing around at the others as they sat looking into their own *eyes*, Mortinan came to the conclusion that none of them had seen anything strange or untoward. Their expressions gave him no indication they were watching something extraordinary.

He therefore surmised none of them had been watching what he had just witnessed.

He was certain the platinum dragon had been speaking with someone before covering more of the ancient forest with her dragon breath, but he heard no words and there was nothing and no-one else in her vicinity.

Looking back at his *eye*, Mortinan continued to watch in awe as she sat back on her haunches and spewed forth more acid fire into the distance. Trees previously untouched by her rage now erupted into flames, as the ground underneath them bubbled.

Mortinan was sure something significant had just happened.

There was passion in what she was doing.

His mind moved quickly through scenarios, but it did not take long for him to settle on one.

Mortinan was aware of nothing within the world itself that was powerful enough to prevent him seeing something occurring on the world of Dark Swell.

Only the Creator would be able to do that.

Why then would he hide a conversation with the dragon?

Mortinan had no doubt she was the destination for their next clue, and he desperately wanted to know what the Creator had said to her.

Was the dragon's reaction one of anger or celebration?

He was torn on whether he should speak with his Champion before he got to the dragon, or risk holding on to his interventions for what was to come next.

He knew it was something he did not need to decide yet, as his Champion still had not left the forest of Glorfiden. But there was no reason he couldn't continue to work his way through every conceivable scenario.

As things now stood, Mortinan believed his Champion would get there first; not counting Mendina's tag-along champion of course. She would invariably get there the same time as his.

Although she had proven herself beneficial at times, her presence and influence over his Champion still nagged at him and would continue to do so until he came up with a solution, or the world of Dark Swell did it for him.

Mortinan hoped she would be required to battle the dragon on her own. He smiled at the thought of that, as his problem would be taken care of very quickly. Mendina's Champion would not last more than a moment against a Platinum Dragon.

He knew his Champion would be devastated by her death, but it would likely make him stronger in the long run. Feelings of love and devotion were not going to help anyone win this game. He fervently believed that. His Champion needed to be hard and ruthless, in the same vein as his father Jarkene. If all went well, he would return to Glorfiden and spend more time with him. The Lord of the Elven Forest still had much to teach his son.

Yet that also depended on whether the Elven Forest still stood when Mortinan was able to return and if his father was still alive.

Mithrak and his hordes moved steadily toward it now. Their numbers made him nervous, considering how few elves now remained. Despite the power Jarkene possessed, he would not be able to hold back, let alone defeat an entire army.

Mortinan had already worked out how long it would take his Champion to reach the dragon and return to Glorfiden, if all went well.

He suspected Mithrak's army will have begun their assault well before then.

What made him feel better about his Champion's potential plight, was that the homelands of his fellow champions did not seem to be faring much better.

The Dark-Elves had finally begun their march down toward the homes of the Barbarians. If Kabir was somehow able to make it back, he may be returning to nothing but the corpses of his family and friends.

The dwarf would fare no better.

Mortinan could see how much stronger the Western Dwarves were than their Eastern cousins. They were also more organised. He believed they should be able to comfortably smash their way through both Dwarven Kingdoms.

Like Kabir, Brindel's champion would be returning to a desolate home, far different to the one he had left. It would also be less welcoming.

Mortinan next looked to Linf's home, but for only a short time.

Although the goblins did not yet face any major specific threat within their realm, Linf's welcome were she ever to head home would be no less hostile than the others.

He found it interesting to see how troublesome things were within each realm. He felt the strength of their realms would still play an important part within this game they played.

As the mighty dragon took flight over her ruined domain, Mortinan switched his view and narrowed it this time to a single champion.

The Barbarian Kabir had almost made his way into the realm of men. He had taken shelter in a farmstead with the plains woman and now a group of soldiers and wizards from Valdor's realm approached them.

Kabir had survived some serious injuries so far, but looked to have somehow came out of them still whole and with his remarkable sword still in his possession. Mortinan may have been concerned about the barbarian, if he were not so far away from the dragon. It would take him a long time to catch up even if the lands were clear, but he had to traverse the western realm, with its armies between him and the ruined forest.

On top of that, he still had no idea where the ruined forest was. Mortinan still suspected the barbarian may even try to go through Glorfiden. Kabir would be forced to use his last entry into the world to stop him from doing that, which would put him at a further disadvantage.

He did not see Kabir's Barbarian as a threat in this game. He simply had too much to overcome and he wasn't strong enough. Take his sword from him and he wasn't much better than Mendina.

Moving his attention to Linf, he knew her situation was even more hopeless than that of Kabir. Smiling at her as she furrowed her brow at whatever she was looking at through her *eye*, Mortinan believed her champion was definitely going to die, sooner rather than later.

Captured as she fled the realm of men, the goblin Linf was at this very moment on her way back to the army of Kritch, and Mortinan was almost certain what her fate would be at the hands of the Ogre-Mage.

It was going to be painful and there was going to be lots of screaming.

The dwarf was the only other Champion who looked to be any chance of making it to the dragon anytime soon and challenging Mortinan's own champion.

As he made his way back out of the swamp with his little companions, he was probably closer at present than his own Champion, however the army of Western Dwarves making their way towards him would certainly slow him down. He would need to traverse deeper into the swamp, or else hide for a time while they went past.

To move deeper would put him in extreme danger.

Brindel's champion was also moving a little slower now. Mortinan had been sure he was about to die when the swamp monsters had pierced him with their darts.

It was pure luck he had been revived in time, but there were plenty more things about that could comfortably finish the job.

Mortinan would not be surprised if he never made it out of there alive.

He was also still seriously toying with the idea of sending his Champion and Jarkene north. It was possible for him to do, and he did not believe it would affect their situation too adversely. Using one of his chances to enter in order to kill off the dwarf was probably worth the price, but he would only consider it if he knew it would result in the dwarf's certain death.

He looked across at Brindel, sitting in front of his *eye* eating a piece of fruit.

He smiled, just as Brindel looked across at him. His fellow gamer frowned at him, before smiling back and waving.

Mortinan turned back to his own *eye*.

Maybe he would do it. He had seriously had enough of his fellow gamer.

Why wait for the Dwarven army?

Perhaps it was time for his Elven Lord to kill off the dwarf once and for all!

DARK SWELL

CHAPTER 1

An Army Awaits

THE RAIN HAD stopped some time ago, but they were all still soaked through to the skin.

The sun hadn't come out since they turned back from the place where Brindel and Kagen had nearly died.

It was a miserable day and none of them were in the mood for chatter. Not even the young dwarf.

It wasn't until late in the day when they finally made their way out of the swamp.

'We need a fire,' Brindel said, breaking the long silence.

'There is still plenty of light left to us,' Granwith replied. 'We do not need to rest yet.' He frowned at the look the older dwarf gave him, before looking down at young Kagen.

The small dwarf had his hood covering his face, which currently pointed at the ground. His body shivered as he stood still. Granwith realised he was waiting to hear what they would do next before getting his body to move again.

'He needs a fire,' a voice growled into Granwith's mind.

'This is a good spot for a fire,' Granwith said pleasantly, looking around for some kindling. 'I'll get some wood.'

Brindel walked up to Kagen and put his hand on his shoulder.

'Sit here,' he said. 'You will be warm again shortly.'

The young dwarf didn't answer. He just sat down on the sodden ground with his legs crossed in front and his shoulders slumped forward.

After Granwith returned and they had a good-sized fire going, the two older dwarves stepped away so they could talk about their next move.

Brindel assumed Feng would keep watch over his young charge.

'What is it we need to discuss?' Granwith asked, before Brindel could say anything. 'I'm coming with you and I am fairly certain young Kagen won't be swayed either.'

'Exactly,' Brindel said. 'I'm sure he looks up to you. Nearly all of the young dwarves do. I often have their parents come see me and ask for armour "just like Granwith's".'

'I think he will care little for what I have to say,' Granwith said. 'Also, our home is not the safe fortress it once was.'

'It is a good deal safer than out here,' Brindel persisted, 'and a bloody lot safer than where we are headed!' He knew he was frustrated, but it was because he was so concerned about the life of his young charge. Kagen was his to take care of now, yet he was struggling to even take care of himself.

'We will keep him safe, and he has his own personal bodyguard don't forget.'

As if he could forget Feng.

'Okay then, if he is still stubborn and insists on coming, then what is the best way for us to go?' Brindel knew the answer, but he wanted to be sure Granwith didn't know of some alternative route they could take.

He didn't like how desperate he sounded.

'Obviously we will run along the edge of the swamplands,' Granwith said, a little confused. 'I already said as much. You aren't suggesting we go above the swamp? That would take a lot longer, and the lands there are full of sneaky hobgoblins, half-goblins and whatever other goblins there are in this world.'

Brindel shook his head and swore loudly.

'No, I'm not.' He didn't add anything else.

'Don't misunderstand me. I enjoy killing sneaky things,' Granwith continued, 'but there are a lot of hobgoblins and it will take some time killing them all.'

'We are not going that way,' Brindel said exasperated.

'Okay then,' Granwith said slowly. 'We should rest up here before we leave. I think night would be a better time to travel.'

A dwarf's eye sight was quite good in the dark. They lived underground and moved through parts that were often dark or even pitch black. Navigating their way through flat grounds next to the swamp would not pose a problem for any of them.

'Agreed,' Brindel finally said. 'I need to try and fix my armour anyway. The best I can without any tools to do a proper job.'

He wasn't pleased about the damage Feng had caused, but he was confident he could mend it sufficiently so it would still provide a good level of defence. The straps had been torn at the side, but he could use what was left to try and fasten it so it didn't hang loose. The main part was still whole and would protect his body from serious attack, but sections at the side would now leave him more vulnerable.

Cursing under his breath, Brindel trudged back over to the fire and removed his armour. He might be lucky enough to get a little sleep before they moved off again.

Brindel was tired, but he found sleeping difficult. A couple of hours were all he got before he finally rose and woke the others.

'*He needs more sleep,*' a voice said within his mind. '*He is weakened from nearly dying, as are you dwarf.*'

'I know,' Brindel said, 'but it is better if we travel through the night. There may be elves in the trees during the day.'

'*What are elves?*' Feng asked. '*I have heard some dwarves talk about the ones in the forest. Are you scared of them?*'

'No, I'm not scared of them!' Brindel said, affronted by the mere thought of it. 'But we travel near their forest and there are some that are powerful enough to be particularly bothersome.'

'*Sounds like you are afraid. Just let him rest.*'

'Okay,' Brindel conceded. 'He can sleep some more, but I'm leaving.'

He heard a growl, but Feng didn't appear and Kagen's friend made no move to try and stop the dwarven smith from walking away.

Both Granwith and Kagen soon caught up with him.

Neither of them said anything, they just fell into step.

The moon wasn't visible through the clouds, but it gave enough luminescence for them to easily navigate their way along the flat grounds next to the swamp. The grass wasn't lush here, but it was considerably better to walk upon than the wet bog.

At times the swamp's border was only a few stone throws from the edge of the forest to their left. None of them spoke aloud as their pace quickened a little, until they were further away again.

Brindel told himself he was wary, and not afraid of what might be moving within the trees. He knew his own armour was a match for most elves, but Kagen's had a few weaknesses, and he didn't rate Granwith's as highly as his own when it came to defensive prowess.

Yet he needn't have worried.

By the time the first glow of a new sun began to show itself, they had travelled quite a distance and without challenge of any sort.

'We should rest within the swamp,' Brindel suggested, coming to a stop.

'I think we are far enough from the trees,' Granwith replied. 'I would rather not spend any more time within that cesspool.'

'Feng agrees with Granwith,' Kagen added. Brindel looked across at him and could see the young dwarf was still quite fatigued. His eyes were sunken and downcast and his walking had slowed throughout the night.

'We are close enough to be easily seen,' Brindel persisted.

'I will scout the swamp when it is light, in case we need to flee inside,' Granwith said.

Brindel thought about it for a time before nodding in agreeance.

As he nodded, Kagen dropped to the ground in exhaustion.

'I'm hungry,' he said, looking up at Brindel.

'Then let's eat,' he said, patting Kagen on the shoulder and sitting down next to him.

Reaching into his carry sack, he pulled out a few morsels and shared them around. Unfortunately, he hadn't packed for three dwarves, so there wasn't a lot to be had.

'I'm sorry there isn't much food,' Brindel said.

'That's okay,' Kagen said. 'Feng has gone into the forest to see what he could find for us.'

'He did what!' Brindel exclaimed, jumping to his feet. 'Has he gone already? Can you call him back?'

'Don't worry,' Kagen said, 'nothing will be able to see him in there.'

'I must side with Brindel on this one,' Granwith said, as he walked back out from the tangled trees of the swamp. 'I don't know a lot about the forest of the elves, but I do know how strong they are in magic Kagen. There are ways to see things without using your eyes.'

Kagen looked worried now.

'He has gone in already. I can't speak to him. He is too far away.' The young dwarf stood up. 'We should go and get him.'

Brindel again placed his hand on the shoulder of the young dwarf.

'Steady on Kagen. We don't know where to look or how far in he has gone.' He paused and looked away. He didn't want to look him in the eyes. 'Like you said, they won't be able to see him anyway.'

'Granwith said they can see him!' Kagen exclaimed, brushing aside Brindel's hand and pulling his axe from his belt. 'He would come and look for us.'

Brindel wanted to tell him that none of them would have been stupid enough to enter the elves' forest, but he didn't. It probably wouldn't help the situation.

'None of us are stepping foot inside those trees!' Brindel said in a voice that meant business. He may as well have been talking to himself.

'I'm going,' Kagen said, as he began walking off.

Swearing under his breath, Brindel quickly caught up to him and grabbed Kagen by the arm. He made sure it was the same arm he held his axe with. He wasn't entirely sure the little hot-head wouldn't swing it at him.

'Let go,' Kagen said, trying to brush his arm off. 'I am going to get my friend.'

'Stop,' Brindel said, pulling him around to face him. 'You are not going into the forest, and I will tell you why.'

Kagen didn't answer. He just continued to stare daggers at him.

'If we go in and there is an elf anywhere nearby, then we are all of us dead. The trees themselves might even do it!' He saw the look of surprise on Kagen's face.

'That's right,' Brindel continued. 'For all we know the trees might come alive and rip us all to shreds. I have heard stories.'

'I haven't heard those ones,' Kagen said, suspicion creeping into his voice. 'Did you just make that up?'

'I don't lie!' Brindel said. There was no pretence in the anger he felt at being accused of that. 'I have heard lots of things about that forest. I have killed several elves on neutral ground, but I have never heard of a dwarf killing one inside there.' He pointed at the forest to stress his point.

'However,' he continued. 'I am not so sure the elves will be as outraged by Feng walking in there. He is not a dwarf, so they may just let it go.'

Kagen stopped and looked to be thinking again.

'But he said he was going to kill some creatures for us to eat. Do you think the elves will be okay with that?' His question wasn't rhetorical. He wanted an answer.

'I don't know if they will,' Granwith said, joining in on the conversation. 'I can tell you this though. If there are elves some distance away, then they probably won't bother themselves going too far just to find one stray...' he paused. 'What exactly is Feng?'

Kagen looked at him blankly.

'You're right, it doesn't matter,' Granwith said. 'However, if they sense three dwarves walk into their forest, I can assure you they would cross the entire length of their forest to find us!'

Kagen's whole face fell, as he turned to look searchingly at the forest and then back at the two dwarves.

'Okay,' was all he said, as he trudged back to where they had been sitting.

Brindel looked to Granwith and gave him a small nod of thanks, before going to sit back down next to Kagen.

CHAPTER 2

Good-Bye Father

THE FIRST PART of their journey was made in silence.

Jarkene led, with Mort and Mendina following a short distance behind.

Their fairie-dragons flew amongst the trees in no particular order or pattern, but they stayed close.

'Who do you think we will meet in the ruined forest?' Mort asked Mendina eventually. He was just making small talk now. They had spoken about it before and obviously had no idea what they would be walking into.

'You are both walking to your deaths,' Jarkene said in answer to his son's question to Mendina.

Neither of them noticed he had stopped and turned to face them.

Mortinan was taken aback to begin with, but quickly straightened his back.

'We are stronger than you think,' Mortinan said. 'We might surprise you.'

Jarkene's expression didn't alter.

'I don't know exactly what it is that dwells within the forest you seek Mortinan, but it is not somewhere I ever chose to go during all my time in exile. I heard stories told about what might be there. None of them give me any hope that either of you will leave there once you have entered'

Mortinan couldn't believe what he was hearing.

'Why are you telling us this now?' Mortinan asked.

'Because neither of you wanted to listen to me before. I already told you it is far too dangerous and foolish to try.' Jarkene's voice softened a little as he spoke now. Mort thought it strange hearing his father speak like that.

'We have our faerie-dragons and I will have your rod,' Mort persisted. 'We will not be defeated easily.'

'The rod will certainly help if you are able to use it,' Jarkene conceded. 'The fairie-dragons are another matter.'

Mortinan waited for him to continue.

He felt Mendina's arm on his. 'I don't think they will be able to accompany us,' she said to him. Mort turned to look at her. He knew his face would be one of confusion.

'Mendina is correct Mortinan,' Jarkene said. 'They are magic-born of Glorfiden. They will not want to leave, even if they were able to.'

Mortinan didn't try to hide his disappointment, letting out a long sigh.

'We will still prevail,' Mendina said, squeezing his arm tightly. It was all Mort needed to hear.

'Of course we will,' he replied, looking down at her and smiling.

Mort looked forward again as his father shook his head.

'You are both of you children,' Jarkene said, but once again without the air of arrogance or degradation in his voice. 'There is so much more for you to learn Mortinan. You have been shown but the tip of the mountain. There are spells that you can presently only imagine being able to perform. Spells that I will teach to you.' He stared at his son for a time, before looking to Mendina. 'I also have much I could learn from you Mendina. Entine was the finest in Glorfiden at working with the trees and all of the remarkable creatures that call it their home.' Mort thought he actually looked abashed as he continued to speak. 'I know that I am responsible for the death of much that you held dear in your heart, but I will do all I can to restore that which is gone. But I will need your help.'

Mort looked at Mendina. Her face remained expressionless as his father spoke. His words appeared to have no impact upon her.

The effect they had on Mort was somewhat different. He had fantasised about hearing those words so many times since Jarkene had left their home all those years ago.

It had always made him sad when his thoughts drifted to it.

Growing up, his favourite pastime was pretending he was a mighty Elven magician and warrior, playing around his home with long pieces of wood, striking down imagined enemies with both magic and sword.

'Glorfiden will need you both if it is to survive what is circling its borders. We have powerful enemies Mortinan, intent on destroying both our home and those few elves who remain.' He spoke now with a fervour Mort had not heard from him since they had been re-united. He was lost in what his father was saying and was at this moment seriously doubting what he and Mendina were setting out to do. What was it they were actually hoping to achieve?

'Perhaps we should wait until the forest is safe again?' he said, looking down at Mendina.

'What we do is important Jarkene,' Mendina said, not looking at Mort. Her eyes looked straight at his father. Mort could see she was still not so easily swayed.

'You don't know what it is you do,' Jarkene said. 'The female who shares your name Mendina, neither of you have seen before. How could you possibly know what her intentions are?' Jarkene spoke with the tone of an Elven Lord again, as he addressed Mendina.

'We are leaving,' she said, still staring straight into the eyes of her Lord.

Mort slowly nodded his head as he turned back to his father.

'We need to do this,' Mort said, although he no longer sounded convinced, even to his own ears.

'Then I will have to mourn you again,' Jarkene said, before turning.

Mendina and Mort looked at each other. Neither of them spoke, but Mort could see that she was as determined as ever to leave.

He nodded his head, before they both began trailing after his father once more.

The three of them moved briskly throughout the rest of the morning, eventually coming to a place in the forest that looked like many other spots they had walked through. There were trees reaching high into the sky above them, with thick foliage growing around their trunks. There was no path here, as there were no paths anywhere else within the elven forest. It was eerily beautiful, as sporadic rays of sunlight penetrated through the branches to the foliage under their feet. It gave enough light, but not enough where you would think it was nearing the middle of the day.

Jarkene stopped and turned to face them once more.

'We have arrived at the outskirts of Glorfiden,' he said.

Mortinan looked towards the way they were travelling, yet couldn't see what lay beyond the trees in front of him. It looked to him like there was only more forest.

'Does the forest lead into another forest here?' Mortinan asked, squinting in his efforts to see through the foliage in front of them.

'No,' Jarkene said. 'The forest is thick where it borders the Western Realm. Prying eyes do not see inside when they come upon Glorfiden.'

Mortinan nodded. The forest never failed to impress him. He would love nothing more than to have the time to explore it all.

'The time has come for farewell,' Jarkene said. His voice didn't betray whether he felt any emotions at seeing his son leave.

Mortinan wasn't sure how he felt about leaving his father.

He was genuinely sad to be leaving the forest though, after finally being welcomed within it. Such an occurrence he had only ever been able to imagine.

He had also met and fallen in love with an elven girl, who in turn felt something akin for him.

These were the happiest days of his life, as it suddenly struck a chord deep within him at what a stupid thing it was they were doing.

In a panic, he also realised it was too late to back out. He wouldn't show that kind of weakness to Mendina. Unlike his father, she actually believed in him. Jarkene had simply told him they were walking to their deaths.

Mortinan stood and watched as Jarkene removed a small rod from inside his jacket. He couldn't take his eyes from it as Jarkene hesitantly held it out to him. As he took the rod in his hand, he could see clouds swirling along it and a breeze coming from its end.

'However you may be tempted to use it,' Jarkene said to him, 'I would advise you wait until you are facing that which awaits you in the ruined forest.' He paused, as Mortinan finally drew his gaze away from the rod and looked at his father. 'I fear even the rod may not be enough to save you both. I would want it at full potency for you to have any chance of defeating it.'

Mort said nothing in response, he just nodded his head.

'The staff is for getting you there,' Jarkene continued, as he handed that to his son also. 'I have filled it for you already. It should suffice.'

'Thank you,' Mort managed to say this time.

'Take care of her,' Jarkene said, indicating Mendina with a jerk of his head. 'There are too few elves remaining.'

Mortinan looked to Mendina, expecting her to say something in response to that, but she just looked at Mort and smiled.

'With my life,' was all he said, as he smiled back at her.

'Follow me,' Jarkene said, and walked a short distance ahead of them.

Mortinan soon joined him, Mendina by his side.

'The way is clear,' Jarkene said.

Mortinan was shocked to see the Western Realm spread out before him.

They stood next to the bough of a large elm tree. Before he had stepped up next to it, Mort could only see more trees in front of him. He guessed there was a glamour cast to hide what was within, not just thick foliage.

Before them now was a plain consisting of short tufts of grass and patches of dirt that stretched out on flat ground. In the distance to the south were a number of small hills and small mountains, but nothing in the direction Jarkene indicated.

Mortinan turned around and looked up into the branches of the elm tree. All of their fairie-dragons were perched within it.

None of them came down to say good-bye. There was no need. The bond between them was strong.

Taking Mendina by the hand, they stepped out into the land beyond Glorfiden.

Mortinan heard a flutter of wings and watched in fascination as *Iska* flew from the trees of Glorfiden and perched on his shoulder.

He looked across at the incredulous look on Mendina's face, before turning to look at his father.

Jarkene had not yet turned to leave and his expression was also one of surprise. Not as animated as Mendina, Jarkene's eyebrows simply rose; before his face took on the look of one deep in thought.

He looked at Mort for a short time, before turning and stepping back into the forest. He disappeared from sight almost immediately.

'How is that possible after what Jarkene said?' Mendina said to him, her eyes scouring the edge of the forest for *Ebo*.

'I have no idea,' Mort said. 'Perhaps it has something to do with how two of them were able to choose me?'

Mendina finally looked away from the forest and back at *Iska*.

'Whatever the reason, we are fortunate to have him,' Mendina said as she gave Mortinan's fairie-dragon a big smile.

All Mort's thoughts and fears suddenly faded as his fairie-dragon began speaking with him, inside his mind.

'I said that we are fortunate to have him,' Mendina said, as she punched Mort in the arm.

'Indeed, we are,' Mortinan said, a big smile on his face as he rubbed his arm and looked at Mendina. He now knew why *Iska* was able to travel with them, and it delighted him. It also explained how he had been able to help Mort when those abominations attacked he and Palir in Glorfiden.

'What happened?' Mendina asked, obviously puzzled as to why Mort was suddenly so happy after ignoring her for a time.

'I know why *Iska* is able to travel with us,' he said.

'How do you know that?' Mendina asked. 'Did he tell you?

'Yes,' he said in answer, as he looked again at his small companion. 'Yes, he did.'

Mendina waited for him to tell her, but he continued to stand there looking at his fairie-dragon with a stupid look on his face.

'Are you going to tell me?' Mendina asked pleasantly.

Mort looked over at her and blushed.

'*Iska* is unlike any of the others. This is why I am able to have two, although I still don't understand why he picked me.'

He looked back at his fairie-dragon as he continued.

'He does not draw any of his power from Glorfiden, therefore he is not bound to the forest.'

'How is that possible?' Mendina asked, obviously confused. 'All of the fairie-dragon are magic-born.'

'Not *Iska*,' Mort said. 'He is so much more than that.'

'Will you just tell me,' Mendina said, less pleasantly. She had run out of patience.

'All the others augment the greatest strength of the elf,' Mort said, 'as you have already explained to me,' he said quickly, holding up his hands to stop her next comment. 'When I was in the forest with Palir and we were attacked, *Iska* was able to...'

'You were attacked?!' Mendina exclaimed. 'When? By what?'

'By orcs and a mage,' Mort said, 'but thanks to *Iska* I was able to defeat the ones that came at me when Palir wasn't there.'

It was Mendina who held her hand up this time.

'Orcs and Mage entered the forest and attacked, and Palir left you alone?'

Mort nodded.

Mendina continued to stare at him and looked about to ask more, when she instead just shook her head.

'Go on,' was all she said instead.

'It was when they were about to break through my shield of air that *Iska* landed on my shoulder and showed me how to use the sun to send beams of light through each one. It burned them all right through, and it was magnificent,' he finished, happy to be able to tell Mendina about it finally. He didn't say anything before, as it had not made a lot of sense to him.

'What exactly are you saying?' Mendina asked, once the initial look of shock seemed to wear off. 'You killed them with beams of light?'

'They were a lot more intense than that,' Mort said. 'They tore through them like a paddle through water, but easier than that.'

'How did you do it?' Mendina asked.

'That is what I am telling you Mendina,' Mort said excitedly. '*Iska* knows spells. He doesn't increase my strength through his link to the magic of Glorfiden. He is able to show me what spells I can cast, even if I have never done them before.'

Mendina didn't answer Mort straight away.

She waited for his words to sink in, so she could think about what he was telling her.

'He can tell you how to cast spells?' she finally asked, in lieu of coming up with a better question.

Mort just nodded again and continued to smile.

'What other spells?' she asked. 'How many other spells?' This could change everything, Mendina thought, as her own excitement began to build.

'I don't know,' Mort said, no less excited. 'All that was conveyed to me is that he knows a great many spells and can tell me how to do one when the time is right.'

'Wow,' Mendina said, staring at *Iska* again. Then a thought occurred to her.

'Why can't he teach you the spells now, so you are prepared when the time comes?' It seemed to make more sense that way.

Mort shrugged. 'That is just how he does it I guess.'

Mendina nodded back at him, seemingly satisfied with his answer for a change.

'And yet *Ebo* has shown me nothing,' she said, thinking about her own fairie-dragon and comparing her with the amazing creature perched on Mort's shoulder.

'Nothing at all?' Mort asked, obviously surprised to hear that.

'Nothing at all,' she echoed. 'But we shouldn't dwell on it,' Mendina said. 'She's not here with us anyway.'

'Okay,' Mort said, looking at her in a strange way. She wasn't sure what he was thinking. 'Should we go?' he asked.

Mendina took a deep breath and looked out into Western Realm. Unlike their first journey out of Glorfiden, this time the fear wasn't as palpable within her. She was certainly afraid of what lay before them, but this time she had more confidence in their ability to defeat whatever horrors lay before them.

Mortinan was certainly stronger now, and somewhat more confident. He was still absent-minded and foolish, but they now had a rod of immeasurable power and a fairie-dragon unlike any she had ever heard told of before.

Her relationship with Mort had also grown in a way that still surprised her. She knew without question how he felt about her, which she had found comforting. Yet now her own feelings towards him had grown to the point where she did not like being away from him.

He was immature, did stupid things and said stupid things, but she wouldn't have him any other way. He had surprised her in many ways the night she had taken him into her bed, none more so by how she felt afterwards.

She was able to genuinely return the feelings he had for her now, which both delighted and frightened her.

Taking his hand in her own, she nodded at him and smiled.

'Yes Mort, we should go now.'

'Off to the Ruined Forest,' he said, squeezing her hand tightly. 'To face and defeat whatever lays in wait for us there.'

CHAPTER 3

An Honoured Guest

THEY HAD BEEN walking for hours when Linf finally decided it was enough. Stopping in protest, she tried putting her hands on her hips and was about to say something, when she felt a sharp pain to the back of her legs. Turning to face the one who had whipped her, she was struck again. Howling in pain, she glared at him from under her hood, before turning and trudging forward once more. Biting back the words she wanted to say, the goblin reached down and tried to rub her legs as she walked. The cords wrapping her arms to her body made it a difficult endeavour.

Linf begrudgingly realised it still wasn't time for her to make her stand. Especially when she couldn't see the ones she was planning to kill.

Their time would come, she thought, as she tried not to think of the pain in her legs and the grumbling in her stomach.

She had been ready to collapse in exhaustion for the past hour at least, before they finally decided to stop and let her rest.

Without any grace, she crumpled on to the ground and curled her knees up into her chest.

The hood was pulled roughly from her head and her restraints removed from her arms, leaving only the ones on her wrists. Some stale bread and plants were thrown on to the ground in front of her.

Linf reached over and grabbed the bread and stuffed it into her mouth. She tried to chew it, but had no saliva in her mouth. She took it out and put a small piece back in, trying unsuccessfully to chew even that much. When a small bucket was placed on the ground next to her, she took the small piece of bread from her mouth and stuck her face in the bucket.

She drank as much water as she could, before trying more successfully to chew and swallow the bread this time.

Picking up the plants, she looked at them.

'What is this crap?' she asked out loud.

'They are roots from the ground,' Gort said in an urgent whisper. 'You should just eat them and try not to get their attention with stupid questions.'

Linf turned to her right and looked behind her a short distance at the orc who had just spoken.

'I see you are brave again now that you think I won't kill you,' Linf snarled at him. 'What are roots?'

'They are from the ground,' Gort said.

'They are not food!' Linf said in disgust, throwing her roots at Gort.

The orc just shrugged and picked up her discarded plants.

Linf drank some more from the bucket, before lying down on her side and closing her eyes for a moment.

Opening her eyes again, she looked over at where a couple of her captors stood conversing. Neither of them had any emotions coming from them. She was sorely disappointed and wondered for a moment if she should try and anger one of them. Her focus was drawn to the one carrying a whip in his left hand. His features she burnt into her memory. That one would die slowly.

He was taller, broader and had an angry look on his face, yet no anger spilled from him. It must be just how he looked, Linf thought. They were certainly an ugly breed, whatever they were.

Not orcs like Gort. Although still large and muscular, orcs did not have the same presence these ones had. It was probably the lack of fear, and possibly because Linf and Gort were their prisoners. Their skin was darker than Gort's and their eyes a dull yellow. Linf admitted to herself they looked intimidating enough. She definitely wasn't afraid of them though. Nothing much scared her now that she was powerful.

Despite this, and going against every instinct within her, Linf knew she needed to be patient. She had grown smarter as she grew stronger and she realised now was not the time to do something stupid. There were too many of them and they were too much like the humans who had helped capture her when she was with Brax.

'Where are they taking us?' Linf asked, looking back at Gort again.

'I would think we are going back to the main army,' he said. She could hear the underlying fear in his voice, although he tried to hide it.

It would be much easier to sneak away when there were a lot more around. An army was just what she needed. There would be plenty of fear and anger within a group so large.

Pleased at the thought of arriving there, the goblin closed her eyes and tried to sleep.

Linf was awoken by a kick in the back. Straightening up, she quickly sat up, as the hood was once more placed roughly over her head.

Swearing inwardly, she was dragged to her feet and pushed in the back to get her moving again. She had planned on draining Gort before they left so her journey would be easier. Linf knew she could do it without seeing, but she didn't want to risk draining him too much. That might raise questions she did not want to answer.

Frightfully hungry, she concentrated instead on simply putting one foot in front of the other. She would be able to feed on his emotions the next time they stopped.

The going was not overly arduous for her this time. For the most part, the ground was level and not too rocky, but she still stumbled regularly and felt the sting of the whip every time she lost her footing completely and fell. Thankfully she now had her arms free, so she was able to stop her face hitting the ground when she did.

A couple of times they needed to negotiate shallow streams. Her captors must have thought it amusing to watch her fall headfirst into the water, as their pushes seemed to be a bit harder than usual as she crossed. Linf now had wet clothes to add to her discomfort.

Added to that, her frustration and anger built each time she was struck.

No matter how hard she tried to temper it, she was still a goblin and getting angry was a part of who she was.

By the time they stopped again and the hood was wrenched from her head, Linf was almost ready to explode. Almost.

Somehow, she was able to calm herself and sit on the ground; a little more gracefully this time; and wait for her food and water to be given to her. Her remarkable power of will surprised her, but it was pleasing. She wasn't ready to die yet.

Looking around at her surroundings, she noticed straight away they had changed.

No longer out in the open, they sat in a deep valley surrounded by trees. That meant the next part would be all uphill.

She saw Gort sitting on the ground not far from where she was. He looked tired and miserable. There was even more fear surrounding him now than the last time they stopped. She assumed it was because they were closer to their destination and he probably recognised where they were.

As she looked at the pathetic orc, Linf knew if she were to drain him too long or too deeply, he probably wouldn't survive another forced march.

Shrugging her shoulders, Linf began to draw small amounts from him. At least she wouldn't be suspected of causing his death.

She started to feel better the moment his fear was absorbed into her, but she still didn't want to drain him too quickly, else that drew suspicion to her. It was a constant effort to remind herself that keeping her secret would be crucial if she hoped to survive when they arrived.

Picking up the bread; while she waited to drain him some more; Linf dipped it directly into the bucket this time before putting it into her mouth.

Once she had finished eating her morsel of food, she drank deeply of the water. Looking across at Gort, she continued with her draining of him.

She allowed herself a small smile as Gort sunk on to the ground the moment he finished eating.

Linf could have drained more, but the renewed energy coursing through her would be enough to sustain her for the next part of the journey.

She was now able to take the time to have a good look around her.

Her guards stood away from her and Gort. A couple of them were speaking quietly together, while the others all stood silently. Some of them ate, while a couple of them just stared at her.

It was late in the afternoon and the valley they were in was filled with lush, green grass under foot. There were a few trees spread throughout, with thick lines of them at the top of the rise all around. No other creatures stirred.

She slid forward a little and kicked Gort in the midsection. He grunted and weakly reached out a hand to swipe her foot away.

'How much further?' she asked him.

He opened his eyes and looked at her, before closing them again.

Linf kicked him again, a little harder this time.

'I will keep kicking until you answer me,' she said. She resented his weakness, regardless of the reason why he was feeling that way.

'How should I know?' he replied. 'Leave me alone.'

She tried to kick him again, but he caught her foot with his hand. Without pause, she launched her other foot into his lower stomach. He groaned and let go of her foot.

'Because you come from these lands idiot.' Linf said, pulling her foot back for another kick.

'I know you did this to me goblin,' he said. She could hear the anger in his weakened voice. 'If you kick me one more time, I will tell them about your little trick.'

Linf obviously didn't want that, but she wouldn't be threatened by this weakling.

'You won't be able to say much if I drain you completely,' she threatened. 'They know you are weak and cowardly, so they will just think you gave up and died.'

The orc looked to think on that for a moment.

'If the army continued marching at the same pace, we should meet up with them in the morning. Now stop kicking me!'

Linf stared at him for a bit longer, before lying down on the soft grass to rest. She stared at the sky for a time, not thinking about much, until she finally drifted off.

Once more she failed to hear the guard approach. Pulled roughly to her feet, she had time to see that the sun hadn't progressed far across the sky, before the hood was shoved down over her head.

Setting off at a steady walk, she felt far more energised this time. The next stage of their walk shouldn't be too arduous.

Linf was wrong about that.

It felt like they had marched throughout the night by the time one of the guards pushed her in the chest, signalling for her to stop.

The energy she had usurped from Gort had left her much earlier in the walk than she had foreseen, and she had begun stumbling again for the last part of their walk. Linf doubted the orc would have lasted. It wouldn't surprise her if he were no longer there when they finally took the mask off her.

She was left to stand for a time with the mask left on however, and she began to wonder what was going on.

Eventually she was shoved roughly in the back again, which set her legs moving of their own volition. Her mind had had enough.

How much further? she thought to herself, as her legs continued to involuntarily move her forward.

As they began to walk up a steep slope, she almost gave in.

Her legs ached and her feet were blistered. Not knowing how far they had to go made it even more difficult, yet she persisted. Somewhere deep inside, the goblin runt found the fortitude to continue. She wasn't ready to die just yet.

A couple of times she fell forward, her hands again stopping her face from hitting the hard ground. Each time it happened, she was roughly jerked to her feet and sent on her way with a hard shove, until finally the ground levelled out and they came to a stop again.

This time they removed the hood and she was able to look around.

Below was a wonderland of lights spread out before her. There must have been more lights than there were goblins within her settlement. Which was a lot.

There was still no sign of the sun, which surprised her, as Linf had been sure they had walked all night.

'Sit,' one of her guards said to her, as he pushed down on her shoulder. She didn't resist him, slumping to the ground. She was still able to see all of the lights even in her seated position.

'I see you somehow made it,' she said softly to the one sitting beside her.

Gort didn't even lift his head to look at her.

'Shall I put you out of your misery?' Linf asked, only half serious.

He managed a grunt in reply this time, but still didn't lift his head.

One of the guards walked over and threw them both a small bone with meat on it. Linf couldn't help but chuckle as Gort managed to catch it. He still had some life left in him yet and was a lot stronger than he looked; considering the amount of energy she had stolen before setting off on last march. Linf was a little bit impressed.

She caught her own bone also, but decided to ask a question before she ate it.

'Why the gift?'

The guard stopped as he turned away and looked back at her.

'Probably your last meal, so our leader thought it fitting. It's also a reward for making it here without dying. It will be entertaining watching what our King decides your fate to be. We don't want you to die too quickly.' He looked like he smiled before turning around this time.

Gort had already begun crunching his bone by the time she began tearing the flesh from hers. There was not a lot of meat on it, but it was better than bread.

'The King?' she asked Gort, when they had both finished eating.

'King Kritch,' Gort said. 'It is his army that sleeps down there.'

The fear was coming off him in waves now. It was hard for Linf to resist draining it all, but she decided to wait until she was amongst the army now. There would be so much fear and anger down there it almost made her giddy thinking about it. She didn't want the loud-mouthed orc ruining that for her. She was still bitter at missing out on the human child that had been promised to her. She was not going to miss out on the feast below.

Linf was woken once more by a kick to her ribs.

Groaning in pain, she opened her eyes and sat up. Her captors didn't bother putting the hood on this time.

'Time to move,' was all her guard said, before walking off to the others.

Standing up, she stretched. Looking out over the valley, Linf was stunned at the immense hive of activity happening below. She stood there a moment to try and take it in, before a hand in her back got her moving.

It didn't take them long to walk down the gentle slope. Although there was no track, it was flat and this time she could see where she was going.

Linf knew she was wide-eyed as they reached the first of those that made up one half of the army of the Western Realm.

The first sensation that struck her was how noisy it was.

Voices yelled at one another as creatures argued and laughed, while others practiced with their weapons. A couple of orcs looked to be doing more than practicing, as they swung their heavy swords at something large that Linf had never seen before. It was ugly and mean-looking, but it was slow, and was struggling to hit its two antagonists.

Yet as soon as they saw the ones escorting her and Gort, their efforts stopped and they stepped back from each other. Many of those who were talking loudly also went silent as they walked past.

Some of them looked at Gort and spat, while others stared at her with snarls on their faces.

Linf returned those looks with a smile, as she drained the myriad of anger and fear from them, increasing her strength to the point where she thought she might explode. At times, she couldn't even be sure what creature she was absorbing. There was just too much of it.

Eventually she gave up on draining them.

Partly because she had enough within her, and part due to the fact those she now passed had less anger about them and very little fear. They were also more organised than the ones she had walked past earlier.

A lot of these ones looked like men, but not the same as those in the towns she had been in.

They looked different, both in their appearance and in the way they held themselves.

Their armour was dark, but clean, and their swords shone in the early morning light. None of them paid her and Gort any attention and they certainly didn't yell or spit at them. Linf was glad she had filled up before coming through here.

Before long they were finished walking past all of the men, as they made their way into a large clearing.

She looked ahead and saw a tent standing by itself in the middle of the space. Linf estimated it would be big enough to comfortably house fifty goblins.

Behind the tent was more space for as far as she could see, other than a number of stationary shadows. Around the tent itself were more guards similar in size and looks to the ones who had captured her.

They walked to within about twenty paces of the entrance to the tent, when a hand grabbed Linf by the shoulder and pushed down with enough force to bring her to her knees.

She didn't struggle against it, but she kept her head up, looking to see what would come from the tent.

She didn't have to wait long, as the front flap was pulled aside and a large figure strode out.

It wasn't man or orc, but had similarities to both. Much taller than a man and taller than her own goblin race, it was also broad at the shoulders. The face was horribly ugly, with teeth that protruded all along the top and bottom. It almost looked as if the teeth were on the outside of his mouth. It had dark armour similar to the others she had just walked past, except this one had red streaks throughout his. Probably because he was the King, she thought. She remembered that Greeble liked to look different to the other goblins as well. Linf had thought he was just showing off, and it looked like this leader was doing the same.

He stopped about ten paces in front of them and signalled to the guards surrounding them.

'What have you brought me?' he asked. Linf was pleased her amulet worked for him too. She needed to know what he said.

'A deserter,' his guard said. Linf knew it was male now, going by the tone of its voice. She hadn't been sure by looking at him. 'And a goblin from the other side of the land. The deserter says it is an emissary.'

'An emissary? That is vaguely interesting. Let us take care of the deserter first, then get back to the goblin.' He looked down at Gort. 'I have a particularly creative death in mind for you.'

Linf looked across at Gort and saw the blood drain from his face. She was curious to see what this creative death was.

Gort looked down at the ground in front of himself, before lifting his head again. 'I am no deserter my King.' Linf was impressed by his lack of fear all of a sudden. Perhaps he had none left.

'That is what every deserter says,' King Kritch said. 'Stand him up,' he said, turning to one of his guards.

Gort was lifted to his feet.

'I brought you the goblin,' Gort said. His voice was remarkably calm. 'The others have gone to get the rest of the goblins to attack Dayhen from the other side. We are scouts, not deserters.'

'Bring it,' Kritch said.

Linf could see the fear had returned now to Gort. His efforts to talk his way out did not look to be working.

A guard walked into the tent, before shortly stepping back out again. He held a small box in his hands, which he handed to his King.

Kritch walked closer to his prisoners.

'The thing inside this box is like nothing you have seen before.' Kritch sounded excited. 'It will give you a death more painful than anything you can imagine deserter.' He leaned in close to the orc. 'You can't even scream,' he said quietly. Only Linf and a couple of guards would have heard the last bit.

Gort's fear had definitely returned in full.

'Tie him down,' Kritch said.

His guards put Gort on the ground, before tying his legs together and then strapping his arms to his body. The orc struggled at first, but was easily overpowered.

Leaning down, Kritch opened the box and tipped something out at Gort's feet. Linf had certainly never seen its like; which was nothing new to her this day. Whatever this thing was, it didn't look too terrifying. Linf assumed it must have some excruciatingly painful poison when it bites.

It looked like a giant ant crossed with a spider, but kind of like a small man as well. Linf was intrigued.

'This will take several minutes,' Kritch said, talking to those within the clearing. 'I will describe what is happening as we go.'

Ling was fascinated by the whole show.

She thought it was a wonderful gesture; that a King would take the time to entertain his men when they were in the middle of going off to fight a war somewhere. She was beginning to kind of like Kritch.

Linf hadn't taken her eyes off the insect, and she watched now as it began to chew at Gort's foot. It took small bites only and the goblin wondered if this was all that would happen.

She looked up at Gort's face as the little creature began to bite him. His eyes immediately glazed over, as his mouth opened. He looked to be screaming, but no sound came out of his mouth.

Gort's body released more colours at once than Linf had ever seen an individual produce. Every pore in his body must have released some, and Linf couldn't help drawing some of it towards her. But before she could absorb it, the colours were suddenly sucked back into the orc's body.

She was physically shocked by it. It had tugged at her, as if whatever was drawing the colours back in, were trying to clasp her own and draw them in too.

'This amazing creature; which I have called a *Crelch*, inflicts immense pain as it slowly eats its victim. It grows as it feeds, eating the entire victim in one go.' Linf nodded slowly as he spoke, taking in every word.

'But what is really clever, is that it lets the pain increase to a point where the body of its victim would normally shutdown because the pain is so much.' He sounded excited as he spoke. 'Yet the *crelch* is able to somehow reverse the pain; to quickly shut it off and start it all over again.' Kritch looked around at his audience now. 'To top that off, it uses some kind of electricity, which stops the wound bleeding as it goes, so the one it is feeding on doesn't bleed out.'

'The pain is at maximum nearly the whole time?' Linf had to ask. It was a remarkable creature and she wanted to know more. She wanted to take one with her when she left. This *crelch* would ensure that nothing and no-one was ever immune to her powers. She was sure she could work out a way to stop it drawing all of the colours back in again. That might be a problem otherwise.

The *crelch* had eaten Gort's whole foot by the time she spoke, and it had grown half as big already, when her face was pushed down and into the ground.

'You don't speak to the King,' a soft voice spoke into her ear.

Linf grunted in response.

When her head was finally lifted off the ground, Gort was no longer there.

Instead, the *crelch* had grown to be half as big as the orc had been.

Two of the guards carefully carried the King's pet back into his tent.

'I have another one of those if any of your answers don't please me,' Kritch said.

Linf decided it would be a good idea not to upset this King.

She nodded once and waited for his first question.

CHAPTER 4

Nice Sword

KABIR WAITED PATIENTLY for the men on horseback to ride up the track leading to the farmhouse, where his bath had just been interrupted at the most inopportune time. There was no longer any light in the sky, only a dim glow from where the sun had disappeared for the night. Those leading held torches in their left hand, which gave off enough light to see who was riding towards them.

They didn't look to have ill intent, as Kabir searched the faces of those in front. Men in armour rode at the head of the group, with two in robes behind them, and two others in simple leather armour at the rear. The two at the rear were shapes of men only, as they held no torches. He couldn't make out any details.

The rest of those they rode with had stopped at the main track where Kabir and Ahlia had first seen them. There were more lights there, with several lanterns fixed to the wagons they had with them.

'Well met,' Kabir said, holding up a hand in greeting.

None of them stepped down from their horses.

Kabir had become accustomed to such rudeness since leaving the highlands, and so he let it pass. The last person to act this way was now a close friend.

'Who are you and what are you doing here? Are there more of you inside?' the man in front asked him. He spoke in a neutral voice and held the torch out in front so they could see more clearly who they spoke with.

'I am Kabir, from the village of Deerstep, and this is Ahlia, Princess to the Plainsmen.' He saw Ahlia cringe as he looked across at her. Perhaps he shouldn't introduce her that way in future. 'We ride alone.'

'What are you doing here?' the man asked again.

Kabir took a deep breath before answering.

'We are adventurers and we are seeking the ruined forest. Have you heard of such a place?' He was excited as he asked. Surely one of them would know.

'If you seek adventure Barbarian, you need not search out a ruined forest. There is plenty to be had throughout King Dayhen's realm.' He spoke without condescension, but also without any humour.

Kabir looked to Ahlia and smiled.

'We are searching for a ruined forest,' Ahlia said, turning to the man on horseback.

'We care not for your quest,' said one of those dressed in a robe. It was tied tight at the waist by a leather belt. Attached to the belt was a sheathed dagger. He could see no other weapons on his person. He was younger than the soldier who had spoken, and stepped down from his horse as he addressed Kabir. 'You are trespassing on the King's land. Looking for adventure and a ruined forest is not a very convincing story.'

Kabir had heard stories of the magic users within the realm of men. Strong wielders of magic, they could burn a man alive with a wave of their hand. He suspected this wasn't someone he wanted to upset.

'I can assure you wizard, this is our only purpose in coming here. We are not your enemies.' He gave a curt bow to show his respect. He was intruding upon their land after all. 'If you can tell us where to find that which we seek, we shall be on our way.'

'Only men loyal to the King are able to roam freely throughout the lands. You are not one of those,' the young wizard said. 'You will relinquish your weapons.'

Kabir wasn't smiling as he looked down at Ahlia this time. She had reached out a hand and put it on his forearm.

'I had heard that men were more welcoming of strangers in the past,' Ahlia said. Neither she nor Kabir made any move to give up their weapons.

'These are not welcoming times,' the wizard said. 'Now slowly remove your weapons and place them on the ground.'

The remaining men dismounted, but stayed behind the wizard. The young magic user had stepped closer to where Kabir and Ahlia stood.

The other wizard lifted something in his hand and suddenly the area in front of the farmstead burst into light. Although not as bright as sunlight, it still made it easier for all to see and to ensure that none were hiding in the shadows surrounding them.

Kabir and Ahlia both took a couple of steps back.

'I will not disrespect my sword in such a way,' Kabir said. 'This is foolish. We are no threat to you.' He paused and thought about not saying anything further, but this wizard had insulted him. 'Not unless you provoke us.'

The wizard held his arm out. The moment Kabir saw him begin to move he reached up and removed his sword, holding it out in front.

The wizard flicked his hand, but nothing happened.

He looked across at Ahlia and saw a startled expression on her face. She appeared to be exerting herself, but was unable to move. Something had trapped her, but had no effect on him.

'Release her,' Kabir said, as he took two steps toward the wizard, his sword held ready now to swing.

He saw a stunned look on the face of the wizard, before he looked to compose himself again.

There was no attempt to hold Kabir this time. He knew the Barbarian was close enough to strike him before any of the others could intercede, so this time flames shot from his fingers.

As close as he was, Kabir knew he wouldn't survive. He didn't have time to even begin his swing.

He was just as surprised as those standing behind the wizard, as he watched his sword absorb the flames. The steel turned a shade of orange, with small licks of flame swirling along its length.

Kabir recovered from the shock more quickly than the wizard, dragging his focus away from his glowing blade and stepping forward again. This time he swung his sword down as he moved, cutting through the upheld arm of the wizard, before following through to his ribs and then his heart.

The young magic-user died with a shocked expression on his face.

Kabir continued forward to where the other wizard stood, a shocked expression also on his face. The two men in armour were slow to move, but he saw from the periphery of his vision the other two moving to flank him.

Kabir stepped backwards instead of continuing his attack. Ahlia might still be unable to move and she would be an easy target for either man.

'Move forward Kabir,' he heard her say from behind. 'I am free again.'

'It is better if we fight back to back,' Kabir said, as he continued walking slowly backward. 'Although,' he said out loud, 'this is not a fight we should be having.'

'You have killed a wizard,' the other one said with a snarl. He had regained his composure. 'This is only going to end one way now.'

'So be it,' Kabir said, as he felt Ahlia's back at his.

He waited for the wizard to try one of his spells, but he stood where he was, as did the two in armour. They looked almost relaxed in their stances.

Kabir looked to his left, as he moved to face one of those that had circle around them. Ahlia moved to face the other, as both men attacked simultaneously.

The one facing Kabir moved with the grace and poise of a very skilled fighter. Like the barbarian, he had only thin leather armour so his movements were not restricted. The highlander knew it would be foolish to underestimate him.

The man's sword was much shorter than Kabir's and he used only one hand to fight, but he was quick and each move seemed to flow effortlessly into the next.

Kabir's sword continued to glow with the fire it had absorbed, as he deftly deflected blows, while managing to strike out a few times with his own.

Although he still wasn't sure how powerful his sword was, he knew it was far superior to the one his opponent had.

After both had tested each other for a short period, Kabir stepped forward and swung in a wide arc. He knew it would leave him vulnerable to a counter attack, but he also knew the man in front of him would not be able to avoid it completely.

He was right. The warrior in front of him held his sword out to deflect the blow, which shattered the steel of his weapon. The follow-through sliced into his side, coming out at the front as his opponent twisted his body aside.

Kabir expected him to fall to the ground, as he drew his sword back for the killing blow. The man didn't hesitate however, leaping forward and driving his foot into the knee of the shocked barbarian. Kabir's leg buckled, forcing him to stumble as he struck again, which meant his effort struck nothing but air. The man continued forward, his fist striking Kabir in the jaw this time.

Although he had been punched many times before and by men much larger than this one, he had never felt a blow so strong. It knocked him sidewards, on to the same side his knee had been kicked, and he went crashing to the ground.

Kabir then felt a knee driven into his throat, before he could even try to move again, as the man above him struck him again to the face. This time he saw stars, before the next blow knocked him unconscious.

'We should kill them now,' Yandow said angrily. 'We have enough to do without babysitting a murderer and his woman.'

'That decision is for our Lord to make,' Methan said calmly. 'They are both from other realms Yandow. We do not need to make enemies of both the plainsmen and highlanders. We have enough enemies already.'

'I believe we have done that already, if it became known what happened here,' the young wizard replied. 'Yet none would know if they were to be buried here,' he said, lowering his voice this time.

'We would know,' Methan said, wiping sweat from his brow as he continued to remove his armour. 'We just need to get the supplies we came for and be on our way.'

'He killed Ethan!' Yandow exclaimed. 'The punishment must be death.'

'And it probably will be,' Methan replied patiently, 'but that is not our decision to make. The Barbarian said she was a Princess of her people. You know as well as I what that means.'

'He lied,' Yandow said with contempt. 'The plainsmen don't have a King. They are savages. What do we care?'

'They are decisions we were not born to make Yandow, and she is near to death anyway. Lord Marcus may not even have to concern himself with her.' If the barbarian spoke truly, Methan hoped she survived.

Kabir awoke and opened his eyes. His head throbbed as he looked around, but he was quickly alert.

He remembered the confrontation with the man who had bested him and he remembered killing the wizard. Looking frantically around, he did not know what had befallen Ahlia.

He was back inside the farmhouse, tied to a beam of wood. His arms and legs were bound and there were several men seated at a table. They all looked at him as he spoke.

'Where is Ahlia,' he demanded, before he caught sight of her lying on a nearby bed. She looked to be asleep, but he could see blood on her clothes.

'If she is hurt...' he began, before one of the men stood up and walked over to him.

'If she is hurt,' he said, leaning down to speak with him, 'then it is entirely your own fault barbarian.'

'Ahlia!' Kabir said in a loud voice, ignoring his antagonist. She didn't stir.

The man leaned in further and struck him across the face.

'You don't speak,' he said. Kabir knew the moment he stood up that he wasn't one of the fighting men. He was probably another wizard, and friend to the one he had killed. He could see murder in the man's eyes.

'If she dies, so do you,' Kabir said, returning the same look he was getting.

The man raised his hand again, but stopped when one of those at the table spoke.

'Sit down Yandow,' the man said.

The wizard continued to glare at Kabir, before turning and taking his seat at the table again.

'How badly hurt is she?' Kabir asked the one who had just spoken.

'Her wounds are grave,' was all he said, before he too turned away from him.

'Use my sword,' Kabir said. He was loath to let them know just how powerful his weapon was, but it was a small price to pay if it saved her life. She had saved his more than once.

The man answered without turning to face him.

'I said her wounds are grave, but she is not yet lost barbarian. I will not be the one to end her life.'

'I do not want her to die,' Kabir said. 'The sword will save her.'

The man turned to look at him this time.

'How will it do that?' he asked. He did not sound convinced.

'Lay the blade against the worst of her hurts,' he said.

The man chuckled.

'I will not be placing your sword where she can grab it and use it against me.' He continued to stare at Kabir. 'I have seen what it can do.'

Kabir took a deep breath.

'You have seen only a fraction of what it can do.' He knew as he spoke that it was unlikely he would ever get his sword back now.

The man stood and lifted Kabir's sword from where he had it sitting on the table. They must have been studying it when he awoke.

'Have your men hold her arms if you must, but you need to lay the blade against her!' He spoke with passion, but the man remained where he was.

Eventually signalling to two of his men, they walked over to where Ahlia lay, each one grabbing one of her arms.

Another walked over from where he stood beside the door and took out a dagger. This one walked over to where she lay and cut away the fabric from her torso, just below her ribcage.

The man with his sword shrugged his shoulders, before laying the end of the blade flat against her exposed skin.

Kabir couldn't see the actual blade, but he saw clearly the glow above her as the magic of the sword healed her wound.

The wizard stood and walked over to look at what was happening.

In a short time, the glow vanished and the man who held his sword withdrew it and stepped back.

Kabir watched on as he stared at the sword in his hand.

'This is a weapon beyond anything I have seen before,' he said out loud to no-one, the awe he felt clear in his voice. He turned to Kabir. 'Is it Dwarven-wrought?'

'It is my sword,' Kabir said. 'Given to me by my father and to him by his. It has been in my family for many generations.'

The man continued to look at him for a time without speaking.

'Her breathing is steady once more,' he said. 'I don't think she will die.'

Kabir nodded his thanks.

'Get some rest Barbarian. We have an early start.'

Kabir let his head fall back against the beam and closed his eyes. Now that he knew Ahlia was safe he was able to find sleep again.

He woke before it was light outside.

It was darker inside now, but there was enough light to see the two men standing guard at the door to his right. They were the same ones he and Ahlia had fought the previous evening.

He wondered again what type of men these were. Did they even sleep?

He was lost in his own thoughts when the others finally began to rise.

By the time they had eaten, packed up their few possessions and ushered him outside, it was still dark.

The carts he had seen at the end of the track to the farmhouse were now just outside the house, people already piling baskets of food into them. None of those who he could see harvesting the food looked like warriors.

Kabir did not know why they were doing it, but they looked to be stripping this farmland of as much food as they could gather.

He wanted to ask questions, but decided against it.

No doubt he would understand what was happening soon enough.

Ahlia had still been sleeping when he was ushered outside, but he looked back now as she slowly walked out the front door.

She looked weak, but her proud features remained, along with her predatory look. She did not walk with the air of one who was a prisoner to these men.

Walking to where he stood, she looked him up and down.

'You look better today,' she said. 'Are you enjoying your latest adventure?'

The smile didn't quite reach his face. She was far from healed and looked ashen in colour.

'Not so much,' was all he said. 'You need more rest.'

'I am okay,' she said. He expected nothing else from her. 'And I don't think we have a choice.'

He nodded.

'Why are we still alive?' she asked him.

'Because you are not from here,' Methan said to her, as he stepped in front of them both. 'My Lord will decide your fate. It will most likely be death.'

'How far is it to this Lord of yours?' she asked. 'I look forward to speaking with him.'

Kabir saw the look of surprise on the face of their Captain.

'I don't know why,' he eventually said, as he held up a hand to stop her next question. 'You will both ride the same horse. One of those giant breeds you rode here on. Yandow was to ride behind you on the other, but the brute would have none of it. He is not in the finest of moods, so if you think to ride off, he will enjoy preventing your escape. You no longer have your sword to protect you.'

Kabir looked over at the wizard sitting atop his regular horse. He had no doubt the Captain spoke truly. The man hadn't stopped glaring at him since he stepped from the farmhouse.

'As I said,' Ahlia replied. 'I look forward to speaking with your Lord.'

They stepped over to his horse and the one who had bested Kabir stooped down behind him and removed the ties around his ankles and those of Ahlia, before assisting them both to mount. Firth moved around a bit with the extra weight, but Ahlia was able to calm him with a few soothing sounds. Her own horse was tied to the back of Firth. She appeared calm now that Ahlia was present.

Kabir didn't know how she did it, but he was in awe at the skill the plainsmen and women showed with their horses.

Methan mounted his own horse and moved to stand him in front of them. He had to look up to address them.

'You will not move unless told to. If you fail to obey all of my directions, or those of my men, then we will not take any chances. You will be killed without hesitation. We need to make haste, so keep up.'

Neither of them said anything, as their ankles were tied together on either side of Firth's torso. If one fell off, the other would quickly follow. It was a clever idea, Kabir thought.

They rode off at the rear of the procession, the carts hardly setting a blistering pace in front of them, despite Methan's words of haste.

Kabir tried not to think about his own hurts as he looked at Ahlia sitting in front of him. She rode straight and proud, but he knew she would be in considerable pain.

Although he had almost died not long ago, the magic of his sword and the new *ginseng* formula had restored him to reasonable health.

The headache he had from being punched hard several times was probably the worst of his current injuries.

He wanted to learn more about the one who had bested him, but for now he was content.

They were still alive, and he was tied closely to Ahlia. She was no longer at risk of dying, although she had looked weak and was already leaning back into him. He had to admit to himself that it bothered him not at all. Her closeness was something he was thankful for.

'Why are you so keen to speak with this Lord of theirs?' Kabir asked, still not sure what she meant by it.

'He will know more than those here with us,' she said. 'If the forest you seek is nearby, then he will know of it.'

'What makes you think he would tell us?' Kabir asked. He admired her confidence, but they would be fortunate indeed if he decided not to kill them on the spot.

'He will,' she said, but offered nothing more. Laying back further against him, Kabir let her rest while he watched the land around them come to life, as the sun finally began its ascent into the sky.

CHAPTER 5

A Lack of Confidence

'IRONIC ISN'T IT,' Mortinan said from where he sat in front of his *eye*, 'that Valdor is gone and yet one who is not even his strongest warrior could be the death of your Champion Kabir.'

Kabir continued to watch on in disbelief as his unconscious Champion had his hands and legs tied and his sword taken from him; yet he decided to bite at Mortinan's taunt for a change.

'Almost as ironic as Mendina's Champion; who you have so vocally derided since the Naming Day; saving your Champion from the tusks of the *Freegol* and then gifting your Champion with the rarest of fairie-dragons. I do believe you would struggle without her Mortinan.' Kabir looked across at him now. He had seen enough of Dark Swell for the moment.

'At least he will still be headed in the right direction,' Mortinan added, ignoring Kabir's retort. 'Perhaps you might catch up some time after the game is ended.'

'You think you are winning this game Mortinan?' Kabir asked. He was trying not to let his fellow gamer get to him.

Mortinan paused in his response this time, before answering.

'Mine is closest to the dragon Kabir. Do you see it otherwise?'

'I do,' Kabir said, 'although I do concede mine is obviously in a dire situation. Again.'

Mortinan chuckled, as he nodded his head.

'So very magnanimous of you,' Mortinan said in response. 'Dire is certainly an apt description, yet who do you think is in a better position than I? Notwithstanding Mendina's tag-along Champion.'

Kabir looked across at Mendina and saw that she didn't intend biting. Her focus remained on her *eye*.

'None of us know what to expect when our Champions arrive at the Ruined Forest,' Kabir said in answer.

'*If* your Champion arrives,' Mortinan interjected.

Kabir ignored him this time as he continued to speak.

'Yet once yours arrives, we will all know. And we can make a new assessment on what to do when that happens,' he said. 'Especially if yours is killed.'

Kabir smiled as he finished.

'He makes a very good point,' Brindel said, before Mortinan could respond.

'I have yet to speak with my Champion. Once the Dragon has killed your young half-breed, then perhaps I can advise mine on how to better tackle the situation.'

Mortinan smiled as he turned to face Brindel.

'If my Champion falls to the dragon Brindel, then I doubt very much yours would prevail. The trinkets your Champion has are not nearly as powerful nor wide-ranging as those which mine possesses.'

'Your "all-powerful" Champion struggled against those "trinkets" the last time they met Mortinan,' Brindel said. 'Perhaps they are stronger than even your all-encompassing knowledge realises.'

'That skirmish was a long time ago in this game Brindel. Much has happened since then, as you well know.' He turned away from his antagonist. 'Why do I even bother talking with you?'

'Because none of the others enjoy talking with you as much as I do,' he replied.

Mortinan ignored him this time.

Mostly because he knew he was trying to get under his skin, but also because of what Kabir had said.

Perhaps he was right. He had been too focused on getting to the ruined forest first, so that he could obtain whatever advantage that entailed.

Yet the advantage Brindel received from winning the last task was not as great as any of them had thought it would be. Even Brindel would have to admit it wasn't much of a bonus.

Maybe this time the reward will again be disappointing, even though the Creator had been forthright in telling them how important it was to get there with as much haste as they could muster.

He was deep in thought now and didn't hear any of the conversation that continued on around him.

What was the Creator's plan for this game? That question continued to nag at him. He had several scenarios in his mind, and his actions could influence his Champion's success in a number of ways; but only if he chose the right option.

Getting to the dragon first had so far seemed to be the most advantageous, but Kabir's suggestion threw a new light on that.

He was no closer to determining why the Creator had hidden his meeting with the dragon, but again he had several theories.

Mortinan eventually decided that he needed to let their current direction run its course. Intervening now would be a waste. Speaking to his Champion in an effort to delay them would not be a worthy use of his opportunity to speak with him. Especially after the efforts he had expended in getting Mendina to enter Dark Swell and speak with her Champion.

That would certainly not please her.

Not that he was overly concerned about upsetting Mendina, but it would show her and the others that he was not in control of what he was doing.

He would certainly not let Kabir influence him. That was beneath him.

His Champion was up to whatever challenge the Creator could throw at him. After all, he said that all of them were still a chance of winning this contest. Assuming that were true, the Creator must believe Mendina to be capable of surviving the next challenge.

His Champion should therefore be able to not only survive it, but excel at it.

Mortinan chastised himself for letting Kabir make him doubt what he was doing.

His Champion was winning this game.

CHAPTER 6

Falling Behind

'I THINK WE SHOULD go back and get their water,' Wilhelm said. 'Even hobgoblins need to drink.'

'It depends if their main party was close by. They may not be carrying anything.' Meghan said. 'We also don't know how long our new 'friends' will be. I think we should keep moving.'

Wilhelm wanted to keep arguing with her. It was frightfully hot on the plains and they had only Meghan's water to share, but she was probably right.

They needed to keep moving and the direction they would now take was towards the mountains. There should almost certainly be some water running off the slopes.

Hopefully it wouldn't take them long to find it.

They walked for a time without incident, Meghan's horse still sore from her stumble earlier. The mare wasn't lame, but even one of them riding on her back would be a burden that could make her condition worse.

They needed their remaining horse to regain as much strength as she could, in case she was needed again.

'Is it getting hotter?' Wilhelm asked.

Meghan looked across at him, but didn't bother answering.

'I think it is' he continued, 'but it is difficult to tell, because it was so ridiculously hot when we first entered these accursed plains.'

Meghan still didn't answer him. She was suffering in the heat, and speaking would simply use up more energy. Telling him to shut up and stop saying stupid things would be a double waste. If it helped him to talk, then she would try not to let it bother her.

'We need to find some water,' he said.

She stopped walking and waited for him to turn, which he eventually did.

'Why are you stopping?' he asked, a confused look on his face. 'Did you see something?' Wilhelm quickly looked around at their surroundings.

Meghan walked up to him without saying a word and put her hands on both sides of his head. Leaning forward and upward, she kissed him gently on his lips, before letting go and walking off again.

She didn't look back at him.

Hopefully that would shut him up for a while.

More hours passed as they trudged through the long grass, the scorching sun still beating down on their burnt bodies.

Both of them had eventually taken their lighter coats from the horse and draped them over their heads and shoulders, but not before their skin had turned a bright red.

At least Wilhelm had stopped complaining, which was a small relief.

The kiss had worked a charm. He hadn't said a word since.

It had taken him a short while before he caught up to her. When he did, all he had done was look at her for a time, before apparently losing himself in thought again.

The sun was high in the sky now, but it would still be some time before it sunk beneath the giant mountain peaks and offered them solace from its heat.

The last of their water was long gone.

Wilhelm had given her the greater share. He was obviously guilty at losing his own water, although it had been through no fault of his own.

They made an effort now to walk well wide of any tree within the plains, despite making their journey even slower and keeping them out under the hot sun even longer. They couldn't be sure if any were the same as the one that had 'eaten' his horse.

Meghan still had shivers thinking back on it. The sound it made as Wilhelm's horse was brutally shoved into the hollow at the top of its trunk was like nothing she had ever heard before; and hoped never to hear again.

As tired, thirsty and burnt as they were, both Wilhelm and Meghan still kept an eye on their surroundings.

She doubted the carnivorous trees were the only horrors within this bleak landscape. They needed to try and remain alert.

When they were still some distance from the nearest mountain, Meghan finally broke the silence.

'We should rest,' she said.

'We should keep going,' Wilhelm replied. 'We are nearly there.'

Meghan sighed. They didn't know for sure there would be water in the direction they now travelled and it would be easier to travel in the shade of the late afternoon.

She told him as much.

'Okay,' he agreed.

She was surprised he gave in to her so easily.

Her horse was happy to stop, as it munched at the base of the long grass.

The two highlanders sat close to her, using her body to shade them from the sun above.

Wilhelm looked like he was about to say something, when the distant sound of a horn stopped him.

They looked at each other.

'That wasn't too far away,' Meghan said.

Wilhelm smiled as he stood and offered her his hand.

She reached her own up and let him help her stand.

'It must be plainsmen,' he said, still grinning. Meghan returned the smile, but more so for the ridiculous look on his face. His mouth was dry and already beginning to crack and his face was redder than any she had ever seen on a highlander before. Fortunately, he had no idea why her smile was really so large.

'They will have water and shelter,' he said.

'They may also have news of Kabir,' she said, the excitement obvious in her voice also.

'Let us go then,' Wilhelm said, as he turned to walk off.

Meghan grabbed his arm and he turned back to her.

'They may not be friendly to us,' she cautioned. 'We know very little about them. We need to be careful.'

Wilhelm nodded in agreeance and then smiled again.

'I am sure my charms and wit will keep us safe,' he said to her, a serious expression on his face now.

She sighed in response and beckoned with her head for them to move off.

The horn blasted out several more times as they walked, so they were certain of the direction they went.

Well before the sun had reached the mountain, the grasses before them began to thin and they could hear the sounds of voices and the thunder of horses running in the distance.

They deliberately walked slowly, so as not to alarm those they first came across. Neither wanted their intentions confused by those they approached.

Their heads were bare now and they walked in front of Meghan's horse.

They were still some distance from where the horn had blasted when they saw several of the giant horses coming towards them. The grass was shorter and thinner now, and their view was uninterrupted. Wilhelm thought the riders looked small in the saddle, their short hair bobbing in the wind. Perhaps they were only children.

As they came closer, Wilhelm could see they were indeed adults. The horses were just bigger than he first thought. He could now see their faces as well, and the look they all shared made him more concerned at the reception they would receive.

All of the riders were female and they had either bow cocked or swords in hand. Their expressions were more than just wary; they looked ready to kill.

Both Wilhelm and Meghan stopped moving and held their hands up to show they held no ill intent. Wilhelm looked across at her. She had obviously read the same expressions on their faces as he had.

There were six riders in total and they stopped about ten paces in front of where the two highlanders stood, spaced evenly apart. One of those in the centre had jumped gracefully from her horse before her mount had come to a standstill, her sword held out towards them.

'Go back from where you came,' she said. 'You are not welcome here today.'

Wilhelm was torn as to what he should say. It was not the welcome he had been hoping for.

'We have no water,' he said. It was a weak introduction, but he wanted to tread lightly. Those few adventurers who had returned to the highlands after travelling through the plains in times past had spoken of fierce warriors who somehow thrived in a brutal landscape. He could see that hardness in the faces of those in front of him.

He could also see the beauty in them. Their features were striking and their figures lean, the skin tanned deeply from living their lives under the hot sun. Their short hair surprised him and he thought it odd, but it just served to accentuate their faces.

It made it more difficult for him to speak. He had always been shy and awkward when speaking to the fairer sex. Even with Meghan at times.

The plains woman who spoke to him turned to look at one of those on their horse. The one she looked at removed a watering skin and threw it on the ground in front of him.

'Now you have water,' she said. 'Leave.'

'We are searching for someone,' Meghan said. 'He may have come this way.'

The plains woman turned to look at her.

'If you will not turn back, then you can go around, but you will come no closer. I would suggest the mountains. There has been no other come this way.'

She turned and pulled herself back on to her horse before either highlander could reply.

Wilhelm was amazed at how graceful she was. Their horses made Meghan's look like a small pony, yet she had no difficulty pulling herself back on to it. He was happy for Meghan to do the talking.

'My horse is sore,' Meghan said.

An arrow thudded into the ground mere inches from her foot.

Wilhelm hadn't even seen who loosed the shot.

The one who had spoken held her arm up. No other arrows were fired.

'I can see that,' she said to Meghan, before sighing. 'Your horse will stay, but you two will leave.'

'You will leave us without a horse?' he said incredulously, finding his voice again.

'I will save the life of that horse,' she retorted angrily. 'If she goes with you, then she will die. She needs rest and healing.'

Two of the plains women got down from their mounts and walked over to Wilhelm and Meghan.

'Remove your things,' she said sharply, the sword in her hand pointed menacingly at Wilhelm.

'You are going to steal our horse?' he asked. 'I had not heard the people of the plains were thieves.'

The plains woman stepped forward and kicked him swiftly in the stomach, doubling him over. Meghan moved to draw her sword, but an arrow thudded into her shoulder, embedding itself deeply into her muscle.

Wilhelm straightened and quickly drew his own sword, as the one who had kicked him stepped back.

This time he saw the arrow coming at him and was able to swat it away, but the second one came at almost the same time, and embedded itself into his side.

The one who had kicked him took a few more steps back, as did the other one who had approached. The plains woman who had first spoken put her hand up again.

'Put your weapons down or you will both die.'

Wilhelm looked across at Meghan and saw that she had her sword held ready in her left hand. She looked at him also.

Both of them dropped their swords on to the ground in front, as the plains woman threw a short rope at Wilhelm.

'Tie her hands behind her back and then move away.'

Wilhelm picked up the rope and moved over to Meghan. The arrow in her shoulder was bleeding, but it had not hit anything that would kill her. He still frowned at it though, turning his look to the one who had spoken. He decided not to say anything, as hard as it was not to.

He could feel his own injury as he moved. The discomfort was intense. He had not been as fortunate as Meghan.

After wrapping the rope around her wrists, he stepped back.

'Turn around and walk backward towards us,' she said to Meghan.

As she got close, the one who had kicked Wilhelm stepped forward and grabbed hold of the rope. She quickly checked it, tightened it and then held her sword to Meghan's neck from behind.

'If you try anything highlander, your woman will die quickly.'

Wilhelm gave a short nod of understanding.

'Now you turn and walk backwards.'

Wilhelm did as he was instructed and had his wrists also firmly bound, before he was turned to face them again.

'You were given the chance to leave,' the one on horseback said. 'Remember that.'

Wilhelm remained silent. Even he knew that anything he had to say would not improve their situation.

They were walked to the plains women's camp at sword point.

Wilhelm's side continued to bleed as his energy quickly left him. The arrow sticking out of his side had penetrated his lung. His breathing was becoming steadily more difficult and he knew his insides were probably filling with blood. Without healing, he knew it would kill him.

He didn't take much in as they entered the camp. His vision was blurring, both from his wound and his dehydration. The smells and sounds of horses were strong, but there was little else. No-one spoke, even though there were a lot of plains people around.

They were taken to a large tent and forced to their knees outside of it.

Wilhelm gave an involuntary outcry from the pain it caused, but kept his head held high. Meghan did the same.

An older woman stepped out of the tent and approached them. She addressed the one who had spoken to them first.

'Why have you brought them here?' she asked. 'We have no time for this.' She didn't sound angry.

'They surrendered,' was all she said.

The older lady looked beyond them. Wilhelm could hear a horse coming towards them.

A male with his long hair tied back walked past him and gave the older woman a long and fierce hug, before turning to face them.

'These two should not be here. Not today,' he said. His face was drawn. 'What happened?'

'They were told to leave, but didn't listen,' said the female standing behind him. Wilhelm wanted to defend themselves to this man, but it seemed he was resigned to their fate already.

The man just nodded and turned to the one he had hugged.

'What are your plans with them?' he asked.

Wilhelm had been right not to assume he was the one in charge. He was glad he hadn't wasted his breath.

'They will be taken away towards the mountains. If they are strong enough to survive then they will, but they will not disturb our mourning again.' She still didn't sound angry or bitter.

'May I ask one question of them?' the man asked.

The woman nodded to him.

He turned to them once more, a strange look on his face.

'Why have you come here?'

Wilhelm's vision was becoming worse. He knew he wasn't far off passing out.

'I am searching for my brother,' he said.

'His name?' the plainsman asked. Wilhelm managed to hear a catch in his voice.

Wilhelm tried to focus as best he could. Why would he want to know his brother's name?

'Kabir.' Wilhelm said.

He saw the man's eyes open wide before he began barking orders.

Wilhelm didn't hear what the plainsman said, as he collapsed face first into the dirt in front of him.

CHAPTER 7

They Will Not See It Coming

A s he had expected, Mithrak caught up with his main force well before they were at the outskirts of Glorfiden. His army was still a full day's march to the forest of the elves.

To their right was the great swamp, and far beyond that was the intended battlefield between Kritch and Dayhen's army.

Those of his forces who would be joining Kritch to the south would make their way around it, while those accompanying him would travel between the forest and the swamp. None would be going through it. That had never entered his mind.

All within the Western Realm knew that only death waited for any who went into the Swamp of Madness, just as assuredly as death used to wait for any that ventured within Glorfiden. He didn't believe the latter to be true any longer, but nothing had changed within the giant cesspool. The swamp remained a place none would enter.

The rest of his army would head north, marching parallel with the forest until all were in position.

'Have there been many deaths during the march?' Mithrak asked the man in front of him. The leader of his army in his absence and his highest-ranked Ve-Karn, Jurg was one he had complete faith in.

'Skirmishes among the orcs and hobgoblins have seen only a few dozen dead my King.' Jurg knew how to keep a report brief and to the point. 'Well within our expectations. There have been some incidental killings by the trolls, and the ogres have slaughtered a few of the mounts, but overall, we are where we hoped to be. Everything else is still as it should be.'

Mithrak nodded. That last part of his report was the most important. It was something he trusted with no other but Jurg and it was key to his success. As he continued looking at his general, he couldn't help marvelling once more at his armour. A one-of-its-kind, it looked to mould itself to his body. Zuroth had done well there. An obsidian colour, the golden jewels and bright emeralds imbued within it, gave a dull sparkle when he moved. It was designed to distract and even stun his opponents. Truly remarkable.

'Deserters?' Mithrak asked next.

'Again, very few,' Jurg said. 'There aren't many places they would feel safe going. Some orcs fled south between the forest and the swamp, while a band of hobgoblins went north.'

'Have they been caught yet?' Mithrak asked. It was up there with his greatest dislikes. Deserters were nearly always caught and made examples of in imaginative ways. His trackers were ruthless and never gave up. He was surprised that any would dare do it.

'No word yet on the orcs, although they may be taken to Kritch if his army is closer when they are found. The hobgoblins have been brought back,' Jurg said.

'Good,' Mithrak said, dismissing him with a wave of his hand.

Jurg left his tent and was soon replaced by all five of his senior mages.

'At first light, we begin our final march. The time is upon us. We will soon know if the elves are still a threat. I suspect not.'

He smiled and all those present did the same.

'Jeosh and Flitch, you two will march north. Jeosh, you will go to the Northern sector. Flitch, you will remain just above Daggertooth Mountain. When your designated time arrives, you will burn the Elven forest to the ground. None inside are to be left alive. Not elves, fairie, birds or even butterflies. I want the forest and everything within it to be nothing but ash.'

Both Mage bowed low, although Mithrak did not fail to notice the flash of anger pass across the face of Flitch. Thrisc was supposed to be the one going to Daggertooth Mountain.

He knew they had their own pecking order within their elite group of dark-mage. Mithrak had been a part of it before he had taken the position he was now in.

Flitch was a powerful mage and highly respected, however Mithrak had always been one who respected initiative as well as power. Those who could think as he did and continually strove to be better and more powerful.

He saw that more in Thrisc than he did Flitch.

Flitch had once shown such drive, but he had become comfortable in his status and position and no longer pushed himself as before. He had not earned the honour to accompany his King and so would need to show Mithrak that he was still worthy. A foray into the forest of Glorfiden could determine that one way or the other.

The younger mage Thrisc, had shown Mithrak on several occasions he was capable of making smart decisions. His strength in magic also grew steadily.

Yet the reason he wanted him by his side and not Flitch, was that he knew the younger mage coveted his rule.

He knew without any doubt that Thrisc would one day challenge him for the right to rule over the Western Realm. Since he had revealed his intention to rule over every other realm as well, he had seen the longing increase exponentially in the young mage's eyes.

He needed Thrisc near to him so that he could study him more closely, and if there came a situation where they were in serious danger, he would become a very expendable dark-mage.

Mithrak knew Thrisc would not rate dying in the defence of his King as a high priority, but he would be given no choice if the situation called for it.

Mithrak's personal guard were unswerving in their loyalty to him. Anyone or anything that threatened his person would not live long afterward, even if they somehow managed to end his life. They would fight for him even after his death.

Flitch didn't ask what his new role entailed.

They had all been told of Mithrak's plans for the forest in detail earlier. He knew what was required when he arrived above the mountain.

'Cordak, you will remain here.'

The mage bowed low.

'Rastiss and Thrisc, you have the honour of accompanying me.'

'You do me great honour King Mithrak,' Thrisc said as he bowed low. 'You will not regret your faith in me.'

'Now you can all get out,' Mithrak said. He didn't need to hear how grateful Thrisc was, and neither did Flitch. He didn't believe any of those in his inner circle would be stupid enough to try anything against another of their order, but he couldn't be sure. Thrisc had a way of antagonising others at times without even trying.

Mithrak had also said all he needed to say and all he wanted to say.

Now he just wanted some time to himself before they left in the morning.

His plan was coming together and he wanted to go over it all once more in his mind; and then go over it all again after that.

There were so many things out of his control. Scenarios that could play out in several different ways, which no-one would be able to predict.

Having things outside of his control both frustrated him and gave him concern.

Yet he had no intentions of changing any of his plans. Most of his thoughts instead focused on what he would do if certain situations played out differently.

Anything he must do to accomplish his goal was on the table. There was nothing and no-one he would not sacrifice to achieve it.

Pushing those plans from his head for the moment, he gave himself a reprieve as he thought instead of how his life would be once he was the ruler of every creature within the land. It would be an amazing time throughout all of the lands, but his battles would not be over.

There would always be those who craved what he had earned; what he will have worked so long and hard to achieve. Dark-Mage like Thrisc, and countless others throughout the lands of those he would conquer.

Yet he looked forward to the challenge.

Mithrak was happy with those he had surrounded himself with. Most were extremely loyal, and they would be rewarded accordingly.

Their loyalty would only grow as their status did, which would attract more as the riches flowed in.

He smiled as he looked at the map spread out on the table in front of him.

Soon there would be no more need for these maps, other than to look upon everything that belonged to him.

CHAPTER 8

Preparing For War

WHEN DAYHEN ARRIVED at the town of Mayfield, he no longer recognised it.

It had been many years since he had been here, but the transformation was incredible.

When he visited the last time, it had been only a small settlement, surrounded by a low, but adequate wall on all sides. Now it was the base for their entire defence of the realm, and the works done to reinforce the walls in such a short period of time were impressive. Add to that the myriad of temporary housing and tents and it looked much, much larger than he remembered.

The destruction of Glorfiden had forced him to consider an attack from the north, something unheard of before now.

The great swamp situated to the north-west of Mayfield would no longer prove to be a factor, despite it remaining an unsurpassable barrier. Not if the armies of Mithrak and Kritch were able to attack him from both sides. Moving an army between the swamp and Glorfiden had not been done before. The elves would not have allowed it. Times had suddenly changed.

He had scouts who watched their progress and reported back regularly, and so far they were bringing back only bad news.

As he had feared, Mithrak's armies were moving towards Glorfiden.

Not smaller parties of creatures either; intent on trying to sneak through; but a great portion of his army, including his Dark Mage and whatever other misbegotten monsters he had scared into fighting for him.

It would stretch his forces if Dayhen had to try and cover the lands south of Glorfiden, and he would have no warning of where they would exit if Mithrak made it through. Or how many there would be. There were far too many scenarios, but he would need to have plans for all of them. Or least those which would impact his realm the most. Did he spread his forces and hope Mithrak did the same, or did he keep his northern army together and hope they were in a position to react in enough time?

Or did he just relinquish his hold on the borders, and fight them at a place of his choosing between here and Lakerth? A complete retreat so he could fight them with every warrior and wizard at his disposal. It was a daunting thought, but one that he was seriously considering. Once Mithrak's army was destroyed, it shouldn't take him long to reclaim all the land he had surrendered.

But there was also the army of Kritch to consider.

His army was less of a concern, but combined with Mithrak's, they could prove his downfall.

Kritch was still camped several days' march away, and did not look to be in any hurry to advance on him. They had been stationary there for a couple of days now. He surmised the Ogre-Mage was waiting for Mithrak to move into position.

Which meant he did not yet have a decision to make, other than supervising the fortifications of his defence and continuing to plan in anticipation of the Western Realm coming against him.

Until he knew how Kritch's army would move, he would not need to disperse his own soldiers and wizards.

'They are up to something,' Thaiden said, looking at the map spread out in front of them. Dayhen had chosen to set himself up in a large tent away from the town of Mayfield. It was quieter.

'Of course they are up to something,' Dayhen said, frustration clear in his voice. 'But what?'

'I don't think we need worry too much about Kritch,' Lord Bantan said. 'He is just an ogre-mage and they are not well known for their intelligence. If Jarkene is able to repel Mithrak, we could advance on Kritch's army before the dark-mage is able to give up on his plan to go through the forest and join up with him. Kritch would not expect us to attack.'

Dayhen liked what Bantan said, but there were still too many 'what-ifs'.

How and when would they know if Mithrak's efforts in Glorfiden had failed?

They may not know for a day or more if Mithrak were successful. By that time, he could be well on his way to Lakerth, while Dayhen's army sat and waited for news.

His capital would be slaughtered before they were able to catch them, yet if he gave up his position here, Kritch would certainly advance behind them. As stupid as ogre-mage, orcs, trolls and his other monsters were, all of them were strong and they could move quickly with the proper motivation. His army would not out-pace them.

Kritch would strike from behind, without any defences between them and his army. They would be slaughtered, and no help would ever come to Lakerth.

'Any word yet of the wizards and Kings Shield from the east?' Dayhen asked.

'None,' Bantan said, a catch in his voice. 'I expected to hear of their departure by now. Something is amiss.'

That news certainly didn't please him. They would be critical if Mithrak won through.

Although no chance in defeating a sizeable force, they might slow them down enough to allow reinforcements from his main army to get to where they were.

'Make it a priority message. Your fastest and best bird,' Dayhen said.

Bantan nodded and gave a small bow.

Thaiden smirked as the Lord of the West retreated out of the tent.

'Aren't all of your birds the fastest and best?'

Dayhen managed a small grin, before the frown quickly returned to his face.

'This could be the end of times for us Thaiden,' he said to his friend.

'I don't think those elves will let them through unscathed.' Thaiden replied. 'If at all. Mithrak and his hordes won't know there's one of those Elven Lords alive in there still.'

'It is a large forest,' Dayhen said. He wasn't convinced even an Elven Lord would be capable of doing more than putting a small dent in Mithrak's army.

'If you were Mithrak and you weren't sure how many elves were left alive inside, what would you do?' Dayhen didn't like having to guess at what the dark-mage might do.

'None of us think like one of his kind does,' Thaiden replied. 'But if he is true to all the other dark-mage before him, he won't care too much about a lot of them dying in that forest, so long as they killed those that were in there.'

'Meaning?' Dayhen asked. He trusted Thaiden's judgement above all others.

'He will send in as many as he can afford to lose, just to see what happens.' Thaiden sounded disgusted by the words coming out of his mouth. 'Mithrak will decide what to do based on how many of them come out alive. He will probably send them in all along the border, to test all of the defences throughout Glorfiden. So long as his army is big enough to throw away so many lives.'

'You think this is likely what he will do?' Dayhen asked. 'I would hope it was true, it will give us more time. Yet I am not so sure. He will need a great number of his army if he has any hopes of conquering my realm.'

'Then perhaps he will just storm the forest with everything he has,' Thaiden added. 'Either way we will know when it happens, because I think that is what the ogre-mage is waiting for.'

'If that happens and he gets through, then we are lost,' Dayhen said. He wanted to sound more positive, but there was just too much at stake. His daughter was in Lakerth.

'Not necessarily,' Thaiden said. 'It's true he could march to Lakerth unmolested, but if his army comes out here, or even here,' he pointed to two places on the map,' their progress will be slowed considerably.'

'We are fooling ourselves if we think he hasn't sent spies throughout the north of my realm before starting a war with us,'

Dayhen said. 'He will have a pretty good idea which places are best for his army to come out.'

'I don't doubt it,' Thaiden said. 'But no spies would have mapped out the inside of Glorfiden, if they were stupid enough to enter at all. If his army somehow survives in large numbers, I am certain they will have no idea where it is they need to come out.'

Dayhen nodded slowly at Thaiden's words.

'They could exit the trees and have no idea where they are,' Lord Kylle agreed.

'If they come out at either of the places you pointed out, not only would it slow them down, it might give us opportunity to come at them with the advantage and obliterate his entire army in one fell swoop.' For the first time in a while, Dayhen began to feel the stirrings of hope.

Only a small sensation, it was nevertheless a vast improvement on the emptiness he had been feeling of late.

Maybe they weren't finished just yet.

Maybe he could somehow win this war.

CHAPTER 9

Play Time

JARKENE SENSED FENG the moment he stepped into the forest. The Elven Lord was quite some distance from where the intruder had entered, and there were so many tasks he needed to do elsewhere, but for some reason he wanted to know what it was doing there.

Mort and Mendina had already left; much to his disgust; and he didn't quite feel up to returning to Corein just yet. Jarkene realised suddenly why he wanted to seek this creature out.

The Elven Lord wanted something to kill.

He didn't recognise what Feng was, but it wasn't from his forest, so it needed to be dealt with.

Not long after he set off north, Jarkene was joined by another elf. Eltrik had known his Lord was nearby and needed to speak with him.

'My Lord, Palir has sent me with tidings.' Jarkene could see the news wasn't good.

He nodded impatiently, beckoning him to continue.

'An army from the West is moving along the border of Glorfiden.' Eltrik waited for confirmation from Jarkene before continuing.

'How many is an army, and what kind of army is it?' His journey to see the intruder might have to wait.

'Thousands,' Eltrik replied. 'There are dark human wizards, fighting men in well-made armour and many other races of misbegotten fiends. They are spacing themselves out along the length of our western border, from above the great swamp.'

'How far along are they?' Jarkene asked. How much time did he have?

'They are past the Waterfall of Dreams, but they move quickly. They have a purpose,' he added.

'Of course they do,' Jarkene said, looking beyond Eltrik to where the hordes of the Western Realm would be amassing. 'Their first strike nearly wiped us out. This next attack is meant to finish the task they began when they sent the storm.'

'Why do they not strike with another storm?' Eltrik asked. Jarkene could hear the fear in his voice. He needed to rid him of that before the defence of their home began. Those of his race who remained would need to be fearless and ruthless when that time came.

Eltrik was the next oldest of them, behind Palir and himself. He would need to set an example. He was a hunter, but he was still strong in magic.

'If they could, they would have already,' Jarkene said, looking the elf in the eye. 'Now they intend to try and attack us using more conventional measures. On foot and in great numbers.' He paused before asking his next question.

'How many of them do you think we can stop before they overrun Glorfiden?'

Eltrik looked confused by the question.

'My Lord?' he asked. 'What does that matter?'

'It matters,' Jarkene said. 'How many?'

'It depends how many there are, where it is they enter and in how many different places they attack us from.' Jarkene could see he was thinking about which places and how many, so he could give a more accurate response.

'No, it doesn't,' Jarkene said, snapping Eltrik out of his thoughts. 'You do know where our power comes from don't you? All elves are taught this on the very first day they begin their training.'

'Yes, my Lord,' Eltrik said. 'The power source comes from the centre of Glorfiden, from within the Glade.'

'Yes,' Jarkene continued. 'Yet that source is accessible from anywhere within Glorfiden. It is Glorfiden! Every inch of this forest has magic running through it. In the water and in the trees Eltrik. It runs deep within the soil and bursts out with every sapling and blade of grass.' He spoke with a fervour now.

'Nothing has ever survived within Glorfiden that was not welcomed under her branches. Do you intend to offer welcome to any of those things amassing outside her borders? Will you let them lay waste to our home?'

'Of course not Lord Jarkene,' Eltrik replied. He looked suitably abashed.

'Then I ask you again,' he said. 'How many of them can we stop before Glorfiden is over-run?'

Eltrik didn't hesitate this time.

'All of them,' he replied, any trace of doubt gone from his voice.

Jarkene smiled at him and nodded.

'Now I go north to meet with something that has entered. I need to do this and I need you to come with me, but I need to get there fast.'

Eltrik looked confused and surprised that his Lord would be heading off in the opposite direction to where the threat came, but he had no more time to explain.

'Catch up to me when you can,' Jarkene said, before he took off at a sprint.

It took until after nightfall before he finally came upon Feng. His vision was excellent in the dark, but he still couldn't make out what it was. The trees relayed Feng's shape and position, but as he looked upon where it should be, he could see nothing. He could hear it moving, but it was invisible to him.

'Show yourself,' he said, from where he crouched on a low branch.

There was no answer and no sound. Whatever it was, it had stopped moving.

Jarkene wasn't sure whether it even understood him.

'If you come within this forest with ill intent, then I will end your life right now.'

'*I come to hunt,*' a voice said within his head. Jarkene smiled. It certainly understood him.

'All creatures within Glorfiden are under my protection,' Jarkene said. 'You will find nothing to satisfy your hunger here. You will find only death.'

The creature said nothing to him, but Jarkene was patient. He knew where it stood, even if he couldn't see it. If it moved to go further within the forest he would act. Until then, he was intrigued by it. What manner of creature was able to disguise itself in such a way? He sensed no magic, so he assumed its invisibility was a natural phenomenon it was born with.

'*What are you?*' Feng eventually asked.

'I am an elf,' Jarkene replied. 'This forest is our home and we are not fond of others entering uninvited.'

'*I have heard talk of elfs before,*' Feng replied. '*Tree-huggers and pretty folk are some of the names I have heard. Do you hug the trees?*' he asked.

Jarkene did not reply straight away. He was able to make a good guess as to where this four-legged creature had come from. A dwarven pet was likely, but why had he never seen one before? If the dwarves had such pets, why had they never used them in battle before. They would be formidable in a fight.

He decided it was unlikely to be a pet, but it had certainly been around dwarves before.

'Where are you from?' Jarkene asked.

'*From the other side of the great mountains,*' it replied.

'You are a long way from home,' Jarkene said. 'Why are you in my forest?'

'*I too have someone that I protect,*' Feng replied. '*but I need to hunt.*'

'You travel with dwarves,' Jarkene said in a pleasant tone. 'If they wish to come into the forest, then I should meet them. None may enter and remain without being welcomed first.'

Again, Feng was slow to reply.

'*We are looking for a ruined forest. It is not here that we look.*'

Jarkene's interest was piqued now. Another that spoke of travelling to a ruined forest. What was it his son had gotten himself into?

He knew he needed to speak with these dwarves. He knew it unlikely they would tell him much, but at the least he would be able to kill something.

'I know what lives within the forest you seek,' Jarkene said. 'I would be happy to tell them about it.'

Feng didn't answer straight away.

'My name is Lord Jarkene and I welcome you into my home,' he said.

His bond with the trees told him the creature had moved off in the direction from which it came.

'*Follow me,*' the voice said to him.

Jarkene smiled, as he took off after it.

CHAPTER 10

No-one Left Behind

'WE NEED TO keep moving,' Brindel said as he walked back over to Kagen.

The young dwarf gave him a bewildered look.

'Kagen, Feng will catch up to us very easily. He would have known we'd keep going, so he's probably hunting further along anyway.' Brindel actually believed what he was saying.

Kagen didn't seem to feel the same way.

'I'm waiting here for him,' he said.

'Okay,' Brindel said. 'Granwith will wait here with you.'

'No, he won't,' Granwith said. 'We definitely need to keep moving. We have a long way to go yet. I'm not sitting around any longer. I'm not a babysitter.'

'I'm not a baby!' Kagen said indignantly.

'Then stop acting like one,' Granwith said. 'Your friend can look after himself.'

'Fine,' Kagen said, picking up his things as he stood.

Brindel's eyebrows rose as he nodded towards Granwith. He was going to say something, but thought better of it. Instead he simply began to trudge off.

The others quickly caught up.

They all walked in silence for a time.

Half way through the night they stopped to rest and have a bite to eat. Feng had still yet to return.

'He's not coming back,' Kagen said forlornly.

Brindel wanted to comfort him, but he was thinking much the same thing. Kagen's friend should have returned well before now.

'What if he's badly injured and can't catch up with us?' Kagen said. 'He might have made it back to where we were but can go no further.'

Brindel had already thought that also.

'We can't go back now,' was all Brindel had.

'He saved my life,' Kagen said. 'And he saved yours! He would go back for us.'

'Yes, he probably would,' Brindel agreed. 'But he is much faster than we are and he chose to wander off without a thought about where he was going. If he had told me first, then I would have told him not to go in there.' Brindel kept his voice low. He felt horrible saying it, but they were the facts. It didn't make him feel any better though.

'I thought you were a better dwarf when I chose you,' Kagen said. 'I think I was wrong.'

'Don't be saying things you will regret later,' Granwith chimed in.

'No need to defend me. He is spot on Granwith. I don't know why he did choose me.' Brindel was tired of talking about it. 'I think it is time we got going again.'

'Yes, let's make sure Feng never catches up with us,' Kagen said.

Brindel didn't even look at the young dwarf. He picked up his things and moved off.

'You haven't travelled very far. I thought you would be further along.'

Brindel was half relieved and half offended hearing those words in his mind.

He turned to Kagen and saw the young dwarf was smiling. Then Kagen looked at him and his smile turned into a scowl.

Brindel couldn't even be bothered telling him he had been right.

'And where have you been friend?' Granwith asked, relief clear in his voice.

There was no answer for a while.

'Kagen,' Brindel said. 'What did he say?' He didn't like the look on Kagen's face. Even in the darkness he could see the panicked look on his face.

'I think we should move into the swamp,' Kagen said. 'We should do it now.'

He began walking towards the dark, swaying branches that ringed the swamp to their right. Brindel wanted to ask more, but he instead just followed the young dwarf.

They all made their way into the swamp, the waters immediately rising up to his thigh, as they took cover behind some trees.

'Why are we here?' Brindel asked.

'Ssh,' Kagen said, looking out at where they had just been. 'Look to the trees,' he said softly.

Brindel didn't like being told to ssh by the young dwarf, but he looked to the forest of the elves. So far, he could see nothing.

They all stayed silent for a time, waiting to see what would show itself to them.

Then a figure stepped out from the trees and stood still.

Brindel couldn't make out features from this distance, but it was almost certainly an elf.

'Feng was followed?' Brindel whispered in close to Kagen.

'Not exactly,' Kagen said.

'What in the god's name does that mean,' he whispered back, trying not to be too loud.

'Ssh,' Kagen said again. 'I will tell you when he is gone.'

'He?' Brindel asked. 'What, they are friends now?'

'Not exactly,' Kagen said again. 'Feng says his name is Lord Jarkene and he wants to meet with us.'

Brindel froze where he crouched behind the tree he was looking around.

An Elven Lord! What had Feng gotten them into?

Brindel turned to Granwith. He wouldn't have been able to hear what Kagen just told him.

'We need to move further into the swamp,' Brindel whispered.

'It is but one elf,' Granwith said, not as quietly as Brindel spoke. 'Why are we whispering.'

'He is an Elven Lord,' Brindel whispered. 'That's why.'

From this close Brindel could see Granwith's face. His comment didn't have the expected result. His Dwarven companion actually looked excited.

Brindel grabbed his arm.

'No,' he whispered. 'I can't say no enough times Granwith.'

The dwarf looked at him for a time before finally nodding in acceptance.

Brindel wondered why it had been such a difficult decision for him. Even Kagen had recognised the mortal danger they were in.

As Brindel continued to look, the elf took a step backwards into the trees and disappeared. The dwarven smith was not going to assume he had simply left. The elf had made the effort to travel all the way to the northern-most part of his realm. He didn't think he would simply step out from the trees and then leave again. He would be watching from within. Waiting for something to happen. He must have been right behind their four-legged friend.

'Are we going to sit here and hide all night?' Granwith eventually said. 'I thought we were in a hurry.'

'We are,' Brindel said quietly, 'but I am not in a hurry to die... again.'

Granwith sighed, but said no more.

Another few minutes passed, when suddenly the entire clearing between them and the forest lit up as if it were daytime again.

Brindel couldn't help shielding his eyes as he moved back behind the tree.

The elf must have seen his movement, as a bolt of lightning crackled above their heads, flying harmlessly above the tree they hid behind.

It was enough for Kagen to jump back in fright, exposing himself to the elf in the forest. Brindel saw the danger immediately, drawing his weapon and standing in front of the young dwarf, as another bolt of energy flew from inside the elven forest. It struck Brindel in the middle of his chest, knocking him backwards into Kagen.

A fierce burst of wind followed the second lightning bolt, sending the dwarves somersaulting backwards through the murky swamp. Brindel sat up and saw Kagen being dragged behind a tree, while Granwith took shelter behind another one.

Brindel however, was unable to move. The bolt that struck him had been more powerful than anything he had ever felt. His armour had managed to prevent a fatal blow, but he was still hurting.

He didn't know how long he lay there for, but eventually he was satisfied no more spells would be coming their way. He had been fortunate at least that he had been knocked back on to a spot where the water was not high and he didn't drown.

Perhaps the elf had decided it was enough.

Just in case he was wrong, Brindel lifted his axe in front of his body as he sat up. To his relief, nothing else came at him from the trees in the distance.

'I must say I am glad I didn't charge at that one,' Granwith said, moving over to stand next to Brindel. 'That looked like it would have hurt.'

Brindel looked up at him.

'Do you think so?' he croaked, as he tried to get his breathing under control again. Looking down, he saw that several of his stones had broken and fallen from his chest plate. 'Another one of those and I would have cooked within my own armour.'

'I was not aware the elf harboured ill-will towards you,' a voice in his head said. *'He told me he wanted to welcome you into his forest. Although I would believe it if you told me you had personally offended him some time in the past.'*

Brindel looked over at where Kagen stood behind the tree that Feng had dragged him to. He assumed Feng would be there with him.

'Elves and dwarves have never been friendly Feng,' Brindel said in a pleasant voice. He realised it would achieve nothing showing his anger. 'We have warred with them for many hundreds of years.'

'I see,' was the only reply he got.

'Well, my boots are already wet,' Granwith said, 'so we may as well travel through the swamp for a time.'

Brindel had nothing more to say. He simply nodded, before gingerly standing up.

'Let's go then,' Kagen said, leading the way. 'We still have a long way to go.'

Brindel looked across at Granwith and shook his head. The other dwarf smiled as he turned and followed the young dwarf.

They walked for a time through the soggy ground of the swamp, before Kagen finally decided that his boots were wet enough.

'Feng has scouted ahead and says there is nothing ahead and the forest looks safe now.' He stopped and turned to look at the other dwarves as he spoke.

'He can detect elves within their own forest now can he?' Brindel asked sceptically. Then a thought came to him. 'He didn't go back in again did he?'

'Of course not,' Kagen said. 'He knows elves are sneaky now. They are not his friends.'

'Good,' Brindel said. 'So then explain to me how he could know if there are no elves around?'

'He smells nothing and there has been no movement,' Kagen said. He sounded convinced.

'And did he know when the elf was about to attack last time?' Brindel asked.

Kagen didn't answer straight away.

'I don't want to walk in this swamp any longer,' he finally said.

Brindel was reminded by the way he said it, that he was still only a young dwarf.

'Neither do I,' Granwith chimed in. 'But Brindel was nearly killed by that elf. We shouldn't risk it again for the sake of dry feet.'

'But...', Kagen began, before Brindel cut him short with a gesture.

'What are those?' he said, pointing behind where Kagen stood.

His vision was good in the dark, but he couldn't make out exactly what it was that moved through the swamp towards them.

Granwith moved up next to him.

'Whatever they are, they move through the swamp at night. I'm guessing they aren't friendly,' he added.

'Are they the same things that nearly killed us?' Kagen asked. He had taken his small axe out and held it ready.

Brindel and Granwith moved forward to stand next to him.

'No, they aren't,' Brindel said. 'They are smaller and thinner. Does Feng know what they are?' he asked in a hushed voice.

'He is further along,' Kagen said. 'He can't smell anything within the swamp. I asked him to come back.'

'They look human,' Granwith said, as they moved closer. They didn't appear to be rushing at them.

'Get back,' Brindel said.

'I want to fight them,' Kagen said.

'I need room to swing my axe,' Brindel said, exasperated. 'Do as I tell you!' he spat at the young dwarf.

Kagen moved to the side to give him room, as Brindel began to swing his weapon over his head.

The man-shaped shadows were almost upon them as Brindel's axe began to burn bright.

One of them moved forward and into his blade. As it was struck, it dissipated into nothing, as if it had never been there.

Even this close, the three dwarves couldn't make out what they were. They were shaped like some sort of hobgoblin or half-goblin, but there were no features. They looked to be nothing but shadows.

Granwith stabbed forward with one of his spears. He wasn't going to risk losing another one in this swamp. As it entered the shadow, it too vanished into thin air.

Brindel struck another as it moved forward. As it disappeared, he saw Kagen a few paces in front of him, swinging his axe low at another of them. His weapon went straight through it, but this one didn't vanish.

Brindel watched on in horror as the shadow wrapped the young dwarf up in its arms. Before he could make his way to it, a spear shot through the night air above Kagen and the shadow disappeared.

The other two were quickly dispatched, as Brindel moved over to the prone dwarf.

As it disappeared, Kagen had collapsed to the swampy ground.

Brindel picked him up and turned him around.

His eyes were open and his chest was still moving.

'Are you okay young'un?' Brindel asked.

Kagen nodded, as he lay limp within the older dwarf's arms.

'Can you talk?' he asked.

'Yes,' Kagen said eventually. 'I just feel really weak. It seemed to drain all my energy from me. I thought I got it a good one,' he added, disappointment clear in his voice.

'You did,' Brindel said.

'Then why didn't it die?' he asked.

Brindel thought he knew the answer, but he didn't say it straight out.

'I will make you a weapon that kills them when we get home,' he said.

Kagen tried to nod.

Granwith lay his cloak on the wet ground and Brindel lay him down in it.

'I need to find my spear,' Granwith said, as he walked off. 'We'll rest here for a bit.'

Brindel sat down next to Kagen as he heard Feng stop next to his young charge.

'I'll take first watch,' Granwith said when he returned, still wiping his spear clean.

Brindel said nothing as he lay down and tried to find some sleep.

He couldn't tell what time it was when he awoke. A thick fog had descended over the swamp, making visibility difficult. There was enough light for him to know that it was already past first light.

Kagen still slept near to him, while Granwith sat staring into the fog.

'I hope you're feeling more refreshed today,' he said, as he continued staring at nothing. Brindel sat up and stretched his arms wide.

'Much better,' he replied.

'Eat some food and then we should be going,' Granwith said, looking at Brindel this time. 'At least the fog will shield us from any prying eyes. We should make the most of it.'

'Agreed,' Brindel said, as he reached over to his bag and pulled out some salted meat and dried fruit.

Kagen must have sensed there was food to be had, as he opened his eyes and sat up.

'I'm hungry,' he said. 'We should eat and then get going.'

They marched through the swamp for the best part of the day. Nothing molested them this time, other than a myriad of insects and several thousand leeches.

It wasn't until late afternoon that a light wind suddenly sprung up and blew the thick fog away.

The dwarves were thankful for the comfort of the breeze. It had been especially humid and smelly as they walked.

Moving across to the edge of the swamp, they looked out across the plain towards the trees.

Glorfiden was still there.

Brindel hadn't really expected to be past it yet, but he had been hopeful they might be able to see the western edge of it. No such luck.

They stopped to eat, before standing up and continuing their journey through the edge of the marshland.

They hadn't gone far when Kagen told them to stop.

'Feng has returned and he has news.'

Brindel waited for the young dwarf to finish communicating with his friend.

He didn't think it would be good news, looking at the expression on Kagen's face.

It never was good news and it was not what he wanted right now.

They were all cold, wet and tired. Despite a decent sleep, Brindel still felt lethargic after all he had been through. A hot meal would do wonders, but he didn't hold out hope for one of those any time soon.

He also needed to repair his armour. The blow from the Elven Lord had left him more vulnerable than he would like. Another blow in the same area would likely go straight through.

The young dwarf in front of him looked as if he needed a hot meal too. His bravery was incredible; even for a dwarf; but he would need more than a strong heart to survive where they had to go.

Granwith, on the other hand, looked like he was out on an afternoon stroll. He still had a spring to his step and a fierce determination to face whatever was thrown at him. Brindel liked him, and he was a mighty companion to have.

He was brought quickly out of his thoughts by Kagen's next words.

'Feng says there is an army of dwarves headed this way.' Kagen sounded confused.

'A what?' Brindel said. Surely Draug hadn't sent a whole battle group of dwarves after them?

'He says there are hundreds of them.' Kagen actually sounded a little excited now.

Brindel didn't answer straight away.

There was no way Draug would leave their home with that many dwarves.

'Which direction do they come from?' Granwith asked. He also sounded a little excited, but not in the same way as Kagen.

'From that way,' Kagen said, pointing in the direction they were headed.

'Western Dwarves?!' Brindel exclaimed.

That couldn't be good.

CHAPTER 11

The Forest Awaits

THE FIRST PART of their journey was uneventful, and the land they traversed was unexpectedly pleasant.

Mendina had been apprehensive about what her senses would encounter within the Western Realm. The elves had never ventured into these lands before, other than Jarkene of course. He had not spoken of it to her since his return and she had not questioned him about it.

The only time he had mentioned it was when he told them they would be walking to their deaths.

Throughout the first day, they had walked through low rolling hills covered in grass. The trees had all been healthy and there was a myriad of small creatures. Most scampered away at their approach, but those that didn't, appeared more curious than threatening. *Iska* spent most of his time curled up on Mort's shoulder as he walked, but from time to time he flew about, scouring the land. Mort told her he didn't know what *Iska* was looking for or whether he did it just for fun. He wasn't even sure what a faire-dragon ate, and as yet he hadn't seen him hunt.

'It is not what I expected,' Mendina said to Mort. The day was almost done and both of them looked around for somewhere to camp for the night. Neither were confident enough to continue walking through the night.

'It is definitely a lot nicer than I thought it would be,' he agreed. 'Do you see anywhere we could lay our heads for the night?'

Mendina hadn't yet seen anywhere, but she wasn't too concerned. There was an abundance of trees where they walked and they had decided earlier it would be best to be away from the ground when they slept. Both of them would be more comfortable within the branches of a tree.

'I don't think we need to stop yet,' she said. 'There is plenty of light and there looks to be plenty of options ahead.'

Mort nodded in agreement, as his hand moved along the smooth rod in his pocket.

He felt powerful with the storm rod in his possession.

Combined with his fairie-dragon and his father's staff, he was confident he could deal with any creature of ill-intent they came across. He almost felt sorry for anything that might choose to attack them.

Although he hadn't used it yet, Jarkene had briefly explained to him how to. At least he had tried. His exact words had been, 'When I first held it, I just knew what I needed to do. If the same doesn't work for you, then I cannot help you further.'

The moment Jarkene had passed it to him and he held it up in front of his eyes, he knew it would respond to him.

There had been numerous times when he had been tempted to 'try it out', but he had stopped himself. It wasn't made to be played with. When the time required it, he would unleash its full power.

They found themselves a safe place to sleep for the night, in the boughs of a large oak tree. There was plenty of foliage to protect them from the eyes of any night-time marauders, and they were high enough to feel if anything tried to make its way up to them. Mort was also confident *Iska* would alert them to any threat, as he nestled on a branch just above where Mort lay.

Both of them slept soundly after their long march that day and woke reasonably refreshed the following morning.

Mort would have liked to sleep closer to Mendina, but there was nowhere with enough room that would support them both safely.

He resigned himself to the fact he may have to wait until they returned home before he could sleep with her in his arms again.

Hopefully it wouldn't be too long. She occupied much of his thoughts.

They looked out through the foliage at their surroundings, before making their way to the ground again.

The land around them was still pleasant, and the sun looked like it would shine throughout the day again.

They had walked barely an hour as the sun rested just above the horizon, when the land in front of them suddenly changed. No longer were there rolling hills with a generous spread of trees.

They stepped to the top of a large hollow and saw below them a marsh land stretching as far north as they could see.

To their left, it stretched for some distance, before joining up with some mountains.

Beyond it in the distance they could see the peaks of much larger mountains. Nothing like those of the Dwarven Mountains to the east of Glorfiden, but they were still daunting.

Mort assumed the forest they sought would be somewhere between the mountains and this swamp that stretched out before them.

This was more like the lands they had expected to come across, but he was still disappointed to see it.

'Can the rod scorch that land which is in front of us so we can walk through without getting our feet wet?' Mendina asked.

Mort didn't think she was serious, but he had been thinking much the same.

'I could try,' he said. 'It would likely kill whatever evils lurk within it as well. Perhaps *Iska* could help.' The fairie-dragon was nestled on his shoulder, staring out at the bog in front of them.

'Or we could go that way.' Mendina indicated to their left, where it moved towards the smaller mountains.

'It is hard to say how far it goes beyond that,' Mort said. 'I would like to, but it may mean we need to go through lands occupied by more than that which we have seen already.'

Mendina didn't look convinced.

'It doesn't feel right,' she said. 'I would rather not go through it.'

'It isn't the right direction,' Mort persisted. He had a bad feeling about going through the swamp, but he was less convinced the other way was a better idea. The time it would cost them aside, it seemed just as wrong as the swamp for some reason.

Yet he couldn't say why it felt wrong, so he had no real argument against it.

'Is the extra time all that important?' she asked.

'It might be,' was all he had. 'But I don't think we should venture too close to any mountains.'

'Agreed,' Mendina said quickly in response, as she started to walk in the direction that would take them parallel to the swamp, but no closer. It looked so wrong even from this far. There appeared to be no joy in the trees and plants that lived there. They looked to be warped and suffering. She certainly didn't want to get any closer. Mendina had seen enough sadness and destruction to last her an elven lifetime.

As they walked down the slope and the sun rose higher into the sky, Mendina looked over at the swamp. A cloud of vapour seemed to descend upon it, or rather rise up from it. Whatever was in it was reacting to the sun, sealing off the life-giving rays. It was why the trees looked the way they did.

The closer they got, the more she knew there was no way she would have been able to go in there even had they wanted to. Aside from the difficulty they would have simply from breathing the stagnant fumes, the attack on her senses from the pain of everything trying to eke out an existence in there would have been too much.

What a horrible place.

She looked across at Mort as they walked, his face one of disgust also as he looked over at the swamp.

'I think we would be better in the mountains than in there,' he said to her.

Mendina couldn't agree more.

As before, their pace was good. So far, the time lost wasn't as great as Mort had feared. They would have moved much slower through the swamp anyway.

But as the sun crossed the middle of the sky and began its downward descent, the land near to the swamp began to change.

The hills remained, but the lush grass and trees changed to patches of coarse grass and hardened dirt where nothing grew. The proud trees gave way to large, spindly ones with little or no foliage and clumps of spiked and thorned bushes surrounded them. They continued to cross over shallow streams making their way into the swampland below, but the water in these was no longer clean. The one positive that he could see, was they were yet to be attacked or threatened by anything. Incredibly, there were no predators to be seen anywhere in these lands.

Mort was pleased by it, but it was concerning. His father had told him there were many horrors within these lands, yet they had been travelling nearly two days and had seen nothing.

'We need to start looking for somewhere to hole up tonight,' Mendina said, interrupting his thoughts.

The land was becoming rockier the closer they got to the small mountains to their left.

'Perhaps we will find a small cave or similar,' he replied. 'I can't see any suitable trees ahead.'

Mendina nodded.

'Keep an eye out,' she said.

Their conversations dried up as the land about them did the same.

It wasn't until it was nearing dark that Mendina drew his attention to an outcrop of rocks at the top of the next rise.

Mort saw it at the same time.

'It will have to do,' he said. There was nothing else within sight that looked to offer any shelter for them and the clouds moving quickly from the north looked menacing. There would be rain tonight.

They made their way quickly up the rocky slope, their feet continually slipping on the loose surface. Elves were sure-footed, but it was difficult to grip when the ground you walked on moved from underneath you.

They eventually made it to the rocks and Mort was pleased to see an opening which led to shelter.

Iska squirmed into a standing position on his shoulder, as Mort lit up the front of the cave entrance with light. The spell was a simple one, but he wouldn't have been able to perform it without his little companion.

The entrance was stone, so neither he nor Mendina were able to see footprints leading inside. They weren't sure whether it was occupied, but there was a pungent smell coming from within.

Mort's light spell shone deeper inside the narrow cave, but the end wasn't visible. It was deeper than he had first thought.

'How far in should we go?' Mendina asked.

'I'm not sure,' Mort said. 'Far enough in to be protected from the storm that is almost upon us. I don't think we should go further than that though,' he added. The smell was even worse as they stepped inside.

They walked about twenty paces, looking around at their surroundings. It didn't appear to be a lair of any sort. Not here anyway. The ceiling was rough, while the floor and walls were smooth. There were no droppings, bones or anything else that would indicate something made its home here. It actually appeared quite clean.

'How much further?' she asked. 'Should we look to see where it ends? I don't want something coming upon us from inside this cave. You cannot keep the light going all night.'

Mortinan was nervous. The smell was sickening now they were so far inside the cave. It smelt of death.

'Perhaps we should find somewhere else,' Mort said. 'This cave doesn't smell right.'

'We don't know what is out there,' Mendina said. 'Perhaps we haven't come upon anything because whatever lives in these parts hunts at night.'

'I know,' Mort replied. 'And perhaps they live in caves during the day.'

Mendina didn't respond.

Mort sighed.

'We will look further in,' he said. 'Be ready.'

The cave was wide enough now for five or six elves to walk side by side. About fifteen paces ahead it turned to the left, all the while slanting downwards.

Mort moved slowly to where it turned, beckoning for Mendina to stay back.

As he turned the corner, the stench became almost too much. The back end of the cave still wasn't visible, and to his dismay it forked. Both tunnels ahead were as wide as the one they walked in and both went down.

Mort stopped to speak with Mendina.

'It goes on for another ten paces before it becomes two tunnels.' He dimmed the light as he spoke to Mendina, pointing it up at the ceiling. He didn't want to blind her. 'I think they could go on for a very long way. And they are damp,' he added.

'What does damp mean?' she asked. Mendina obviously had no experience with caves. Nor did Mort, but he was beginning to understand this one a little more.

'I think it means it may not be such a great protection from the storm outside. Look at how smooth the stones are at our feet.' He shone the light down.

'These tunnels may have been formed from the rain flooding inside.'

Mendina looked at him and he saw the truth of his words dawn on her.

'Let's go,' she said. 'We will find somewhere else.'

Mort nodded in agreeance, as they made their way back to the entrance.

It had already begun to darken outside when they poked their heads out.

Not from the sun setting, but from the storm clouds above them. The first heavy drops of rain had also begun to fall.

'The slopes will be slippery,' Mort said. 'Watch your step.'

He was about to step outside, when Mendina grabbed hold of his arm in a tight grip.

'What are they?' she whispered, pointing at a group of creatures making their way up the slippery slopes towards them. They didn't appear to be having any difficulty climbing. They were only short, but there were at least twenty of them. Mort didn't think they had spotted them yet.

'We should make a run for it,' he said. 'They don't look to be very fast.'

'They will be faster than us on these slopes,' she said quietly. 'I don't like it, but we should head back into the cave.'

Mort didn't want to go back in there, as it was obviously the home of those things. It seemed illogical to try and escape something by running into its home, but perhaps she was right. He would be able to defend against them better in a dry place where he could see them all coming. Or he could try something from where they now stood.

'I could use the rod and sweep them away from us. A gust of gale force wind will certainly test their footing.' He even managed a grin.

'Does it work that way?' she asked. 'Will it answer your call that quickly? Jarkene called it forth from a great distance when he tried to destroy Glorfiden.'

'The storm is already here,' Mort said. 'I just need to concentrate it, but I will need to do it now before they get much closer.'

Mendina nodded at him. She looked like she really did not want to go back into the cave. A weather rod would also not help them in there.

Mort pulled the storm rod from his pocket and pointed it not at the small humanoid creatures making their way towards them, but at the sky above them.

His mind opened to the storm as he let it pull him toward it. The rod became an extension of his being, a conduit to the powers above him.

Although he knew that he still stood on the ground below, he felt himself within the clouds above. The concentration of wind and electricity was intense and something more powerful than he had ever felt before.

It was different to when he used his magic. The control he felt was certain and complete.

Directing it downwards, it struck just above the slope the humanoids were walking up. The wind struck with such force, that the ground beneath it erupted. The lightning strikes that followed, lit up the entire valley beneath the cave.

It was all Mort could do to stop it boring its way into the hillside.

With a monumental effort, he pulled the rod back down to his side, shutting himself off from the storm above.

The lightning stopped and the wind went back to a strong gust, as it had been before he harnessed it to his will.

He looked down at the rod and could feel there was still so much power left within it. He could also sense that it was aching to be let loose.

Quickly putting it back inside his jacket and securing it within his pocket, Mort looked across at Mendina. The expression on her face was both horrified and relieved, which mirrored his own emotions in some way. The only ones she lacked were those of accomplishment and satisfaction. He had mastered the storm rod on his very first attempt and it had been incredible.

He followed Mendina's gaze down into the valley.

There was no chance any of them had survived what he had just cast down upon them. A small crater was now visible in the gloom, at the point just above where he had seen them last.

Mort let out a sigh.

'We should be moving now,' he said, as the rain started to come down even harder.

Mendina shook her head.

'There are more coming,' she said, pointing to the opposite side. The side they were intending on going. These ones were moving faster and they were already closer than the others had been.

Mort took the rod from his pocket again, but Mendina grabbed his wrist.

'They are too close,' she said. 'We need to go back into the cave.'

Mort sighed, but eventually nodded, as he saw more of the small creatures coming from directly in front of them as well. Without the rod, he couldn't hope to kill them all. They may have defences against certain forms of magic and there wouldn't be time to second guess.

He waited until they were well into the first part of the cave before he lit up the way before them. Hopefully they chose the right tunnel and the creatures about to return to their cave didn't know they were in here.

'Which way?' Mendina whispered frantically, as they came to the fork in the tunnel.

'Where is the smell of death coming from?' he asked.

Mendina pointed to the left.

'Then we go right,' he said, as they took off at a run.

CHAPTER 12

Fight to the Death

'SO HOW ARE you going to entertain us?' Kritch asked with a wicked grin.

He stood directly in front of her as he looked down. The ogre-mage was much taller than the largest goblin, of which Linf was not even close.

To those looking on, it probably looked like a parent talking to his child.

Linf just shrugged her shoulders. Until she worked out how the mind of this King worked, she thought it safer to say nothing. That he was brutal, was obvious, but she didn't yet know what triggered his anger, so she didn't want to test him.

'I don't think you are an emissary, so what are you doing here?'

Linf knew this time she had better answer him. She had thought about what she should say while her face had been pressed into the ground.

'The goblin armies have been raiding the lands of men for many, many years great King,' she answered. 'There was talk that now was the time to make war against them. I was sent to see where the best places to attack were.'

'You are just a scout,' Kritch said. He sounded disappointed. 'It looks like you went a bit too far to report back to those you serve.'

'I was captured and brought to one of their big towns,' she replied, unflustered. 'I saw how they live. They are weak.'

Kritch chuckled.

'Then you are a spy for the humans,' he said, motioning to one of his guards.

Linf was grabbed roughly from behind and forced to her knees.

'I escaped,' Linf said quickly, before her face was pushed into the ground again.

'You are a spy,' Kritch said. 'Spies are always good entertainment when they are captured.'

Linf tried to speak, but couldn't. She tried to curse. This hadn't gone as she had expected.

'I have something special for you spy,' Kritch said.

Linf didn't want to find out what his new special thing was. Gort's death had been 'special' enough. It was time to try something different.

Kritch's guard was powerful and had enormous strength, but Linf had absorbed as much of her own power as she could, prior to her arrival before King Kritch.

Gritting her teeth, she began to push back against the hand that held her. The pressure increased as she pushed back, but she managed to lift her face off the ground and look directly in front.

'If I could say one more thing,' Linf said calmly, as she straightened up into a kneeling position.

She waited for the blow to come and tensed herself, as the guard struck her with his free hand to the side of her head.

Linf flinched from the blow, but it did nothing more to her.

She saw Kritch lift his hand, as the guard allowed her to stand.

'You are stronger than you look goblin,' Kritch said. 'I will let you tell me how you escaped.'

'I would prefer to show you instead,' Linf said. She managed to maintain the calmness in her voice, which both delighted and surprised her.

She had the King's attention now. She could tell by the way he looked at her.

'And how would you do that?' Kritch asked.

'Pick any of those here and I will show you how I killed the humans, before I just walked out of their town.' Linf guessed Kritch responded better to strength. She had seen the look on his face when she took the blow to the side of the head.

'The humans have wizards goblin,' Kritch said. 'Did you manage to kill any of those?'

Linf nodded and smiled.

'He looked just as surprised as the one who I will kill here today.'

Kritch remained silent for a time, staring at the goblin. Linf knew he would accept now. He didn't seem in any hurry for his army to be going anywhere. Linf was curious why that was, but she knew she needed to focus on the here and now. She had been forced into offering this challenge. The alternative was her certain death.

Eventually Kritch smiled. She assumed it was a smile anyway. His large jaw widened, showing a mouth full of long, sharp teeth.

He looked beyond Linf and pointed behind her.

'You will fight this goblin,' he said. 'But I expect you to take your time killing it, as I think it is simply trying to get a quick death.'

It was Linf's turn to smile now. She didn't even bother looking behind to see who it was she would be fighting. She continued to look at the King, before the one holding her let go his grip and stepped away.

Linf took her time turning, before she finally faced the one she would have to kill.

It wasn't one of those who had brought her here, for which Linf was surprisingly relieved. For all her bravado and positive reinforcement, she was still only relatively new to her powers and those ones seemed to be immune to them. And despite her strength, those ones would know how to wield the weapons they had, whereas she did not.

Looking the one in front of her up and down, she tried to give off an air of disinterest. It looked similar to the King, but smaller. She had no idea what it could do, but at present there was no anger or fear coming from it. It wore scaled armour, but with no helmet. A short sword hung from each hip, but it made no move to touch either of them, as it looked at her with complete disdain.

Linf turned back to the King and bowed before speaking.

'Will I take my time killing your warrior?' she asked.

Kritch sniggered. 'Of course, goblin. I want to be entertained. Else you would be dead already.'

Bowing again, Linf turned back to her opponent.

This time she could see a tiny aura of anger seeping from its body, but there wasn't enough to draw and weaken it.

Linf looked at some of the others wearing the same armour standing to the side.

'I can see why this one was chosen. You all look far weaker. Would have been easy meat.' She finished by spitting on the ground in their direction.

She drew the anger surrounding them without hesitation, balling it in front of her as quickly as she was able.

There was so much of it she could have used more, but her opponent stepped forward and held a hand out in her direction. She realised it wasn't to shake hands, as a searing ball of fire shot out towards her.

It aimed low, and Linf was only just able to drop her defensive ball of energy in time to impact it. She thought it strange it attacked her legs, but then remembered that Kritch wanted a show. Linf thought he had been kidding.

She felt the heat from the fireball, but suffered no hurt from it.

The second fireball was a different story, as it quickly followed the first.

Linf wasn't able to gather enough energy quickly enough. The ball she hoped to use was more of a thin shield. It prevented the fireball from blowing a hole in her leg, but the impact scorched her and knocked her leg out from under her.

She tried to silence the yelp of pain, but the burn was intense and the noise from her mouth was involuntary. She looked up at her opponent, as he stood there grinning at her.

There was no more anger and certainly no fear.

The anger surrounding her had also dissipated into the air around the clearing and she was unable to grasp on to any of it.

Linf realised she was out of options. She was going to die here.

'Stop!' Kritch said, as his ogre-mage stepped forward towards her, drawing both swords as he did. He froze at the words of his King and put both arms down by his side.

Linf turned her head to face him.

'What is this?!' he asked. There was anger and disappointment in his voice.

Linf saw the swirl of emotions emanating from him.

'You lied to me goblin,' Kritch said, looking down at her.

'Your magic; whatever it is; is weak.'

He stepped forward until he was within arms-reach of her.

Leaning down as he looked at her, Kritch stepped down on her injured leg. Another involuntary gasp of pain was released, before the Ogre-Mage reached down with his gauntleted hand and grabbed her around the throat.

Lifting her off the ground, he pulled her face in close to his own.

'There is no sport here,' he said angrily. 'You are not entertaining.'

Linf couldn't breathe, his grip closing off her airway immediately.

Yet she could still see him, and the intense anger bursting forth from him.

Anger which she grasped on to, before sucking it in like she had been starved of it for a very long time.

She saw the confusion in his eyes, as his grip loosened and her feet touched the ground again. None of those looking on would have known what was going on.

Not until Kritch fell to his knees and Linf quickly moved to stand behind him, her left arm snaking its way around his neck.

Several of his guards moved towards them, but stopped at her words.

'I will snap his neck,' Linf snarled at them, as she continued to draw from him. His anger had turned to fear, but it was all the same to her.

Her strength returned quickly, as the pain in her leg subsided.

The ogre-mage in front of her now stood with both swords held out in front. They were no defence against the concentrated ball of energy she cast at him. Squeezing it smaller than she had before, it was almost solid as she sent it flying across the clearing. It tore through his armour like he wasn't wearing any, the power of it ripping right through his chest and out through his back.

'I'm sorry for ending the contest so quickly King,' she spoke softly into his ear. 'Now tell all of them to get back.'

She reduced the pressure on his neck so he could speak.

'Get back!' he snarled, before the squeeze was put back on.

'Now I need time to think,' Linf said in a quiet voice. Only Kritch would have heard her.

Linf realised she had but postponed her life for the moment.

If she killed Kritch, she would be the next one to die. She had learnt that lesson after killing her father.

Yet if she let him live, he would not forgive this. She could only imagine how long and painful her death would be. Much longer than Gort's.

'I don't want to die today,' Linf said to the ogre-mage kneeling in front of her.

'Tell me how we can both live through this.'

Kritch didn't answer her, as she desperately tried to think of a way out.

'You,' she said, pointing at one who looked like one of those that had brought her in. He appeared to be the serious type.

'How does one become ruler of your kind?' An idea had come to her. It wasn't likely to work, but she had nothing else. 'Where I come from, if you kill the strongest, then you are made leader.' She pointed at Kritch with her free hand. 'I assume your King is the strongest?'

'He is the strongest of his clan,' the guard said. 'The strongest clan leads the armies into battle and speaks for all the others.'

'Then my plan didn't work,' Linf said out loud. 'Will you cowards kill me if I let him go, or have I proven myself? If I can't be your ruler, then I am happy to just be alive.'

'Get your arm away from me goblin,' Kritch managed to rasp. Despite his weakness, he had maintained his rage. Linf had stopped draining him, but he would take some time to get his strength back.

'Not until you tell them I am not to be killed,' Linf replied. She had nothing to lose now, so she gave up trying to be nice. 'And I need to believe it.'

'You again,' she pointed at the one who had answered her question, before Kritch could say anything. A bit more pressure on his neck assured her he wouldn't say anything until she was ready for him to speak. 'What words will bind you all and him not to kill me?'

'I don't know what you are talking about goblin,' he replied. Linf didn't like his tone this time. It sounded as if he thought her stupid.

'I want to know that I won't be killed or tortured if I let your King go.' Her hopes of surviving were still very low.

'That is up to the King to decide,' he said. 'You should let him go.'

Linf nodded.

'Here me King,' she said into his ear. 'I could have killed your man any time I wanted, but I was hoping instead to be their new ruler. Now that isn't going to happen, I won't try and kill you again. But hear this well. If you or any of yours try to kill me, you will be the first to die.'

Linf loosened her grip a little, but didn't let go yet.

Instead she began draining him again, until he looked ready to pass out.

'Say the words to them now,' Linf said quietly to him, 'or we both die now.'

'Don't kill the goblin,' he managed to croak.

'I'll need that a bit louder,' Linf said.

'Don't kill it,' Kritch said in a louder voice. Linf looked up and saw several of his guard's nod.

'Sleep now,' Linf whispered, as she drained him into unconsciousness, before letting him sprawl into the dirt.

The goblin expected fireballs to rain down on her then, but none came.

She stepped back as several of Kritch's guards moved forward and picked him up, before carrying him back into his tent.

Several more stood around Linf in a circle, their weapons drawn. Linf didn't bother moving. She let the blow to the back of her head knock her forward on to the ground.

Feigning unconsciousness, she felt herself lifted off the ground and taken away somewhere else, her wrists and ankles bound as she was carried. Eventually she was tossed onto the hard ground, before she heard their footsteps as they left her there.

'We have been told not to kill you goblin,' a voice said to her from close to her face. She had been about to open her eyes and sit up. 'You will have to wait until Kritch is ready to do it himself. Think about that in your dreams. It will be a manner of death talked about for a long time.'

Linf remained motionless, with her eyes closed.

She still had reserves of strength within her, which she would need for her escape.

She knew it would have to be soon.

CHAPTER 13

An Unlikely Ally

ETHAN HAD SPOKEN truly when he said they needed to make haste.

It was not yet evening and they had already visited four farmsteads, loading up their carts with food and mustering whatever farm animals remained.

So far it had been orderly and without mishap, yet there was still an underlying urgency in their movements. Kabir could sense that none of those doing the labour wanted to be here. Nor did most of the soldiers.

He didn't consider those few who had bested him and Ahlia as soldiers. They were obviously more than that. He had not fought their like before.

Ahlia's condition didn't worsen throughout their day on horseback, but Kabir felt weakened from the constant jolting and lack of exercise. The only comfortable part of the journey for him was that he was tied so close to her. Even though it was cut short, her hair constantly flicked his face, but he didn't mind. Her scent was both soothing and arousing to him, despite the situation they found themselves in.

Methan finally called for a meal break after the fourth farmstead had been stripped, and Kabir and Ahlia were permitted down from their horse.

A glaring Yandow shadowed them, as did two of their warriors.

'Sit,' Yandow ordered, pointing to a piece of dirt a few paces from Firth.

'I would rather stand,' Kabir retorted. 'I have been sitting long enough.'

Kabir felt a tightening around his knees, which pulled them together. An invisible weight then forced the back of his knees to buckle and send him to the ground.

'Better,' Yandow said, the look of pure loathing stuck to his face, combined now with one of satisfaction.

'Cowardly wizard,' Kabir muttered under his breath.

'Cowardly?' Yandow said to him. 'Are you cowardly when you use your greater strength to better a man half your size?'

'It is my natural strength,' Kabir replied. He didn't know why he was letting the wizard get under his skin. Probably because the man wanted him dead and was more than willing to let Ahlia die earlier.

'Magic is my natural strength barbarian. I use it to best weakling barbarians when they no longer have their 'magic' weapons to hide behind.' He smirked this time. 'You are an arrogant fool, and I am going to be there when you are hanging by your neck from a tree.'

Kabir didn't respond this time. Instead he moved off his knees and into a seated position.

'He will get his sword back wizard and when he does he will bury it deep in your stomach, so you die slowly and painfully.' Ahlia was not so reticent.

She had already sat down next to Kabir.

Yandow walked up to her and slapped her across the face.

Their wrists were still tied behind their backs, but the bonds on their ankles had been removed prior to getting them off Firth.

Yandow wasn't quick enough to avoid the kick to his stomach from Kabir's boot. It doubled him over, leaving his face exposed for the next strike. Blood spurted from his nose, as his head jolted backwards.

Yandow managed to step back a couple of paces, a hand going to his face.

Kabir remained where he was, waiting for whatever would come next.

The wizard lifted his other hand and extended it forward towards Kabir, but whatever spell he had in mind was stopped, when one of his guards moved swiftly in between them.

'Methan has ordered they be brought before our Lord for judgement.' He said nothing more, but it was enough.

The wizard stalked away, probably to check on his hurts.

'Thank you,' Ahlia said.

The warrior turned to her. 'I do not require nor want your thanks. My duty is to my Lord and my King. Whether you live or die is not my concern.'

'Where are you from?' Kabir asked. 'You are not regular soldiers. I have not fought men like you before. Your skills are impressive.'

'We are from the Kingdom of Dayhen of the Storm. We are the King's Shield and we live and die defending his realm.' He paused for a moment. 'Are your people enemies of ours?'

'We are not,' Kabir replied. He was taken aback by the question, but trying to look at things through this man's eyes he could understand the question.

'Then why did you fight us?' he asked.

'We were provoked,' Ahlia said. 'We sought no quarrel from you. Why would we want to battle so many? We are not fools.'

'Yet here you are,' the King's Shield said, before taking up a position behind them once more.

They were given food to eat with their bonds removed briefly, before Methan gave the order for them all to move off again. Without his sword, Kabir was not considered a threat to the King's Shield who watched over him.

After being assisted on to Firth, Kabir watched as Ahlia leapt on without assistance. Even with himself already seated on the back of the stallion and her hands tied behind her, she had no difficulty. He was dumbfounded and amazed at her agility, which shifted his thoughts to other things.

He was quickly brought back to their current situation when one of Methan's soldiers rode up quickly from the direction of the last homestead they had visited.

Kabir couldn't hear what he said to Methan, but Methan's reaction told him plenty. He began barking orders, as the wagons;

both full and empty; started moving off. The workers who had been collecting food and walking behind the carts in between farmsteads, now jumped into the remaining empty ones.

Only a few soldiers on horseback moved with them. The remainder came together near where Kabir and Ahlia sat on their horse.

This time they could both hear what Methan had to say.

'Our scouts have returned. There is a goblin hunting party headed in this direction. They know we are here. They are at least fifty strong.'

'We cannot outrun them with the carts,' Yandow said.

Methan looked to his only remaining wizard.

'I know that,' he said, trying to keep the anger out of his voice. 'But Shadow Hill needs those supplies. It will be up to us to stop them getting through.'

'What else?' the King's Shield asked. Kabir liked that he didn't waste words, unlike the wizard.

Methan turned to him.

'They are led by one of their blind trackers, all have horses and there are half a dozen *Krett* in their pack. We will be pressed to beat them with our numbers,' he finished.

'Take off these bonds, give me my sword and I will beat them all for you,' Kabir interjected.

'You two are prisoners and will remain so,' Methan said. 'As for your weapon, I was going to use it myself, but you speak truly in one regard. It should be in the hands of one who is best equipped to use it.' He turned back to his King's Shield.

'Atriol, the weapon is yours for this battle.' He drew Kabir's sword from its sheath at the side of his horse and handed it to his King's Shield.

Atriol took it with a nod, swinging it a few times to get a feel for it.

'I do not usually fight with a two-handed weapon Captain, but this is like no sword I have ever held.' He bowed lower this time. 'Thank you for the honour.'

'I look forward to seeing you use it Atriol,' Kabir said, as Yandow glared at him. There were already bruises coming through under each eye, but his nose didn't look broken. 'Do not forget whose sword it is though. I will have it back.'

Atriol turned to him and to Kabir's surprise, nodded to him in respect.

'If your life is not forfeited by my Lord, then this weapon shall be returned to you.'

Kabir nodded back. He respected this one.

'That is not a decision for you to make Atriol,' Methan said. 'Our Lord will decide who keeps it.'

'Of course, Captain,' his King's Shield replied. 'I will but remind him that we do not steal things that rightfully belong to others.'

Methan looked as if he was going to reply, but let it be.

'As for you two,' Methan said, turning on his mount to face Kabir and Ahlia. 'If you attempt to flee you will both be killed. We will not wait for our Lord's judgement.'

'We do not run from a fight,' Ahlia spat back at him. 'Your insults are what put us in this position to begin with.'

'Nevertheless,' Methan said. 'You have been warned.'

'Give us both a sword,' Kabir said. 'I give you my word we will fight to the death against these creatures.'

'I am afraid your word is not enough for me,' Methan said. 'I don't know you well enough and you have killed one of my wizards already. You will not have a sword.'

'I have never broken my word before,' Kabir said, real anger in his voice as he spoke. 'It is part of who I am. Who we are,' he said, indicating Ahlia. 'Do you have no honour.'

'I believe him,' Atriol said.

Methan sighed.

'No sword. You stay where you are.' He turned back to his men.

Kabir let it go. He was not going to change his mind. He was a fool.

Three King's Shield, one wizard and fifteen soldiers. The odds were certainly not in their favour. It made no sense to leave he and Ahlia perched on their horse with their arms and legs tied. He may as well have executed them already.

'Only fifty goblins,' Kabir said in a quiet voice to Ahlia. 'It doesn't seem too many against three warriors of Atriol's ability and a wizard. He also has my sword.' Perhaps they weren't finished yet, now that he thought more about it.

'If the goblins are on horses, they will be the better fighters from their settlement,' she replied. 'We are told they have some natural built-in defence against the human wizards and the beasts they call *Krett* are not easy to kill.'

'What else?' Kabir asked. He wanted to know as much as he could about their enemy, and hadn't been aware Ahlia knew so much. She continued to impress him in many ways.

'They are not naturally gifted on horseback, but they are better than you.' He saw she had a small grin on her face as she turned her head to look at him. 'The *Krett* are some kind of lizard hybrid, a foul beast that I have been told is immune to the spells of wizards. If there are six of them it will be difficult. I would look to kill them first. The *Crintin* are primarily used to track, but are still strong and ferocious and have excellent movement and skills.'

Kabir knew she was thinking the same as he. They needed to get free of their bonds as quickly as possible and arm themselves.

If would not be easy. They would need to wait until the battle began, else the wizard would look to stop them. He would not require much of an excuse to scorch them where they sat.

The straps that held them were a strong leather, tied skilfully by one of the King's Shield. They would also need to be cut.

'How long do you think we have until they are here?' Kabir asked.

'Not long,' she said. 'I can hear their horses already.'

Kabir looked around. There was no advantage to be had with the land they stood on. The farmhouse was no defence and it would burn too easily.

There were a few fences to keep their farm animals in, but not enough to funnel the goblins towards them. They would be forced to fight them on open ground, which gave the goblin's superior numbers a huge advantage.

Hopefully the wizard had some tricks which might help them.

If Ahlia was not confident, then Kabir knew their chances were not great.

He also had reservations about Atriol using his sword. The man had unbelievable fighting skills, but the use of a two-handed sword required a completely different fighting style to that of single-handed combat. Kabir was proficient in both, so he knew.

Hopefully the King's Shield was able to adapt.

He would need to, else this fight would be over very quickly.

CHAPTER 14

Hard To Keep Up

A LOT HAD HAPPENED since the Naming Day. Decisions made to influence the fate of their respective Champions had kept the game moving at break-neck speed, along with things completely out of their control.

Linf now found it a challenge simply keeping up, let alone trying to anticipate what might happen next and making decisions to influence those possible outcomes.

Her own Champion continued to go from a desperate situation to a hopeless situation and then back again to a desperate one. The fact Linf was constantly in danger at least made her own decision not to speak with her somewhat easier. She simply hadn't been permitted to try.

Her *eye* was nevertheless constantly changing from one part of Dark Swell to the next. The situations her fellow Gamer's Champions found themselves in were in some ways no better than her own.

Kabir was still a long way from the Ruined Forest and his situation was grim.

Brindel was close to the Ruined Forest, but surrounded by creatures of evil intent on all sides, and now Mortinan and Mendina found themselves in a place that made her less upset about her own Champion. She would not want Linf to be trapped inside those caves. Like all of those seated around the circle, she knew what lurked inside.

They were also aware of the new creatures appearing throughout the world; monsters never before seen within the world of Dark Swell.

The Creator had ramped things up recently, and Linf still wasn't entirely sure why. To make things harder for their Champions was an obvious reason, but she had a feeling there was more to it than that. This game had many more levels to it, with a number of those levels not made clear to any of them until later on.

Linf was sure this was another one of those levels.

Testing the strength and resilience of each of their homes was one theory that had been thrown about, although they discussed things less amongst themselves since they had been given the ability to enter the world and influence the game again.

Yet why did Valdor's realm continue to be tested, when he was no longer in the game.

She had spent considerable time speculating on such things, but in the end, most of her thoughts returned to how her Champion was going to get to the Ruined Forest. Was there anything else she could do to influence that end?

At the moment, the answer was no. But she continued to run scenarios through her head in case an opportunity did arise. When it did, she would be ready to act.

Now that her Champion was resting, Linf paused for a moment to look at all the others in the circle. And by 'resting', she meant that her Champion was waiting for Kritch to regain his strength and slowly torture her to death. The term resting comforted her more.

The other Gamers had all been quiet for a long time, as they watched their own Champions struggle to get to the Ruined Forest. Conversation had been non-existent. If only each of their Champions knew what awaited them in the forest, they may not be so intent on getting there.

Her perusal of the other Gamers was interrupted by a solitary figure making his way towards their circle, from the direction of the forest where they all once lived.

The Creator moved slowly, casually looking around at the landscape as he did. He looked like he was out having an afternoon stroll, without a care in the world.

Linf didn't take her eyes off him, but she was still able to sense the others turn their attention to him.

Although he had surprised them with visits previously, she honestly hadn't expected to see him again until the death of another Champion, or the game itself came to a conclusion.

She would have been lying if she told anyone she wasn't both nervous and excited as he stepped into the middle of the clearing.

All of their *eyes* became translucent as he began to speak, a solemn look held within his gaze.

'When first you learnt of this game many years ago, I told you all the reward at the end would be greater than any one of you could ever imagine. A prize beyond imagining. You spent years studying the world of Dark Swell and then more years crafting realms in which to house your chosen race.'

'You have given all you have so far, and your efforts have exceeded my expectations. For that I congratulate and thank you.' He stopped speaking as he turned to acknowledge each player and nod his head in appreciation.

Linf was delighted hearing those words come from the mouth of the Creator. It was the highest praise he had given them and she couldn't help smiling.

'When I gave you the ability to enter the world and speak with your Champion, I did it both as a reward for your efforts so far and to give you another opportunity to prove your worth in this game. To impress me with your foresight and ingenuity. I have been intrigued so far at how it has played out.'

He paused, as his face took on the look of one in deep thought.

'Yet it is not enough,' he said in a softer voice, but still loud enough for them all to hear.

He paused again; as did Linf's heart; as she waited for his next words.

'This time I offer you all the opportunity to do more than simply enter the world of Dark Swell and offer advice and information.'

Linf was certain his pauses were for no other reason than to build the suspense within them all. It worked remarkably well with her.

'Your opportunity to enter the world and relay your messages still stands as before. Nothing there has changed. As a further boon and test, you will each be given an extra chance to enter and influence the game in an entirely new fashion.'

The solemn expression changed, but Linf couldn't read his emotions this time. Possibly one of pleasure, or maybe even a mischievous look. She had no idea, but she gave up trying to read him as he spoke his next words.

'You all now have the ability to influence the game directly, in a physical sense. One time only you may enter and assist your champion as you see fit, but there are limitations. And there are risks.'

A scroll appeared in his hand. Linf had not seen it before he held it up.

'On this scroll is a list of powers available for each of you to choose from. You may choose one only and you may enter only once to help your Champion. This time it matters not if they are in danger. In truth, that is when they are most likely to need you.'

Linf took in everything he said. Drank it in as if his words were water and she was dying of thirst.

And yet all she wanted for him to do now was leave, so she could look at the scroll in his hand. Not only would it enable her to save Linf from her current situation, it may allow Linf to trust her enough when the time came for her final visit to Dark Swell.

'To those of you who think this may be unfair to the few who have visited Dark Swell already, I strongly disagree. Those who have yet to visit have held off for a reason and deserve to still have their opportunities. The playing field remains level.'

Linf didn't think that way, but perhaps others might.

'One final thing I feel is only fair to add.'

This time he was certainly expressing joy.

'You are all susceptible to hurts sustained while on Dark Swell.'

Linf was grateful for that piece of information, and alarmed at the same time.

'Also, if you die on Dark Swell,' the Creator continued, 'then you will not return alive in this world. Dead means dead.'

Then he vanished.

Five scrolls remained on the ground where he had been standing.

CHAPTER 15

The Western Dwarves

THEY HAD MARCHED through the flat lands of the Western realm for two days and two nights without pause, before finally resting for a short period during the middle of the following day. Their constitution was remarkable and they only stopped now to socialise with a meal and look upon the land before them.

Zuroth also saw it as a great place to speak to his army again. There was a large rock formation in the middle of the small plateau where they rested, which would enable most of those present to hear what he wanted to say. He took a position upon it after his dwarves had finished their meal.

'Our destination is now visible in the distance,' he bellowed, indicating the mountain range beyond the Elven Forest. Even from this distance they could all see the silhouette of the mightiest mountain range in the land.

'We have been promised riches and wonders beyond our imagination and a new home for any who wish to stay.' Those surrounding him let out a roar in unison. 'And all we have to do is dislodge the current occupants.' This time there were pockets of laughter among the roar of approval. 'Hopefully their females aren't as scary as ours.' The whole place erupted into laughter at that comment. Even from the females among them.

'We will be upon the Elven Forest soon, and although we hold no fear of the pretty ones, nor are we foolish enough to walk among their trees. We go north above the forest, but if any poke their head out, feel free to lop it off.' Zuroth was enjoying himself, and he could see his audience was enjoying it too.

He rarely got the opportunity to address so many of his dwarves in the one place, but he knew they were all keen to get to their destination. He would save the rest of his speech for when he was within the throne room of the King of the Eastern dwarves. He was super excited at the thought.

'Now let us march some more, so we can show our weakling cousins what a real dwarf is made of!' He took out his two double-edged axes and struck the blades together.

The sound of clashing weapons and roars of approval rung out over the plateau, as Zuroth's Dwarven army clashed their own weapons and shields in response to their King.

Their war-cries continued to ring out, as they re-commenced their march towards the Mountains of the East.

Sometime during the following night, they reached the upper eastern corner of the elven forest.

Zuroth had wanted to keep some distance between his army and the trees, but the swamp to their left flank was a lot closer than he had been told.

Walking through the swamp was an unknown prospect and would certainly slow their progress dramatically. He cursed out loud, before turning to those in front of him who waited patiently for his direction.

'We stay close to the swamp, but not inside it. Call our scouts back to the main force. If there are elves about they will be easy pickings for their cowardly arrows.' He paused as he thought about the risks of having no scouts. The strength of his main force should negate the risk of not knowing what was ahead. He didn't want to lose any dwarves unnecessarily. He decided it would be worth the risk.

'How wide do we march?' one of his captains asked him.

'Thin lines,' Zuroth said. 'Four wide, shields held up on the right flank. I want them all to stay tight while we are so close to the Elven forest. Make sure they don't attack unless we begin to take casualties. I don't want any dwarves drawn into the forest. You and the other captains space yourselves out and be ready to move along the flank. You few hold the key to our passage through here if we are attacked.'

His High-Captain and those in front of him moved off to pass on his orders and organise their march.

Zuroth wasn't afraid of those inside the forest, but his fight wasn't with the elves unless they attacked first.

Not yet anyway.

CHAPTER 16

A Choice To Be Made

MORTINAN WALKED QUICKLY toward the centre of the clearing the moment the Creator disappeared.

He knew he had no time to waste.

His Champion was walking into a situation he was unlikely to walk out of alive.

This scroll could be the difference between life and death for his Champion.

Yet it could mean his own death if he rushed in without preparation. He saw it as no coincidence that the Creator had chosen this time to introduce a new facet of the game. All of their Champions were in a dire situation.

He believed on the face of it, that this opportunity was designed to be used sooner rather than later.

He unwound the scroll and began reading it before he had even sat back down in front of his *eye*.

'You will have no longer than ten minutes within the world of Dark Swell to use your selected power and return to the clearing.'

Sitting down in front of his *eye*, Mortinan continued to read.

'You are not permitted to communicate with any of the selected Champions in any way and you will not be visible to them or any of their close companions. You will however, be visible to every other creature on Dark Swell.'

'When you are ready to enter, simply say the name of your selected ability and step through. You will be transported to where your Champion is.'

There was nothing further to indicate what would happen at the end of the ten minutes if you were still there. He assumed they would simply be removed from Dark Swell and returned to the clearing. Yet assumptions could be dangerous in this game.

Sitting back down, he began to scroll through the list of powers which had been allocated for them to choose from.

There were more than he had expected, but in his mind that only made the decision more difficult.

He thought about entering and using one of his earlier granted abilities and simply tell his Champion to leave the caves and try their luck with the creatures returning from the swamp. Those ones could be tough to kill; he accepted that; but they were nowhere near as powerful as that which dwelt at the end of the tunnel Mortinan and Mendina were making their way along.

Yet he was reasonably certain that would not be permitted. They were clearly in danger and the rules stipulated he couldn't appear when his Champion was in peril.

He went through the list a second time.

A few jumped out at him, but he needed to pick one that would not only assist his Champion to survive, but keep himself safe also.

Invisibility would keep him safe, as would *speed*, but they wouldn't help Mortinan defeat the *Lokaan*. That would require something special and there were only a couple of abilities within this list which could enable him to vanquish it. Unfortunately, they would also leave him vulnerable to attack. Attacks not just from the Lokaan; he would need to be wary of any spells his own Champion would cast at the monster if he were too close.

The risk would be no different for Mendina, who looked his way at the same moment he looked across at her. He wanted to ask her whether she would enter the world with him, but there was no time.

So far, they had been given nothing but time to make decisions and choices. His game had been planned meticulously, with changes made and then those plans altered even further.

Now he truly had no time. His next decision would need to be made within moments or his game could be over.

He stood up and was about to speak the word and step in, when he second-guessed himself once more.

Mortinan's fairie-dragon had been extremely resourceful so far. There was a good chance he would pick the spell Mortinan needed to slay this monster.

'A good chance' he thought. Since when did he rely on 'a good chance'.

They were almost at the entrance to the large cavern.

He looked across at Mendina, who also stood in front of her *eye*.

Without further hesitation Mortinan stepped through.

As he did he spoke a word out loud.

'Earthquake'.

CHAPTER 17

A Little More Time

U NLIKE MORTINAN, KABIR did not step straight into his *eye*. Instead, he remained staring into it, as Mortinan stepped through his.

He still hadn't decided on an ability.

Looking across at the empty space in front of Mortinan's *eye*, he was momentarily surprised to see Mendina still standing in front of hers. She hadn't followed Mortinan into Dark Swell. That would be an interesting confrontation when his fellow gamer returned; if he returned.

Smiling to himself, he turned away from her and went back to studying his scroll. The goblins were still several minutes away from his Champion and he needed to get this right.

Simply removing their bonds was not going to be enough. Ahlia and his Champion would still be weapon-less and vulnerable. He needed to find a way to help defeat the horde of goblins heading their way; and their pets.

Like Ahlia, he knew they were his most dangerous foe. Adding to that dilemma, he also had to ensure his own safety. That piece of information from the Creator had been a shock and made his decision even more difficult.

If he chose an attacking ability, it would have to be powerful and should be aimed at the *Krett*. Yet that would still leave him vulnerable to the swords and arrows of the goblins.

He mulled over the list for a time, yet was still unable to commit to anything. He had narrowed his choices to a couple of attacking spells and two defensive ones, when the panic began to set in.

The goblins were close now.

If he didn't decide soon, they would be upon them and his defenceless Champion would be an easy kill.

Taking a deep breath, he pushed the doubt aside.

Striding over to the table where their food was laid out, he picked up a sharp, carving knife. He hoped he would be able to take it with him.

Trying to be remain calm, Kabir casually walked back over to his *eye* and stood in front of it.

He didn't step in however. For all his indecision, it wasn't quite time yet. The goblins hadn't arrived and he didn't want to enter too early.

Looking intently into his *eye* at the advancing raiding party, Kabir counted the goblins at closer to sixty in number and eight Krett, not six. It was going to get ugly. He hoped he had chosen correctly.

Out of the corner of his eye, he saw Mendina step through her *eye*, but he paid it no more heed than that thought. His entire focus was on his own Champion and the goblins thundering towards him.

Yet even with the life of his Champion on the line; and possibly his own; Kabir stepped through with a smile on his face.

'Shield' he said, as he finally left the clearing and stepped into the world of Dark Swell.

Kabir arrived on Dark Swell standing next to his Champion's horse.

Although he had been here before, the size of Firth still surprised him a little. It would make cutting their bonds more difficult, but he was relieved the knife was still in his hand.

Firth shied away a little at his appearance, but was quickly calmed by the soothing voice of Ahlia and the subtle pressure from her legs.

'There are more than fifty,' Ahlia said to the barbarian behind her.

'Great,' he said sarcastically. 'We really need to find something to cut these bonds.'

Ahlia slipped from the back of their horse and landed gracefully on the ground, looking around as she did.

The G.O.D. Kabir used the opportunity to step behind her and quickly cut the bonds on her wrists. She turned as soon as she felt the pressure; the knife slicing into one of her fingers; but it also sliced cleanly through the leather.

Looking around, Ahlia was startled to see no-one standing there, her hands now free.

Quickly composing herself, she told Kabir to get down. He slid off, also landing on his feet thanks to Ahlia's assistance.

'How did you get free?' he asked her, bewildered.

'I don't know,' she replied, 'but trust me when I tell you to stand still and not move.'

He looked at her strangely, but did as she bid.

Fighting the urge to move when he felt pressure on his bonds, he managed to remain motionless as his hands were also freed from their bonds.

'What was that?' he asked her, looking around.

'Perhaps you have more than one being looking over you Highlander,' she said, 'only this one is invisible.'

He didn't know if she was joking or not.

'No time to ponder,' he said, as the goblins arrived. Their horses didn't slow, as they charged into the small party standing before them, firing arrows as they rode.

'We need to get closer and use the weapons of any who fall,' Ahlia said, motioning him forward as she walked quickly towards the fray.

Arrows were thick in the air now. A couple of soldiers fell to the ground with arrows jutting from their neck and chest, despite the shields they held. The goblins had spaced out and were shooting from different directions.

Kabir and Ahlia continued to move forward, when suddenly something exploded in front of them.

The barbarian looked to where it came from and saw a bewildered look on the face of Yandow. Frowning, he shot forth another ball of energy at them. Yet again, it shattered upon an invisible shield before them. The look of anger and astonishment on the face of the wizard was quickly replaced by one of pain and fear as an arrow thudded into his side, another following quickly after, piercing his shoulder.

Neither were mortal blows, but they were enough to knock him from his horse, his head striking the ground as he fell. Moments later, one of the *Krett* pounced on his prone body and began shaking it, its sharp teeth tearing him apart.

A sword through its head put a stop to its feasting, but not before the life blood of the wizard gushed out of his body and began soaking into the ground.

They had lost their wizard quickly. The battle was not going well. Perhaps he should have concentrated his efforts on their real enemies.

Kabir and Ahlia made for the two fallen soldiers, the wizard no longer in their thoughts.

Crouching down, Kabir took one of the swords, while Ahlia helped herself to that of the other.

Standing up, Kabir moved to dodge an arrow coming straight at his head, but once again it struck something in front of them and fell harmlessly to the ground.

'Powerful allies indeed,' Ahlia said. She sounded stunned, but excited also. 'It will be fun to kill all of these abominations knowing they cannot touch us.'

Kabir looked across at her and grinned.

'Let us see if Atriol is happy to swap with me.'

Ahlia nodded her agreement.

'Stay close to each other,' Kabir said. 'We don't know how far this invisible barrier stretches or how long it will last for.'

'And don't assume it will stop everything,' Ahlia added. 'I don't want you to die with a stupid look on your face if something comes through and you are just standing there expecting this barrier to save you.'

Kabir laughed, as they moved off to find the King's Shield.

As they did, one of the *Krett* moved in to strike at Ahlia. She swung her sword at it, anticipating its move, but the shield stopped both its flailing tail and her sword stroke.

'We cannot attack them either,' she said. Kabir heard the disappointment in her voice. His feelings mirrored her own.

How could they kill them if the shield stopped their attacks?

'I need my sword,' he said. If anything could penetrate this shield, his weapon could.

He looked around for Atriol, as the goblins ceased firing their arrows and joined the melee. Long poles with wicked axe-heads or spear-points were their weapons of choice. Excellent for ranged combat, but cumbersome when in close.

Kabir saw Atriol standing about twenty paces away.

He was no longer mounted and had three goblins and a *Krett* surrounding him, yet he still looked to be the one in control.

He was using Kabir's sword to keep them at bay for now. Although his swings were text-book, Kabir could see he didn't know how to use it to maximise its effectiveness. He was better with the shorter sword he had used to best Kabir.

'With me,' he said, as they sprinted over to where the King's Shield fought. His two companions were equally besieged, but they were also holding their own.

Looking across at the rest of the battle, Kabir could see the soldiers were not faring as well.

Three more had fallen, while the others were doing all they could just to defend. As he looked on, another fell from his horse as one of the *Krett* took the legs out from his mount. Another of the *Krett* shot in and grabbed his throat in its jaws before he was able to stand.

Kabir continued forward, as one of the goblins pulled its horse up before them, swinging its wicked axe-blade as it did. The blade swept through the shield, as Ahlia only just got her sword up in time to stop it slicing through her.

Her blade jarred in her hand and fell from her grasp.

Kabir stepped in front of her as the goblin swung again. His sword blocked it, striking the shaft just under the blade and pushing the weapon downwards. The goblin was unhorsed, but managed to land on its feet.

With its weapon held up in front, the goblin stepped through the shield, stabbing this time with the point of his axe-blade. Again, Kabir hacked downwards on the shaft, before deftly stepping forward around it and driving his own blade into the goblin's neck. Two other goblins moved in to help, but the shield blocked them both.

'Grab that weapon,' Kabir said without turning.

'Atriol!' he called out. 'I need my sword!'

He saw the King's Shield glance in his direction and give a barely perceptible nod.

'Keep moving,' Kabir said to Ahlia, who patted his shoulder to indicate she followed still.

They met up with Atriol, who stepped through the barrier without pause. Those he had been fighting began to rain blows down on Kabir's shield, but none were able to breach it this time.

'I confess this weapon is not what I am used to fighting with,' the King's Shield said. 'I did not know you had a wizard with you,' Atriol added, looking beyond both Kabir and Ahlia.

'You can see him?' Kabir asked, stunned.

'Of course,' Atriol said. 'A young man stands behind you. I assume he is the one putting forth this shield.'

'What does he look like?' Ahlia asked.

Kabir thought it an odd question at this time.

'Dark hair and dressed in a strange robe,' Atriol said. 'I did not see him arrive. He looks to be rather excited, which is odd.'

Ahlia looked at Kabir and smiled.

'He seems to have something in common with you,' she said.

'My sword?' Kabir asked, bringing them back to the situation at hand.

Atriol handed the sword to the barbarian with a nod.

'It is yours for this battle,' the King's Shield said.

Kabir nodded.

'Perhaps this is more to your liking,' Kabir said, indicating the blade Ahlia held in her hands. 'It will also get you through the shield surrounding us.'

Ahlia's mirth quickly disappeared as she gave him a scathing look, before handing over the weapon.

Kabir just shrugged.

'It is only fair,' he said in defence. 'He returned my weapon to me. Our friend will keep you safe.'

'Enough talk,' Atriol said, stepping back outside of the magic barrier, slashing goblins as he went. He seemed much more comfortable with his new weapon. Holding it almost half way along the shaft, he was able to strike with the blade and defend with the bottom half. It was a whirlwind in his hands.

Kabir followed straight after him, his sword moving almost as fast as that of the King's Shield. He was relieved to be fighting goblins and *Krett*. The look Ahlia had given him after his last comment was truly frightening.

Despite the threat of imminent death, the G.O.D. Kabir couldn't wipe the smile from his face.

When the goblin breached his shield, he had involuntarily jumped backwards, but it only served to increase his adrenaline.

A destructive spell would have been exhilarating, but he was content to stand within the protection of his shield and watch as the goblin party attacked.

He had wanted to speak with Atriol, as the King's Shield stared at him, but it was all so chaotic, he could think of nothing to say.

Instead he just watched, as his Champion and the King's Shield moved through the goblins like a whirlwind.

Their styles were poles apart, but each was a natural born fighter, and nearly all of their strokes were effective in crippling or killing their opponent.

It took them little time to reach the remaining soldiers. None of them were mounted any longer, and all had serious wounds, but four of them were still alive and fighting by the time Kabir and the three King's Shield made their way to them.

In the frantic melee, they were unable to form up into any kind of defence, but the goblins now looked to be less sure of an easy victory.

One of them squawked something in their guttural language, and those that were left, pulled away from the men.

There would have been more than thirty goblins alive, twenty of them still on horseback. Only two of the *Krett* had been killed.

Ahlia moved quickly to where Kabir and the other survivors stood, huddled tightly together now.

'Get behind her,' Kabir said to Methan and the others. The Captain of their group was one of those who still lived, although he had a gaping wound across his chest. The soldiers all reacted to the voice of the barbarian, even though he had been their prisoner only minutes earlier.

'The young wizard has a shield,' Atriol said, as the other King's Shield remained where they stood. 'You need to get behind them.'

They both moved quickly to stand behind Ahlia with the other soldiers.

Kabir and Atriol stepped back into its protection.

The goblins had re-grouped a short distance away before turning to face them.

Without pause they began shooting arrows at them again, all of which struck the shield and fell harmlessly to the ground.

'We have a stand-off,' Kabir said, looking down at Ahlia. She still didn't look happy, but the thunderclouds above her had gone.

'I am afraid not,' she replied, indicating for Kabir to look back at the goblins.

They had quickly given up on wasting their arrows, and instead took off at a gallop to the right of the shield. The ones on foot doing their best to keep up.

'They are fleeing,' the G.O.D. Kabir said with a smile. 'You have won the day.'

Atriol looked at him without expression.

'We have not wizard,' he said in a calm voice. 'They will look to ride around us. Those that have gone before us will not fare as well as we have.'

'Look for any horses that can still be ridden,' Methan barked. 'We need to protect the carts.'

Kabir turned to Atriol.

'Are you speaking to this wizard?' he asked.

'Of course,' Atriol said. 'Did you not hear him speak?'

'I did not,' Kabir said. 'Did you?' he asked Ahlia.

She shook her head.

'Can you ask him a question for me?' Kabir asked.

'I can hear what he says,' the G.O.D. Kabir said, 'but I cannot answer him.'

'He hears you barbarian, but he will not speak with you,' Atriol said.

'We need to move!' Methan said, his wound didn't appear to have slowed him down yet.

The goblins had already stopped riding south, and had turned back in the direction where the carts were headed.

The G.O.D. Kabir looked around and saw they would struggle to find enough fit horses to carry them all.

Firth was still okay, but only a couple of other horses looked capable of being ridden. The goblin arrows and their pet *Krett's* had crippled or killed all of the others.

'The barbarian and his wizard need to get on the large horse,' Atriol said. 'Without his shield, it will be difficult to prevail.'

'I am going,' Ahlia said, walking with Kabir over to where Firth patiently waited. She swung herself into the saddle before any of them could say a word in response.

'The wizard will have your horse,' Atriol said to one of the soldiers who was about to jump into the saddle. 'Can you ride wizard?' The King's Shield seemed to ask as an after-thought.

The G.O.D. Kabir was intrigued at how Atriol had taken over command. Methan didn't even question his orders.

'I can,' he replied, 'but I won't be coming with you.'

Atriol's forehead furrowed. It was the first real facial expression he had seen on the man.

'Where are you going then?' he asked, before turning to Kabir. 'Your wizard says he is not coming.'

The G.O.D. Kabir was shattered by the look he had given him, but he knew his shield would not last long enough. He would disappear back to the clearing well before they caught up with the carts. He had completely lost track of time with all that had just happened, but he knew he would have only a few minutes left at most.

His Champion was still in serious danger, but at least he had given him a fighting chance.

'I have to leave,' was all he said to the King's Shield. 'And with me, so too does the magic shield.'

After he had finished speaking the word 'shield', the G.O.D. Kabir vanished from the world of Dark Swell.

CHAPTER 18

Unity Is Hard

'THEY SHOULD HAVE been here,' Fargesh said, as he trudged through the muddy snow. It was the third time he had said it in the last hour.

It was a sunny day in the highlands, and the sparse cover of snow had begun to melt on the track they all walked on. They had used this track to move their cattle up and down the hillsides for as long as he had been alive.

'You have said that already several times,' Herid replied. He tried to keep the exasperation out of his voice, as he understood why Fargesh was nervous. His eldest son had gone with his uncle and cousin to help bring the herd down. It was the first time he had been permitted to go. Herid would be just as worried if it had been his own son.

They had agreed it was possible the men and boys had spent time rounding up strays, but it shouldn't have taken them four whole days.

When they were three days late, Dougal had sent this small party to find out what had happened. He wanted to send more, but he had already sent a large party to meet in Wolfsbane. The rest were needed to safekeep their home.

Only six others walked with Fargesh and Herid.

They had left their horses at home, thinking it wouldn't be long before they ran into the missing barbarians on their way down.

Now the day was almost over and still there was no sign of them.

They had all started to worry long before now.

Fargesh was the first to see his slain kinsmen and women, left where they had been killed by the dark-elves. Their bodies were covered in a fine layer of snow, hiding most of the blood which had been scattered throughout the clearing only two nights earlier.

'No,' he rasped, running towards the first of the dead.

Fargesh moved quickly past him and on to the next body. He didn't stop moving until he had been to the other end of the field and back again.

His son wasn't among the dead, but it gave him little relief.

It may mean his fate had been worse than those lying here.

'I haven't seen injuries like these before,' he heard one of the men say. It brought the barbarian out of his trance. He had paid little heed to how they had been killed.

Now that he knew his son wasn't among them, he wanted to know what sort of creatures has done this to so many of his kinsmen.

He walked over to where the body of Krith lay. The snow had already been swept from his body, leaving his horrific wounds visible to those looking on.

'It wasn't a wild animal, that is for sure,' Herid said. Wild animals wouldn't have left the carcasses behind.

'What then?' Fargesh said. He knew he sounded desperate.

'I know not,' Herid replied.

'Nothing smart,' one of the others said, holding a helm up in his hand. 'If they were, they wouldn't have left this behind.'

'Whatever they were,' Fargesh said, 'when we catch up with them, I will put my sword through the heart of each and every one of them.'

None of the others said anything. They all remained silent as they stared at the surrounding bodies.

Fargesh looked around at those who stood with him, staring down each man and woman in turn.

'We are not going back without the boys they have taken,' he said.

'We don't know what has done this,' Herid finally said. 'And there are only eight of us.'

Fargesh moved quickly to where Herid stood, his face pushed up close to that of the other Barbarian. 'Are you a coward?' he asked.

Herid refrained from pushing his friend away.

'You know I am not Fargesh,' Herid replied, 'but we need to be smart about this. We need more warriors. Then we will return.'

'We don't have time for that!' Fargesh said, his voice rising as he spoke. 'What if it were your son Herid? Would you wait before seeking him out?'

'If we make haste in returning to gather more men and horses, we will be back here before the sun is at its peak tomorrow,' Herid said, but without much conviction this time. Fargesh could see his words had impacted him.

'Send one back to get men and horses and they can track where we have gone,' Fargesh said.

Herid hesitated still, but eventually he turned to one of the others.

'Brinn, you are the fastest, so be quick about it.'

The Barbarian didn't hesitate, taking off at a slow run back down towards their village.

'Let's find their trail,' Herid said to Fargesh, clapping him on the shoulder. 'We will find your son and the other boys, or we will die trying.'

'Not until they are all dead will I let you die,' Fargesh said, clasping his friend's shoulder in return. 'We will burn the pour souls of our kin on our return.'

They continued walking upwards, until the light of day was completely gone.

After seeing what had happened to their brethren, none of them thought it worth the risk to light a fire. Which meant nothing to light their way; which in turn meant they had no choice but to huddle down for the night.

As soon as the first sign of light showed itself in the darkened sky above, Fargesh was up and prodding the others to get moving.

It had been a freezing night, and it took a while for them to warm up, but they made good time.

Most were familiar with the area, having brought their livestock up here many times before.

Presently they were heading for the Twin Pass.

As good as their prey was at covering their tracks, Herid was their best at tracking and he was confident they were going in the right direction.

'Are you sure the trail continues this way?' It wasn't the first time Fargesh had asked, nor would it be the last.

'They headed for the Twin Pass,' Herid replied patiently. 'Same as us.'

'Good,' Fargesh said.

'We should stop and eat,' Herid said. 'I'm hungry.'

Fargesh turned back to him.

'Can you tell how far behind we are?' he asked.

'No,' Herid said. 'They cover up well, despite the cattle they herd. Maybe a little too well, but I can't say how long ago they were here. The snow is not consistent.'

'Then until you can tell me how far, we should keep going.' Fargesh turned and began trudging off again.

Herid didn't follow him.

'If I could tell you how long Fargesh, would you be okay with eating?' He continued on without waiting for an answer. 'If we were close you would want to go faster so we could catch them. If they were a day in front, you would want to go faster so we can get closer. We are stopping to eat,' Herid said, as he pulled off his pack and started to rummage inside.

Fargesh swore under his breath, as he stopped and returned to stand with the rest of them.

None spoke as they ate. All of them were tired, their thoughts consumed with their unknown enemies.

'What could do that to so many warriors?' Freta asked, speaking to no-one in particular. She had no children of her own yet, but had younger brothers and sisters. It horrified her as much as it did the others, what fate may have befallen those who had been captured.

'I would wager whatever did it, came upon them at night and took them when they weren't expecting attack,' Herid replied. 'Whatever manner of beast, they are cowards. We will not be surprised.'

'We are the hunters now,' Fargesh replied in agreeance.

'Speaking of which,' Herid said, holding the helm out to his friend. It was the greatest treasure they had in their village. 'Until it can be returned to his eldest son, the helm is yours to wear.'

Fargesh didn't take it. 'You should have it,' he said. 'You are the strongest here.'

Herid shook his head.

'You will be first to battle them Fargesh, of that I have no doubt.' He smiled thinly. 'You will need to kill as many as you can before we all join the fray. It is best you have it.'

Fargesh hesitated, but then reached out his hand and took it.

'I can't promise there will be any left for the rest of you,' he said, as he stood once again and placed the War Helm on his head, the mighty curved horns glistening where the sun's rays struck it.

Herid knew he wasn't joking when he said it. He hoped it came to pass, but he was nervous.

He wasn't afraid of fighting, or even of death.

He was nervous for those he stood here with, and for those left behind in their village.

Something within was telling him these first deaths were only the beginning.

He feared something terrible was coming for them all; that his people were in serious danger.

And here he was, leading six barbarians to face this evil on their own.

This may not be the slaughter Fargesh was hoping for.

CHAPTER 19

Shaking The Earth

THE G.O.D. MORTINAN appeared in the tunnel, his Champion by his side and Mendina to his left on the other side of Mort. They weren't far from the opening of the cavern, but to his relief Mort and Mendina slowed as they approached it.

Mortinan sprinted ahead of them. As much as he wanted to stop and absorb where he was and who he was with, time was his enemy right now.

He entered the cavern, the front part of it lit up by his Champion's magic. He was unable to see the back part yet, but he knew what lurked there and where it stood.

He was no more than five paces inside when he heard a crashing sound behind him. Turning, he saw that a large portcullis had crashed down into the ground below, cutting off any exit. He hadn't known that was there. He suddenly wished he had spent more time investigating this particular cavern.

The light cast by Mort had stopped just beyond the metal gate, but it still shone through into the large cavern, lighting it up completely now and revealing the hulking form of the Lokaan as he turned to face it.

His Champion and that of Mendina, were stuck behind it.

'Something doesn't want us going in there,' he heard Mendina say. 'We should go back.'

'What is that?' Mort said.

What indeed, Mortinan thought to himself, as the gravity of the situation he found himself in began to dawn on him.

Standing almost ten feet in height, the Lokaan was made completely out of iron. As was the gigantic sword it held in its right hand. It had no facial features, but possessed the form of a large man.

It had been put there by the Creator many hundreds of years ago, to guard an artefact of tremendous power. There were similar artefacts strewn around the world of Dark Swell, within other dark and foreboding places.

All of which had different kinds of monsters guarding them.

It was how the human Brax had accumulated such a wealth of powerful items in his travels.

Mortinan would love for his Champion to have what was nestled in an alcove in the wall behind the Lokaan, but that would not be happening today. As soon as his Champion left to leave, he would take with him the only illumination within this space. He would not be able to see where the treasure was.

Yet that would not be his major concern once the light left. It would leave him alone with the Lokaan and with no way of seeing where it was. He knew the Lokaan required no light to see. It lived in the dark.

That meant he would have no choice but to use his spell straight away or risk his own death within this dark and foreboding cavern.

Although he had been given no instruction on how to use the ability he had chosen, he knew how to make it work the moment he arrived on Dark Swell. He didn't understand how he knew; he just did. And as the true nature of its required destructive force dawned on him, Mortinan believed he knew now what real terror felt like.

Why had he chosen it?!

As he looked on, the monster began to move.

Painfully slow at first; as if it was stuck to the floor; Mortinan knew it would increase in speed. He was thankful he had taken the time to at least read up on it.

Yet as he stood before the Lokaan, watching on as it made its way slowly toward him, he hesitated.

With the portcullis down, his Champion was no longer in any danger from it. All he and Mendina had to do was turn around and run back up the tunnel.

They were actually in more danger if he were to use his given power. The entire tunnel could easily collapse on top of them. Mortinan had known it was a possibility when he chose his spell, but in his panic, had somehow discarded it. He had convinced himself he would be able to focus it at the Lokaan only, but now he knew better. He had been a fool. It was likely the entire cave system would crash down on top of them, killing both Champion's instantly.

All he wanted to do now was shout at them to run, but he knew they wouldn't be able to hear him. Just as they couldn't see him, even from only a few paces away.

Panic seized him still. What had he done? If only he had known the portcullis was there, he would have used a defensive spell to keep himself safe and no more.

Mortinan and Mendina would have simply left, and he would be safe from this monstrosity that was slowly making its way toward him.

Now he was beholden to use his ability. It was one of the conditions of entering. He could not leave until he did. Unless he remained for ten minutes, and Mortinan was under no illusion he could survive that long.

He knew they should leave now, yet curiosity got the better of Mort. The light remained within the cavern, as Mortinan's Champion stood there staring at the giant, iron guardian.

'We should go,' he heard Mendina say.

'There is strong magic in this,' Mort said, touching one of the thick steel bars of the gate in front of them. 'I think we are safe behind it.'

'Why did it close before we got in there?' she asked. 'It would appear it was designed to keep intruders in, not keep them out.'

'I agree,' Mort said. 'I guess we got lucky.'

'Then let us not push our luck,' Mendina said. 'We need to go. Look,' she said.

Mort turned to her and followed her gaze to the ground at their feet. Water was trickling past them and into the large cavern.

'You said the water probably carved out this cave. It might get a lot stronger and a lot deeper if we do not hurry back outside.' There was panic in her voice, but Mort wasn't feeling it within himself. He wanted to know what this thing was and why it had suddenly swung its sword in a large, slow arc around itself.

'What is it doing?' he said out loud, as the huge man-shaped monster turned around, continuing to swing its sword as it moved.

Its speed of movement was steadily growing faster, as the mighty sword sent off sparks each time it struck the ground.

It turned again to face in the direction of the closed gate, swinging its sword once more in a wide arc.

'Something is in there.' Mort said to Mendina, not taking his eyes from the inside of the cavern. 'That is why the gate closed and why it is swinging the sword.'

'I don't see anything,' Mendina said. 'We should go!' She was more frantic now. The trickle of water now covered the entire tunnel. Mort could feel it under his feet, but he wanted to know what was in there.

He could feel *Iska's* talons starting to dig into his shoulder, telling him that his fairie-dragon was also keen to leave this place.

'A moment longer,' Mort said, as something floated towards him from within the cavern. As it came close to the gate he could see it was a necklace with a pendant attached to it. It floated through one of the gaps in the gate and Mort snatched hold of it.

'Let's go,' Mort said, turning to leave, as the sword of the giant guardian smashed into the portcullis. Mort shone the light back there for a moment and saw it had turned away from the gate already and was moving back into the centre of the cavern. It hadn't appeared to damage the gate at all.

They were indeed fortunate, he thought. They would never have gotten out of there.

'Run,' Mendina said. The water was rising fast now.

They were almost at the fork in the tunnel, when they both heard a deafening crack behind them and the ground under their feet started to shake.

They both stopped running at the same time, coming to a stand-still in order to balance themselves from the movement of the tunnel.

So too did the dozen or so small humanoid creatures, only ten paces in front of them.

CHAPTER 20

Call To War

'I AM GLAD TO see you have decided to join us,' Flek-Niht said to the dark-elf standing in front of her. 'You will be glad you did.'

Clen-Joint tilted her head slightly. An acknowledgement of her thanks, nothing more.

None gave fealty amongst the Dark Elves. There was loyalty to the family and nothing more. Some families were stronger than others, but none ruled.

Flek-Niht stood at the entrance of the great cavern, looking out at those assembled before her. She was dressed in her family's ancient battle-armour.

It would be the first time she had worn it at a time when they were leaving for war.

Before today, it had served as nothing more than ceremonial dress-wear for as far back as her mother's stories went.

The headpiece covered none of her face, but it wound itself around her head, the thin horns curving up and then down along the side of her head, their points facing forward in front of her breast plate. Her shoulder plates had spikes pointing outward, while the armour continued to snake along her arms, all the way down to her wrists, where they became wrist-guards and gauntlets. They looked flimsy and thin, but they were crafted of a long-forgotten material and were incredibly hardy. The darkest of blacks, they would change to a blood-red when she moved.

Clen-Joint wore her own battle-armour, as she moved to stand beside Flek-Niht, joining her in observance of those who would leave with them today.

Numbering almost a thousand strong, Flek-Niht had never seen so many of her kind in one place before.

Warriors from three of the great houses were about to march down into the lowlands for the first time in history.

They were finally going to bring war to the barbarian tribes who had kept them within their rocky domain for so long, too wary to risk showing themselves.

Yet that was in the past. They were strong enough now to challenge the barbarian hordes. She corrected her own thoughts. They were strong enough to do more than simply challenge them. She intended to wipe them out.

Flek-Niht wanted to say something stirring to them all before they set out, but their plans had been discussed the night before and nothing else needed to be spoken. She knew what lay in the hearts of those assembled. Stirring words were not required. They would be skilful and they would be fierce.

The small council had decided to attack the closest of the barbarian villages, a place their people called Horned Peak. A couple of the barbarian children had eventually opened up to her about where the barbarians lived.

There were six settlements in total, the largest and strongest furthest west.

That one would be the last to fall.

Although it was early morning now, they would wait until night before launching their assault. They were strongest at night.

If all went to plan, it would be less of a battle and more of a slaughter.

The barbarians would not even know what had come upon them until it was too late.

Walking from the entrance she moved to stand before her mount.

His name was Jext, and he was the largest and most powerful of his kind.

He was one of the *telquin,* and he had been captured and tamed by her many years ago. Their kind ranged much further north, in the desolate place between the mountains and the black ocean, but of late they had started to appear within her own lands.

As a result, many dark-elf warriors now possessed *telquin* of their own, which would prove to be another advantage during the upcoming battles.

Their usual stance was upright, but those who had been trained for an extended period of time, were able to run with their heads pointed forward, allowing their riders to be far more efficient and flexible in their options of attack when mounted.

Many of the recently acquired *telquin* still ran standing straight up, which made them more challenging to ride and looked ridiculous, in her opinion. Still, it was considered an honour to have one, so their riders were not embarrassed.

Jext pushed his head forward and bent his knees as she approached, allowing her to easily move on to his back, her saddle already tied firmly around his mid-section. Due to their lack of arms, the saddle was placed near the base of their backs so their balance could be easily maintained.

His powerful legs straightened, as Flek-Niht took her position, lifting her up above those standing around. Jext was easily half her height again when upright.

There was no fanfare as she began to move out, the members of her clan falling in behind her.

The cowardly clans who had decided to stay had not come out to see them go. Flek-Niht hadn't expected them to.

She was glad Clen-Joint would be coming though. Aside from the extra numbers it would give them against the barbarians, it would also make it easier for them to return home when they had secured the land below them.

If there had been a greater number stay behind, they would have wanted to share in the bounty that was to come. With the inevitable loss of dark-elves in the ensuing battles, it would have been difficult to deny them.

But now it would be shared among the three great houses who were travelling south. Those remaining would not dare to try and impose their will upon them on their triumphant return.

They would get nothing, and they would deserve nothing.

No words were spoken by any dark-elf as they left their ancestral home.

Travelling in silence, they moved out, grim expressions on the faces of all.

Flek-Niht remained silent and expressionless also, yet inside she felt an exhilaration unmatched before in her life.

She was saddened her son was not at her back, but the first fifty kills she would dedicate to him, penance for the life taken from her.

The rest she would do for her own sheer pleasure.

Flek-Niht had already vowed to herself she would not smile or rejoice until she held within her hands the severed head of the last Barbarian Chieftain.

Not until the village of Deerstep was razed to the ground.

CHAPTER 21

Surrounded

B RINDEL GENUINELY FELT his was the most difficult decision of those playing the game. He also felt strongly that once again he had been cheated by the Creator. As hard as he tried to suppress the notion, it continued to bubble up into his mind.

That the Creator believed it was fair to all in giving them this added opportunity to not only enter the world, but influence things directly, was plain wrong.

It was not only plausible that every Champion of his fellow gamers was about to be killed, it was highly likely. That would have left only his Champion alive, and victory his by default.

How was that fair?!

Admittedly, his Champion was pitted against an army of Western Dwarves, an Elven Lord and a myriad of creatures that called the swamp their home.

Presently the Dwarven Army was steadily approaching his position and one of the most powerful creatures on Dark Swell was in the trees almost adjacent to him, waiting for his next opportunity to try and kill Brindel's Champion and companions.

However, there was no immediate threat from any of them.

A couple of abominations would definitely pose a serious threat, if his Champion was to come across them before getting clear of the festering swamp he walked through. But that was not assured. Not by a long way.

The more likely scenario, was that his Champion would stay where he was until the threat of the Dwarven army had passed.

Then another thought struck him.

Perhaps it wasn't enough to simply be the last one alive in the game. Maybe they needed to achieve some goal before they could be crowned victor.

If that were the case; and the more he thought about it, the more certain he was; then perhaps this extra ability could prove a tremendous advantage.

Turning his thoughts back to the game, Brindel believed it may be better for him to select a defensive ability.

He knew he had no chance of attacking any of those on his list and surviving, let alone doing sufficient damage to allow Brindel to pass unmolested. He would also likely get himself killed trying.

Yet if he were able to hide his dwarf, then perhaps the Western Dwarves, the Elven Lord and the inhabitants of the swamp, would all just move on without paying him any mind.

Unfortunately, he had a window of ten minutes in which to do whatever it was he was going to do.

Not nearly enough time to keep his Champion safe.

Fortunately, he had time to think on it.

His Champion was far enough into the swamp that Jarkene wouldn't be able to see him from the forest, and the Dwarven army was still some distance away. His Champion had also just been forewarned about the dwarves coming, so he doubted they would look to show themselves any time soon.

For now, so long as they stayed where they were, his Champion wasn't in any immediate danger.

With a bit of luck, he may not have to intercede at all.

As much as that should delight him, he looked across and saw that Mortinan had already stepped through his *eye* and into the world of Dark Swell.

That left him as the only one yet to enter, so instead of happiness and satisfaction at the thought of saving his chance to enter, he felt only sadness and bitterness. He wanted it badly. More than anything else he could ever remember wanting. He knew he was being petulant, but he couldn't help it.

As he continued to ponder his predicament, he saw Mendina also step through. Letting out a massive sigh, he turned to look at his *eye* to see what had forced both Mortinan and Mendina into the world.

As he watched his fellow G.O.D.'s on Dark Swell, the feeling of self-pity soon passed.

He could enter the world any time he chose. At any time and place he wanted, and with the ability to cast a spell to help out his Champion.

It would make things so much more intriguing; deciding exactly when the right time would be. If he paid attention and used his smarts, he needn't worry about not being able to enter the world. It would happen right when he was needed most.

He had been caught up on the rules associated with his ability to enter and converse with his Champion only when it was safe. This was different. Although unable to converse with them, he would have the ability to intercede directly in what was happening. It was an amazing gift from the Creator. A gift he should be grateful for.

As his attitude shifted, another thought occurred to him.

What if he were to intercede when his Champion arrived at the Ruined Forest? The Creator did not say when and where they could use it. They were given a list of spells and told they would have ten minutes in which to use it.

He had guessed at the time, that all of the other G.O.D.'s would need to enter and use it, due to the circumstances each found themselves in.

It had only occurred to Brindel a short time ago, that he may not have to use his at all just yet.

Now he had thought about it in length, he was suddenly very happy with his situation.

He might actually be able to help his Champion against the dragon, and if Mortinan and Mendina got there first, so much better.

It suddenly felt to him like he had only just now received a reward worthy of winning the first task set to them, and he began to wonder whether the Creator had been thinking exactly the same thing when he gave it out.

He should probably be more careful with his thoughts, as he looked around at no-one and said sorry.

CHAPTER 22

Another Chieftain

RAIF FINISHED THE final stitch to his forearm, before standing up and looking around at the bloody scene before him. The blood had been free-flowing, making his efforts slow and slippery, but he had done so many times during his life that it no longer bothered him. The claws on the creature had been sharper than he thought, but he was able to limit the damage done by driving his sword through its face.

It was still light outside, although the sun seemed to be hurrying to its sleep for the night. Raif felt like doing the same. He was desperate for his own bed. It had been a long day, but well worth the pain and fatigue.

The creatures that had been killing his goblin villagers were finally dead.

Their heads now rested on the spear points of three of his warriors, the filthy carcasses left to rot where they lay. None would risk eating that flesh.

Raif was fascinated by them, and horrified at the same time. After they had been put on the spikes, he had taken the time to stop and examine the heads from up close. Each had four eyes in the front of their skulls, two of them almost at the side, so their range of vision was excellent. Their mouths were only small, but housed sharpened fangs inside, the likes of which he had never seen before. There were four smaller ones at the front, but they were still bigger than his own. Next to these on either side was a pair of even longer fangs, almost the length of his finger when fully exposed. As he held its mouth open, he could see where they withdrew into the gum when not being used, but could be made to elongate with small muscles around them when used to attack. These are what they used to suck the blood from their prey, and due to their size, they were able to do it quickly. He had seen goblins die within seconds from being drained. As he had looked down at the carcass of this one, he wondered where all the blood went. Their bodies didn't look large enough to absorb so much blood in such a short period of time.

He had refrained from slicing them open however. There didn't seem to be any point in that. The blood of the goblins they had killed was obviously in there somewhere. He didn't need to see it and neither did the goblins around him.

He was just glad none had gotten hold of him and sunk those fangs into his flesh.

One of the surviving goblins had called them *louckrift*, meaning blood-drainers. It seemed to fit, so that is what he decided they would be called.

The goblins who died quickest had been the ones who had the blood sucked directly from their heart. The fangs were long enough to penetrate through leather armour, and yet thin enough to get in between the ribs.

The ones bitten on the thigh lasted a little bit longer, but not by much.

His warriors who still lived stood proudly nearby, waiting for Raif to give them the word to move off back to their home with their trophies. There would be a celebration tonight, even though they had lost many more goblins in the battle.

Yet it was only due to Raif bringing such a large number of goblins, that they had finally won the day.

That, and their leader's sword.

Raif had sacrificed many of his own in order to get close enough to drive his sword through the throat or face of each one.

No other weapon among those that fought had been able to kill the creatures. Only his.

The rest had served only to keep them busy long enough for Raif to act.

His heroics would be told and re-told tonight. He was sure word would spread throughout the larger goblin settlements as well.

'Raif the Demon Slayer' they were already calling him.

He liked the sound of that. A name to cause fear in those who would think to challenge him.

Not that he was coveting anything more than he already had. It was challenge enough keeping his leadership where he was.

Raif still wasn't foolish enough to try and take the Chieftain title in their main settlement, but from time to time some little upstart thought he was strong enough to challenge for leadership of their own small goblin hovel.

He knew one of them would probably try and steal his sword; now word would spread that it was magic; but he wasn't too concerned with that.

Nervous fear was different to ordinary fear, and he would see those ones coming.

'Shall we leave?' one of his warriors asked. This goblin had one of the heads on his spear, its black oozy blood still running from the hole in its neck

'You can, and most of the others with you, but I need five to come with me.'

They all looked at him like he was crazy. None stepped forward to volunteer.

'Five of my most loyal will stay,' he said. This would be interesting, he thought.

Those standing around all looked at each other. He could see they were trying to work out what was going on.

Eventually Shathez stepped forward.

'I'll stay,' he said, though his voice betrayed his suspicion.

Raif had expected him to volunteer. He was a good dog.

Four others stepped forward as well. Friends of Shathez, they only did it because he had.

'Any more of you, or is that all?' Raif asked.

There were no more, but they all looked decidedly nervous. Every one of them knew how quick Raif could be to anger. They had all been scared of him before this battle, but he could see a couple of them actually trembling where they stood.

'Cowards', he thought, but it didn't really bother him. He had given them the opportunity to stay. That was all he had really wanted to achieve. Five should be enough.

'Okay then,' he said. 'The rest of you get back and start preparing for when I return. Nothing starts until I get there.'

He was confident most of them would heed him, but he honestly didn't care that much. It would show him which ones were somewhat trustworthy. A good test for them.

He would enjoy beating the ones who disobeyed him when he returned.

Those that were going didn't waste any time with good-byes.

'Oh, except for you Gurth,' he said. The goblin and his *crintin* stopped in their tracks. 'You and your pet will stay.'

Reluctantly Gurth turned and walked over to where Raif stood.

Once Raif was satisfied the rest had all left, he looked to those that stayed.

'I can't believe how stupid they all are,' he said, shaking his head. 'Do you know why we are still here?' he asked.

He shouldn't have been surprised this lot was just as stupid, as he looked upon nothing but blank expressions. Yet they were goblins, greedy and selfish by nature. They should have at least been able to guess.

'You are a little bit less stupid than the others, because you stayed,' he said. 'These things we just killed were powerful, do you agree?'

They all nodded.

'And they live in caves,' he added. Still nothing.

'We are going on a treasure hunt,' he finally said, putting them out of their misery.

'But they had nothing on them,' Shathez said. He looked disappointed with the reason Raif gave to keep them here.

'Do you think those they have killed might have had things with them?' Raif was convinced they would have a horde somewhere in the caves they lived in.

'Or how long they have been doing it?'

There still wasn't a lot of interest on their faces. It had been a long day.

'What if there are more of them way back in the caves?' one of Shathez' lackeys asked. Raif couldn't remember his name. He looked scared.

To be fair, Raif couldn't be sure there wasn't. The ones they had just killed had rushed them not far from the opening to the cave. Who knew how far back it went or if there were more of them in there.

'That is why we have the *Crintin*,' Raif said. Gurth's hound had sounded the alarm early, before the creatures had arrived. It could obviously smell them, because they made next to no sound when they moved. It would also help him to track where their lair was.

'You want me to go in there on my own?' Gurth asked. He didn't look too happy about it.

'We won't be far behind you,' Raif said. 'You might get second pick of the treasure if you do a good job.'

Gurth wasn't stupid enough to argue with Raif about it.

'Now move,' Raif yelled. 'The feast will begin soon and I want to get back there.'

The cave was dark once the entrance was out of sight, but goblins could see well enough without light and the *Crintin* could smell exceptionally well. If there were more of them, Raif was confident he would have time to get out of the cave. His chances of beating more than one of them with only this many to assist were not good enough for him to risk fighting them.

They had walked farther into the cave than he had hoped when they set off, before he finally heard Gurth bellow something from up ahead. The *Crintin* master didn't sound alarmed, so Raif quickened his pace.

Turning the next bend in the cave, they came into a small cavern-like area, except there was no exit on the other side.

As Raif looked around, he knew he had found their lair, and there were no more of the creatures here.

Just bones and more bones. He couldn't even begin to guess how many dead numbered within this small area. They had definitely been at it for a long time!

Raif turned on the men who had come with him.

'Go and stand by the entrance and keep guard while I look around.' He could see the anger coming from them after he said it. 'I will select a few things and then the rest of you can have at it.'

The anger dissipated for the most part.

Raif thought it best not to try and be too greedy, but that all depended on what he found. Not that it really mattered. If one of the others found something which he missed and later wanted, he would just take it from them anyway. But to be sure none of them tried to hide anything really valuable or powerful, he would be the one to look first.

'You too Gurth,' he snarled, as the *Crintin* handler continued to rummage through some of the bones on the far wall. He moved slowly back to the entrance, the anger thick in the air around him.

Raif scanned everything in the cavern, before his eyes came back to a large piece of rock jutting out, away from the wall.

He walked over to it and saw that there looked to be a large space behind it.

He walked behind it and stopped. That was why he hadn't seen anything as he looked around. It was all stacked up here, behind this natural piece of rock that jutted up out of the ground.

There were weapons and armours the likes of which he had never seen before, and all sorts of trinkets and jewellery. They had definitely been here a long time, and looked to have travelled to who knows where to get a lot of this stuff. A few things he recognised as possibly belonging to goblins, but most was almost certainly from the other realms.

The *louckrift* had killed countless creatures in their life-time, and yet Raif had been the one to end them. He felt a smug self-satisfaction at that. Now that he had found their treasure, it didn't occur to him to give any credit to the many goblins who had died so he was able to do it.

He turned to look at those who had accompanied him and sighed. He should have brought more. Seven would not be enough to carry all of this.

Raif thought for a moment about killing them all. Then he could take a few pieces back with him now and collect the rest at his leisure. There would be no sharing it then.

Yet for all their stupidity, there was six of them. And the fact they were all still alive meant they were all capable of looking after themselves.

Raif doubted he would be able to kill them all, and then he would be dead and left with none of it. He didn't want that.

Back to his original plan then.

He would take the rest of what he wanted later. For now, he would choose those he thought were the best of the lot.

'Come on over,' he said to them. 'There is more than we can all carry, so let's spread it out and see what is worth taking now.'

None of them hesitated, as they moved quickly to stand next to Raif.

As they looked upon their find, Raif saw that not one of them had even the slightest amount of anger or fear left in them.

'Greedy bastards', he thought, as he grabbed a couple of swords and took them to the centre of the cavern. This might take some time, but he wasn't in the least bit worried. He was no longer in a hurry.

Let the others enjoy their feast.

They would all choke on their food when they saw what he had brought back, and none of them would be getting any of it.

Well, maybe those who had helped fight against them. They wouldn't deserve it, but he knew better than to have that many of his goblins conspiring against him.

Looking at his riches, he decided he could afford to be a little bit generous.

He knew he would probably need them when goblins from elsewhere heard about what he had won for himself.

Thinking more about the frenzy such rumours would cause in the larger settlements, he thought maybe he should be more than a little bit generous. They would fight harder if they had their own treasures to defend.

CHAPTER 23

Patience

ELENDA WAS CERTAIN now that the words she so desperately needed were not going to magically appear.

The instructions to complete her masterpiece were out of her reach.

The one she had sent north to Draug's Kingdom had not yet returned, and she no longer held out much hope that he would. If he had found what she had sent him to find he would have been back by now.

She was at a momentary loss as to what she could do. Brayden was her most trusted dwarf and a very good thief. If he had failed, they would be wary of more coming. And as trusted as Brayden was, Elenda did not believe he would keep his tongue still for Draug. The King of the Northern Dwarves had a reputation for getting what he wanted.

Elenda had thought of going herself, but that would be risky if Brayden had talked. Stealing was something Dwarves didn't do, especially the Northern Dwarves with their strict codes of conduct. Their rules were far more stringent than those within her own realm. She hadn't really understood a lot of their more obscure traditions and laws, and did not agree with many of the ones she did understand, but now that she was going to be the new Master Smith of the Southern Dwarven Realm, she had begun to see the appeal in a few. Those that would ensure her longevity and power she would look to take on board.

She was broken from her thoughts by a knock on her door.

Elenda had still kept her own room. It was much too soon to move into Brangold's much larger and more lavish rooms. Not until she was officially named Master Smith would she do that.

'Come in,' she said.

'A message for you Elenda,' Jorwen said, as he strode arrogantly into her room.

What was he doing delivering letters to her? That would soon stop.

Snatching it from him, she checked to see the seal was still intact. It looked to be, but she wouldn't put it past this one to know how to open and seal a letter without the recipient being any the wiser.

'When did this arrive?' she asked.

'Some hours ago, Elenda. Unfortunately, I was unable to locate you at the time and had other tasks to attend to.' He smiled at her.

This one will be joining Brangold soon enough, she told herself, as she struggled to contain her anger. He would definitely have had the time to open it.

'Still no word on the Master Smith,' Jorwen said, 'just in case you were interested.'

'I am well aware of that,' she replied pleasantly. 'I seek my counsel and advice from others more trustworthy. You can go now.' She waved her hand in the direction of the door as she moved to her desk to retrieve a small dagger.

Looking up to make sure Jorwen had left, she sliced the dagger through the seal and began reading.

'*We caught your man trying to steal. If you want him back Elenda then you need to come here and get him. Bring whatever you think he is worth and enough also to pay the fine for his crime. And something for the time and expense on tending to his many injuries. King Draug.*'

Elenda scrunched it up and threw it into her burning hearth. She watched as it quickly burst into flames and turned to ash.

An invitation from the Northern King to come and get her man.

Leaving now to head north with riches in tow would raise far too many questions of those here in her own Kingdom. There was zero chance she would risk a journey like that, let alone leave those such as Jorwen to scurry around whispering in the ears of other influential dwarves while she was away.

If she did decide to pay Draug a visit, it wouldn't be until after she was declared Master Smith.

Once the position was hers, she would be free to do as she wished and not even Draug would dare harm her.

She needed to be patient.

Brindel's book would be hers.

Not soon enough, but eventually it would be. It had to be.

CHAPTER 24

Sacrifice

THE MOMENT MENDINA heard Mortinan utter the word *Earthquake* and step into the world of Dark Swell, her stomach dropped.

'*What was he thinking?*' she thought to herself. She had momentarily thought to do the same thing, but quickly realised the danger it would put both of their champions in.

They stood in a tunnel, under the ground! And Mortinan was going to set off an earthquake! It would certainly put an end to the Lokaan, but it would almost certainly kill both of their champions as well.

Mendina looked into her *eye* and saw the giant gate crash down behind Mortinan.

She hadn't expected that, but it suddenly gave their Champions a chance.

If they started sprinting now and Mortinan held off on his ability, they could be out of the tunnel before it crashed down around them.

Yet to her horror, Mortinan's Champion remained standing at the gate, looking inside. Her champion was trying to get him to leave, but he wouldn't. What was he thinking? He was as foolish as the one who had gone to save him.

She knew at that moment she would have to act.

They would not get out in time.

Trying not to watch Mortinan walking toward the rear of the cavern, she ran the scenarios of her decision quickly through her mind.

'*He is going for the necklace!*' she realised in horror, as her thoughts scattered momentarily, before another one occurred to her.

If Mortinan died within the cavern, there would be no earthquake. That would be preferable to anything else that might happen.

Yet she didn't have time to watch and hope for her fellow G.O.D. to be struck down by the sword of the Lokaan.

She had to assume he would use his ability, and that he would do it soon.

He would not survive within the cavern for his allotted time. The Lokaan's movements were already quickening.

Mortinan had acted stupidly, but he would not sacrifice himself for his Champion, and certainly not for Mendina. There would be no point to that. He would rather both Champion's died, than he himself.

As Mortinan handed his Champion the necklace and they both finally began to run back up the tunnel, Mendina had made her choice.

Looking into her *eye* she spoke a single word before quickly stepping inside.

Both Mort and Mendina were still running up the tunnel as she appeared next to them. The water rushing past her feet was ankle high now and the pressure of it made movement difficult, but she quickly caught up and matched their pace, as all three moved towards the fork in the tunnel.

The G.O.D. Mendina knew the moment Mortinan used his ability she would have to act.

She didn't have to wait long.

The crack of hardened stone from the cavern behind them was deafening, as the entire ground shook.

Looking ahead, she saw the startled look on the faces of the dozen or so *Fetchlings*, as the tunnel around them began to shake.

'*Slow*,' she said out loud, her hands held out in front.

Mendina wasn't sure holding her hands out was necessary, but it felt right.

Regardless of whether she needed to do it, the moment she spoke the word, everything around her slowed. The breaking of the roof tunnel, the flow of water at their feet, even the Fetchlings in front of them, all slowed to such an extent they almost looked frozen in place. The noise within the tunnel also stopped.

Unfortunately, so too did Mort and Mendina.

This is where Mendina was hoping her memory had served her well.

Reaching out, she put her hands to the back of both Mort and Mendina.

To her tremendous relief, both of them caught up with her own movements, and neither of them looked to be able to feel her touch, as she had hoped. That would have been another distraction she could do without.

'What is happening?' Mort said, looking around at their surroundings, his light following where he looked.

'There is magic at play,' Mendina said. 'Perhaps the same one who was in the cavern and handed you that necklace.' She indicated the piece of jewellery still clasped in Mort's left hand.

'The tunnel is collapsing,' Mort said, shining his light upwards. The roof of the tunnel above them had cracked and pieces were beginning to fall towards them. 'Run!' he said, shining his light forward again.

Mendina had already begun to sprint ahead, before she looked back over her shoulder, just a couple of paces from the small humanoids in front of her.

Her first thought before she turned was hoping they didn't spring to life all of a sudden and attack her while she had her back to them.

Then she saw Mort, moving as slowly as the creatures were now. The roof of the tunnel continued falling ever so slowly, as the floor itself began to shoot upwards and crack under their feet. The water was also no longer such a hindrance.

Mendina moved back to Mort and grabbed his arm. He immediately began to move quickly again.

'Hurry,' he said to her, seemingly oblivious to what had just happened to him.

Clasping hands, they ran together this time.

With the water slowing, they moved quickly now, although the floor was becoming more unsteady as the ground burst slowly apart.

They turned into the last part of the tunnel and looked towards the exit.

Or where the exit had been.

It was no longer there.

Whatever was happening where they had first started their sprint from the cavern entrance, looked to have already occurred here. The dust from the collapsing tunnel filled the air, although it too moved slowly now.

'Whatever magic has slowed the world around us, didn't extend this far,' Mendina said, as they both stopped before the caved-in exit.

'How much of this do you think we need to get through?' Mort asked her.

From memory, Mendina felt they were still at least twenty paces from where the entrance to the tunnel should be.

It may as well have been a thousand.

'I can try to start moving it,' Mort suggested.

Bereft of any other idea, Mendina nodded her head.

'Iska?' Mort asked his companion, but his fairie-dragon remained silent where it perched on his shoulder. That just added to his worry.

Reaching out with his staff, Mort began to use the wind within the tunnel to lift a large chunk of stone in front of them.

Yet the moment the spell left his staff, it moved with the same speed as everything else around them.

The roof continued to fall above them, the floor bursting asunder, while his spell moved slowly toward the first stone in their long barrier.

'It won't work,' Mendina said, truly panicked now.

'What then?' Mort asked, the panic obvious in his own voice. 'This will not be our tomb,' he added, staring into her eyes.

Mendina stared back at him. There was still hope and determination in his eyes, yet she had no answer for him.

Looking back at the wall of rock in front of them, all she could think of was the word 'tomb' echoing in her mind.

She was convinced they would be buried here. There was no way out.

CHAPTER 25

What A Stupid Thing To Do

MOMENTS AFTER HE spoke the word *earthquake*, Mortinan was spirited out of the cavern and back in front of his *eye*. 'What have I done?' he said softly to no-one, the moment he realised where he stood.

Glancing across the clearing, he saw that Mendina was no longer in front of her *eye*. Turning to look into his own, it immediately took him to his champion.

He quickly took in all that was happening.

Mendina had slowed things so that what was happening around her almost stood still.

He nodded his head. As hard as it was to swallow, he had to admit to himself she had been much smarter than he when it came to dealing with their champions predicament within the cave.

Yet despite her quick thinking, he could see what their Champions were headed towards.

He knew how this spell worked and knew it would slow Mortinan's magic the same as it did everything else within its scope.

His Champion would not be able to use any spells, even with the help of his fairie-dragon.

He tried to think of a way in which they might still get out of the tunnel, but he couldn't think of anything and there was nothing more Mendina could do.

In less than nine minutes her spell would no longer keep them safe and there was every likelihood the game would be over for both he and Mendina.

Why hadn't he simply tried to freeze the Lokaan? A spell of cold may not have stopped it, but it would probably have slowed it enough in its movements where it would pose no real threat. Yet he had second-guessed himself. What if the cold spell did nothing? The Lokaan were born of magic and would have a high resistance to any spells, but surely it would have been a smarter alternative than bringing the cavern and tunnel down on top of his Champion.

With no time to think, he had somehow overthought the situation and now his Champion was going to die. For all his bragging that he was the smartest among them, at a time when he needed to act quickly he had failed. Even Valdor may have done better in the circumstances.

He watched on as his Champion attempted to move the rocks in front of them. Mortinan knew it wouldn't work.

He sighed and sat back, helpless now, as he prepared to watch his Champion die.

CHAPTER 26

It Is Safe Again

THE DWARVEN KING walked into the dark tunnel in front of him.

He put his hand to the pile of rubble which now blocked their main route into the eastern reaches of their home.

It had been a necessity at the time, but looking at it now, he regretted the decision.

There had been no further incursions into the main parts of his domain for several days now and he was thinking about re-opening some of the tunnels he had ordered collapsed.

After taking time to think and plenty of wine to drink, he now felt it was wrong for them to hide and cower within their own home. Within his very own Kingdom.

His race were renowned for their strength and endurance in combat, yet here they were, frightened by a few creatures springing forth from the darkness and a pack of hobgoblins attacking from the north.

'This shouldn't take long to clear,' Draug said to the few expert stonemasons he had brought with him.

'Not more than a few hours,' one of them said. 'Then a day or two getting it back looking the way it did before.'

Draug nodded.

'Best get to it then,' he said. 'I'll send some warriors here for when you break through. Just in case,' he added. 'Send for them when you are nearly done.'

'What else?' he asked, turning to the dwarf standing next to him.

'The western gate,' Branwen said. 'The works haven't even begun, so we are still vulnerable. We have a few guards staggered back from it, but that is all.'

'What do we fear from the west?' Draug asked. He had grown bored hours ago, and now just wanted to return to his room and have a drink.'

'There was nothing to fear from the east, north and south until recently,' Branwen said.

'The elves will never leave their forest, and nothing will go through it, so I think we are pretty safe on the western side at least.'

Branwen didn't respond. He just looked at his King with the same droll expression.

'Can we spare any that are clearing the tunnels we collapsed?' Draug asked.

'We can,' Branwen answered. 'It will mean the tunnels will take a little longer to be cleared and repaired, but it is a small price to pay to ensure our exposed western gate is secure.'

'You really have a thing for this western gate don't you,' Draug said. 'You can throw as many dwarves as you want at it, but not until after the tunnels are cleared and repaired.'

Branwen sighed and then nodded.

'Now is there anything else?' Draug asked, before raising his hand to silence the old dwarf. 'Anything else important?'

Branwen looked to be thinking, but eventually shook his head.

'Good,' he said, as he walked back down the tunnel towards his waiting room, Branwen shadowing him as he went.

'What news from the southern walkways?' Draug asked.

'They are all but cleared of the ooze,' he said. 'Your message to Elenda will have gotten through without any difficulty.'

'Good,' Draug said. 'I bet she will be beside herself when she reads it,' he said, chuckling to himself.

'Oh, I will need you to send another,' Draug continued.

'To Elenda?' Branwen asked.

'No, to the Master Smith,' Draug said. 'I want you to tell Brangold that I need more armours and weapons supplied to us, and whatever other new things his smiths may have come up with.'

'Anything in particular?' his steward asked.

'No. Whatever they think will help my warriors fight off whatever comes at us next. I want it brought up as soon as he gets the letter,' he said.

'How will you pay?' Branwen asked. 'We cannot spare too many to send and help defend their kingdom, if they even require it. Brangold has also forbidden any of his dwarves leaving the mountains.'

Draug stopped and turned.

'I will not be paying them anything Branwen.' He'd had enough of the greed of his southern cousins. No more. 'And we won't be sending any more dwarves either.'

'I doubt Brangold will allow that,' Branwen said. He looked shocked by the suggestion.

'Don't look at me like that,' Draug ordered. 'We have lost much already, so I want all of my dwarves here equipped properly to defend against anything else that may come at us. Tell him if he doesn't want us funnelling every monster and miscreant we come across down their way, he will send us what we need.'

'I have never known a southern dwarf to respond well to threats Draug,' Branwen cautioned. 'I have especially never known one to give something valuable away for nothing.'

'You are right,' Draug said. 'Tell him also that if he doesn't honour us with what I ask, I will call back every northern dwarf currently in the south helping them to keep their own kingdom safe.'

Branwen again didn't respond straight away.

'They are there in payment for much of what we have already,' he said. 'They are honouring deals already struck.' He sounded appalled at the suggestion.

Suddenly a dwarf came barrelling around the corner right in front of them and nearly slammed into his king, such was his haste.

Draug held his hands out to stop him.

'Slow down,' he growled.

'A message for you King Draug,' he panted. 'The hobgoblins are coming again.'

'Get a hold of yourself,' Draug said. 'Where are they this time?'

'They were marching on the Northern Gate when I left,' he said. That would have been several hours ago at least.

'And?' Draug asked. He had sent lots of reinforcements up there after their first incursion. If they weren't inside the gate, then it shouldn't be cause for alarm. 'How many of them?'

'It looked to be all of them,' the dwarf said.

Draug turned to Branwen.

'Send the letter and send it now!' he said. 'If he refuses, then tell him I will come down there myself, along with the entire Northern Kingdom, and we will take it all from him.'

Branwen bowed his head and took off at speed toward his quarters.

'Go and rest,' Draug said to the dwarf.

'I am good,' he said, as he turned to lead his King back from where he had just come.

'I will need to stop and collect a few things,' Draug said. 'While I do that, you need to collect as many warriors as you can and get them to the Northern Gate. Go to the food hall. There should be plenty of them there.'

'At once,' he said, taking off at a lope with his King running after him.

CHAPTER 27

Mistakes Are Made

ORT WAS AT a loss. He could think of nothing, and as his panic increased, his mind gave him even less. The fact *Iska* remained silent just added to his dread.

Even though the fracturing roof and floor moved at such a slow speed that it almost didn't register, it still didn't help. Watching their deaths happen in slow motion was probably more frightening than were it to happen at normal speed. At least they would not have been able to watch it slowly coming at them. To be able to think of nothing but their impending deaths was a truly horrible experience.

'Mort,' Mendina said. He heard a catch in her voice, as she squeezed his hand tighter.

He turned to look at her and saw a glimmer of hope in her eyes. He tried to steel himself, to forget about his own demise so that he could find a way to save Mendina. The determination in her eyes shamed him.

'Just after we heard the loud crack and the tunnel began to erupt, you moved as slowly as the floor and roof. It wasn't until I grabbed you that the spell no longer had an effect on you.' The hope in her eyes remained as she spoke.

Mort took a moment to let her words sink in.

Lightning.

He heard the word echo inside his mind. Mendina's words had awoken his fairie-dragon.

Mort understood before his little friend had any need to explain further.

'Touch the large rock in front of me,' Mort said to Mendina. She didn't hesitate, moving forward and placing her free hand on the boulder. Her faith in him lent him even more confidence.

He moved his own hand just in front of the rock, reaching his two fingers out so they also touched it.

Drawing the magic from within, he pooled what he thought would be enough and sent the bolt of lightning into the rock.

It exploded in front of them, but the moment it shattered, the pieces of rock stopped, slowing to the same speed as the rest of the tunnel.

Mort began swatting the pieces out of their way, as he reached out to the next one.

Looking across at Mendina, he couldn't help returning the smile she now had on her face. Pulling his hand away from the rock, he placed it under her chin and pulled her toward him. He was surprised she didn't stop him. They still had a long way to go, but she curled her own hand behind his neck and kissed him long and deeply. He was the one who finally pulled away, breathless.

'There will be that and more when we are out of here,' Mendina said to him seductively, as she put her hand to the next large rock in their way. Mort didn't want to look away. Her smile always sent a shiver down his spine, but the look she gave him now almost made his heart stop. Her perfect features were not marred by the dirt on her face, nor her hair falling across her face.

He could have continued to gaze at her forever, but first they needed to get out of this tunnel. He no longer thought of it as a tomb.

Putting his fingers to the next rock, he exploded it the same as the one before.

Mendina swept the fragments away this time, the smile still on her face.

The G.O.D. Mendina felt a little uncomfortable watching her and Mortinan's Champions kiss while she still had her hand resting on her Champion's back.

That feeling soon passed though, as the incredible feeling of relief continued to sweep through her body.

She had already estimated in her mind how long it would take them to break through to the other side and she was confident they would have time. So long as they didn't stop to kiss after every rock was destroyed.

The G.O.D. Mendina even managed to smile herself when she heard her Champion's words to Mort. It had the added bonus of Mort doubling his efforts in a bid to be free even sooner.

It was strange standing this close to her Champion and feeling what she did at this moment.

She had cursed herself more times than she could count for not choosing Jarkene as her Champion. She had suspected he would still be alive when Naming Day arrived, but did not want to risk choosing a Champion who might also be dead. That would have ended her game before it even began.

Standing with her hand on her Champion's shoulder, she could not have been prouder, nor more delighted at her choice.

The young elf may not be able to compete one-on-one with any of the other Champions in a battle of strength, but her determination and fortitude for one so young and inexperienced in life, was, in her opinion, unequalled by any of the others. Her genuine love of life was also something that gave Mendina a closer connection to her Champion than any of the others had with their own.

She knew at this moment, she would hold her head up high, no matter the final outcome in this game.

Yet the further the game went, the more confident she grew.

Mortinan's Champion grew stronger every day, and continued to accumulate powerful weapons, making him a formidable Champion, no matter the contest.

Standing this close to the two intertwined Champions, Mendina could see so clearly how deep his love and devotion for her Champion was.

And to her own shock and surprise, the G.O.D. Mendina also felt something for the half-elf. Whether those feelings were somehow passed on vicariously through her Champion, or simply a genuine affection for the man he was becoming, she couldn't say.

Mendina had often wondered how he was so different from his G.O.D., but now she saw why.

Mortinan had not had any influence on his race, because he did not have one. His was a hybrid of two other races, one of which was her own.

It therefore made sense she would feel some kinship and affection towards his half-elf, yet it still surprised her.

Mendina was brought from her thoughts by a loud crash behind her.

Another part of the tunnel had fallen, giving her a momentary panic, before she realised that as Mort and Mendina moved forward, the tunnel at the edge of her spell would be collapsing.

Her panic quickly turned to relief.

The more crashes she heard, the better it would be for all of them.

Mendina calculated there was probably just over one minute remaining on her spell, when they finally crawled through the last part of the collapsed tunnel and into the night air beyond. It had taken a little longer than she initially thought, but thankfully they were out now.

The rain was still heavy, but neither Mort nor Mendina seemed concerned by it, as they collapsed on to the ground in exhaustion. They didn't even bother surveying the land surrounding them, but fortunately there was nothing to threaten them lurking out there. Not in this weather.

Physically it hadn't been too demanding, but mentally they both looked exhausted.

Mendina smiled as she let her hand fall from her Champion.

Looking down, both of them now looked as if they were frozen in time. Her spell continued while she remained there, but she was in no hurry to leave.

It was amazing being back down on Dark Swell.

She took the time to look around and breathe deeply of the air around her.

The forest they sought wasn't too far away now, but there were more dangers lurking between here and their final destination.

That was something she was not looking forward to, but it was a worry for another day.

Mendina looked lovingly at her Champion one last time, before she was spirited away. In an instant, she had gone from looking down at her elven Champion as she rested her face in Mort's shoulder, to looking once more at the clearing, and her fellow Champions standing or sitting around their respective *eyes*.

As Mendina looked over at Mortinan, she saw him looking back in her direction.

He did not even acknowledge her, before turning back to look into his *eye*.

For all the joy she felt at her accomplishment, and spending time with her Champion, that was the last straw. After so many years of putting up with his arrogance and belittling comments about her decisions and overall lack of skill in playing this game, that was all it took for her to finally decide she could take no more.

Never wanting to give in to his taunts and bring herself down to his level, Mendina had always strived to ignore him as best she could. She had been pleasant to him when he was rude, or else she had simply smiled at him or ignored him outright.

But not this time. This time he was going to be told.

Striding over to his *eye*, she could sense the others watching her.

Mortinan looked up as she approached and actually looked a little bashful. He must have seen the look on her face.

'What were you thinking?!' she said in a raised voice.

'I don't think he was,' Brindel chimed in before Mortinan even had a chance to respond.

Mendina turned on him.

'Stay out of this Brindel!' she said, pointing a finger at him.

Brindel raised both hands in a gesture of peace, the smile still on his face.

Mendina turned back to Mortinan.

'Well?' she asked, as he sat there looking at her.

'I made a mistake,' he eventually said.

Mendina took a couple of deep breaths.

'A mistake,' she said, her voice controlled now and not as loud. 'You made a mistake. Is that all you have to say? You are usually more forthcoming than that in your opinions Mortinan.'

'What would you have me say?' he asked, a little more fire in his own voice now. 'I had no time to think and had to choose quickly. I chose wrong, but our Champions are still alive and so are we.'

'We?' Mendina shot back. 'When have you ever thought of 'we'?'

Mortinan remained silent, before turning to look back at his *eye*.

Mendina stepped closer and grabbed him by the shoulder, swinging him around to look at her again.

'Don't you dare turn away from me,' she said. 'I have not finished speaking with you yet,'

Mortinan stood this time. He was considerably taller than Mendina and looked down at her now.

'How dare you touch me,' he said to her in a quiet voice. 'I can see you are upset, but that is no excuse. You had best go and sit back down.'

'Or what?' Mendina asked, standing on her toes and leaning in closer to Mortinan.

Mortinan took a step back from her.

'What are you doing?' he asked. 'I apologised already, so there is no need for this.'

'Apologised?' Mendina said, incredulously. 'You have never apologised in your entire life, you rude pig. I am tired of your smug arrogance. Admit that you nearly got us both killed and if it weren't for me our game would be over.'

Mortinan looked taken aback for a moment, before his eyes narrowed and his chin raised defiantly.

'I will not,' Mortinan said. 'Mistakes have been made by all of you and none of you ever needed to apologise. I was the one who saved our Champion's from the Lokaan. If not for me they would have walked into the cavern and been trapped. Where are my thanks for that?'

Mendina tried to control her temper, but it had already been unleashed and she hadn't finished yet.

'I bet you didn't even know the gate was there!' she said to him. 'What is wrong with you? You think you can turn this around?'

'What were you doing when I acted?' Mortinan asked, his arrogance back in full now. 'I will tell you what you were doing. You were looking into your *eye* and wondering what you could do to save your Champion.'

'Then you retrieve the necklace for your Champion,' Mendina continued, ignoring his last comment. 'That was time where they could have been running back up the tunnel. In what world did you think that was a smart move?'

'They are alive and Mortinan now has the necklace,' Mortinan replied calmly. 'In what world Mendina, is that not a smart move?'

Mendina stepped back from Mortinan and shook her head.

'Why do I even bother speaking with you,' she said, most of the fire gone from her voice now. 'I was hoping for some gratitude and acknowledgement. Nothing more. I should have known better and not lost my temper. You are selfish and my ire is wasted on you.'

'The slow spell was a good move,' Mortinan said in reply. 'I am happy to acknowledge that Mendina.' He looked to turn back to his *eye* again, but paused. 'So it would seem we have both done well and I agree your anger was unnecessary.'

Mendina opened her mouth to respond, but stopped herself.

Turning around, she walked over to the refreshment table to get herself a drink and a snack.

Why did she let him get to her like that? She had just experienced something extraordinarily special with her Champion. She should have been smiling and basking in her own victory, but that look on Mortinan's face when she returned had triggered something Mendina didn't realise she had been holding inside of her.

It had been released now, but she felt no satisfaction.

It would be best if she just ignored Mortinan from now on, or at least spent time pondering every word he said to her in future.

Her Champion depended on his for survival, she knew that, but in no way did it depend on her fellow Gamer.

Her game was her own now.

Taking a long drink of water, Mendina tried to re-focus her thoughts on the time she had just spent on Dark Swell.

She still had one more chance to visit, and she would not be wasting it.

CHAPTER 28

Call To Arms

K ABIR WAS IN awe at the speed and endurance of the three King's Shield. Although they were unable to keep up with the galloping horses, the speed they maintained was not natural.

It gladdened him though. He did not really want to fight the goblin party without them.

Kabir had been involved in a lot of battles recently, but he had enjoyed that one the most. Fighting side-by-side with those three men had been an experience he would not forget.

Looking ahead, he feared what they would come upon when they caught up with the carts. The goblins had a start on them and would kill everyone escorting it, if they didn't move as quickly as they were able.

'If they are all dead when we arrive, do we wait for the others?' Ahlia asked him as they rode. Firth had left the other horses behind already, her smaller cousins unable to keep up.

Ordinarily Kabir would have said no. He was confident in his abilities and never tried to think about the odds, however he had another to think about now. He would never let her know of his concerns of course. Ahlia was fierce and a magnificent warrior, but the feelings were still too raw when he thought about how he felt when he thought she might die. He did not wish to experience that again so soon. Or ever.

It was why adventurers never had companions. Kabir had never intended to take up with anyone, but Ahlia hadn't really asked for his permission.

He had resented it a little at first, but she had not taken long to grow on him. Kabir did not want her to leave his side now.

Yet it made him pause now to consider any reckless decisions he might otherwise make.

'Without the magic shield, we will be vulnerable to their arrows,' Kabir conceded. 'Perhaps running headlong into battle is not the best option this time.'

'You are worried harm may befall me,' Ahlia said. It wasn't a question. Kabir had been afraid she would see right through him.

'I would ordinarily show you what I think of a man trying to shield me from danger, but on this occasion, I am pleased it has allowed you to make a wise decision.'

Kabir relaxed a little.

'Your attitude to chase glory at all costs has had me concerned,' she continued. Kabir didn't think she sounded angry. 'I think you have mistaken glory with honour. Honour is what you should continue to strive for highlander. It is what makes someone great, and you are an honourable man. It is also greater than a stupid death.'

Kabir knew he had a lot to learn from her. She was wise for one so young. A lot smarter than he was.

'I will follow your lead, my Lady Ahlia,' Kabir said.

'Don't call me that,' she said in an irritated voice. 'However, I will lead on this occasion.'

Kabir smiled as he looked at the back of her head, her hair bouncing from the movement of the horse underneath them.

'Why do you think the wizard left us so soon?' Kabir asked, changing the subject.

'Those are questions for another time,' Ahlia said. 'I can see them up ahead.'

Kabir looked over her shoulder at the scene ahead, not knowing exactly what to expect. He knew there would be death ahead, he just didn't know if they were in time to help any of them.

He could make out the goblins and their pets in the distance, but no carts.

Either the goblins had stopped to wait for those on foot, or else the guards had made a stand and sent the carts on ahead.

As they neared, it appeared the latter was true.

All of the guards were dead, with only a couple of goblins lying dead among their corpses. They must have fought bravely, but never stood a chance.

Before Kabir and Ahlia got close, the goblins had already taken off in the direction the carts had gone. It wouldn't take them long to catch up.

Ahlia put her boots into Firth's midriff, urging him to go faster.

'We will at least catch up to the ones on foot,' she said. 'We must kill them off quickly. Watch for archers,' she said, as she took her bow out from where it was strapped to their horse.

There were more trees where they now rode and the track wound through them, so the goblins weren't able to take aim with their bows until Firth was almost upon them. Ahlia put an arrow into the face of one before he could shoot his own.

The only other goblin with a bow was too panicked at Firth bearing down on him and his shot went wide. She didn't give him a chance at a second arrow.

Ahlia was forced to stop before they got too close, to allow Kabir to dismount. She feared he would break his neck if he tried to jump as he rode. It was something they were all taught to do as young children, but the barbarian's grace didn't shine until his two feet were firmly on the ground.

The goblins were heartened by the lack of any visible magic shield around them this time, so they charged the moment Kabir hit the ground. They still outnumbered the barbarian and plains woman six to two.

Ahlia spurred Firth forward when Kabir was clear, turning her so that she moved to the right of the furthest goblin. She was able to cut him down as she rode past, turning quickly for another run at them.

She needn't have bothered.

Kabir swept through the remaining five like they were standing still, his giant sword arcing through the air, its blade not even slowing as it cut through leather, skin and bone. None of the goblin swords came near him.

Checking quickly to make sure they were all dead, she beckoned the barbarian to her, holding out a hand to help him mount.

As soon as Kabir was on, Firth took off at a gallop again.

Hopefully those they rode to help would not all be dead this time.

After rounding a few more turns, they came upon the carts and the goblins attacking them.

If there were any guards left, they hadn't been able to put up much of a fight.

The *Krett* had already finished killing the last of the farm folk and had begun feeding on a couple of their bodies. The goblins had only just started hoisting the remaining dead bodies on to the carts. Human carcasses were more to their liking when it came to food. The baskets of fruit and vegetables lay scattered on the ground, cleared from the wagons to make room for the bodies.

Kabir was surprised they believed themselves safe enough to take the time to stack up the wagons. They must have been aware there were still men coming for them. Surely, they knew they would be getting chased by those they hadn't killed earlier. Or were they really that stupid?

Ahlia stopped Firth about fifty paces away, at the spot where they had first seen them in the distance.

Two of the *Krett* looked up at the barbarians and without hesitation began running towards them. A whistle from one of the goblins had the rest of them sprinting after the first two. The goblins took a little longer to find their horses and begin their gallop towards Kabir and Ahlia. By the time they started their charge, the *Krett* were almost upon their prey.

Kabir had already dismounted, while Ahlia stayed atop Firth.

'I can shoot my arrows from here,' she said in response to his look. 'Firth is also a much smarter animal than the horses ridden in this realm. I will be safe.'

'You don't need to justify yourself to me,' Kabir said, looking towards the oncoming beasts. Ahlia wouldn't have been able to see his smile, but he could visualise her scowl.

Stepping forward to make room for himself, Kabir waited patiently for them to reach him.

The first crashed to the ground barely three paces in front of him, an arrow sticking out from its eye. From that range Ahlia's shot was an easy one. She knew she would have no time to fire off another, as she drew her sword and leaned back in the saddle. As she did, Frith lifted his mighty front hooves as the first *Krett* leaped at them. Frith fell forward as it did, his hooves impacting its head as the *Krett's* teeth tried to find purchase on his leg. Fortunately, the strike was enough to shatter its skull, killing it almost instantly.

Ahlia was shocked to see another following right behind. She wasn't in position to strike, as it too came at Frith's face. She knew his effort to stand would be too late this time, when a sword suddenly impaled its body, bringing it up short. Ahlia looked down and across at where Kabir stood, his sword no longer in his hand. He had thrown his weapon to save her horse, leaving him to face the last of the *Krett* unarmed. She knew she shouldn't be shocked any longer to see the stupid grin on his face, before he turned to face his circling adversary. Shaking her head, Ahlia took out her bow again, as the goblins began to close in.

Before she removed the arrow from her quiver, Ahlia changed her mind. Leaping quickly from the back of Frith, she ran to where Kabir's sword lay imbedded in the dead *Krett*. Pulling it out easily, she marvelled to herself again what a magnificent weapon it was, before looking across at where Kabir lay on the ground, trying his hardest to keep the powerful jaws of the *Krett* from tearing his face off.

Ahlia was truly surprised to see the barbarian holding his own against it, but she knew it was going to be difficult for him to kill it with just his bare hands.

Sprinting over to where he was, Ahlia drove the sword through the creature's back, stopping herself from shoving it all the way through and into the stupid barbarian lying underneath it.

She watched as he threw the carcass off, a broad smile still on his face. A smile which quickly turned to one of horror.

Ahlia felt the pain in her side, but didn't immediately understand what had happened, until a second sharp jab hit her just underneath the other one.

She saw Kabir jump to his feet and snatch his sword from her suddenly weakened grasp, before roughly shoving her to the side so that he could stand with his back to her.

The next sensation she felt were her legs losing all strength, followed by her breathing suddenly becoming difficult, as she collapsed to the ground. She looked up in time to see the galloping goblin riders upon them.

Kabir looked up in horror as the arrow pierced the side of Ahlia's thin leather armour. Before he could move to stand, another struck her just below the other. He knew that if they had somehow missed her heart, they would not be far from it.

Leaping to his feet, he grabbed his sword from her, before gently moving her behind him, just in time for him to face the oncoming goblins.

Two more projectiles arrowed at him. Fired from such a close range he acted on instinct only, swatting them aside. Gritting his teeth, he waited for them to reach him, when suddenly shadows flew past him on either side.

The King's Shield had arrived, leaping into the air to strike at the charging goblins. As much as he would have liked to watch them kill all of the goblins, Kabir turned around to Ahlia, confident in the ability of the three men now behind him.

Dropping to his knees, he chopped away the ends of the arrows so he could lay his sword against her broken skin.

The moment he did, he saw the familiar glow from the magic within the sword, as it worked its way into Ahlia.

Kabir hoped he was in time, as it was difficult for him to tell if she was still breathing. When the bleeding stopped and her scars began to close, he was able to breathe a sigh of relief. Laying her comfortably on the ground, he removed his sword once he was satisfied her wounds had healed.

Looking at her closely, Kabir was confused at a lack of any response. He had expected her to have opened her eyes by now and begin chastising him at throwing his sword at the *Krett*. Leaning down, he put his ear to her mouth. To his horror, Kabir could not feel her breath coming out.

Sitting up in a panic, he was at a loss as to what else he could do. The sword should have saved her!

He sensed more than heard Atriol move to his side.

'What has happened to the Lady Ahlia?' he asked.

'Two arrows pierced her chest,' Kabir said. He could hear the panic in his voice. 'The sword healed her but she no longer breathes.'

'You removed the arrows?' Atriol asked.

'I cut them away,' Kabir said. He was finding it difficult to think.

'Perhaps the head of the arrow still sits in her heart Barbarian. The sword may not be able to heal that.'

Kabir didn't hesitate, as he used the edge of his sword to make a cut along her side where she had only moments ago been healed. Reaching in, he found the first of the arrows and carefully pulled it out. Blood began spurting everywhere, but he knew he needed to get the second of them before he tried to heal her again.

Before he could move to get the second, a hand slid past him and into Ahlia's gaping wound. The second arrow came out quickly this time and with less of an explosion of blood.

'Your sword,' Atriol said firmly to Kabir, bringing him out of his stupor.

Surely not even his sword could save her now, he thought, as he placed it once more against her side.

The blue glow seeped inside her once more. It took longer for the wounds to close this time, but eventually they did. Kabir lifted the sword from her, looking down and hoping beyond hope that her chest would begin moving again.

He was horrified, but not surprised, to see that it still did not move.

'Move back,' Atriol said to Kabir. 'Her heart needs to be started again.'

Kabir did as he was bid, as the King's Shield moved to kneel above her.

Placing his hands above her chest, he began to thump her chest.

Kabir remembered seeing their healer doing this to one of their warriors when he had been badly injured during sword practice. He had not been able to save him, and Kabir held out little hope that Atriol would be able to do more than their own healer had achieved.

Ahlia was dead and he was responsible.

When he heard Ahlia cough, it was the sweetest sound the barbarian had ever heard.

Opening her eyes, she took her time to look around.

Groaning as she sat up, Ahlia had no idea what had happened. She remembered Kabir flinging aside the *Krett* she had killed, but nothing after that.

'We need to stop putting ourselves into situations where we are constantly saving each other,' Kabir said. Ahlia wasn't sure if he was crying or it was the dust from the track they had just fought on.

'What happened?' she asked. Her side hurt like crazy, but she could see no hurt on her skin, other than a faint scar. She didn't remember having a scar there, or having her leather armour torn away.

'Did your sword just save me again?' she asked, when no-one answered her.

'You were struck with two arrows Lady Ahlia,' Atriol said. 'One of them went into your heart.'

Ahlia shivered involuntarily. She had almost died again. If not for Kabir's sword, she would have.

Before she could say anything in response to the King's Shield's answer, Kabir knelt down next to where she sat. Atriol stepped back and walked off to assist his men with the supplies.

'My sword will always be here for you,' he said. His eyes were definitely watery.

'I hope not to have to need it again anytime soon,' she answered. 'It still hurts.'

'Then I will carry you,' Kabir said, no sarcasm in his voice.

'No, you will not!' she said fiercely. 'I will walk anywhere I need to go. Or run if I have to,' she finished.

'Of course you will,' Kabir said, a large smile on his face now. 'Shall we walk over and give those men a hand then?' He held his hand out to help her up.

Ahlia looked up at him for a moment, before accepting his hand and slowly rising to her feet.

'We shall,' she said, before walking gingerly over to where the King's Shield had busied themselves already.

Methan and the other men turned up not long after Kabir and Ahlia began assisting the King's Shield in re-loading the carts. They had spent the rest of the time prior to their arrival, removing the dead bodies of the farmers and remaining guards. As much as they would have liked to take them home for a proper burial, the supplies scattered on the ground by the goblins were more important to those who still lived. Methan also wanted them back to Shadow Hill as quickly as they were able. Digging graves was not an option.

There was little talk as they re-loaded. Most of the supplies were still in good condition, despite their treatment.

Methan wanted to make sure those who had sacrificed their lives had not done so in vain.

They eventually finished packing what they could still take and set off once more.

They arrived in Shadow Hill before it was dark, the gates opening to let them inside. Other than that, there was very little in the way of a greeting or welcome.

Kabir saw nothing but frightened faces, as he looked around at the people within this settlement. They looked like people who believed death was likely waiting for them around the next corner, or possibly the one after that.

Going off that observation, he was surprised to see so many wagons and carts packed high with personal belongings. It looked like many of these people had decided to leave the one place that might offer them some level of protection.

None of them paid the strange looking barbarian and his plainswoman any attention other than a passing look.

Kabir and Ahlia were eventually taken to a large hall, where an older gentleman looked to be waiting for them.

'Stay here,' Methan said to them, as he approached the old man. Atriol and another of the King's Shield remained standing either side of them.

Both he and Ahlia had been made to relinquish their weapons prior to entering, but Atriol's assurance they would be returned was enough for him to believe it would not be stolen from him.

'My Lord, as you have probably already been told, we have suffered grievous losses. Despite that, we have still managed to secure most of the provisions you sent us to collect.' Methan sounded tired as he spoke.

'I have been told nothing,' Lord Marcus said to him. 'But I have sent orders for the carts you brought to remain untouched. We are not staying.'

'Who is not staying?' Methan asked, obviously confused.

'None of us,' his Lord replied. 'The whole place is being emptied and we are to make for Havern.'

Before Methan could ask more questions, Marcus held up his hand.

'Now, who do we have here?' he asked, looking directly at Kabir and Ahlia.

'They are from the lands to the East,' Methan said. 'The Lady Ahlia is from the plains, while Kabir is from the hills to the north of the plains.'

'Lady Ahlia?' he asked, emphasising the 'lady'.

'I am no lady Lord. I am a rider from the plains, nothing more.' Kabir could see her stance stiffen.

Marcus nodded to himself.

'Why are they here?' Marcus asked. 'Are there more of them coming to help us? That would be welcome news. I hear both the plainsmen and barbarians are fierce warriors.'

'We have seen first-hand just how fierce,' Methan said, 'but unfortunately, despite their help in fighting off a horde of goblins, they are here to face your justice my Lord.'

Marcus sat back in his seat.

'Does it have anything to do with why neither Ethan nor Yandow accompany you?'

Methan nodded.

'The barbarian Kabir is responsible for the death of Ethan, Lord Marcus.'

'I do not have time for a trial!' Marcus said, before sighing and sitting forward in his seat. 'So that I get the short version, tell me what happened Atriol?' he asked, looking at his King's Shield.

'We came upon them in a homestead,' Atriol began, as he stepped forward. 'Kabir was asked to give up his sword by Ethan. Kabir refused. Words were exchanged, before Ethan cast a spell at Kabir. The spell was ineffective due to the power of the sword the barbarian has. Kabir then drove this sword into Ethan, killing him. Yandow was killed by goblins,' he added, before stepping back again.

'So, Ethan was killed by Kabir the Barbarian after Ethan cast a spell at him. He was acting to defend himself, is that correct?' Marcus said

'It is,' Methan said.

'Yet he also disobeyed a direction to give up his weapon, when directed to by a wizard of the King's Realm. Is that also correct? he asked.

'It is,' Methan said again.

'Then the killing was as a result of Kabir's unwillingness to give up his weapon, therefore acting in defence of himself is not a valid reason for killing my wizard. The penalty is death.' Kabir could sense both of the King's Shield tense as the last words were spoken. He knew they were ready to act if the order was given or he did something stupid. He knew without his sword, he would be no match for them. Probably not even with his sword, as had already been demonstrated to him.

'If I may,' Kabir said, remembering something one of the men had said as they were travelling, not long after they were first captured.

'Were we taken prisoner within this realm or in the goblin realm?'

'Anywhere that men loyal to King Dayhen have made their home is part of his realm,' Marcus answered.

Kabir had nothing else.

'Ahlia had nothing to do with what I did,' Kabir said, even though he knew it would anger her.

'What role did the plainswoman play?' Marcus asked Methan this time.

'She also refused to give up her weapons, but she was bested by Mikael. She did not land a blow on any.'

'Nevertheless,' Marcus replied. 'She also disobeyed a wizard, and was fighting with the Barbarian. Her life is also forfeit.'

'You can't do that!' Kabir roared, stepping forward. He was quickly restrained by Atriol and another of the King's Shield. They were so much stronger than they looked, Kabir thought, as they pulled his arms behind his back and bound his wrists.

'We have been told Ahlia may be the daughter to the Leader of the Plainsmen,' Methan said to his Lord, after Kabir had stopped his ranting.

'I have no title,' Ahlia finally spoke. 'Whatever fate Kabir is given, I will share.'

'You will not!' Kabir said. 'You will not lay a finger on her!'

'You will be gagged if you speak again,' Marcus said calmly, before looking back to Ahlia.

'Is the ruler of the plains your father?' he asked her.

'My father is Chieftain,' Ahlia replied, 'but I am no Lady.'

'That makes it a little tricky,' he said. 'Only King Dayhen can try royalty. Although you claim no title, it is obvious to me you are equivalent to a Princess in our realm.' He paused in thought.

'Fortunately, we are heading to Havern, so you will accompany us. Others will escort you on to the Capital.'

'The King fights in the West, Lord Marcus,' Methan reminded him.

'I am aware of that Methan, but the Princess Areana sits in his place. She can pass judgement in his stead.'

Methan nodded, before asking one more question.

'The barbarian my Lord?'

'His judgement stands. He will die tonight.'

CHAPTER 29

Where Are They?

EVERYTHING HAD HAPPENED so fast of late and Areana was still trying to come to terms with what was going on around her. Her mind seemed to be constantly spinning from all of the changes to her life.

It seemed like a lifetime had passed since she left Loftenberg on her journey home to Lakerth.

Areana kept trying to convince herself of the importance in staying strong, but deep down she could not shake the terror that gripped her.

She was terrified of what might happen to her father in the far western reaches of the realm, and to the rest of those brave souls who had gone with him to defend those who remained.

She was also scared of what might be coming for them if the King was unable to drive them back. The death of Valdor had shown her just how vulnerable they really were.

She was even terrified of the decisions she would have to make in her father's absence, despite having Heridah to lean against once more.

That moment he had tried to choke the life from her was almost a distant memory, and something she tried not to think about anymore, but it was another incident that gave life to the fear eating away at her.

Heridah also had many things requiring his attention elsewhere, and he was often away seeing to those. These were the times when she felt the fear and uncertainty most acutely.

Since she had returned from Loftenberg, Areana no longer enjoyed her own company as she once did, and at the same time, she was also warier around people.

Fortunately, there was a new constant in her life which allowed her to function and attend to the duties required of her. Without her, Areana would likely never want to leave her own room.

Her own personal Shield, Catlin now shadowed the princess wherever she went.

And unlike Heridah, she had no other tasks to attend to. Her sole purpose and duty was to keep her Princess safe.

'Thoughts?' she said, turning to her Princess' Shield.

'They obviously have too much energy and not enough to keep them occupied my Princess,' Catlin replied. Areana had grown to love her no-nonsense approach to everything. Although she never advised her on what to do directly, Catlin always said enough to assist Areana in making many of her decisions. She trusted her without reservation, as Valdor had.

'You remain here to keep the peace,' Areana said, turning back to look at the four men standing before her. 'Not to add your own disturbances to the uncertainty within Lakerth.'

The men before her were not the kind of men who would normally be left to patrol the streets of Lakerth, charged with protecting its people from thieves and cut-throats. Prior to the current upheaval, they were most likely those very same thieves and cut-throats.

However, with most of the able-bodied men sent west to fight against the monsters from the Western Realm, she had been given the leftovers with which to try and keep order.

Those of the Kings Shield who remained could not be everywhere, and most of the soldiers still in the city were either too young or too old to be effective in policing the city.

'You will report to the outer walls and help with the works there,' Areana continued. 'Fail in this and I will send you, under escort, to join the rest of your King's army, where you will be sat in the front line to await Kritch's horde.'

None of the men said anything.

One of them bowed and began walking backwards. The others quickly mimicked him and scuttled from the throne room.

'I think that is enough for today,' Areana said. 'I need to get out of here for a while.'

'Where would you like to go?' Catlin asked.

'I don't know,' she said. 'I just want to walk for a time. When will Heridah be finished with his wizards?'

'The wizard doesn't tell me such things,' Catlin replied. 'I will have someone tell him what you are doing when he finishes.'

'Thank you,' Areana said. She didn't think Heridah would want her wandering around the city. In fact, she knew he wouldn't. Catlin on the other hand, didn't seem to care as much. She was still cautious, but she was also confident in her own abilities to keep her Princess safe. Areana also believed her Princess' Shield preferred to be out of the keep as much as she did.

'Shall we go now then?' Areana said.

Catlin nodded and moved off to inform the guards of their intentions.

The guards would of course follow, but at a discreet distance, as per the Princess' instruction.

A few other unarmoured soldiers would scout discreetly ahead. The Princess was unaware of these men, but Catlin was not one to take chances.

Her Princess had certainly matured a great deal in the short time she had sworn fealty to her, but she was still only a girl who had grown up coddled and protected from the evils of the world.

Catlin was impressed with how quickly Areana had accepted things, but she knew that inside, her Princess was still only a scared little girl.

They walked out through a smaller gate at the side of the keep. The fewer eyes that saw them leave, the better. It was not yet the middle of the day, so there would be plenty of people about.

Even with most of the men gone from the city and many traders accompanying them, it was still busy

The Realms' best smiths and most skilled craftsmen had gone with the army, as had many of the finest bakers and cooks. People from all walks of life were required to assist with the upkeep of those who had gone to fight.

Areana walked past all of these. She hadn't come out here to shop.

She just wanted to walk and not think about anything for a time, while still trying to take in the mood of the city and her people.

The traders who remained were still full of voice.

Previously second-rate wares were suddenly in high demand from the citizens of Lakerth. Areana knew that these people would at least be satisfied with their lot now, if not entirely happy. There were few people happy within the walls of the city in these days of war. Very few families and households would have no loved ones fighting against the Western hordes.

So despite the appearances that everything was business as usual, Areana was able to feel the tension in the air. The people were also scared.

Yet it gave her own fears no comfort knowing she wasn't alone in her feelings of despair. Instead it seemed only to feed it.

Nevertheless, they continued on for a time, Areana content to let Catlin lead the way.

After about an hour of walking, they turned off into a narrow, but well-worn street. There was an open gate at the end of it and she could see people within. It looked to be a large area inside, but she couldn't tell where it was they headed.

Walking to the gate, Areana stepped through and looked around.

There were large targets at one end of the area. They would have been at least one hundred paces away. Other targets were closer and spaced all around.

Catlin had brought her to an archery range.

'Why are we here?' Areana asked. She noticed there was no-one lined up to shoot arrows. In fact, apart from a man standing next to a bucket full of arrows, and two small boys standing behind him, there was no-one else within the whole range. She initially thought it was because everyone was away at war, but then she looked across at Catlin and saw her nod to the man next to the arrows.

Catlin had brought her here for a reason. To shoot arrows? Why would she do that? She had never held a sword or used a bow before. It was not something a princess did.

'You are here to shoot arrows,' Catlin said, in her no-fuss manner. 'Darid here will show you the basics. He is proficient.'

Now that he stood closer, Areana could see that Darid was one of the King's Shield. His garb had been why she didn't recognise it the moment she saw him.

He now held a slender bow in his left hand and had the bucket of arrows in his other.

'Why would I want to shoot arrows?' Areana asked, although it wasn't really a question.

'Because there is not time to teach you how to use a sword,' her sworn guard replied.

'Apologies Catlin for my cryptic question. I will try again.' As much as she liked having Catlin around, sometimes she could be frustrating. 'Why do I need to learn how to shoot arrows? I have yourself, Heridah and what is left of the King's Shield and King's Guard to protect me. Am I in more danger than I am already aware?'

'We are all of us in danger my Princess,' she said. 'More danger than ever before in this Realm.'

That wasn't comforting, but she knew how bad things were. It would take more than a few words to increase her current level of fear.

'I am aware,' Areana replied. 'I don't however, think that by learning how to shoot some arrows I will be able to make a difference. I have more important things to learn, such as how to rule this city until my father returns.'

'If we are besieged and I and all of your guards kill everything that attacks us, but fall at the same time and there is one of them left and it is running at you with a sword in its hand, what would you do?'

If she didn't know her better, she would have thought Catlin was joking.

'That would not happen,' Areana said.

'But what would you do?' Catlin persisted.

'If you were all dead around me I would probably panic and freeze where I stood.' Catlin always brought the honesty out of her.

'Yes,' Catlin replied, 'and you would die. Or even worse, you would be captured.'

The thought of being captured sent a shiver up her spine.

'Or you could draw an arrow and fire it into the creature's heart,' Catlin said.

'And if you miss, it would at least be forced to kill you rather than risk trying to capture you.'

'So, you would like me to learn archery so that I would be killed,' she said, her eyes wide open.

'It is preferred to being captured my Princess,' Catlin said.

Areana believed that was probably true. She had heard stories from other children what some of the monsters out there did with people they killed. She didn't really want to think about what they did to people that were caught alive.

'It is still a preposterous scenario,' Areana said, 'but as we are here already, I will humour you.'

'Thank you,' Catlin said, not a trace of mockery in her voice.

Darid stepped forward so that he stood to her left side, after taking an arrow from the bucket.

'A demonstration first my Princess,' he said. 'You need to place the end of the arrow into the string here, before pulling it back using these fingers.' He did as he described. 'Your left arm needs to be held straight as you pull back the arrow, until the string is taut.' He pulled back the arrow. 'You then visualise where the arrow is going and let go.'

Darid loosed his arrow, which struck the nearest target directly in its centre.

Proficient indeed. The King's Shield modesty was legendary. She suspected every arrow he let go would end up in the exact same spot.

If Areana wasn't so happy to have them protecting her with their lives, she would probably resent how good they were.

'My turn?' she asked. Darid nodded and handed her the bow.

'Practice pulling back the string first,' he suggested. 'It can seem difficult to begin with.'

Areana wondered at what age this man had difficulty pulling the string back for the first time. When he was 3?

He was not wrong.

Although she did not consider herself weak, Areana had never been involved in warfare-like training before.

As hard as she tried, she could not get it all the way back.

'Try this one,' Darid said, handing her a smaller bow.

'A child's bow?' she asked, offended and humiliated. 'I would rather just leave.'

She handed the bow back, but did not take the smaller one he offered.

'Just a smaller bow, my Princess,' Darid replied, unflustered by her words. 'It is used by those unable to effectively control a larger bow. There is no shame in using it. The arrow shot from this bow can still kill the one it is aimed at.'

Pulling forth another arrow, he turned and let loose in one fluid motion. The arrow pierced the target right next to his last shot.

'It is easier to carry long distances and through rough terrain. I have used it many times before.'

Areana sighed, before holding out her hand to take it.

This time she was able to pull the string all the way back, holding it near to her face as Darid had demonstrated.

Taking an arrow from him, she nocked it as he had done, before pulling the string back again.

'Now empty your mind,' Darid said. 'Think only of..' he continued, as Areana let fly with her arrow.

To her delight, it struck the bottom of the target. Although not a 'kill' shot, she had seen children practicing before. Many of them couldn't even hit the target after practicing for some time.

'Another,' she said, holding out her hand.

Darid gave her another arrow.

This time she took her time once the string was pulled back.

'Control your breathing,' Darid said. 'Visualise your target.'

She listened to him this time, as the bulls-eye became larger in her vision.

Letting loose, Areana watched as it struck just above her last arrow.

'Once you are stronger, you will be a fine archer,' Darid said, offering her another arrow.

Areana did not take it from him. Instead she handed him back the bow.

'That is enough for today,' she said. 'I will return when I am stronger.' She tried to keep her tone civil.

She turned to Catlin, who had remained silent the whole time.

'We are going now,' she said, not waiting for Catlin for respond, as she walked toward the entrance of the training arena.

Her 'bodyguard' soon caught up with her, as Areana slowed her pace. For all her anger at being treated like a child, she still had enough wits about her not to want to walk through the streets on her own.

'I thought you may have wanted to practice some more,' Catlin said.

Areana stopped to look at her.

'So your friend could ridicule me some more?!' She was not happy at her treatment.

'Ridicule?' Catlin asked. 'How were you ridiculed Princess?'

'A child's bow? And then he called me a weakling.' She knew she sounded petulant, but was unable to stop herself.

'All of us need to continue to learn. Especially when we are young,' Catlin said. 'Why is it important to learn?' she asked.

Areana stared at her for a moment.

'I am not here for a lesson,' she said. 'I have enough of them from Heridah. I also have to look after the city. I don't have time for this Catlin.'

'How did you feel when you hit the target the first time?' Catlin asked.

Areana was about to walk off again, but she didn't want to upset Catlin. If it were anyone else she would have.

'It felt good,' she admitted, 'but it will not help me rule.'

'If you could hit the centre every time, how would that make you feel?' Catlin persisted.

'Even better,' she replied, but still with little interest. 'Yet it would not help me.'

'If you could run and fight as Valdor did, how would you then feel?'

Areana had no idea where that question came from, but it struck a chord within her.

'Every man and woman would love to be able to fight like he did,' she said. 'Why are you asking me these things? I will never be as good as Valdor, nor as good as you are. Never.'

'Do you think he was born that way?' Catlin asked.

'Of course not.' Areana answered, a little annoyed now. 'I know he would have worked hard and suffered a lot to become that good, but I am not a King's Shield, nor am I a warrior. Being able to shoot an arrow will not help me to rule!' This had gone on long enough.

'Having the skill to defend yourself against others in not just for warriors,' Catlin said. 'And it does a lot more than simply giving you that skill.'

'What are you trying to say?' Areana said. 'We need to keep going.'

'I am trying to say that learning these skills give you a new level of confidence in dealing with many different situations. But it is not something you can learn from words.'

Areana was surprised at how much Catlin was saying. She was not usually one for long conversations. This was obviously important to her, so Areana decided she would stay and listen for a little longer.

'Then what do you want of me?' Areana asked. 'To learn the bow and arrow?'

'That would be a good beginning,' the King's Shield said to her. 'But just a beginning.'

'And what would be the end?' Areana asked, thinking herself clever.

'Death is the end,' Catlin said. 'Before that, there is only learning.'

Areana didn't like hearing that. There had been enough death lately, and likely much more before this was over. She didn't really have the time to spend practicing how to shoot an arrow.

'I have many other things to learn,' Areana said again. 'How to run this city is all I have time for.'

'Then you will forever be dependent on others and you will always be afraid,' Catlin said.

Areana was really taken aback at her words. Is that really what Catlin thought of her. A child who couldn't look after herself?

Her first impulse had been anger, quickly replaced by sorrow and then as she thought about it, acceptance. Catlin was right. She was afraid.

'I do not blame you for the fear you have,' Catlin continued. 'It is normal and to be expected. You have been given responsibilities you are not equipped for, at a time when strength and courage is needed more than anything else.'

'Okay then,' Areana finally conceded. 'Let us return to the archery field. Let us see if my shooting an arrow straight will help me rule this Kingdom.'

Catlin nodded to her, but said no more, as they walked back to see Darid.

The King's Shield also said nothing as he held out the small bow for his Princess to take.

'We stay until I hit the centre circle,' Areana said, as she took an arrow from Darid and nocked it to her bow.

Catlin did not reply, as the Princess let loose with her arrow.

CHAPTER 30

Need To Catch Up

MEGHAN HAD BEEN permitted to sit by Wilhelm's side during the day, but was forced to stay in her own tent during the night. Despite her protestations, the plains people were steadfast when it came to men and women sharing a tent before they were promised to each other. They would not allow it under any circumstances, regardless of whether she was tired or not.

When she went into his small tent on the third day, after two full days watching him sleep, Wilhelm finally awoke.

'You are even lazier than I thought,' she said to him, as she entered the tent and saw him sitting up. He was allowing a woman of the plains to spoon broth into his mouth.

The lady stood when Meghan spoke and reached out with the bowl and spoon. Meghan looked at her with a confused look on her face.

'You feed him. Now that he will live, you can promise yourself to him.' She walked past Meghan, but turned before she left. 'Then you may sleep here,' she said with a small smile, before leaving the tent.

Wilhelm was also smiling at her, as she squinted back at him.

'Promise myself to you? What have you been saying to her?' Meghan asked, before she sat down and put the bowl gently in Wilhelm's lap, so that it wouldn't spill.

'Are you not going to feed me?' he asked, clearly disappointed.

'I will tip it over your head,' she said pleasantly.

Wilhelm groaned as he tried to stifle his laugh.

'Try not to move,' she scolded him. 'You need to get better faster so that we can leave this place.'

'Are they mistreating you?' he asked.

'No, they have been remarkable, considering what they have been through.'

Wilhelm waited for her to continue, but she just stared at him and remained silent.

'What happened here?' he asked her in a soft voice.

'Something so horrible I cannot speak of it. Maybe when we have left I will have the strength to repeat it.'

Wilhelm could see she was genuine, but he knew they could be touchy, so he needed to know what had occurred.

'I don't want to say the wrong thing,' he said. 'You need to tell me what not to talk about.'

'Don't ask about their children,' was all she said, before leaning over and hugging Wilhelm, the side of her head resting against his.

After a time, she finally sat back up.

'You need to finish your broth,' she said.

Wilhelm took the spoon in his hand and continued eating the watery stew they had given him.

As they sat quietly together, the door flap was pulled aside and a man strode in.

'Denizen,' Meghan said, bowing her head as she stood.

'Please sit,' he said, beckoning towards the bed. 'I was told your friend was awake now. I would like to speak with him if that is all right with you?'

'Of course,' Meghan said, taking her seat once more on the bed.

Wilhelm tried to sit up straight, but groaned in pain and gave up trying.

'Thank you for looking after us,' Wilhelm said, as he looked at Denizen. He assumed he was their leader. The man carried himself with the same confidence his brother did. He had the look of a strong warrior and leader of men. His long hair was tied back with a leather strap and he walked with his sword like it was a natural extension of his body.

'I am not to thank for that privilege,' Denizen said, 'but I will pass on your words to the one in charge of us here.'

Denizen moved to stand at the foot of the bed.

'You are weakened still, but I understand you are both wanting to leave as soon as you are able.'

'We are searching for my brother,' Wilhelm said. His memories of being brought to this place were still a little foggy, but he remembered being told they were to be sent away. Something had obviously changed, and Meghan hadn't had time to fill in the gaps. Yet she was obviously familiar with this plainsman, and the bow she gave told Wilhelm she respected him.

Wilhelm trusted her judgement most of the time, so he was satisfied they were no longer in danger.

'Meghan has told me all. I am not sure what she has since told you,' Denizen replied.

'He has only just awoken,' Meghan said. 'I have not yet told him anything.'

Denizen nodded and turned back to Wilhelm.

'Your brother Kabir came to us weeks before today. He fought with us and nearly died with us, but he was well the last time I saw him. In his name, you are an honoured guest here.' This time Denizen bowed his head.

'My brother is here?!' Wilhelm exclaimed, once again wincing in pain as he tried to sit up.

Meghan put a hand out and touched his arm.

'Stop doing that,' she said, but not harshly. 'Kabir is not here. He is a long way from here.' Wilhelm could clearly hear the disappointment in her voice.

'Kabir had something to needed to find,' Denizen said. 'He rode towards the realm of men, accompanied by Ahlia.'

'What did he need to find?' Wilhelm asked, confused. 'Adventure? Surely there is enough of that here.'

Wilhelm couldn't help but notice Denizen tense at his words.

'We have had more 'adventures' here than we would care for,' Denizen said, a dark look in his eyes now.

Wilhelm didn't know why he had angered him, but he was ashamed still.

'I apologise for my words,' Wilhelm said, truly abashed. 'I spoke wrongly and without thought.'

'You are desperate to find your brother, I know,' Denizen said. 'As I said, Meghan has told me much.'

'Who is Ahlia?' Wilhelm asked. He thought it a safe change of the subject.

'She is one of our best,' Denizen said. 'He is in good hands, although she is as big a loss to our people as your brother is to yours. Especially now.'

'Are you able to help us search for them?' Wilhelm asked. 'We intend to bring them back.'

'We cannot.' Denizen said. 'And I doubt they would return,' he added.

'They will when we tell him what is happening at home,' Wilhelm said.

'Something else is drawing your brother away from here Wilhelm,' Denizen said. 'Something or someone requires something of him. I do not know who or what it is they want, but I saw the same look in his eyes as I see in yours now. I wish you well, but I do not think he will be swayed.'

Wilhelm had no idea what he was talking about. The plainsman spoke in riddles. A tight squeeze of his arm stopped him asking his next question.

'I am glad to see you awake, young barbarian. I will leave you to rest some more. You need to regain your strength. We cannot send anyone with you, but we will help how we can when you are ready to travel.'

He turned and left the tent.

'What is he talking about?' Wilhelm asked. He was trying to work out what Denizen's words meant, but his mind was still a little foggy and fatigued.

'He was not able to tell me much more than he just told you,' Meghan said. 'But I can tell you other tales he has spoken to me of about Kabir. Would you like to hear those?' she asked. 'It will pass the time until you sleep next. I am hopeful we will leave tomorrow at first light.'

That got Wilhelm's attention. Tomorrow was better than he had hoped for, but it just added to his confusion. Meghan was tough, and as much as he wanted to be moving, he wasn't sure his body would be ready. He hated to admit it, but he was certain he wouldn't be physically able to ride out at dawn.

'Tomorrow?' he asked. 'You think I will be ready?'

'Ordinarily, of course not,' she said. 'You nearly died Wil. Your body has only just started to heal itself, but I have been assured the plains people have a substance that will give your body a special energy, without depleting it of that which it needs to heal.'

'Magic?' Wilhelm asked.

'No, Wil. Not magic. It will enable you to sit a horse, but not much else. Your wounds will still need to heal. I will be there to make sure you do nothing more.' She spoke seriously now. 'I will box your ears if you try to do anything stupid. Denizen has assured me as best he could, that the first couple of days travel is through lands they have just come through. We should be safe from anything wanting to kill us.'

'Wow,' Wilhelm said. 'Why can I not take some now so we can leave today.'

'Because I had to beg them to give it to you at all,' Meghan replied. 'I told Denizen you were at least as stubborn as your brother, probably more so. He laughed and said you could not have any until a full day has passed from when you wake.'

Wilhelm nodded in acceptance.

'Thank you,' he eventually said. 'I hope you were okay about lying to them.'

'Lying to them?' Meghan had a look of confusion on her face.

'That I am as stubborn as my brother,' he said.

Meghan stared at him without expression.

'Are you sure you don't want to spoon feed me?' Wilhelm asked, as he scooped out another mouthful.

'How about I tell you what your brother has been up to since he left Deerstep,' she said in response. 'That way I don't leave you here now and set off on my own to find Kabir and his Princess.'

'Princess!?' Wilhelm exclaimed, nearly choking on his soup.

'He wasn't long entered the plains,' Meghan began, ignoring Wil's question with a small smile on her face, 'when his horse tripped and your brother was nearly killed before his adventure had even begun.'

Wilhelm continued to eat as Meghan replayed the tale told to her by Denizen, of how Kabir the mighty Highland Barbarian, almost single-handedly killed the feared queen of the insect-creatures.

CHAPTER 31

Making Friends

L INF WAS UNCEREMONIOUSLY awoken by a swift kick in the ribs. Groaning, she sat up slowly, cursing the one standing above her. After rubbing her eyes and looking around, she noticed there were several others present. They were not taking any chances with her this time.

Nor should they, she thought to herself. She was powerful now and deserving of their fear.

Standing up, she was led out of her makeshift pen and back towards where Kritch had his tent set up.

It was nearly dark now, and torches lit the space where she had spent her morning entertaining the Ogre-Mage King.

She saw no sign of him as she searched the shadows, before being thrown down on to the dirt, a bit further away from the entrance this time. They really were a bit jumpy, she thought to herself.

Despite the beating she received after knocking Kritch unconscious, she felt full of energy as she waited for him to appear. Since her escape from the human town, she had learnt how easy it was to take the power from others at great distances and without even being able to see them.

Not that she had to do that here. The camp of Kritch's army was brimming with anger and fear. It was such an amazing feeling to have it all around her. To have more than she could ever hope to hold.

It was just so easy to get and she had well and truly taken her fill prior to arriving here.

Linf was ready for whatever would come next.

After a few minutes of having her face almost held into the ground, Kritch finally exited his tent, quickly flanked by the four who had been standing guard outside.

Linf had lifted her face just enough so she could see in front of her. The goblin's strength was greater than the one holding her, so after a couple of tries, he had given up trying to force her face into the dirt.

The four guards surrounding Kritch were all similar to the ones who had brought her here from the lands of men.

Linf smiled to herself as he approached. She could see the level of anger Kritch held within him, but it was easily matched now by his level of fear.

That aside, he looked to be showing no ill-effects from their previous encounter.

Linf had already decided she would kill him before he killed her.

Those around him would be no protection. Not from the small ball of condensed energy floating mere feet from him already, hovering stationary in the air until Linf was ready to cast it through his ugly face.

Not that she wanted to die. Linf was enjoying her life more now than she ever had previously; she just didn't see a way out of this. Better to go quickly, than by one of his excruciating tortures. She had suffered enough during her short life already.

Kritch stopped only a few paces away from his tent before he began to talk.

'The goblin in front of us has shown extraordinary courage and has powers I would be foolish to waste. It will accompany our forces and be allowed to kill as many men and their wizards as the rest of us.'

He raised his arms to silence the voices calling out in disbelief.

'If any of you disagree with my decision, step forth and tell me all about it,' he roared above the noise of voices. As expected, all of the voices fell silent and none stepped forward.

'Good. Make sure none of you filth do anything stupid to the goblin, or you and your clan will answer to me. Now off with you all. Go and find something to do. We are heading to war soon!'

With that, he turned and walked back towards his tent.

The ball of energy hovering in front of Kritch disappeared, as the King stepped back into his tent.

Linf remained kneeling in the dirt as those around her began walking off in different directions.

What in the pits of the Arkinsh Cess Pools was going on? She suspected that Kritch was probably setting her up for a laugh. She would go to leave and then be grabbed before she could go very far and brought back again, to the laughter of all those that were in on it. Clenching her jaw, she was determined to kill not only Kritch, but every single one of the swine who would laugh at her.

Yet after a while, she wasn't so sure.

The area in front of the King's tent had emptied of all but his four guards and a few others on the edges talking in small groups.

She eventually stood and looked around some more.

What was going on?! Not only was she not going to be killed, but it appeared she was free to do whatever she wanted.

Linf decided to test how free she was, still suspecting some form of treachery.

Looking in the direction leading away from Kritch's tent, she began walking there, turning in circles as she did. None tried to stop her, although one large ogre-looking thing with a very long, axe-looking weapon began trailing after her. So, he was the one who would grab her and bring her back, she thought.

Linf decided there was no fighting it, so she decided to play along for now.

She continued outside of the clearing and soon walked near to a group of orcs. She knew what they were, because one of them looked very similar to Gort.

They were sitting on logs and eating some kind of watery meat out of a bowl.

She decided to stop and test whether Kritch's order had been real.

'Give me some of that,' she said to the one seated closest to her. It stood up and stepped closer to where Linf stood.

'Why don't you try and take some?' it said menacingly, before looking behind Linf. With a grunt, he turned around and sat back down.

Linf also turned around and saw the large ogre standing behind her. Here we go, she thought.

'What are you doing?' she asked. She didn't fail to notice this one had no anger and no fear about it. She didn't like anything without emotions. It wasn't normal. Yet she didn't need to draw anything from it. Not while she remained within reach of Kritch's army.

'I am here on King Kritch's orders to make sure you are not killed and to make sure you don't kill anyone else.' He even spoke without emotion.

'What if I kill you?' Linf asked. 'Who watches over me then?'

It didn't answer her, but still no emotion was forthcoming.

'Okay then. Is that all you are here for?' Linf asked sarcastically.

'No,' he replied this time. 'I am also here to make sure you don't try and run away like a coward before you get your chance to kill men.' She could hear the emotion in that comment, but still couldn't see any. He probably wasn't happy Kritch had let her live, but he was obviously a good soldier and did as he was told without question.

'What about food?' she asked. 'Did your King tell you to get some for me as well. I'll need my strength to kill all those men.'

Maybe the faintest trace of anger was visible around him now.

'You get your own food goblin. I don't care if you are hungry.'

'And how am I supposed to get food if you are going to stop me killing anything?' She wasn't that hungry at the moment. Her powers kept the hunger somewhat at bay.

The ogre shrugged his shoulders and turned his side to her.

Linf mimicked him, before walking off to explore more of the camp.

The G.O.D. Linf had longer than most of the others to choose her ability, and to decide upon a plan on how best to implement it.

Nothing stood out the first time she looked over the list, but on the second time through she took her time and decided on one the moment she re-read it.

It was neither a defensive nor attacking ability, but it would suit her need perfectly. She held out little hope of saving her Champion after the first read, but she was more confident now.

Having seen already that Kabir had been able to take a knife in with him, she gathered a large, thick coat from their store of clothes. Some of the nights on the creator's world could be chilly and there was an abundance of clothes for them all to choose from.

Walking back over to her *eye*, she waited for the right time to make her move, not that it was terribly important exactly when she did it. Unlike the others, she did not necessarily have to be there at the critical time.

She watched inside Kritch's tent, waiting for the Ogre-Mage to wake.

When he eventually did, she watched patiently as he summoned one of his guard.

The moment his guard left the tent, Linf put on the coat, pulled it over her head and stepped up to her *eye*.

'*Charm*' she said, as she stepped into the world of Dark Swell.

Linf was still asleep when she arrived next to her.

Smiling down at her rude, annoying goblin, Linf began to make her way toward Kritch's tent.

Linf hadn't been sure how she would cast the spell before stepping through her *eye*, but as soon as she was standing on the dirt of Dark Swell, she knew.

She need only say the word once more.

'Charm,' she said quietly to no-one.

Now she had only ten minutes to get to the tent of King Kritch and convince him to free her Champion.

Even with her face hidden, Linf knew she would stand out.

She was much smaller than any of the monsters and beasts within the camp, so she was relying on her ability to get her where she wanted to go.

Yet she knew if she were seen by too many of those present in camp, then her ability may not be enough to save her. If she was discovered and outed, then she would be in mortal danger. If she was stopped by only a few and her identity kept a secret, then her plan should work.

The thought of imminent death after spending so many years in perfect safety and serenity gave her a sense of dread as she set off, but also a feeling of excitement she had never felt before. To have such conflicting emotions within her was remarkable.

Linf had never felt so alive before and was unable to keep the large smile from her face.

Fortunately, there didn't seem to be many walking about at this time of the evening. There was still enough light to see easily, but it was beginning to darken.

Linf sighed deeply as she continued to galvanise herself for the task in front of her and immediately regretted it.

After spending so many years on the picturesque world of the Creator, the stench within Kritch's camp was an assault on her senses. Taking a deep breath made her slightly dizzy for a moment.

Taking shorter breaths and pulling her hood even lower, she continued on past the sounds of things eating, laughing and arguing.

She hadn't walked far when she was roughly grabbed by the shoulder and spun around. Linf almost cried out, such was the shock she felt.

She tried to stop herself looking up, but couldn't help it.

A Ve-Karn looked down at her.

One of the soldiers Mithrak had sent south as a token of his supposed good-will towards Kritch. They were deadly warriors, their weapons crafted by the grey dwarves living in the mountains near Mithrak's home.

Linf panicked for a moment. If he thought her a human magic-user, then he may run her through without hesitation.

Fortunately, she came back to herself before he had the chance.

'You need to escort me to Kritch's tent,' she said. 'He will reward you for taking me there.'

The Ve-Karn paused for a moment, and Linf's heart almost stopped.

She knew there were restrictions to how the spell worked. There had to be some part of what she sought to be believable to the one she intended to charm, along with other things. She knew her words would need to be chosen carefully, even when she had little or no time at all to think.

He reached out and grabbed her arm, turning her roughly away from him, before grabbing her other arm.

Linf did cry out this time, as his fingers dug into her arms. He began to march her off in the direction she had been walking.

'He wants me there unharmed,' she managed to say, causing his grip to loosen slightly.

They hadn't walked far when Linf passed those who Kritch had sent to fetch her Champion. None of them paid her any heed, for which she was thankful.

She would have only a couple of minutes at most with Kritch before they arrived back, if they let her inside the tent straight away.

And if she did manage to make it safely inside his tent, Linf would need to have time alone with Kritch to convince him to release her Champion. She would need to get his guards to leave.

All of a sudden, time was no longer her friend.

It had not been her preferred plan to be escorted to his tent, but in hindsight it was probably the quickest and safest way for her to get there unmolested. Fortune was shining on her so far. She would need it to continue.

They arrived at the King's tent without incident, two of Kritch's guards stepping forward with their weapons held out. They were both ogre's and they were huge.

'King Kritch is not seeing any one', one of them said.

Linf kept her head down, the hood covering her face still.

'She is to see him,' her Ve-Karn escort said to them. 'She is not to be hurt.'

'Who sent you here?' one of the ogres asked, stepping forward and lifting her hood away.

He stepped back and grunted.

'Where did you get this from?' he snarled, the Ve-Karn not yet having answered his first question.

'I was taken from my home of Mayfield and brought here for your King to play with. He will be pleased with you for taking me to see him.' Linf looked across and saw a couple of ogre-mage making their way over.

The ogre grabbed her by the shoulder and began walking her into the tent.

'The others should wait outside,' she said. 'I am no threat.'

'Wait here,' he said to the others.

'Stop' one of the ogre-mage called out, as they increased their pace.

The guard turned to look at them.

'The King needs to see this one,' her guard said, turning back toward the opening of the tent.

'Stop!' the mage yelled, as they moved quickly to stand in front of the guard, blocking his way. The other guards moved in menacingly.

The ogre-mage held a hand up to them.

'It is our duty to protect the King as much as it is yours,' he said. 'What do you have here?'

Linf tried not to look at any of them, as she focused her eyes on the ground in front of her feet.

'A plaything for King Kritch,' the guard said. 'You need to move.'

'Why are you in such a hurry?' the ogre-mage asked. Linf knew he was suspicious. She was beginning to panic. They were powerful wielders of magic. One quick spell and she would die where she stood.

Linf needed to think quickly. She didn't know how many she would be able to charm at once, or how long the spell would work. There were varying degrees of the spell, depending on the strength of the caster. She hoped beyond hope that the Creator had given her a higher spell.

'I was told the King gets angry if he is made to wait,' she said. 'You should let him pass and wait out here.'

This time she looked up.

The ogre-mage behind the one who had spoken nodded his head.

'We should let her inside,' he said to his fellow mage.

The ogre-mage turned to look at the one who had just spoken, before turning back to Linf. She could tell by the look on his face the spell had not worked on him. He must be too strong for it.

'Assassin,' Linf said quickly, lifting her hand and pointing at the ogre-mage, as he began to lift his arm also. 'Sent by Mithrak to kill your King.'

'Die witch,' the ogre-mage said, moments before a sword impaled his neck.

The fireball died on his fingertips.

'Quickly, into the tent,' the guard said, as he shoved her through the opening.

'None are to approach the tent,' she heard the guard shout from outside, as feet scurried about. None of them entered the tent. Amazingly, she was suddenly free of his guards.

Linf took a deep breath as she gained her footing and looked at her surroundings. She knew exactly what the inside of Kritch's tent looked like, and where he would be sitting, but she was enthralled nevertheless. It was one thing to look at it through her *eye*, another thing entirely to be immersed within it. If she were ever permitted to stay for an extended time, she didn't think it would ever grow old.

Kritch stood from where he lounged and eyed her suspiciously.

'What are you doing here?' he asked, looking beyond her for the guards that should have accompanied anyone entering his tent. 'What is happening out there?'

Linf was suddenly extremely nervous. Kritch was the most powerful of the ogre-mage, which is why he was their King. She now had serious doubts about her spell being powerful enough to influence him. If the dead ogre-mage outside the tent had been too strong for it to work, then she rated her chances of charming the King as not good to slim.

'You need to let the goblin go,' Linf said, without thinking. She had made it to where she needed to be and impulsively spoke the words she had needed to say. There was no thought put into the words and she immediately regretted them.

Kritch grunted, and then snarled at her before she could say more.

'Who are you to tell me what to do?!' he roared. 'I'll have you torn apart with that goblin.'

'Why would you waste the goblin that way?' Linf asked. She had quickly realised her error and tried to correct it before he called for his guards.

The spell didn't work unless there was some desire within the other to begin with. Kritch had no desire to see Linf go free.

Kritch looked to stop what he was about to say. Linf guessed he had been about to call for his guards. She would be lost if that happened.

'Waste it?' he asked. 'The goblin tried to kill me! And what and who are you!'

'Which is why you should let her fight for you,' Linf replied. 'Let the goblin kill as many of Dayhen's soldiers and wizards as she can before they kill her.' Linf had given up on trying to free her Champion. That was not going to happen today.

'I want to end the stinking vermin myself,' Kritch said, but not with as much heat in his voice as before.

'Dead is dead,' Linf said. 'You will still be able to watch.' She could see he was swaying now. 'What better spectacle than watching wizards and men die, and then the goblin being cut to pieces by some of Dayhen's King's Shield.'

Kritch continued to snarl, but she thought she had him now. The spell was powerful, but there needed to be more of Kritch's own desire within her words for it to work against him.

At least her Champion would live for a while longer. She had survived difficult situations before.

'Who are you?' he asked again, his suspicion returning.

Fortunately, Linf had thought of an answer to that question before arriving, and was able to answer without hesitation.

'Mithrak sent me. I have information about his progress.'

'What information?' Kritch asked, the suspicion still there. She knew he had little trust for the dark-mage.

'That it is time for you to move. That all is in readiness. He asked me to tell you "the human realm is now ripe for the taking."' Linf paused for effect. 'He said he will meet you inside Dayhen's city before the next full moon.'

Kritch looked less suspicious, more excited now.

'You are one of Dayhen's humans. Why do you do Mithrak's bidding?'

'I want to be on the side that wins, and Mithrak has promised me great treasures.' Linf smiled, but realised she needed to get back on topic.

'I believe they have the goblin outside now great King,' Linf said as she bowed. Hopefully she had timed it right in her head.

Kritch nodded and swept past her without a further glance in her direction.

The G.O.D. Linf remained in the tent. She didn't dare look out in case it drew the attention of others to her. Others who had not yet been charmed.

She could hear clearly everything Kritch said to her Champion.

The smile stayed on her face long after she had been whisked back to the Creator's world.

Striding over to the table of refreshments, she poured herself a large glass of juice before moving back over to her *eye*.

Linf didn't envisage being able to return to the surface of Dark Swell any time soon. Her Champion would still be in danger for the foreseeable future.

Taking a long drink, she sighed and sat back, the adrenalin from her adventure still coursing through her body.

CHAPTER 32

Take The Fight To Them

JARKENE CONTINUED TO stalk the edge of the forest, hoping to come across the dwarves again.

He was surprised the one he hit with his energy bolt had somehow survived. He begrudgingly admitted to himself the dwarf's armour must be quite a remarkable piece of work.

He would like to get his hands on it so it could be studied. A defence such as that could be invaluable in the coming conflict.

Yet he was also painfully aware that throughout the ages, when dwarves had been killed and their possessions taken, no elf had ever been able to come close to replicating what the dwarves could do with steel, stone and jewels. Their craftsmen were unparalleled to anything he had seen come out of the Western Realm or that of humans. The elves concentrated on magic, so weapons such as those the dwarves made were not as important. Elves were left to concentrate their craft on arrowheads and light armour that did not impede their movements through the forest. It was well wrought, but no match for the little folk in the mountain.

It did not usually end well for an elf if a dwarf was allowed to get too close.

Yet even with their magic, Jarkene knew that powerful, lightweight armour would be invaluable in the thick of battle in case of a random arrow or spear.

It had been some time since he had glanced the three dwarves trudging through the thick fog of the swampland.

It didn't offer him much of a shot at them, and he wanted to wait until the moment was perfect before he tried again.

Jarkene did not want to spook them into travelling further into the swamp. Eventually they would be confident enough to think he had gone and would come closer to where it was easier to walk on the ground between the swamp and Glorfiden.

After a while longer, the Elven Lord decided it might be smarter for him to move further ahead and wait for them to come to him. That way he wouldn't risk their invisible friend warning them of his approach.

Especially now that Treille had joined him once more.

Running swiftly through the branches of the trees, Jarkene and Treille arrived at the place he had chosen to wait for the dwarves. He expected they should arrive within the next hour, so the two elves made themselves comfortable.

After waiting only ten minutes, a sound reached his ears, but it came in the opposite direction to where he had expected it.

It didn't take long to come into view and at first, he didn't believe his eyes.

'It cannot be,' he said to Treille in a quiet voice, unable to take his eyes from it to gauge the reaction of his fellow elf.

'There are so many of them,' Treille finally said, before falling silent again.

'A Dwarven Army!' Jarkene exclaimed. 'And they dare come this close to Glorfiden.' His full voice had returned as the initial disbelief was quickly replaced by anger.

Sending out his senses, Jarkene quickly determined there were no other elves close enough to assist them.

They would need to fight the entire army on their own.

'They cannot be permitted to enter the trees,' Jarkene said, looking across at his fellow elf this time. He had expected to see fear on the face of Treille, but was gladdened to see the opposite.

He looked both determined and excited, but not afraid.

'We will kill a great many of them Lord Jarkene,' Treille replied, taking out his bow.

Jarkene put out an arm.

'Not yet,' he said, as they watched the dwarves come closer, comforted in the knowledge that none of those outside of the forest would be able to see them. 'They are not coming towards us.'

Treille didn't respond straight away.

'They are not spacing out to stretch their attack either,' Treille commented.

'Their formation is defensive,' Jarkene said. 'It looks as if these dwarves are trying to sneak past this forest without having to get their feet wet in the swamp.' He smiled at Treille. 'We may not have to give them a reminder of what happens to any who enter the forest uninvited.'

'Where then are they going Lord Jarkene, if not here?' It was a good question.

'Where do you believe they go?' Jarkene asked, as he thought about his own answer.

'To the Dwarven Mountains,' Treille replied. 'To fight the other dwarves.'

Jarkene slowly shook his head as their true intent dawned on him.

'They have seen the storm strike our home from wherever they dwell in the distant west,' Jarkene said. 'They now seek to join with the Eastern Dwarves to move against Glorfiden, thinking us weak and almost all gone.' Jarkene knew he sounded bitter, and he was. As hard as he tried not to constantly dwell on it, he found it very difficult to stop thinking how it was entirely his fault they were now so vulnerable to the outside world.

So weakened by the destruction he had sent forth, they could do nothing while an entire Dwarven Army walked casually past the trees of Glorfiden unmolested.

Such a tale spoken to the Eastern Dwarves would have them all scurrying out of their mountains, confident in an easy victory.

Unless they were no longer allowed to continue on unmolested.

The Lord of the Elves was still confident of his own safety within Glorfiden, even were these dwarves foolish enough to enter with their entire army. The forest was not a welcoming place for any stranger, let alone a dwarf. He had spells that would see them separated and lost, wandering aimlessly until they were picked off and slaughtered.

Yet he doubted the dwarves would even try and enter. They would instead run and pass on to their brethren in the east that the elves continued to rule within Glorfiden.

The dwarves would still know that entering this forest meant their death.

'When I give the word, you will begin to fill their ranks with arrows,' Jarkene said. 'I do not care whether every arrow kills its target, I want you to shoot as many arrows as quickly as you can. Do you understand why?'

'So they believe there are more than just the two of us,' Treille said.

Jarkene nodded, pleased that his fellow elf did not question his orders and possessed enough smarts to know what his Lord's intentions were.

'What will you do my Lord?' Treille asked.

'I will make them wish they were back safe within their hole in the Western Mountains,' he said, turning slowly to look at Treille as he finished speaking.

Treille took the first of his arrows from his quiver and turned to face the approaching army.

'Let us show them what happens to a dwarf who thinks it safe to come near Glorfiden,' Jarkene said, as he began to draw from the pool of magic deep within the forest.

Looking intently at those leading the dwarves, Jarkene chose his spell and picked his mark.

'Loose,' he said to Treille, as he cast his spell.

The ground beneath the dwarves blew apart, as dozens of their warriors flew into the air, their shields falling from their hands as Jarkene followed up his first spell with a barrage of lightning bolts.

Several dwarves exploded before their bodies had time to fall back to earth.

Treille cast a quick glance across at his Lord as the first dwarves died. His eyes were aflame as he cast his spells.

Ordinarily it would have scared the elf.

However, facing a Dwarven army with just the two of them, he was gladdened.

He feared only for those dwarves standing across the field from them.

He would not have wanted to face such a foe. Not with ten armies behind him.

Then a thought occurred to him, as he suddenly realised they would no longer be simply sending a message to this dwarven army.

His Lord was now in such a state, he will no longer be able to stop.

Not until his enemy were vanquished.

The realisation hit him that they would remain here until every last dwarf had fled or died. Or until they themselves were killed.

As powerful as he was, he did not believe even Jarkene would be able to defeat such a force on his own.

Turning away quickly, and left with no other recourse, Treille continued shooting his arrows as fast as he was able.

His best hope was that the army would simply retreat into the swamp and Jarkene would not then follow them.

Treille obviously did not know dwarves well at all.

CHAPTER 33

For The Realm

JARON WATCHED FROM his balcony as his envoy left.
His most trusted wizards and fifty of his personal guard; those
most loyal and well-paid; rode from the square below him.

Their mission would make or break his city.

His continued rule depended on them diverting the wizards and
King's Shield sent from Shadow Hill. If they got word of Dayhen's
order to his own King's Shield and remaining wizards, then he would
be lost.

Aside from a probable charge of treason, it would leave the city of
Havern vulnerable to the outside world. He doubted Dayhen would
accept his excuse of not receiving the message.

Four other birds had arrived after the first message was sent, each
one more urgent than the last.

Why Dayhen would think to order away nearly all of his wizards
and King's Shield still bewildered him, no matter how many times
he had run it through his mind.

As bad as things were in the Western part of the realm, he
believed things were certainly just as dire here. Letheris had been
evacuated and every farmstead east of Shadow Hill now stood empty,
their provisions ripening and rotting with none to harvest it.

Dayhen should be sending them more of The Shield, not taking
away what they already had!

If both Shadow Hill and Havern were to be overrun, those wizards and King's Shield Dayhen wanted to help bolster Lakerth would make no difference. The capital was too big to properly defend with so few.

More reinforcements in Havern made far more sense.

His King was a selfish fool, which is why Jaron had decided upon his current action. He risked death by doing it, but he believed the risk of death greater if he didn't do it.

He did not regret his actions. Hopefully time would prove him correct and those future consequences might be avoided when all was right again within the realm.

If he was really lucky, Dayhen and his spawn would be killed in the coming war and there would be none to bring him to task about his treason.

All Jaron had to do now was wait to hear how his men went, or it could all be over a lot sooner than he hoped.

Lord Marcus had been horrified when he received the message from his King. Three quarters of his King Shield and three of his four wizards were to make for Lakerth without delay. It was a difficult order to obey, considering two of his wizards were off escorting those collecting provisions from the now-empty farmsteads. Fortunately, his King had not asked for more soldiers, as those he had left were made up mostly of old men and boys anyway.

The majority of his best soldiers were away escorting the wagons east or had already been subscribed into the King's Army during the preceding months.

Losing that many wizards and Shield would leave Shadow Hill almost defenceless, but he had no choice. His King had ordered it and Marcus had no reason to doubt the urgency of his decision.

'Should we evacuate the entire town?' Mikael asked him.

An elderly King's Shield and leader of what remained of his forces at Shadow Hill, Marcus considered Mikael his oldest friend. He was talkative for one of the Shield and was never backward in giving his opinion.

'I am seriously considering it,' Marcus replied, running his hands through his hair. 'But we cannot go anywhere until they return with the wagons.'

'We can begin preparations,' Mikael said. 'We could be ready before they are here.'

'We don't know how long they will be,' Marcus said. 'I would rather not send away our only two remaining wizards and most of your order before then, but King Dayhen ordered without delay.'

'He would understand if he knew the circumstances,' Mikael said.

'I thought you were a King's man,' Marcus said, chuckling. 'Did you just encourage me to defy an order from our King.'

'No,' Mikael said, his tone still serious. 'However, a small delay would mean receiving more than he has requested.'

'Why the urgency?' Marcus asked. It was rhetorical and so Mikael refrained from answering him again.

'He knows how bad things are here. If things are worse in the west, then it must be serious.' He turned to look at Mikael.

'Make the preparations to have everyone leave,' he said. 'But send Brycen and Palinda, along with the remaining King's Shield, without delay. As ordered,' he added.

Mikael nodded, before turning and leaving the room.

Brycen rode his horse out front, the twelve King's Shield and his fellow wizard Palinda, riding behind him.

He had been loath to leave Shadow Hill, but Derekia had co-signed the note, just in case there was any doubt as to the legitimacy of the order.

They would go through Havern on their way to Lakerth, but Brycen would have expected Jaron's reinforcements to have left prior to their arrival.

He would have liked to have travelled with them. In these dark days, even two wizards and a dozen King's Shield were at risk of being attacked. The fate of those escorting the Princess from Loftenberg and the death of Valdor spoke volumes of the danger they were all in.

Brycen himself had wanted to remain until the carts returned, so they could ride escort for the evacuation of Shadow Hill, but his Lord had been firm. They needed to make haste.

They made good time throughout the day, with nothing to slow them down. There was no traffic on the roads these days, not even between two of the realms largest towns. It wasn't safe anywhere.

As evening approached, Brycen thought he saw something coming towards them from a steep hill to their right. The land they rode through was punctuated with pockets of trees, but it was rocky land, and for the most part sparse, with only mounds of bushes and spiky grasses. The track they rode on wound its way along the lower ground, but every now and then they had to traverse small hills.

It was as they were riding over the top of one of these hills, that Brycen thought he had seen movement ahead, and to their right. The sun was low in the sky, and there were shadows all around them now, but he was almost certain something was out there.

He slowed his horse and waited for Patric to join him. He was the most senior of the King's Shield accompanying them.

'You have seen something?' Patric asked.

Brycen knew his posture would have given him away even before he slowed his horse.

'Over there,' he said, pointing in the direction where he had seen the movement.

'We will scout ahead,' Patric said, turning around and summoning two others to ride with him.

'Wait,' Brycen said. 'We don't know what is there. I think we should all go.'

'We can move quieter with just a few,' Patric replied, but he stayed where he was. The wizard had been given command of this group, and he wouldn't go unless told.

'I think it would already know of our coming,' Brycen said. 'We will all go, but you may ride in front.' He didn't need to tell them to stay alert.

They continued riding, Brycen scouring the land ahead. There was no other movement as they rode, until they had almost reached the point level to where he had first seen the shadow move.

Without warning, Patric and the other two King's Shield jumped from their horses and took off at a run towards a copse of trees nearby.

Brycen wanted to follow them, but the terrain was rocky and would be dangerous for his horse.

Readying his spell, he stood in his stirrups and watched as the three King's Shield approached the trees.

Arrows suddenly came shooting out at them, the three King's Shield effortlessly dodging or swatting the projectiles away.

Patric lost sight of them, as they stepped under the branches. He heard yells coming from inside and turned to see if any of their fellow King's Shield had jumped from their own horses to assist. They all still sat upright, surveying their surrounds in all directions, but otherwise looking relaxed.

A few minutes passed before Patric and the other two King's Shield stepped back into sight again. They moved at a jog back to where Brycen and the rest waited, before casually lifting themselves on to their mounts.

'A dozen or so hobgoblins I believe,' Patric said, 'although they looked different to any I have fought before.'

'Did they flee?' Brycen asked. 'It is hard to see from here.'

'None escaped,' Patric said, 'although they fought better than the usual hobgoblins. These ones were stronger and faster.'

Patric had never gotten used to the casual manner of the King's Shield when it came to combat. None of them had a sweat up or looked to be fatigued in any way. They had just killed a dozen hobgoblins without injury to any of them.

He was extremely grateful to have them with him.

He decided this would be a good spot to rest their horses for a time and get some sleep. Unlike the King's Shield, he felt fatigue, and being in the saddle all day was not his idea of fun.

It was well before dawn when Brycen was awoken by Patric. He had asked to be woken early in the morning so they could continue to make haste.

Perhaps he should have been more specific with his instruction, but now that he was awake, Brycen decided they may as well keep moving.

There was sufficient moon, enabling them to easily make out the track they rode on. Although it increased their risk of running into something undesirable as they rode, that risk was still there if they remained where they were.

The small party rode throughout the rest of the night without incident. It was now mid-morning and they were not far off arriving at Havern, when Patric signalled for them to stop.

Brycen had let the King's Shield lead this time. Their eyes and ears were sharper than his, so it made sense.

He looked ahead and could see a large number of men riding towards them.

They would have to be Jaron's men, this close to Havern and in such numbers. He was curious to see why they were riding in this direction.

As they came closer, he could see at least three of his fellow wizards among them. That was odd. Why so many? And there could be even more within the following ranks. He was surprised to see no King's Shield with them. That at least explained the large number of men.

The lead wizard stopped before reaching them and walked his horse forward. Brycen went forward to speak with him.

'Gareth,' he said in greeting.

'Brycen, it is good we have caught you before you got to Havern,' he replied.

'Why so?' Brycen asked, his curiosity piqued now.

'There is a pestilence running rampant. The whole town has been quarantined. We assumed you would be coming, after we received our own summons from the King.' He spoke quickly and with emotion.

'Why are there no King's Shield with you?' Brycen asked. 'Are they sick?'

'Unlikely,' Gareth said, followed by a short laugh. 'Most have left for Lakerth already. The rest are helping to maintain the quarantine, as they are least susceptible to it.'

'That is extremely unfortunate news' Brycen said, 'both for the people of Havern and for those in Shadow Hill.'

Gareth looked at him with a confused look, as Brycen continued.

'Lord Marcus has ordered Shadow Hill be evacuated. We cannot defend it, so all will leave.'

'They cannot come here,' Gareth said, a startled look on his face.

Brycen wasn't sure what was going on, but he was certain Gareth wasn't telling him everything. Lord Marcus made no secret of what he thought of the Lord of Havern. *Sneaky and consumed with his own power* was one of his favourite descriptions.

'We thought to help bolster the ranks of Havern, and Lord Marcus waits for carts full of provisions to arrive from the east.' Brycen knew the risk to those in Shadow Hill would be even more extreme if they had to march all the way to Lakerth.

'There is nothing I can do to help,' Gareth replied. 'I have my orders, as do you. You will need to go north of Havern. It should not add too much time to your journey.'

Brycen didn't answer straight away. He knew there was nothing he could do for those who would be coming from Shadow Hill. His Lord would be in a better position to argue with Gareth. He actually felt a little sorry for his fellow wizard. He wouldn't want to be the one telling Marcus he wasn't allowed into Havern.

Good luck with that he thought, as he nodded at Gareth's last words.

'We will stay north,' Brycen said. 'Are you continuing on to Shadow Hill to inform Lord Marcus?'

'No,' Gareth said. 'Our orders were simply to speak with your group. We will return now, but I am sure Lord Jaron will send other messengers once he is made aware of the situation in Shadow Hill. Provisions will be made for their safe housing.'

'I am sure he will,' Brycen said. 'Shall we be going then?' he asked.

'Yes,' his fellow wizard said. 'We will escort you before your turn off.'

'Thank you,' Brycen said, trying to sound as sincere as he was able to in the circumstances.

Gareth breathed a giant sigh of relief, as he turned his back to Brycen and rode back to his group of wizards and soldiers.

His orders had been to divert this group around Havern. If he was unsuccessful in doing that, his next order had been to ensure they never reached Havern.

Even with five wizards, fifty soldiers and the element of a surprise attack, he was still not certain they could have killed them all without severe losses to his own group. The thought of attacking and trying to kill a dozen King's Shield, not to mention two of his fellow wizards, was appalling to him.

Yet so was the thought of disobeying his Lord. He had witnessed first-hand what happened to traitors in Jaron's employ.

He managed to smile at his fellow wizards as he re-joined him, while his heart rate continued to drop.

CHAPTER 34

Off You Go

'YOU MUST RETURN and warn Draug,' Brindel said again.

'I heard you the first time,' Granwith snarled, looking down at his feet. 'You need to come too,' he added, as he looked up at Brindel.

'I have to keep going,' Brindel said. 'You will be needed there Granwith, I won't be.'

'You underestimate your worth Master Smith,' Granwith said with a smile. 'This quest you are on can wait until we have dealt with these Western upstarts. I am sure the treasure will still be there.'

Brindel sighed. He would actually prefer to return home, rather than continue on his own. In the short time they had travelled together, he had actually begun to grow accustomed to their company. Maybe even enjoyed it a little bit at times.

'I don't think it can wait,' Brindel said. 'I fear I am taking too long as it is.'

'We will return when it is done,' Kagen said, trying to re-assure Granwith.

Brindel looked down at the young dwarf.

'You are going with Granwith,' he said, holding up his hand to stop Kagen responding. 'Every dwarf able to swing an axe will be required to defend our home,' Brindel said to him, lacking true conviction in his voice. He wasn't going after all. Predictably Kagen noticed.

'You can swing an axe and you're not going back, so neither am I and neither is Feng.' He stood with his arms folded on his chest.

Brindel knew they had been here before, and he was certain the young dwarf had exactly the same pose and look on his face the last time he was told to go home.

'He's right Kagen,' Granwith said. 'I need you to come with me. If something were to happen to me on our way back, then only you will be able to warn them.'

'Nothing will happen to you,' Kagen said.

'It's true Granwith is one of our greatest warriors,' Brindel said, 'but there are things out there which might be too powerful even for him to kill.'

'Who is a better warrior than I am?' Granwith asked.

Brindel looked over at his companion, surprised by his question and by the annoyed look on his face. They were trying to convince the young dwarf to go home, and he was picking at Brindel's comment.

'What?' Brindel asked. 'How does that matter right now?!'

'You said I was one of our best warriors. Who is better or equal to me? You better not be suggesting Draaf.' He looked seriously offended. 'Or do you believe Crandle my superior?'

Brindel chose to ignore him, turning back to Kagen.

'Although Granwith is easily the best dwarven warrior throughout the two kingdoms, he will need Feng to scout for him,' Brindel continued. 'And Feng won't go anywhere without you.'

Brindel looked over at Granwith, the dwarf's eyes narrowing as he did and the angry expression on his face still present.

'Are you suggesting there are dwarves in this Western army greater warriors than I am?'

Was he for real? Brindel thought.

'I have never met any dwarves from the West,' Brindel said in response. 'Can we get back to what we were talking about?'

Granwith continued staring at him for a bit longer, before finally looking back down at Kagen.

'You are coming with me,' he finally said. 'The defence of our home is more important than some fools quest that may result in nothing but a glorious death.'

'Then why doesn't Brindel come with us?' Kagen asked, still not won over.

'Do you think the entrance we left from will be able to repel an army of dwarves?' Granwith said, raising his voice. 'We are going home young dwarf!'

Kagen didn't respond for a time, until eventually he nodded and then turned his face away from both dwarves.

'Take some food with you,' Brindel said, opening up his satchel and pulling out a heap of food bundles.

'How much junk have you got in that bag of yours?' Granwith asked, as Brindel handed him over the food. 'I have been meaning to ask all this time. You are always pulling stuff from it.'

Brindel paused as he began to seal it off.

'I have things I now realise I don't need,' he said, opening the bag again. Reaching in, he pulled out what looked like a book, wrapped in leather.

'What is that, and why are you taking it out?' Granwith asked.

'It is a book of sorts and it has been in my family since before the two Dwarven Kingdoms broke into two.' Brindel looked admiringly at it. 'When I left the mountains, I didn't know where I would go, so I brought it with me. I would like you to take it back for me if that's okay.'

Granwith continued to look at the book, before looking up at Brindel.

'What kind of stories does it have in it?' he asked.

'Not stories,' Brindel said. 'It shows how to make weapons and armour, using ancient methods.'

'I bet that is what he was after,' Granwith said, half to himself.

'Who?' Brindel asked.

'The thief,' Granwith said. 'The one I caught in your room looking through your things.'

'What are you talking about?' Brindel said. 'When did this happen?'

'Elenda sent a thief to try and steal something from you,' Granwith explained. 'I caught him in the act and now he is rotting in a hole, but I bet that book of yours is what she wanted. I never did trust her,' Granwith added. 'Too full of herself.'

'Why would the Apprentice to the Master Smith want my family book?' Brindel said, genuinely perplexed. 'There has been nothing written in it for a thousand years.'

'I don't know,' Granwith said, 'but I remember her taking quite the liking to your things. Pretty embarrassing the way you two were gushing over each other's stuff.'

Brindel chose to ignore him, as he un-wrapped his book.

He hadn't checked it since he first left and he wanted to make sure no water had gotten into it, or anything else.

Opening the pages, all seemed good as he flicked through them, ensuring no small insect had nestled itself between the pages.

Everything was as it had been, as he finished flicking.

Furrowing his brows, he opened it again, looking once more at the last page.

He was intimately familiar with almost every page; he had read it so often. Yet as he flicked through the last few pages, something twigged in the back of his head. He thought he had seen something that didn't look right.

Opening the book to the last page, his eyes almost popped out of his head.

He placed a hand on the page and began to read words he had previously never in his life seen before. On the page behind it were drawings and further instructions.

'What is it?' Granwith asked him several times as he read. Brindel didn't register his voice, so he couldn't acknowledge his question.

Kagen was the same, as he chimed in a couple of times.

'What is it Brindel?' he asked, followed quickly by, 'I'm not going with Granwith anymore.'

After a couple of minutes, Brindel gave a deep sigh and closed the book again.

'This is definitely what she was after,' Brindel said, looking at Granwith. Why was he scowling at me? he thought.

'What does it say then?' Granwith asked.

'Who wrote it?' Kagen asked.

Brindel looked at Kagen. His was an excellent question. Who wrote it indeed?

The writing looked to have been done with the same hand as that which was written a thousand years ago. Brindel was in fact quite sure the writing was done by the same dwarf. But how was that possible?

'I can't answer your question Kagen,' he confessed. 'That is a complete mystery. But if I were to guess, then I would say it was by something not of this land.' He saw Kagen's eyes widen and his mouth fall open.

'From the stars?' Kagen asked. 'Or across the far reaches of the dark waters?'

All Brindel could do was shrug and leave Kagen to his imagination.

'What does it say?' Granwith asked again, his voice serious.

'They are instructions on how to make a breast plate,' Brindel said, still a little stunned as he thought more on what he had read. 'But a piece of armour unlike any other ever made.'

'How so?' Granwith asked, still serious.

'I'm not sure exactly,' Brindel replied, 'but if I'm right, then it could make its wearer almost invincible.'

It was Granwith's turn for his eyes to open wide and his mouth fall open.

'What do you mean by invincible exactly?' Granwith asked.

'I mean, it will stop any weapon; even magic-wrought. It will stop any spell and it will protect against attacks of the mind.' Brindel wished he had the time to study it at length.

'Except for the parts not protected by a breast-plate,' Granwith added.

'No,' Brindel replied. 'It doesn't say what it is, only that the central piece, when placed into the centre of the breast-plate, will spread the protection to all parts of its wearer. It will surround them as if it covered every inch of the body.'

'I am pretty sure I know what this central piece is,' Granwith said.

'How would you know that?' Brindel asked. It was his turn to be confused.

'We met up with my brother not long after you left us in the southern mountain,' Granwith said. 'She had sent one of her underlings with him to trade with the Lord in Havern. He told me what they got. What Elenda had insisted he not leave without.'

Brindel had stopped breathing as Granwith told his tale.

'A diamond larger; and with a greater purity; than any other jewel throughout the land,' Granwith finished, almost drooling at the thought of it.

'Whoever wrote this must have told Elenda what she needed to make the armour, but it didn't give her the instructions on how to do it,' Brindel mused. 'Why do that?'

'Who knows,' Granwith said, 'but she is not going to get her hands on this book. I will guard it with my life,' he said.

Brindel felt a sudden chill, as the realisation hit him that he would be handing his book over to another dwarf. He certainly trusted Granwith. The dwarf had saved his life after all. But he suddenly didn't feel comfortable giving it up.

'Maybe I should hold on to it, so I can read it again and see if there is more to what it says.' Brindel knew it should be returned to his home.

'I will take good care of it,' Granwith assured him in a soft voice. 'You can quickly read it again if you like, before we leave.'

Brindel nodded. 'That would be good,' he said, as he opened the page back up and began pouring over the new writings again.

'I'm not going back home,' Kagen said again, but Brindel didn't even hear him.

'I think we should go with the warrior dwarf,' Feng said.

'We agreed to stay with Brindel,' Kagen replied. He spoke the words in his head, so only Feng could hear him. His friend had shown him how to do it not long after they met. It wasn't hard, but he had to be careful at times. No dwarf wanted their every thought communicated. Some were private.

'It is too dangerous now,' Feng said. *'Brindel cannot keep you safe and it is harder for me to do when I need to hunt.'*

'I can take care of myself,' Kagen said. *'You don't have to be around all of the time. We will be fine. Once the army of evil dwarves has gone past, then we will get to this forest and Brindel will get our treasure. Then we can go back home.'*

'We are going back,' Feng said.

Kagen was taken aback by the tone his friend used. He had not heard it before.

'I will not watch you die again,' Feng said.

Kagen was stunned for a time, before finding his thoughts again.

'He will not survive without us,' Kagen said, only realising he had spoken out loud after the words had left his mouth.

'Who won't?' Granwith asked.

'No-one,' Kagen said, looking across at Brindel. The Dwarven smith hadn't heard him. He still had his face in his book.

'You are coming with me,' Granwith said. 'If I have to go, then so do you.'

Something seemed to snap inside him hearing Granwith's words again. It wasn't what he said, it just hit home that it was what he had to do. Brindel didn't want him going with him, and he had a duty to the Dwarves to get back there and warn them.

'You stay with Brindel,' he said to Feng. The sadness he felt as he spoke the words in his mind was overwhelming, but Brindel was going to need him.

'I am staying with you,' Feng said. *'We should get moving.'*

'You need to stay!' Kagen yelled in his mind, but his companion was no longer talking to him. Kagen knew he had probably already taken off to scout back the way they had just come.

'I am going to go back with Granwith again,' Kagen said, turning to look at Brindel, just as the older dwarf lifted his eyes from the book.

He nodded at Kagen's words as he began to wrap the book back up in its leather cover.

'I will get back there as quickly as I am able,' Brindel said to him.

'You will probably die,' was all Kagen said, as he stood up and went after Feng.

Brindel didn't call him back. It was probably easier to say good-bye this way.

'He is just scared that you are off on this dangerous journey by yourself,' Granwith said.

'I know,' Brindel said, handing the book over to Granwith. 'You best be going then.'

Granwith nodded and held out his hand.

Brindel took his wrist and forearm in a firm grip, as Granwith returned the gesture.

Without another word, he picked up the rest of his things and trundled off after the young dwarf.

Brindel watched them walk off, and just like that he was on his own again.

His next plan was simple. Move further into the swamp and wait for the Dwarven army to pass by. Then he would get himself back out on to solid ground.

Hopefully there would be no more swamps and forests between here and the ruined forest.

CHAPTER 35

Sound The Horn

IT WAS A strange feeling riding this close to the Elven Forest. All his life Mithrak had been told he needed to fear it; that it would be his death if he ever walked under the trees.

Now here he was, a small army in front and a small army behind him, readying themselves to charge into the very same forest that not all that long ago he would never have thought to do.

'Do your final sweep and then return with your report when word arrives of Kritch's army,' Mithrak said to his General. Jurg nodded and moved away.

Everything was nearly in place, he thought.

Very soon now and they would be under the branches of Glorfiden. He prayed there were still enough elves alive to give him and his army some sport. They would definitely enjoy slaughtering elves.

As to whether they would be able to defeat the elves if there were still a large number of them within the forest? There was no doubt in his mind they would prevail. The six realms were his for the taking.

This was his time.

Thrisc looked at the back of his King and smiled.

He was thrilled to be given the 'honour' of accompanying Mithrak wherever it was they were going, yet he also knew he deserved it.

Thrisc had always thought quite highly of himself, and due to this arrogance, had needed to be able to back it up. Fortunately for his survival, he had always been able to do just that.

Now he was only a couple of steps below the highest rung in the Western Realm; possibly all of the Realms sometime in the near future.

He was under no illusion Mithrak was by far the most powerful dark-mage in the realm, however Thrisc still needed to make sure he was positioned suitably, should anything untoward ever happen to his liege.

Mithrak turned as he was looking at him.

'You will send the signal when Jurg returns,' he said.

Thrisc couldn't hide the smile this time, as he looked across at the other two dark-mage.

Cordak did not seem fussed, but nothing seemed to worry him. He was a closed book, yet Thrisc confidently believed the man was satisfied with his current station in life and actually didn't care that the younger dark-mage had been given this honour.

Rastiss was the opposite of Cordak. He made it clear to all that he was Mithrak's second; his right-hand.

This was a huge slap in the face to him and Thrisc could see it in the look he gave him. Thrisc almost flinched from it, thinking the old dark-mage might actually try something against him.

Looking away, he tried to put the old mage out of his thoughts.

He was a problem for another day. Thrisc would not allow Rastiss to ruin this occasion for him.

Looking beyond his King once more, he smiled at the thought of what they were able to do.

Once through the Elven forest, there would be nothing to stop them.

They were going to kill everyone and anything that dared to challenge Mithrak's army.

It was going to be amazing and Thrisc had one of the best places to watch it all from.

Smiling still, he waited patiently for Jurg to return.

CHAPTER 36

Sound Judgement

LORD MARCUS SAW the barbarian flinch when he told him he would die tonight, but Kabir said nothing in response. He actually looked a little relieved. He obviously cared a lot for the plainswoman.

Marcus genuinely felt bad for delivering his sentence, but the barbarian had given him no choice. Even in these troubled times, the laws of the land still needed to be upheld. Killing a wizard could not go unpunished, especially after he had only recently sent away all of his remaining ones. It left them too vulnerable, even with his King's Shield and the magical items the spy Brax had so gracefully gifted him. He had yet to fully try out his new helmet, so its effectiveness was still largely unknown. Plus, all but one of the rings had been given to his wizards.

These thoughts had no doubt added to his foul mood, but Marcus still felt sympathy for the barbarian. Their ways were obviously different to those in Dayhen's Realm. In his own mind it did appear the barbarian believed he had done no wrong.

'Why does this Princess not judge Kabir also?' Ahlia asked him. She spoke clearly, but without the emotion the barbarian used.

'Because he is not royalty,' Marcus replied, indicating for Atriol to remove them from the hall.

'I will get word to my father,' Ahlia said, as she was grabbed by the arm. 'There is one there who owes a blood debt to the Barbarian. He will bring many warriors with him.'

Marcus held up his hand and the King's Shield stopped, turning Kabir and Ahlia back to face their lord.

'Are you threatening me?' Marcus asked.

''Yes,' she answered.

'And you think they would fight us to avenge his death?' Marcus asked. He wasn't overly concerned, but it was worth investigating.

'They are much better warriors than the goblins and their pets,' she said. He could hear contempt in her voice now. 'They would kill many more of your men than the goblins did.'

Marcus knew he could do without making more enemies. He wasn't stupid.

Justice could still be seen to be done, even if it was by the Princess. It would probably be good for her development to face these two down.

On the other hand, he did not like going back on his decisions once he had made them.

There was silence for a long time while he thought on what she said. He didn't want those present to think he backed down after being threatened by this woman.

'Your thoughts Atriol?' he asked. Even though the man never seemed to show emotion, he got the impression those men who had brought the prisoners back respected them, perhaps even liked them.

Perhaps it was worth the time to find out why. The plains woman had forced him to listen, if nothing else.

'Without them, we may not have made it back alive,' Atriol said. 'I believe them both to be honourable and they would be helpful in keeping many alive while we travel to Havern. Without any wizards, his sword will be needed.'

Marcus didn't fail to notice it was the second time the barbarian's sword had been mentioned.

'His sword?' Atriol's Lord asked.

'A sword like no other,' Atriol replied. 'As I said earlier, Ethan's spell had no effect upon him. The sword also heals mortal wounds, weighs as much as a long dagger and is incredibly sharp My Lord.

I know not what else it does, but I would not be surprised if it did more.'

If it wasn't already, Marcus' attention was focused now. He would like to have such a sword. Resistant to magic?!

The Lord of Shadow Hill quickly made up his mind. He realised now, after speaking with his Shield, that none of those who had travelled with the barbarian would judge him harshly if he were to leave his fate up to Princess Areana. They would probably be happy about it, and anything that lifted the spirits of those in his town was a good thing right now.

'Kabir will accompany us to Havern. The Princess will decide the fate of both.'

Ahlia gave a small nod of her head, but said nothing, as they were turned around once more.

'Bring me his sword,' Marcus said to Methan.

They left early the next morning, Lord Marcus leading the procession of soldiers, masons, bakers, smiths and all the other traders and craftsmen. Women and children and the elderly followed behind them, the few remaining King's Shield spaced out along their length.

Lord Marcus felt terribly vulnerable riding out front without his usual escort, but with his new helmet and magical sword, he felt the risk to himself was much less than those trailing behind him.

They would be moving slowly, adding to the risk, but there was no other option. He knew if they stayed, they would sooner or later be over-run. It was simply a matter of time. They would stand a greater chance behind the larger walls of Havern.

Lord Jaron would also still have wizards and more King's Shield.

It had not been an easy decision to leave, but he knew it was the only one he could make.

Kabir rode once more on the back of Firth, Ahlia in front of him.

Lord Marcus had tried to usurp their horse as well, marvelling at him when he caught sight of Firth earlier that morning, but Kabir's horse had not wanted any part of that. As soon as Marcus put his foot in the stirrup, Firth had bucked high and turned his head to look menacingly at the Lord of Shadow Hill.

Marcus had not made another attempt.

A couple of others tried, with the same result, before he gave up and let Ahlia and Kabir both ride him.

'You are welcome to the cursed beast,' Marcus muttered as he walked off.

Ahlia sneered at him as he left, while Kabir was less subtle. He had laughed out loud as each man tried unsuccessfully to mount his horse.

'Your first efforts would have been no different without the help of a plainsman,' Ahlia said softly to him when he laughed the first time.

'I know,' Kabir had replied. 'Which makes it even funnier!'

'Get up,' she said, shaking her head, the smile reaching her face too once his back was turned.

Firth walked slowly in the middle of those who had just left their home.

'This is going to take some time,' Kabir lamented. 'Even though there is nothing pushing me toward my goal this time, it still requires some urgency.'

There were too many leaving Shadow Hill for every person to ride a horse, or travel in the back of a cart. They were moving everything they owned and places for those in the coaches and on carts were reserved for those who were unable to walk a great distance.

'I share your frustration Kabir,' Ahlia replied, 'but we are fortunate to still be alive. Perhaps we should be happy with small mercies.'

'I was happy when given that mercy,' Kabir said. 'Now I just want to gallop. As does Firth. I can feel his restlessness.'

This time Ahlia laughed softly.

'You feel nothing of the thoughts of this mighty animal,' she said. 'He is hungry and far from home. His thoughts are of that.'

'You are probably right there,' Kabir conceded. Firth felt no different under him than he usually did when walking.

Kabir looked around at the poor souls accompanying them to Havern.

They would be feeling things much worse than simple frustration.

Forced to abandon their homes at a time when evil walked the land as never before. Scared for themselves and their loved ones. An uncertain future, but one that was going to pit them against monsters intent on taking their lives.

Kabir felt a little chastened at his selfishness, but those feelings soon passed. Life was supposed to be difficult. He had been taught this from a young age. "*Life tests everyone,*" his father had often told him.

It does indeed, he told himself again, as he looked beyond the people walking beside him for any signs of danger.

Without a weapon of any kind, the barbarian felt naked, but he knew if it came to another skirmish or battle, he would be able to find a weapon of sorts somewhere.

At least they were no longer bound.

Atriol and Methan had convinced Marcus their word was their bond, after both Kabir and Ahlia had given Lord Marcus a promise they would not try and escape, nor attack any of those they travelled with.

He had stopped short of providing them with weapons.

They were still his prisoners.

There was nothing to threaten them the entire day, although Kabir thought he had seen movements among the trees, at a place they had passed only a short time before Marcus called for a halt.

There was still sunlight left, but Kabir knew it would take time to plan a defensive position while they stopped for the night.

The soldiers and guards would be spread thin, no matter what he devised, but he would need to try.

'Give us weapons and put us on the outside,' Kabir said, when he saw Atriol walking past them.

The King's Shield stopped to acknowledge him.

'My apologies for your sword not being returned to you barbarian, but my Lord has the right to claim it until the Princess has decided your guilt.'

'You have no reason to apologise Atriol,' Kabir said. 'It is no different where I am from. If you are captured by those from a different village, then all that you have is forfeit. I did not expect to have it returned. I will get it back when this is over, but another lesser sword in its place would be appreciated.'

Atriol paused.

'I will ask,' he replied, much to Kabir's surprise, acknowledging Ahlia with a slightly lower bow before walking away.

'I fear this night will not be a restful one,' Ahlia said to him, as they stood next to Firth. No-one had given them any directions so far, as to what was expected of them.

Kabir had the same feeling, but he was curious to hear why Ahlia thought so.

'A feeling?' he asked, 'or something else?'

'There has been a lot of movement from afar as we rode,' she said. He should have known she would see more than he did. 'I think they have been waiting for the night.'

'We will need weapons,' Kabir said, speaking the obvious out loud.

'There are many here who have them, yet I doubt they know how to use them properly. We may have to wait until they fall and then take them,' she said.

Kabir stared at her for a short while, before she turned to him and returned his stare.

'What is it?' she asked, a little irritated. Possibly from the way he was looking at her.

'Or, we could take them before they are killed and help to defend them,' he said. 'They have shown no ill-will towards us,' he added.

'I will defend you Kabir, and if that means they are defended as a result, then that might be better.' She smiled, which just confused him. Was she jesting? He did not bother asking. She would probably try and confuse him some more.

'The old couple over there,' she said, indicating behind him. Kabir turned to look. They sat together, the man with his arms around the woman. They looked to be well beyond fighting age, yet Kabir could see the sword next to him. The sheath was well looked after, so he assumed the sword would probably be the same. He may have been a fine warrior, many years ago.

'You will need a weapon too,' he said to Ahlia.

She laughed softly at him. 'What makes you think I wasn't going to take that one. They will probably be asleep soon.'

'Okay,' Kabir said. He was not going to tell her he was the better of them with a sword. Not a chance.

'I will look for another,' she said, still smiling at him. 'You are better with a sword than I am.'

'Don't sell yourself short,' he replied. 'You are very skilled with a blade.'

'You think me better than yourself?' she asked, the smile no longer there.

Sometimes he should just say thank you and then not talk.

'We should get some rest,' he replied. 'You need to sleep first. I will keep watch.'

Ahlia looked like she was going to say something, but instead put out her blanket and lay down. Kabir sat down next to her, and was happy when she put her head on his thigh. It felt nice having her so close to him.

Unfortunately, their sleep did not last very long.

CHAPTER 37

Separate Ways

THE NEXT MORNING, Meghan was up and on her way to Wilhelm's tent before the sun had even begun to rise.

She was surprised to see Denizen already waiting outside.

'He is awake and preparing himself for your departure,' the plainsman said, as she stopped in front of him.

Although much older than herself, Meghan still found the plainsman to be a striking man. He looked to be as fit as anyone she had seen; even those men many seasons his junior; and held himself in such a way that she always felt nervous in his presence. Now was no exception, especially as there appeared to be no-one else around. Just the two of them.

'I should wait here then,' she said, trying to sound sure of herself and not at all like a young, teenage girl.

Denizen smiled at her as he nodded his head slightly.

'This is by far the nicest time of the day or night here,' she said. 'Not too cold, but also not hot enough to burn my skin through to the bone.'

'You suffered such hurts?' Denizen said, looking suddenly worried.

'Oh no,' Meghan said, mortified by her poor joke. 'I meant only that it..' she stopped mid-sentence as Denizen's grin grew wider.

'My apologies,' he said, holding up his hands to show he meant no harm. 'The sun can of course burn, especially on one so fair. Your body was not made for the plains.'

Meghan was almost insulted by his words.

'Is it not true that your people once lived in the highlands, before the breaking of the tribes a thousand winters ago?' She asked it as a question so she would not offend him, but all knew it was true.

'I heard a different tale when I was growing up,' Denizen said.

'Something fanciful, like most children's stories I would imagine,' Meghan replied, hiding her own smile.

'Indeed,' Denizen said, his smile disappearing and replaced with his usual forlorn expression.

'I would still like to hear it,' Meghan said, as Wilhelm stepped through the front flap of his tent.

Meghan couldn't believe how remarkably well he appeared, considering the wound he had sustained. His eyes had the look of someone who was ready for battle, and he seemed to move without discomfort.

'If only I could take more of this with me,' he said, lifting up the small vial of liquid he had been given.

'That should be taken sparingly,' Denizen said seriously. 'It is not gifted lightly.'

'I will make sure he does as instructed,' Meghan said to Denizen, as Wilhelm placed the vial in a pocket within his cloak.

'I cannot thank you enough,' the young barbarian said to the plainsman. 'For all you have done for us and for my brother.'

'There is no need,' Denizen said. 'I can never hope to repay the debt to your brother, so anything I can do to help his friends and family is an honour for me. Now let me take you to where your horses await.'

The horses they were given were two of the largest beasts Wilhelm had ever seen, and they were faster than their own and much smoother in the saddle.

The farewells were short and without fanfare, and the two highlanders were soon on their way again.

The sun had just crested the horizon, and they had been travelling slowly for the best part of an hour without conversation, when Wilhelm finally broke the silence.

'What do you make of the plainsmen?' he asked.

'Why do you ask that?' Meghan replied defensively.

Wilhelm was a little confused by her reaction.

'Because we just met them for the first time ever and I was curious.' He doubted he would ever understand the way a girl's mind worked.

Meghan didn't answer straight away and she chose not to look at him when she finally answered.

'I think it is way too hot here,' she said. 'They have adapted well to it, but I could never see myself spending much time here.'

'Definitely far too hot,' he agreed, 'but I asked what you thought of them as a people?'

'Do you mean the ones who almost killed you?' she asked, looking at him this time.

'Yes,' he said, smiling at her as he replied. 'Despite that little incident, I thought they were pleasant.'

'Because you were spoon-fed and fussed over,' Meghan said. 'Typical.'

'They were also quite easy on the eye,' he added. 'I admit I found their darker skin a little odd to begin with, but their women are quite comely. I think one of them took a fancy to me,' he finished with a short laugh.

'You would think that,' she said drily. 'You probably thought the same about the one who put an arrow in you.'

Wilhelm laughed loudly this time.

'She was besotted with me,' he managed to say in between laughs.

Meghan shook her head, but couldn't stop herself smiling, as she looked ahead once more.

They stopped a couple of times while the sun still shone bright, to stretch their legs and have a bite to eat. Unlike the plainsmen and women, they were unaccustomed to being in a saddle all day long. Especially in a saddle on top of horses the size of those they were riding. Their inner thighs in particular were hurting, as well as their calves.

They talked more of the plains people and also of where they thought Kabir would be by now. He was nowhere near as far ahead as Wilhelm had feared.

A handful of days only, and if Kabir moved slowly, Wilhelm hoped to catch up with him in less than that.

Overall, Wilhelm was feeling much better about things than he had in some time.

He and Meghan were young, and healthy once more, and riding through lands they had never seen before was exciting. Wilhelm found it hard to hide his excitement, and he could see his enthusiasm had rubbed off somewhat on Meghan.

She no longer spoke of their haste to return home, although he knew it was still in the forefront of both their thoughts. They just no longer needed to mention it, so they were able to enjoy the journey they were on.

To their relief, the plains through which they rode were free of predators and other nasties, as Denizen had predicted this part would be. He and his warriors had only recently ridden through it, but none could guarantee they would not be molested.

As the sun sunk behind the mountains to their right, they decided it better not to ride in the gloom of evening and stopped to camp for the night.

Both of them slept well throughout the night and woke refreshed for the next part of their journey.

They were off early, hoping to get through the plains before the end of the following day. Denizen had said it should take no longer than three days at a good pace.

It was another day of easy conversation without anything threatening them.

The heat was still intense, and both suffered a bit from it, but they were happy to put up with it when they knew it should not last much longer.

Denizen had assured them the temperature would drop once they reached the lands of goblin and men.

After what they had faced since leaving home, Wilhelm was glad to be given this opportunity to regain his strength. The liquid tonic given him by Denizen was a godsend and they had gotten used to riding easily on the back of their giant mounts.

Wilhelm had no doubt there would be plenty of adventures to be had before they made it back to Deerstep.

'You would not have thought this to be such a dangerous place,' Wilhelm commented, as the sun neared its resting place for the second night since they left the plainsmen's settlement.

'Do not invite fell things to us,' Meghan said to him, her tone displeased.

'We are nearly out of it,' he replied. 'I think it safe now to say such a thing.'

He smiled as he looked across at her riding next to him.

'Surely we are not so unlucky that misfortune would strike us now,' he said. 'Not after all we have been through so far.'

'I would agree with you,' she said, her voice taking on a different tone as she spoke. 'If it were not for the giant-looking predators heading our way,' she said, pointing to his left.

Wilhelm believed she was trying to trick him, as he casually looked to his left.

'I am not as silly as that,' he said, as he turned to look in the direction she pointed.

Three creatures were bounding towards them. Despite the long grass, they were easily visible from where Wilhelm and Meghan sat.

'What are they?' Wilhelm asked. 'They look like large cats,' he said. They had domesticated cats in the highlands, but they were no higher than a man's knee. These ones were bigger, and their fur a dull yellow. One of them led the other two, and was largest of the three.

Without pause Wilhelm grabbed his bow and nocked an arrow.

Their horses were battle hardened, but Wilhelm's mount was skittish as the three giant cats bounded towards them. It moved under him as he fired off his first arrow, which flew harmlessly over the top of them.

It was too late for them to flee. Even the plains people's horses would not out-run these. As they got even closer, Wilhelm could see they were almost as large as the horse he rode on. His next arrow needed to not only hit it, but strike somewhere critical.

The second arrow was more accurate, as he got the horse under control long enough to aim, but it did not strike the eye that he was aiming for. The arrow instead thudded into flesh, just above the right leg. Its run was halted however, as the big cat it slowed to a walk and began to limp.

The other two roared their displeasure, as their speed increased further.

Wilhelm's third arrow went wide, as his horse bucked backwards in an attempt to turn around and flee what was coming at it. Despite its training and bravery, it must have seen these cats before and did not want them getting any closer.

'Your sword!' Meghan cried out, as the two cats were upon them. The first struck Wilhelm with a solid blow to the midsection, knocking him from his horse on to the dry, hardened ground below.

He was able to put his hand to the pommel of his sword and get to his knees before he was struck again, this time to the head.

Wilhelm saw stars and then nothing more.

The heat of the morning sun woke Wilhelm from his sleep.

Opening his eyes, he had no idea where he was, or what had happened. His head hurt, as did other parts of his body, as he tried to lift himself up on to his elbows.

Looking around, he saw his horse chewing grass about twenty paces away.

Meghan and her horse were nowhere to be seen, as the events of the previous evening began coming back to him.

They had been attacked by giant cats and he had been knocked from his horse. After that everything was a blur.

How was he still alive?

Why did they not eat him? He remembered putting an arrow into one of them. Surely that would have been sufficient to anger them enough to kill him even if they weren't hungry?

Standing gingerly, he called his horse over. It did not move from where it was eating. Cursing under his breath, he hobbled over to where it stood and reached into his saddle bag. Pulling out the tonic of the plains people, he put it to his mouth and drank a small amount. Even in his condition he remembered the words of Denizen.

"You can die if you take too much. A small amount will help more."

It didn't take long for his energy to return, as he got on his horse to better survey the surrounding area.

Perhaps Meghan lay injured nearby and her mount had been what they had fed on.

He was wrong about Meghan, but a hundred paces away he found the corpse of her horse. There was little left of it. He assumed three cats that size would make short work of a horse. Even one as big as that Meghan rode.

'Meghan!' he yelled out into the plains. Perhaps she lay injured nearby?

He continued yelling as he searched, but after an hour his voice was too hoarse to yell anymore and he had still found no sign of her.

So where was she? He had seen a blood trail earlier that lead away from what was left of her horse, but it had soon disappeared. Could she be injured and they took her with them? He doubted that had happened.

More likely, it was blood from the cat he had put an arrow in.

Trying to yell out her name again as he looked around once more, he suddenly saw the silhouettes of men riding toward him in the distance. They came from the direction he and Megan had travelled from.

As they neared, Wilhelm was able to make out their forms until finally he was able to recognise Denizen. Four other plains people accompanied him, both men and women.

'Well met,' Wilhelm croaked.

'Where is Meghan?' Denizen asked, scanning the grasslands as he spoke. 'Is that her horse?' he asked, leaping off his own and walking to where the corpse of her horse lay.

Wilhelm jumped off his horse and walked after the plainsman.

Denizen turned as Wilhelm arrived to stand next to him.

'What happened here?' he asked, a frantic look on his face.

'We were attacked by giant cats,' he said. 'I was knocked out and when I awoke Meghan was gone.'

Denizen looked both surprised and concerned at the same time.

'The *Scrithon* do not ordinarily attack us,' Denizen said. 'Tell me in detail what happened.'

'I told you already,' Wilhelm said. 'Three of them attacked us. I shot one with an arrow. One then knocked me off my horse and I don't remember anything until I awoke this morning.'

'You are lucky you were still alive this morning,' Denizen said. 'I should not have let you ride off on your own.'

'What are you doing here?' Wilhelm asked. His head was still sore. The confusion of what was happening here was not helping.

'Our mourning period finished,' Denizen said. 'We rode to make sure you both made it safely out of the plains.'

'What has happened to Meghan?' Wilhelm asked. 'Why didn't they kill me?'

'I told you already. The *Scrithon* do not attack men and women of the plains. That you shot one with an arrow and still they showed you mercy is testament to that,' Denizen said. 'I do not believe they would have eaten Meghan, nor taken her for food,' he continued.

'Mitchall!' Denizen said in a loud voice, turning back to those who had accompanied him. 'Find their tracks. We will follow them.'

'Follow them where?' Wilhelm asked.

'We will track them until we find Meghan,' Denizen said. 'Hallor!' he hollered again, and another plainsman approached him.

'You will make sure our barbarian friend makes it safely to the realm of men. Then you will find us.'

The plainsman nodded as he sat atop his horse looking down at Wilhelm.

'I am not leaving,' Wilhelm said eventually, horrified at what Denizen suggested. It had taken a little while for Denizen's words to sink in. 'I am going to find Meghan.'

'I promise you I will not stop until I have found her safe and brought her back to our home,' Denizen said. Wilhelm was taken aback by the man's vehemence.

'I am not leaving her,' Wilhelm repeated. 'What kind of man do you think I am?'

'I think you a good man,' Denizen said, 'and a smart one.'

Wilhelm didn't answer him straight away. It was not the response he had expected.

'If you try and come with us, you will slow us down. Your horse is sore and fatigued and cannot keep up. You also need to speak with your brother and we are heading in the other direction.'

'I can keep up,' Wilhelm said, but without the same conviction as a moment ago. He had learnt already how much these plains people knew about their horses, much to his detriment last time.

'The *Scrithon* live far to the east barbarian, near the black waters themselves. We may be riding for days before we catch up to them. They move as fast as our horses do and they have no riders on their backs.' Denizen would not be swayed. Wilhelm could see he was simply trying to be polite and not embarrass him.

'You best leave now then,' Wilhelm said, conceding that no-one else would have a better chance of finding her. 'I pray you find her safe and I can return to see her soon.'

Denizen nodded, before moving over to his horse and jumping into the saddle.

'Say hello to your brother for me,' Denizen said. 'Look after him,' he said to Hallor, before turning to the others. 'You have their tracks?' he asked Mitchall.

The plainsman nodded.

'Lead on then', Denizen said.

Mitchall put his heels into his horse's belly and the others quickly followed him.

Wilhelm watched them ride away with a heavy heart.

'Lead on,' he said to Hallor as soon as he was back on his own horse.

CHAPTER 38

A Re-Cap

THE MOOD WITHIN the clearing was unlike anything any of them had experienced before.

The elation of being able to enter the world of Dark Swell again had created such a stir, especially amongst those who had already entered.

There had not been such heated exchanges before, nor had there been such an outpouring of joy.

Except for Brindel.

He had been forced to watch his fellow-gamers entering the world; not the first time for some of them; while he sat in front of his *eye*, hoping for a reason to step through and speak to his own Champion.

But the opportunity had passed, and now he wasn't sure when the next one would present itself.

Now that his Champion had found a nice safe spot to wait out the marching Dwarven army, Brindel took the time to look around at his fellow gamers.

Although she was trying hard not to show it now, he could see that Mendina was still simmering underneath after her exchange with Mortinan.

Mortinan however, looked the same way he always did. Arrogant and aloof.

Kabir was more upbeat than he had been for some time, despite his constant challenges, while Linf had only just now stopped smiling. Her joy was contagious at times, but at other times it irked Brindel. He wanted to experience exactly what it was that gave her such pleasure. He felt sure he would feel similar to how she did.

Two opportunities to enter for information and advice, and another to assist his Champion with a spell. It was a lot to still have, compared to the others. He knew how lucky he was to have them all but that fact didn't really help his current mood.

Only Mortinan had yet to use one of his opportunities to meet and speak with his Champion, but he had still seen them up close.

Brindel was seriously toying with the idea of entering just for the sake of meeting his Champion. If he could justify it in any way, then he had almost convinced himself to do it.

He was sure when Mort and Mendina finally confronted the waiting dragon, he would have more of an idea of what was required.

If they were killed, he would probably need to enter in order to help his champion defeat her. He had spent a good deal of time trying to work out a spell which could be beneficial to his champion against the dragon, while at the same time not putting himself at too great a risk. It was proving to be quite the challenge.

Ever since Kabir had told Mortinan it may not be such a great advantage being first to the dragon, Brindel had convinced himself he was right.

He wished Mortinan and Mendina's champions would just hurry up and get there.

'I wonder if the dragon is the final challenge?' Mortinan said out loud.

It took Brindel by surprise. All of the gamers looked to be lost within their own thoughts, as they often were. A sudden outburst was unexpected. Especially from Mortinan.

'That is a random thought Mortinan,' Linf said. 'And one we have all discussed before.'

Brindel looked across at Mortinan. His face was expressionless.

'Apologies,' he said, looking over at Linf. 'You're right, I don't know what came over me.'

'I guess both yourself and Mendina will be awarded the prize,' Brindel said, playing along. He was smart enough to know Mortinan was simply trying to rattle them. More specifically, he was trying to rattle him. Brindel's champion was obviously closest behind his and he still had all of his visits into the world remaining. 'Perhaps you could cut it in half.'

'Joke all you like Brindel,' he said, some expression on his face now, 'but wouldn't it be a shame if you lost the game and didn't once get to enter the world. I guess you could ask Valdor what it was like when you join him.'

Brindel chuckled at his last comment, but inside he wanted to walk over to Mortinan and punch him in his smug face.

'When I do finally decide to enter, I am reasonably confident I won't try and kill my Champion. I might even be able to help him.' Brindel heard Kabir chuckle, but looked at Mendina when he said it. She looked anything but happy, as she continued to look into her *eye*.

'If you ever decide to enter,' Mortinan said, apparently unflustered at his words.

Brindel was going to say more, but didn't trust himself not to do something stupid. Although the Creator had never specifically forbidden them from hitting another gamer, it would probably be frowned upon.

Instead he brought his attention back to his own *eye*.

Still thinking about their brief interaction, if nothing else, it had steeled him now not to waste his interactions within Dark Swell.

Mortinan may have done him a favour, although he knew that would never have been his intention. What then had been his intention? Brindel had thought at first it was to get him to use one of his entries into the world, but Mortinan was never that transparent.

Perhaps it was simply to anger him and throw him off his game.

Again, it seemed fairly obvious and at a time when Brindel's champion was in very little danger.

Maybe he had been bored?

Stop it! Brindel said to himself. He was letting the annoying twat get into his head.

Relaxing his mind, he pushed all thoughts of Mortinan away, as he began going over scenarios for how he could insert himself into the game.

Back to where he was, he realised nothing had changed from how he was thinking before their little chat.

The one thing he was almost sure of was that the dragon was not going to be the end of this game.

If it was, there was nothing he could do to get his Champion there before Mortinan and Mendina anyway.

CHAPTER 39

The Reckoning Comes

'KRITCH'S ARMY IS on the move King Dayhen,' Lord Bantan reported, as he stepped into the makeshift war-room.

'Where to?' Dayhen asked. Finally, something was happening. Although it probably meant war was upon them, it was preferable to the waiting.

'They move south, towards the High Fort.' Lord Bantan's tone was the same now as it always was. A true soldier, the man never got flustered.

'What more do we know about their army?' he asked.

'There have been a few new reports,' Bantan continued. 'Their numbers are greater than we first thought, but Mithrak's army has not arrived. It would appear Kritch has grown impatient and intends moving on us without him.'

That was both good news and somewhat concerning.

Latest reports had some of Mithrak's army moving toward southern Glorfiden. His chief advisors now believed Mithrak was planning to use all of his army on an assault into Glorfiden. It was why only a small portion of them had been sighted by his scouts. The rest were probably ranged out along the forest.

It would make their task in defeating Kritch much less daunting, but Jarkene's task formidable. As powerful as the Elven Lord was, Dayhen doubted he could hold out against an entire army entering his home from areas right along its western border. It did not bode well for his realm.

It was probably the reason why Kritch was moving away from here and towards the High Fort.

It would be far easier for Dayhen to defend there, than where he now stood inside the newly constructed defences just outside of Mayfield.

Kritch would be stupid to want to fight them there.

High Fort had stood for hundreds of years, chosen due to its vantage point and narrow path through.

An attacking army would have to march uphill and then fight through the narrow pass between cliffs. In past wars, the hordes of the Western Realm had only once chosen to try and get through there. Those that did had been swiftly repelled.

'Do you think it a decoy to draw the greater part of my army away from here?' Dayhen asked.

It was Derekia who answered this time.

'Probably,' the wizard said, all eyes turning to him now. 'They probably won't even attack,' he continued, 'but if you leave it vulnerable and Kritch does march on it, they may win through.'

'Now that we have a more accurate report on their strength King Dayhen, I believe we need not send such a large part of our army,' Bantan said. 'A smaller force could hold the High Fort against just Kritch's army.'

'It could,' Thaiden interjected, 'but what if the ogre-mage decides to continue moving south? There are other places for them to enter this realm less secure than the High Fort. That would draw our army even further away.'

'And if we don't send it now and they move quickly south, they could be through before we are able to catch them,' Dayhen finished for him.

'My King' a voice hollered from outside of the room.

All eyes turned to see who was entering.

A man dressed in riding gear stepped inside, Lord Bantan moving over to speak briefly with him.

When the man had left, Bantan relayed the message to his King.

'The number may not be accurate, but there are at least five hundred Ve-Karn within Kritch's army.'

The room went silent for a moment.

'Then my Shield will have their work cut out for them,' Bilsont eventually said.

Dayhen had not accounted for that. They were Mithrak's finest warriors and none of those assembled here had expected him to let Kritch have them.

Without his full complement of King's Shield to repel them, five hundred Ve-Karn; supported by all of Kritch's Ogre-Mage; would wreak havoc within his army.

'Then we have no choice,' Dayhen said. 'The army will march, and they will continue marching until Kritch finally has the stomach to try and fight us.'

None of those present had any more to say. The King had made up his mind based on the advice given to him. No-one there envied him his position.

'And when they do, we need to slaughter them as quickly as we can. I fear we may need to return to Lakerth without pause. The future of the realm may depend on it.'

CHAPTER 40

The Final Stretch

IT WAS DARK and still drizzling when Mort awoke. His back ached from the small rocks that had been digging into it for the last several hours, but he stopped himself from moving to alleviate it.

Despite their ordeal, her hair smelled wonderful and the ache quickly disappeared the moment he realised Mendina was curled up in his arms.

She must have felt him stir, as she sat upright next to him.

He couldn't see her face; just an outline; as he reached his hand out to touch her cheek.

'I remember you saying something about when we got out of the cave,' Mort said quietly.

'We barely escaped the cave with our lives Mort. Then we fall asleep just outside that very cave, while it is still dark, without even checking our surrounds, and that is the first thing that comes to mind when you wake?' She didn't sound angry or annoyed though.

'Did you hear the tunnel collapsing as we went?' Mort asked, the memories of the night before flooding back into his mind. 'The protection offered us must have only been surrounding us for a short distance. We are now perfectly safe from anything wanting to get out of the cave.' Mort tried not to sound condescending. He was aware she didn't like it when he was.

Mendina sighed, before leaning forward and kissing Mort on the lips.

'What about outside the cave?' Mendina asked, as she drew back from him.

'I had a quick look around before we went to sleep,' Mort said sheepishly.

'It doesn't matter now,' Mendina said. 'We are somehow still alive and need to keep moving.'

Mort begrudgingly agreed with her, standing up gingerly. The hurts and aches had returned with a vengeance.

'Have you any idea what those creatures were that we saw in the cave?' Mort asked, as he tried to stretch out some of his aches. Mendina didn't seem to be suffering the same as he, as she stood without any apparent discomfort. Using him as a pillow probably helped her, but he didn't begrudge it.

'You would know I have also never seen their like before,' Mendina said.

'I know,' Mort said, 'but maybe you could take a guess.'

'Should we leave now, or wait until we have more light?' Mendina asked, choosing not to continue the conversation of the now squashed creatures they had seen yesterday evening.

With his aches subsiding a little, Mort began to try and shake some of the water from his clothes, hoping it might help his discomfort. It did not. Fortunately, the weather was not cold, so being wet through was not as uncomfortable as it could have been.

'We may as well go now,' he replied. 'I can light the way ahead for us.'

'And send a beacon to anything out there with ill intent,' she said.

'The light wouldn't travel far in these conditions,' Mort said, a little hurt that Mendina would think him so foolish. 'I can make it a small light, enough to help with our footing.'

'Okay,' she eventually said. 'Just so long as you remember how far away that swamp is and take us nowhere near it.'

'Of course,' Mort said in a serious voice. 'Or I could use the rod and send this weather out over the swamp and away from us.'

'We have had this discussion already,' Mendina said, before Mort could say he had only been joking.

They moved off into the darkness, the small light Mort cast forth lighting their way enough to stop them stumbling and falling head over foot down the slope below them.

Eventually they made their way to some relatively flat ground, and began walking in a direction they believed to be parallel with the swamp.

Not long after, the dark of the night was broken by the morning sun making its way over the horizon.

Mort was able to switch off his spell of light.

Within minutes the soaking rain also stopped and the clouds cleared, allowing the half-elf and his elven companion to finally begin drying off.

It also allowed them to look at where they were headed.

The end of the swamp was still out of sight, but it gave them a different perspective of the land they walked through.

The land ahead was tougher than it looked from their previous vantage.

They would need to traverse some higher land before reaching their destination. It wasn't mountainous, for which Mort was thankful, but it would certainly be a trek.

Both were surprised at the lack of anything dangerous where they walked.

The land was far from inhospitable; quite the opposite; yet apart from smaller animals who were easily spooked by their passing, there was nothing threatening.

It was a strange sensation, and although they were grateful not to be challenged by anything powerful, it was also a little disconcerting.

The fact that smaller animals scurried away at hearing their approach, told them there were predators in these parts. But where were they?

'We still need to be vigilante,' Mendina said to Mort, breaking the silence of the past hour.

'Of course,' Mort replied. He was constantly checking their surroundings for anything that looked remotely like it might attack them.

Iska spent less time on Mort's shoulder as they walked, choosing instead to fly ahead of them. Mort was confident his fairie-dragon would warn them if he saw anything, but he still remained wary.

'If we come across something, you must remember the power of the rod needs to be saved. Use your staff instead.' Mort could hear the fear in her voice and wondered where it was coming from.

'I know that,' he said to her. It was something they had discussed in length. He didn't know why she felt the need to remind him again now, but something niggled at him.

'Are you okay?' he asked her, grabbing her gently by the arm and stopping.

She turned and looked at him, a strange expression on her face.

'I don't know what it is,' she said, her voice shaky. 'I don't want to keep going this way.'

Mort was perplexed. Other than the swamp; where he knew she certainly did not want to go under any circumstances; this was the only way.

'There is no other way,' he said softly.

'We could go back,' she said, a hint of desperation in her voice. 'Perhaps Jarkene was right. Glorfiden needs us.'

Mort looked intently at her, before looking at the land surrounding them.

She was not herself and he didn't know why. It was uncomfortably similar to when Jarvis had taken control of her mind.

'Iska!' he called out loudly, risking something else hearing him. He would prefer not to yell, but he couldn't see his fairie-dragon anywhere and he needed him. Perhaps he might know how to help. It was possible something had taken control of Mendina's mind, or that something else was causing the fear and uncertainty to manifest itself within her.

'You shouldn't yell,' she said in a whisper. 'It is not safe.'

'Not safe from what?' Mort asked, hoping Mendina might know what was frightening her.

'Glorfiden is safe,' was all she could offer.

Mort was glad to hear the soft flutter of wings, as *Iska* landed gently on his right shoulder.

He began communicating with him, telling his companion of his fears.

'*Iska* has told me there is no threat to us here,' Mort said. 'It is a long way back to Glorfiden.' The fairie-dragon sensed no ill-intent and was unable to help. Mort remained confused.

'I just want to go home!' Mendina said in an impassioned voice. 'There is nothing good awaiting us where we go Mort.'

Mort agreed with her, but he knew they had to push forward regardless. Mendina knew that too, but something seemed to have changed within her.

'We have to keep going,' was all he had.

'Please,' she said. 'We should go home now.' Her voice had lost its urgency. She was pleading with him now.

Mort didn't know what to do. He suddenly wished his mother was here. Corein would definitely know how to get to the source of Mendina's fear. Mort paused to think. How would his mother deal with it?

She would take her time and let Mendina tell her. His mother would gently draw it from her.

'What has changed?' Mort asked, staring into her eyes as he took both of her hands in his.

'Nothing has changed Mort,' she said. 'Don't patronise me. We just need to go back.'

Why did she need to return so soon? He firmly believed they were closer to their destination than they were Glorfiden.

'And when we get back to Glorfiden, what will we do then?' he asked.

'We will be safe there,' she said in a calm voice. 'Our family is there now.'

As he listened to her; truly listened to her without distraction; Mort suddenly thought he knew what ailed her, and it broke his heart.

At first, he thought it may have been something as simple as homesickness.

Although she had been away with him before, they had the compulsion driving them. This time they did not.

Then as he thought more on it, he realised it was nothing so basic as that. It was not simply someone missing their home, although an elf's relationship with their forest was intrinsic to their being.

Not the way Mendina was acting.

She was a young elf outside of her element and place of comfort and she had been through extraordinary loss. Her entire family and almost all of her race had been murdered by his father. She had been upset by it, but he suddenly realised she had never had a chance to properly mourn them.

Add to that, Glorfiden's current peril. The forest was under siege by armies of monsters from the Western Realm, threatening to run through her home and kill all of those elves who remained.

Then to top everything off, just last night they had almost been crushed to death within a dark tunnel. A long way from her home, in an environment she was not comfortable in.

Squeezing her hands firmly in his, Mort guided her on to the ground so they were sitting side by side. He freed one hand and put it around her waist.

Tears were beginning to well in her eyes.

'We are going to finish this quest we have been set,' Mort spoke softly, but with strength in his words. 'Then we will return to Glorfiden together. Our new family will be waiting for us Mendina. We will help them defend the forest against anything that would dare think of setting one foot under the leaves of your home.' He swung around so he could face her directly and take her other hand in his.

'This is no hollow promise I make to you Mendina,' he continued, as the tears flowed freely from her eyes now. 'We will have a life together once all this is over.'

He gave her time to let the words sink in, just holding her hands and staring into her eyes.

'Our home,' she said eventually, trying to wipe the tears from her eyes.

Mort was confused and thought her still panicked, before he realised the meaning behind her comment.

He smiled at her.

'Our home,' he echoed, as he leant forward and embraced her.

They stayed holding one another for quite some time, before Mendina finally pulled away from him.

The sadness and fear still remained, but she felt capable of moving on again.

Mendina had no idea what had just happened, but Mort's words had managed to find a way through the panic she felt and soothe the greatest part of it. She knew he meant all that he said, and there was a part of her that believed what he said. Yet there was also a part that knew they had no control over what happened in Glorfiden while they were away.

She could only hope Jarkene could keep the evil at bay until his son was able to return and help him.

Jarkene would need the rod, and if they returned in time, he would then be able to use it.

She and Mort had talked about its return to Glorfiden on a couple of occasions since they departed. Mendina had even suggested they return sooner, pretending to have found it and give Jarkene the rod. They could then try again for their quest.

None of the other elves would doubt they had been successful in taking it from the one who had used it against Glorfiden. The story would be plausible, and none would ever need to know the true source of its origin.

Yet Mort would hear none of it.

'We will need it where we are going,' he had said. 'I will not risk your life by returning it to my father.'

Mendina had let it go. She knew he would not be swayed.

'The necklace!' Mort said, suddenly remembering the treasure he had been handed inside the cave. 'You should be wearing it,' he said.

Mendina looked at him, a shocked look replaced quickly by a frown.

'Don't startle me like that,' she said crossly, before softening her look. 'Why? What does it do?'

'I have no idea,' Mort said, a little abashed at frightening her. 'But it has strong magic, I can see that much.'

'It may not help if we don't know what it does,' Mendina said, as she let Mort place it around her neck. He struggled with the clasp, before Mendina took over.

'That creature was put there with no other purpose but to guard it,' Mort said, the excitement back in his voice. 'Whatever it is, it is powerful,' he said. 'I feel better with it around your neck.'

'Okay,' Mendina finally said. 'Hopefully we don't get to find out what it does too soon.'

They continued on unmolested for most of the day, with Mort regularly making small talk with Mendina to re-assure himself she was still doing okay. Although she spoke softly and sparingly, the dark panic she had felt that morning didn't return.

As the sun made its way towards the far horizon, the land before them began to change once more.

The swamp remained steadfast to their right, however the land they walked on began to slope upwards and more trees appeared, blocking out much of the swamp from their vision. Mendina was quick to say how much that pleased her.

The greater prevalence of trees made them both feel more comfortable, and at the same time, more vigilant. It would be harder to spot any threats approaching or lying in wait for them.

Mort suspected their luck couldn't last forever.

Sooner or later something was going to attack them.

They finally found a suitable tree before night fell and nestled high up in the branches. Both slept peacefully, before the rising sun woke them.

They climbed down, had a quick bite from their provisions and continued on their way.

It wasn't long before they came upon a small village. Aside from small animals, it was the first sign of any civilised life since they had left the cave.

Both scurried up a tree the moment they saw it, wanting a vantage point to look upon it in safety.

Fortunately, none of those within the village had seen them as they approached.

As Mortinan and Mendina looked on, the occupants began to awaken and move around. They were large, muscly creatures, with wicked teeth and pale skin. They were shaped like men, but looked to be some kind of abomination. Mortinan did not think they would be friendly. They did not look friendly.

'Do you know their kind?' Mendina whispered to him. 'I don't like how they look.'

'Nor I,' said Mort. 'I do not know what kind of creature they are, but I think we should go around.'

'Yes, of course we should go around,' she agreed.

Quietly climbing down to the ground, they moved back the way they had come for a short distance, before walking in a direction that would take them well wide of the village.

They were quiet in their movements and wary, in case some of those in the village began wandering away from their home.

They saw no more of the large, ugly humanoid things, as the trees began to thicken even more, until they were suddenly within a thick forest.

The undergrowth was not too restrictive, so they were able to continue making good time.

It wasn't long before they heard the sound of rushing water.

'I was just beginning to get thirsty,' Mort said, smiling at Mendina. She returned the smile, as they walked toward the sound.

They came upon the stream within minutes, as it snaked in amongst the trees. The water wasn't too deep, but it was wide and gushed quickly over small, rounded rocks.

'It is clean,' Mendina said, almost sounding surprised, as she knelt beside it and cupped some water in her hands. 'There are fish,' she said in between slurping the cool water.

Mort knelt beside her and did the same.

'There is a waterfall ahead,' she said. 'There will be more fish pooled there.'

'Then we will be able to catch and eat some,' he said, as he put his face in the water and began to drink deeply.

After a while, he stopped and stood up.

Mendina was already standing and looked to be waiting for him.

'Let's go then,' she said.

They walked along the side of the stream for a short distance, before coming to the waterfall. It was not as high as she had feared, but still looked difficult enough to ascend. There was sheer rock all around it, as if the land had been cut clean by a giant axe, but fortunately there were vines running down it which should hold their weight.

The pool itself was large and looked to be very deep. The stream they had followed was one of many that ran out of it.

'I don't see any fish,' Mort said disappointingly. 'I don't fancy diving into waters I am unfamiliar with.'

'We can throw lines and see if we have any luck,' Mendina said. 'It is a lovely spot for a quick break.'

Mort was suddenly in no hurry to face whatever it was that awaited them in the ruined forest. He still hoped it wasn't too far away, but for now he was content to rest here with Mendina.

Skilfully, she stripped one of the vines, until she had a piece to use as a fishing line. The hook she crafted quickly from a piece of wood on the ground.

Digging into the rich soil, she quickly located some prize grubs, before sliding her bait through the hook and dangling it into the water.

It didn't take long for her to get a bite and pull out a good-sized fish. Neither had seen its kind before, but it looked healthy, with two rows of sharp teeth. Both were glad they had chosen not to take a swim.

'Your turn,' Mendina said, handing Mort the fish.

He laughed as he took it from her.

'Would you like me to light a fire also?' he asked, 'or do you eat your fish raw?'

Mendina looked at him as if he had gone crazy.

'We will definitely need a small fire,' she said. 'I will collect some wood while you prepare the fish.'

'As you command my lady,' Mort replied, slicing his knife into the belly of the fish and beginning to pull out its innards.

For the first time since they had left, Mort was feeling at peace.

This is exactly how he imagined things were going to be with Mendina once this was all finished with. Whatever this was?

Hopefully it would not be too difficult a task. He was looking forward to their return to Glorfiden.

He still had so much of the forest to explore, after he helped his father make it secure once more.

CHAPTER 41

A Time For Battle

INF CONTINUED TO walk behind her new '*friend*'.
They stood apart from the main section of the army; as she
was considered to be a magic user; and so walked at the back
of Kritch's force. Linf herself walked behind a group of Ogre Mage
and a few bald humans who could also cast spells. There were also
fifteen or so Lava-Orc's, though none of those were as big as the one
guarding her. At first she had thought them ogres, but having had
a few brief conversations with him, she had learnt a little bit more
about the one sent to watch over her. He had also told her his name.
Rark.

Linf's permanent position was at the rear, 'where your station in
this life has placed you,' Rark said to her earlier. 'But worry not. You
will be able to go to the front when we get there.' He had smiled
after he said it.

Linf had not seen him smile before and she hoped to never see it
again. What a horrid and unfortunate looking thing he was. He was
better off never trying to be happy.

'Have you fought in many battles before goblin?' Rark asked her.
They had stopped for a quick bite and so Linf was happy to chat, as
she wasn't given anything to snack on. Hopefully it would help with
the boredom and growling of her stomach. She had not yet seen any
opportunity to try and make her escape.

'I have not had to fight in battles,' she said. 'But I have killed plenty.'

'Killing something is a lot different to a battle,' Rark said. 'In a battle, everything is trying to kill you and it comes from every direction.'

Linf didn't respond.

'Do you have eyes in the back of your head goblin?' Rark asked.

Linf continued to look at the Lava-Orc as if there was something seriously wrong with him.

'You will need them when everything is trying to kill you,' Rark said.

There he goes with that smile again, Ling thought, cringing.

'Do you have anything helpful to say?' Linf asked.

'Grow eyes in the back of your head before we get there,' Rark said, still smiling.

'What is wrong with you?' Linf asked, not really wanting an answer to her question. She could see what was wrong with him. He was trying to be funny, but he was just stupid.

The smile left his face.

'I am looking forward to seeing you get blasted by the wizards and then chopped up by the men. What do goblins taste like?' he asked.

'We don't eat each other,' Linf said. 'Do you?' she asked.

Rark didn't answer straight away.

'No, we don't,' he finally said. 'But I think I would enjoy goblin,' he added, before turning away from her.

Linf had nothing else she wanted to say to him at that exact moment. She didn't really understand him, not that she wanted to. Yet getting to know the one set to guard her might be useful when her time to escape came.

Rark still hadn't shown her any fear or anger, so she initially thought him to be simple, like the big human she had killed just before she saw Brax for the last time.

Yet she thought there was probably a lot more to this one. She knew the Lava-Orc had some smarts, although she wasn't yet sure just how smart this one was.

Rark certainly looked like he would go well in a fight and was quite a bit taller than she was. And he was all muscle. If she wasn't so powerful, Linf might have felt a little scared of him.

The weapon he carried looked like it would do serious damage to an opponent, yet she suspected he was also capable of magic. Why else would they be walking in this group? The dark-red colour of their skin was what she assumed gave them the name lava-orc.

Before they began their march, she had seen only a few other Lava-Orc's within King Kritch's army. Not that she had seen the whole army, but perhaps the ones walking with them were the only ones here.

Initially she thought them guards, but why would all of Kritch's users of magic need guards? Another reason why she thought them part of the magic group.

'What magic do you have?' Linf asked him to his back.

He didn't turn or even look around.

'Just keep working on growing those eyes in the back of your head little goblin,' was all he said. 'You don't ever have to worry about me.'

'I wasn't worried about you,' Linf snarled back at him. 'I just want to know who I am going to be fighting with.'

This time the Lava-Orc stopped and turned around.

'Let me be clear goblin,' Rark began. 'You fight for no-one except yourself. Nothing here will try to help if you are in trouble. Nothing here will be doing anything but trying to kill men and keep themselves alive. If you get in my way, I will run straight over the top of you. You are nothing to me and even if we win, you are going to be horribly slaughtered in this war.' He paused before continuing. 'Any more questions?'

Still there was no anger emanating from its body, so she figured it was safe to ask him another question.

'When do we get there?' Linf asked.

Rark smiled down at her again. She physically cringed at it this time.

'We are already here,' he said, as shouts and horns began to ring out.

Those Linf had been following came to a sudden halt, as did the Lava-Orc in front of her.

'Come with me,' he said, indicating for her to step to the side of the Ogre-Mage and walk towards the front.

Reluctantly, Linf did as she was asked. She told herself she was asked, but deep down she knew there was no freedom within this army for her. She had been brought here to die, and Rark was her executioner; even if he wasn't the one who would be striking the killer blow.

It didn't take long for them to get to the front. There were hundreds of creatures already making their way down the gentle slope to the enormous patch of flat ground ahead.

For the first time, Linf was able to look over at those she would be fighting.

There were not as many as she thought there would be, although there could be any number of them behind the walls. Kritch's army looked like it would still be much bigger than the one they faced.

There might be a chance for her after all, so long as they didn't try to get over the walls.

If the men came out and Kritch sent enough of his army all at once, they should over-run their foes straight away and she may somehow survive.

If that happened, Linf could then just keep running through the land of men, until she got home.

Except those at her home wanted her dead as well, which was going to be a problem.

There were other goblin settlements scattered throughout her lands, but they were distrusting of outsiders, and as a rule generally killed them as soon as they came near.

Another problem.

There was also the issue of that human cow wanting her to go north.

Linf hadn't seen her since she had been caught by the orcs; which she was pleased about; but she had a feeling she would be back again soon if Linf kept going in the wrong direction.

She decided that first she would live through the battle coming up, and then she would choose which way to go.

Maybe she could go into the realm of men just a little way, before going back where the witch wanted her to go. It wouldn't take too long to find a house out by itself or in a small village. Linf still hadn't tasted the flesh of human child and she was determined to do so before she left this area for good.

Marching down the slope, Linf looked curiously at a group of small orcs bound together by chains. They looked to be only children, with several of them crying. The rest stood as if they were frozen, horrified looks etched into their faces.

'What are they doing there?' Linf asked Rark, as he moved to stand closer to the frightened orc children. The rest of the Lava-Orcs moved over to stand behind them also.

'They are our other weapons,' he said with a determined look. No grin this time.

Linf obviously had no idea what he was talking about.

'You will see,' he said to her, before turning his back on the goblin again.

'What do I do now?' Linf asked. She wasn't as nervous as she knew she probably should be.

'Now we wait,' Rark said. 'And then you die.'

Kritch's forces began spreading out along the flat ground before them.

Linf was surprised to see them move in such an orderly fashion. There were large orcs bellowing orders, and other bald men on horses doing the same, as they rode up and down along the front of Kritch's army.

Linf remained where she was, standing beside the Lava-Orcs and their 'weapons'. The other users of magic she had marched here with had spread themselves out along the front line, while a large number of darker-skinned men moved to stand to her right. They had shiny armour on and masks covering their faces.

So far, she had seen no sign of King Thrisc, but she hadn't expected to. He certainly wouldn't be anywhere near where the fighting was going to be hardest. If she was King, Linf would be right at the back with lots of guards surrounding her. Somewhere she could watch and see what was happening, so if things were going bad she could get out of there as quickly as possible.

Unfortunately, she wasn't the leader of this army. She was as far removed from the leader as you could get, except perhaps for those young orcs tied together. Her attention was constantly drawn to them, as they whimpered and cried.

Linf didn't feel sorry for them, she was simply curious what their purpose could be. What powers did they have? None of them looked like weapons. All she could see was the fear pouring from them. Pure and thick.

If she wasn't already brimming from the fear she had absorbed, Linf would have drawn it into her without hesitation. It would have been difficult not to.

Turning her attention away from the young orcs, she looked ahead at those who opposed them.

She could see men scurrying about on their towers and along the walls before them. Still some distance away, she couldn't tell if they were warrior or magic-user, but there didn't seem to be a lot of them.

Looking at where they were set up however, she didn't think there would need to be many of them. A steep slope led up to the cliffs along which the walls stood. The towers stood to the side of a massive gate, which she assumed led through the passageway and into the realm of men. It wasn't an overly wide passage either.

Why had Kritch chosen this place to fight them? It made no sense. As she stared and thought more about it, Linf realised there was no way she was going to survive an assault against that.

She would be cut down by arrows or magic, or whatever else they decided to throw down at her.

All she had seen within her own army that could do damage to the walls were some large trolls with massive slings. They were probably capable of throwing things a long way, but it wouldn't be nearly enough to get them through that gate.

After a long sigh, she turned back to Rark.

'What are we waiting for?' she asked.

'We wait for the word from those who lead this army,' he said, turning around to face Linf. 'Are you in a hurry to die?'

'I don't think I will die today,' Linf said. She didn't really believe the words coming out of her mouth, but she had always liked to talk things up, even when she was a runt growing up. Which wasn't all that long ago. 'I will probably kill a lot of men though,' she said, before pausing. 'And who knows what else.'

She smiled up at the Lava-Orc this time.

'Let us hope so,' he said. 'It will be entertaining to see them die before they eventually put a sword through your face.'

'Is your face immune to swords?' Linf asked. She wasn't worried about upsetting him anymore. What did she have to lose?

He chuckled at her, before turning back to face their enemies across the plain.

Linf did the same, but on this occasion, she decided to take some time to continue trying out a few new ideas on how to use her powers. With an endless supply of energy around her, it seemed like the perfect time to do it.

Perhaps she could also test how far she was able to push the big Lava-Orc by killing one or two of the young orcs.

She smiled as she began trying to form a shield around herself.

CHAPTER 42

Cousins

ALTHOUGH THEY WERE prepared for an attack, Zuroth hadn't expected the incredible power that came with that first bolt of energy. It sent half a dozen of his dwarven warriors flying backward, killing the two who had received the most direct impact. Even their magic-resistant armour had not been able to absorb much of it.

'Shield wall!' he bellowed at the top of his lungs.

Standing only a few rows back from the front of his marching army, one of the dwarves who was flung back, had bowled into the dwarf at his side.

Helping him back to his feet, Zuroth pushed him forward into the breach.

Dwarves scurried to make a straight line again, their shields turned to face the forest and extending to a height greater than that of the tallest dwarf among them. Each shield had a latch which allowed it to slide upward and then lock into place.

But before they could get into line and link the shields, another bolt of energy smashed into their ranks, sending more dwarfs catapulting into the ones behind them.

'Get the shields locked!' Zuroth roared again, this time moving into the newest breach himself.

Thumping the bottom of his shield into the dirt at his feet, the dwarves either side of him were able to lock theirs into his.

The shields began to buzz, as the magic forged into them took hold. Others were able to link theirs as well, but still the bolts of energy came, leaving gaps in the wall.

Arrows began to fly over the shields, but they weren't able to penetrate the dwarven armour. As the Western Dwarf King watched them zing through the air, he was surprised at their lack of precision. He had heard the elves were masters of the bow.

Looking down the line, he was relieved to see the shields were finally linked. The bolts of energy continued to hammer against them, but they were no longer smashing through and into his armies ranks.

The buzz of the shield wall changed suddenly, as the line joined all the way along the entire army.

Zuroth knew what would happen now, as one of his warriors took his position on the wall. The Dwarven King stepped back with a wicked smile on his face.

Treille looked across at his Lord, as his bolts of energy stopped smashing into the dwarves below them. Their shields had suddenly began absorbing the magic he was casting at them. Jarkene paused to think for a moment.

'Do you believe that enough to make them think twice about entering Glorfiden?' Treille asked. He had run out of arrows, not that any of them had killed anything, let alone injured even one dwarf. That had not been his main focus, but it was still disappointing.

'If I can't kill more than what I have, I don't think it much of a deterrent at all,' he said.

Drawing his arms back, this time the bolts of energy became lightning bolts. Enhanced through the power of his fairie-dragon *Linn*, the bolts made the middle of the day shine even brighter. Treille watched them crackle from his Lord's hands. The power was intense.

Arcing across the field, they struck the dwarven shields.

To the shock of both elves watching, this time the shields did not absorb the magic.

This time they repelled it straight back into the forest from where came.

Jarkene had only a split second to react, as he saw his magic coming straight back at where he and Treille stood.

Fortunately for them both, the lightning spread as it hit the shields, and the power was lessened because of it. The Elven Lord was able to put up a shield strong enough to prevent what did come directly back at them from turning both he and Treille to ash.

The impact was still strong enough to knock both elves from the tree and on to the soft forest floor below them.

Gingerly standing back up, Jarkene brushed the leaves and twigs from his clothes.

He looked across at Treille. The younger elf had suffered more hurts than he, but he was able to stand; blood from a large gash pouring down the side of his face.

Moving away from the scorched trees above them, Jarkene found another vantage point in a tree not too far away.

Treille followed him up.

'They think themselves safe behind their shields,' he said in a dread voice. 'Let us see how safe they are when their shields are no longer able to protect them.' He spoke softly, but even Treille felt a chill at his words.

Jarkene spread his arms wide and began to chant.

Looking away from his Lord and back to the Dwarven Army; their shields shining a bright blue; he waited to see what would happen next.

The Dwarves did not move, safe in the knowledge they were secure from any further spells and arrows coming out of the trees. For them it would be a waiting game, if they had nought else to throw at the elves.

Treille's head pounded from the blow he had received, but his mind was still clear. It took a little time for him to realise what his Lord was doing.

He almost felt sorry for their enemies.

For a time, there was no sound but the soft crackle of the Dwarven shield, as Zuroth's army stood motionless behind their barrier.

Then after several minutes had passed, Treille began to hear a rumbling and saw the Dwarven shields begin to move as the ground before the dwarves began to crack apart. They were only small lines in the ground at first, but they quickly grew into larger ones. Small pieces of dirt began to shoot out into the air.

Treille stood stunned at how far ranging the spell was and the damage it began to inflict on the earth itself. He had believed it to be a different spell his Lord was casting. What he looked out upon horrified him.

Jarkene had cast one of those destructive spells which was forbidden within Glorfiden.

He was going to shatter the earth beneath them.

Although the lightning and energy spells were also destructive, he had cast them out of Glorfiden. This spell would resonate back among the trees, possibly even tearing some of their roots out of the ground.

'My Lord!' Treille exclaimed. 'You cannot do this. It is wrong.'

Jarkene looked across at him, his eyes now a deep crimson.

Staring at his Lord's eyes, Treille felt a deep horror take hold within him. He knew there was nothing he could do to stop was happening, but he tried anyway.

'It will be felt in Glorfiden as well! You will kill the trees!'

Jarkene turned back to the Dwarves. Treille doubted he even heard him.

'Balls and chain!' Zuroth roared. 'Throw them when ready. Aim high and low!'

After the lightning had been repelled back into the forest, he thought for a time that the elves might have given up.

No more arrows came at them and no more spells were cast.

The dwarves continued to hold their line. None would move until Zuroth gave the order.

Then the King of the Western Dwarves felt the first rumbling of the earth and he knew it had been wishful thinking. Whatever was in those trees, it was powerful, and it wasn't going anywhere.

Zuroth would have liked to let those in the tree know they were only passing by, but he knew it was too late for that.

He watched on as those behind the front shield barrier moved frantically, but with an orderly purpose, in setting up their line of attack.

The balls of iron were placed into their shallow cups, which were in turn attached to small catapults. These were designed so they could be quickly assembled and ready to fire. Although heavy and cumbersome for those given the onerous task of carrying them, he was glad he had chosen to bring them.

'Shield wall, on my command, get down!' Zuroth bellowed. He would wait until each was ready to fire, although the rumbling was getting louder and the ground beginning to move under them. It would be difficult to stand soon, let alone fire off their catapults. Their shields would also lose their ability to repel the magic if those holding them were no longer able to stand steady.

His soldiers looked to be moving in slow motion now, but the catapults were finally readied.

'Fire high and then low on the second volley,' Zuroth roared, before following it with the order to fire.

The shields at the front were lowered as the first volley of balls were shot over their heads and into the trees beyond them.

Jarkene was concentrating on the crumbling of the earth before him, but he still had his wits about him, as he continued to watch the Dwarven Army below him.

As the shields were lowered and the first volley of iron balls flew towards them, he paused his spell long enough to watch them approaching.

With the grace of an Elven Lord he deftly jumped to the branch above, as the ball crashed into the tree he was standing on. It impacted where he had been, smashing its way through the thick trunk. Jarkene was both horrified and angered by the damage it was able to do.

It wasn't until the last moment that he saw the thin wire attached to it, joining it to the iron ball that had struck to his left.

Looking down, he saw that Treille hadn't seen the wire until it was too late.

The younger elf would have had no difficulty dodging the iron ball, but he must have leapt to the side instead of up or down, the wire slicing through him like he was made of water.

It broke Jarkene out of his trance.

Another elf dead because of his arrogance.

He looked again at the dwarves as they fired off another volley of the deadly missiles.

These ones were lower, but they still cut through the thicker trunks.

Jarkene could feel their pain. This needed to stop.

Leaping down on to the ground he stepped out of Glorfiden and into the open.

His spell had ceased, so another volley was not forthcoming yet.

Jarkene held his hands up and projected his voice out to the Dwarves in the common tongue. He wasn't sure whether they would understand him, but he spoke it anyway.

'Enough!' he said.

The shields were raised once more, however no more iron balls were thrown in his direction.

'Do you have one who speaks for you?' Jarkene asked. Asking for a truce was painful for the Elven Lord, but the death of another elf had shaken him.

The shield at the forefront of the army, facing east, moved aside and a dwarf stepped out, level with the shield wall facing Jarkene.

'I am King of this Dwarven Army,' Zuroth said. 'Say your peace elf,' he said.

'If you try and enter my home you will all be slaughtered,' Jarkene said, 'but if you turn and go back to the caves you crawled out of you, I will allow you to leave unmolested.'

Zuroth was wondering what the elf was hoping to achieve by talking to him now. Had they inflicted so much damage that this one had already had enough? He didn't think it likely. Not when he knew how powerful the elf was.

'We are going that way,' Zuroth said, pointing towards the distant Dwarven Mountains. 'Going into your forest interests me not one bit.'

'Not yet,' Jarkene said, 'but I think it likely you are looking to align with your Eastern kin and try your luck then.'

Zuroth couldn't help but chuckle at the thought.

'You think we are going to join forces and then attack your forest?' he asked, truly shocked. At least it made some sense why the elf had attacked them.

'Why would you not?' Jarkene asked.

'Because our home isn't big enough anymore. We want a bigger one,' he said. 'And we don't intend on sharing it with our "kin"'.

Zuroth shook his head before continuing.

'Walking into your forest is the last thing I would want to do,' Zuroth said, smirking now. 'Not that we fear your kind elf. There is just nothing interesting in there.'

'You have been warned,' Jarkene said, as he backed into the forest and disappeared from sight.

'Keep the shield up,' Zuroth bellowed, as he stepped back behind the line of shields. It might be a trick. Elves were not to be trusted.

Either way, he was happy to wait here for a time. If the elf was going to attack again, he assumed it would be soon.

On the other hand, perhaps he was simply buying time while more of his kind arrived.

That could be a problem.

Thinking for a time, he finally decided it would be best if they continued on.

After they had buried their dead.

'Small graves,' he said. Each warrior would be encased in steel so the graves would not be desecrated before they could return and give them a proper burial in the mountains of their home. He would not leave any of them to rot out here.

He had brought many of the makeshift coffins with them on wagons, yet too many had died already at the hands of the elf.

Although Zuroth wouldn't enter the forest; he had meant what he said; he intended to smash and burn as much of it as they were able to when the time was right. His warriors' deaths would be avenged, he assured those standing around him. The word would be passed along the ranks.

They still had a lot of ground to traverse before they were clear of the trees, so he got his army moving again as soon as the grim task was finished.

The ranks were tighter now, and they moved slower, but he decided they would march throughout the night if they had to.

He was more determined now than ever before, to take over the realm of the Eastern Mountains.

All of those dwarves who opposed him would be put to the axe.

The others he would allow to serve him.

Then the elves would get what was coming to them.

CHAPTER 43

This Doesn't Feel Right

BRINDEL HAD MOVED quite a distance in to the swamp. Not as far as he had first intended, due to the smell and dampness, but still far enough that he was no longer able to see the clearing between the forest and the swamp.

Based on what Feng had told them, the Dwarven Army should appear within the hour, so he sat on a relatively dry spot of ground and waited for them to pass. He knew he would be able to hear that many dwarves walking past at once.

After an hour of boredom and swatting at insects, both flying and crawling, he still hadn't heard anything nearing where he sat.

A short time ago he heard loud rumbling and what he thought were muffled voices yelling in the distance, but it had gone quiet and he had heard nothing more since.

Brindel decided it was worth the risk to move back closer to the clearing and try and see what was going on.

He moved slowly, trying to be as quiet as possible, before stopping short of the edge of the swamp.

He could see nothing moving out there, so he decided to walk along the edge of the swamp for a bit until he did.

It wasn't long before he heard the steps of the approaching army.

Lying low, he found a spot where he could see, but was confident none would be able to spot him. Not unless they walked into the swamp and stood on top of him.

He didn't think that wasn't going to happen, as the dwarves would have no reason to go into the swamp.

An army that size would take forever to traverse the bog he lay in.

He saw only shadows through the tangled branches of the swamp, as the Dwarven Army finally began to trudge past his position.

They moved slowly, and it seemed to take forever before the last of the dwarves and carts they were dragging moved past him.

He waited another ten minutes, to make sure there were no stragglers, before he decided it was safe for him to step out of the stinking swamp.

He immediately looked to his left and saw the thin line of dwarves walking off into the distance. He hoped Granwith and Kagen arrived back at the mountain in time to allow Draug time to prepare his defence of their home.

If they were somehow delayed, or worse, then it was going to get very ugly when that army arrived. There were a lot of them.

Taking a deep breath, Brindel turned back towards the west and began his journey once more, this time just outside of the swamp. He decided it was worth the risk.

If the Dwarven Army had gone this far unmolested, then perhaps the elf had given up.

Less than half an hour into his travel, Brindel came upon the spot where Jarkene and Zuroth's army had fought.

Brindel knew straight away there had been a battle here. The earth was shattered where he now walked, and the ground soaked with blood. Looking across at the forest, he could see trees badly damaged, some had even fallen from the harm inflicted upon them.

'This was what I heard for sure,' he said to himself. 'I wonder what happened to the pretty elf?'

Looking around for a bit, he came upon recently dug ground. He knew immediately that a number of dwarves had been killed here. Less of them for Draug to kill, he thought. Perhaps he would thank the elf if he ever saw him again. He chuckled at the thought.

He was about to continue on, when curiosity got the better of him.

Digging into the dirt, it didn't take him long to unearth one of the makeshift coffins.

They hadn't buried them very deep. Brindel was disgusted at the lack of respect shown to a fallen dwarf, even one from the Western lands.

Opening up the lid, he looked in at the dead dwarf lying inside.

His hair and face were scorched, the lightning bolt from the elf having torn straight through his armour. Brindel couldn't help feel a burst of pride at how strong his own armour was in comparison.

Aside from their skin colour, which was a darkish grey, the dwarf looked little different to his own race. This one's face was a little longer and his shoulders not as wide, but they could easily have been cousins.

Brindel was also quick to notice he had not been buried with any of his weapons. That was disappointing. It was one of the main reasons he had decided to dig it up.

Closing the lid, he covered it back up with dirt, before moving off.

He was more confident at moving outside of the swamp now. It would be unlikely the elf would be wasting his time on a solitary dwarf. He would probably be keeping tabs on the army he had just fought against, or else he was off trying to get some more of his elf friends to help him.

If there were enough of them left.

Looking across at the forest one more time, another thought occurred to him.

There was a lot of damage done to those trees. What had been used intrigued him, and Brindel regretted not getting closer to the passing army and seeing what it was they used to do that. He would wager he would be able to make an even more powerful version.

He also thought the elf may not be doing anything more than lying dead on the forest floor, just out of sight.

He could only hope.

With one last look at the shattered ground around him, Brindel moved off, a lighter spring in his step at the thought of the elf lying broken in a pool of his own blood.

His good spirits quickly soured, as the storm clouds from the west finally broke above him.

He had only been walking a few hours, when the sky opened and the rain quickly soaked into his clothes.

He may as well have walked through the swamp, he thought, as the ground beneath him turned soggy. He did concede to himself the smell was still somewhat better out in the open.

Despite the rain and wind, the old dwarf still made good time.

His footing was sure, and he was nearly at the end of the elven forest by the time the sun sunk beneath the horizon.

With the land seemingly free of anything resembling a threat, he decided it safe enough to continue through the first part of the night.

When he was finally clear of the forest to his left, he decided he would have a short rest.

Finding a spot under a tree, nestled into the bank of a small hill, he lay his blanket out and closed his eyes.

When he awoke, the night was still dark, but he had a feeling he might have slept longer than he intended.

As he set off and the land began to grow lighter, he knew he had almost slept the entire night through.

Cursing at the lost time, he quickened his steps as he set off once more.

The rain had stopped during the night, but his clothes were still wet and his boots soggy. It was an uncomfortable walk, but he persevered without complaint. He had no-one to complain to after all, and no-one would care even if there had been a dwarf to complain to.

As he continued to quicken his speed, he wondered after a while why he was in such a hurry.

He had initially told himself it was so he could return and help with the defence of his home.

But he realised now, that no matter how quickly he was able to get to where he was going, he would never get back in time.

The Western Dwarven Army would be approaching the Eastern Mountains already. Unless he was able to sprout wings and fly, the battle would be over long before he returned, and he had no desire to ever fly again.

What he would be returning to filled him with dread. Despite his joy at travelling the lands, the knowledge he had a home to return to had always re-assured him and spurred him on in his endeavours.

The army that had walked past him had been huge for a Dwarven host.

His own Kingdom had little practice in large-scale warfare. And when he said little practice, he meant none.

They were swords for hire and powerful warriors, but the dwarves he had seen walking away looked to be organised. A large unit marching towards a single goal. He feared that goal was not to make friends.

That they had only lost a few warriors to the power of an Elven Lord, showed Brindel they had excellent defence capabilities, and the destruction wreaked upon that small part of the forest told him they were equally proficient at inflicting damage.

Draug would have his work cut out if they found their way into the mountains.

As he walked, Brindel thought about numerous scenarios that could yet play out, depending on where they got in and began their attack.

Yet despite this very real threat, his mind also kept returning to the discovery of those new pages within his journal. It was a welcome distraction.

Armour that could make its wearer almost invincible! He selfishly knew it was probably the real driving factor behind his haste.

He wanted to get back and start making it.

Then his thoughts would inevitably drift to Elenda. Was Granwith right? Is the only reason she was kind to him and offered him use of her forge, because she suspected he might be able to make the armour for her?

He tried to tell himself otherwise, but it made too much sense.

She wanted him only for his book. Once she had that, he didn't doubt she would send him on his way.

He cursed loudly at her deception. He had actually liked the girl.

He thought then that perhaps Granwith was mistaken, before cursing himself for being old and stupid each time he thought it.

Maybe she was like him though. He would have done the same would he not, if it meant being able to create such an incredible piece of work.

He decided to leave the door slightly ajar for Elenda. Perhaps her love of crafting magical items was as strong as his, and she would actually like to share in its wonder with a fellow dwarf worthy enough to assist.

He sighed and continued walking.

He wouldn't trust her, but he would give her a chance to explain why she sent someone to steal from him.

She had better be convincing.

It was late in the afternoon when he came upon the swamp again.

He had continued to travel directly west after leaving the forest behind him, the swamp snaking its way to the north. He had been delighted to see them both disappear into the distance either side of him.

Now the swamp had snaked its way back down to where he was headed.

It would create only a small direction shift to avoid it, but he was annoyed nevertheless.

Although he didn't know exactly where this forest was that he looked for, he believed it was further north.

That meant he would need to go around the swamp, which meant it would take him even longer to get there.

Yelling long and loudly at the sky above him and the land surrounding him, Brindel released some of his frustration, before trudging off again.

He didn't even care right now if anything heard him.

Perhaps fighting something would lift his spirits a little bit.

He had no such luck for the rest of the day.

CHAPTER 44

Strangers No More

THE SMALL GROUP of barbarians were not yet at the base of the Twin Peaks, when Freta noticed something moving ahead of them.

They moved slowly through the deep snow and trees, shadowing the flatter ground fifty paces away. Herid believed they needed to be more cautious now. It had taken a little while to convince Fargesh they were better arriving late than not at all.

Although only a quiet sound, it was enough for the rest of her party to freeze where they stood.

They were soon able to make out a shape, and then three other similar shapes spaced out either side of the first one.

Fargesh had never seen their like before. These creatures were not what any of them had been expecting.

They were thin and darker skinned, almost a grey. Each of them walked without much effort through the terrain, graceful in their movements.

Fargesh had no doubt they were responsible for the deaths of his fellow barbarians and the capture of his son.

He wanted to take one of them alive. The rest would need to die.

They continued to move forward as the Barbarians crouched down waiting for them. The newcomers appeared oblivious to the threat awaiting them.

Fargesh and the others had all huddled down, their movements incredibly slow so as not to draw the stranger's attention. They would pass by their position shortly, which is what the barbarians were waiting for.

They wanted none of them running back the way they had come and warning the others that probably followed further up. These ones moved like scouts.

When they had walked past; the nearest of them only a few paces from where the barbarians huddled, almost invisible against the snow; Fargesh began to move across to where the furthest of them walked. The others fanned out behind him. Apart from himself, there would be two barbarians against a single one of these trespassers.

When he was satisfied they were all in position, Fargesh gave the signal and the seven Barbarians moved down towards their prey.

The one below Fargesh heard him coming well before he reached him, but the Barbarian was no longer trying to stalk his prey. He was in kill mode now, as he crashed through the small snow-covered undergrowth.

The skinny human-shaped creature turned on him and immediately drew a bow that was slung across his shoulder. Nocking an arrow, he fired as Fargesh stopped. Concentrating on the direction the arrow pointed and the moment it's hand let go, Fargesh was able to move his torso to the side, drawing his mighty sword as the arrow flashed harmlessly to the side.

The second arrow he smashed aside with his blade, as he continued to close in. The dark-elf did not get the chance to fire off a third before the hilt of Fargesh's sword smashed into the side of its head.

The dark-elf slumped to the ground, motionless.

Fargesh bent down and picked it up by the front of its thin black armour.

The features were not familiar to him, but the pointed ears were the same as the elves he had heard about in stories. Creatures of the forest that lived across the other side of the mighty Dwarven Mountains.

What were elves doing in the highlands? He had been told they only ever left their forest to hunt.

Dropping the unconscious creature back on to the ground, he looked across to see how the others had fared.

They were all still standing, while he could see none of the elves, other than one on the ground in front of Herid, who stood closest to him.

'Do any of yours live?' Fargesh asked as quietly as he could.

He waited for word to make its way back to Herid.

'None,' Herid said. 'Freda has taken injury, but no others are hurt.'

'Mine lives,' Fargesh said, indicating for them all to join him.

While he waited for the others to walk over, he looked back down at the one on the ground in front of him. The bow it carried was small, as would be suited for its thin build. He pulled an arrow out of its quiver and inspected it closely. Made of a dark stone, it was nothing he had seen before. It looked sharp. He wondered how durable it was.

Throwing it to the ground he reached down to pull its short sword from the scabbard, but Herid's hand stopped him.

'Do not,' he said.

Fargesh glared at him, but stood up straight again.

'The one we fought had a similar sword which dripped with some kind of black substance. It could be dangerous. An acid perhaps.'

'Why would they put acid on their blades?' Fargesh said. 'It would dull the blade.'

'Their weapons are not made of the same steel we use,' Herid said, before changing the subject. 'We should wake this one.'

'Agreed,' Fargesh said, removing the armour from its body, before driving his elbow into the centre of its chest.

The dark-elf groaned, before opening its eyes and attempting to swat away whatever was causing it pain. Fargesh caught its wrist in his left hand, while using his right to grab it around the throat.

The dark-elf began to wheeze, so Fargesh released the pressure a little.

'You will answer me when I ask you a question,' Fargesh said. 'Do you understand me?'

The creature he held looked frightened to begin with, but after Fargesh had finished speaking, it looked to relax somewhat.

Even still, it did not answer him.

Fargesh took his dagger from his belt and held it inches away from the right eye of the dark-elf.

'Where did you take the children? Are they still alive?!' Although he spoke quietly, there was desperation in his voice.

The dark-elf spoke only a few words, which Fargesh could not understand.

'They have their own language,' Herid said, resting his hand on the shoulder of his friend.

'I thought most intelligent creatures spoke the common tongue,' he said, frustration in his voice. 'Maybe this one is playing with us. Hold his arms,' Fargesh said, as he let go of the dark-elves' wrist.

Placing a hand over the mouth of the one he held down, Fargesh slowly pushed his dagger into one of its shoulders. He could see the pain it felt as he looked into its eyes.

'The next thing I put my knife in will be your eye,' he said, his face only inches from that of the dark-elf.

Releasing his hand from across its mouth, the dark-elf spoke again.

'*Shikk-ra*', it said, before smiling up at Fargesh.

The Barbarian didn't hesitate, as he drove his dagger through the eye of the dark-elf until the hilt stopped it going any further.

'We need to keep moving,' Fargesh said, as he stood and faced the others. 'We are definitely close now.'

'These look like scouts to me Fargesh,' Herid said. 'We need to be mindful that there may be too many of them for us to kill.'

'What are you suggesting?' Fargesh asked.

'We need to warn Dougal. The whole village may be at risk!'

'Because of these few?!' Fargesh said, disgusted at the thought of going back.

'You can return and warn Dougal that we faced a few skinny elves. I go on.'

'These are obviously not the ones that killed Krith and the others,' Herid continued. 'Tell me what you think these ones were doing?'

'They were probably checking to make sure no-one followed their tracks, which they were right to do,' Fargesh would not be persuaded.

Herid remained silent for a time.

'We go on then,' he didn't sound very sure still. 'But if we see an army of these things, we will be going back.'

Fargesh grunted as he pushed past the others.

'Single file again,' Herid ordered, as he took up position just below Fargesh.

They walked for another twenty minutes, slower now and even more cautious. Herid was relieved he didn't need to ask Fargesh to slow down. For all his anger and urgency, he was still an experienced hunter and knew that carelessness came from haste.

He wanted to find his son, but he wasn't going to risk all their lives unnecessarily.

A hand gesture had them all crouching where they stood.

Herid slowly made his way forward until he was level with Fargesh.

'Can you feel that?' he whispered.

Herid nodded.

'There is an army coming,' Fargesh said. Herid could see the disappointment in his face. 'You should all return now.'

'We should all return now,' Herid said.

'I will wait for them to pass. If the children are not with them, I will continue on.' Fargesh looked less angry now, as if he had been warring within himself up until now.

'That will be your death,' Herid pleaded. 'We have a better chance of defeating them at home. Then we all come back and wipe them from the mountains for good. If the children are still alive, we will find them.'

'I will wait for them to pass,' Fargesh repeated, 'now get going!' he hissed, 'before it is too late.'

Herid stopped his reply, grabbing Fargesh tightly on the forearm.

'I will see you again soon,' he said, before moving stealthily back to the others.

Fargesh watched them go, before huddling down in the snow.

Hopefully he didn't have to wait too long. He was eager to kill some more of them.

Herid and the others hadn't walked far, when Freta again motioned to the others that she had seen something. Only this time it was below them, and this time they had been seen first. These elves had been waiting for them.

Four of them were mounted on some kind of creature with no arms. The rest were spread out around them. He estimated at least fifty elves stood between them and their village much further down the slopes.

'One of us needs to make it through,' Herid said. 'We run sideways as fast as our legs will take us. Keep going until you think it safe to head down. Hopefully we can spread them out enough so one or two of us only have a couple to fight past.' He spoke quickly, but all of them understood what was required.

'Get to Horned Peak,' he said. 'Warn the tribe!' he hollered, as they all set off as fast as they could through the treacherous snow.

One of them had taken only a few steps, when an arrow through his neck dropped him to the ground.

Herid glanced down the slope and saw that none of the elves had moved up towards them yet. They were moving easily over the snow, keeping pace with the barbarians as they tried to flee.

Realising the hopelessness of their situation Herid changed tact, and headed straight towards them.

Screaming his battle cry, he took two arrows to the chest before he had gotten halfway to where the elves stood. The third one pierced his heart, while the tenth one finally brought him down.

Barking orders, the Dark-Elf Captain set off to kill the remaining few barbarians.

He would ensure none of them made it past.

His elder would prefer the barbarians were not warned of their impending annihilation.

He had never failed her before. This would be no different.

CHAPTER 45

No Choice But To Rule

R AIF HAD DECIDED before he left the cave of the *louckrift*, that it wouldn't matter if he made a spectacle of himself when they got back to the village.

A show of such wealth and power generally got a goblin killed and the treasure stolen, but he had no fears within his own home. Those with him had been given a fair share of what they found, and there was still more to give to others with strength and influence.

Word would quickly reach the main goblin settlement, and when it did he would be getting visitors. What sort of visitors and their intent wouldn't be known until they arrived.

Unless the entire main settlement stormed his village, Raif was confident he would be able to kill off any challengers.

As he approached the outskirts of his home, Raif wasn't really sure of the reception he would receive. He could see a huge bonfire already burning strongly in the centre, several animals of various sorts staked to the ground. Much of the good meat had already been ripped from their carcasses, but he hadn't expected anything less. They had taken their time collecting the treasures and hiding those they couldn't yet carry back with them.

They all went silent as he and the others entered. Goblins stopped what they were doing and turned to look at their triumphant leader as he strode in with those goblins who had chosen to stay with him

outside the cave. He knew how resplendent they looked, dressed
as they were in mythical armours decorated with jewels, gold and
silver. Much of it didn't fit the wearers, but those who now possessed
it didn't much care.

When some of the goblins caught sight of the makeshift carts
being pulled behind them, stacked high with more treasures, they
suddenly burst into cheer and began moving forward to see what
they could grab.

'Stay where you are!' Raif bellowed

Most listened, but a few ignored his command.

One of those was Grath, a large goblin who had fought with
them, but chose to return before the treasure was found.

He walked up to Raif, his chest puffed out.

'I killed, so I get my share,' he said, moving to walk past Raif.

Raif put out a hand and shoved it into his chest.

'I will decide who gets what. This is going to sit outside my shack
until I have had my fill of food and drink.'

Grath didn't seem pleased with that.

'I'll take my share and you can give the rest what is left,' he
snarled, swatting away Raif's hand. Two of his brothers had stepped
forward to stand behind him. Both had their weapons out and murder
in their eyes.

Raif growled softly under his breath, before pulling a jewelled
dagger from the sheath below his left rib-cage and shoving it deep
into Grath's eye. He moved so fast, the two brothers only had time
to raise their swords, before Raif had stepped forward past the falling
body of Grath. Drawing a second dagger from the sheath under his
right rib-cage, he thrust forward with both, each embedding itself
in the throat of a goblin.

Their downward sword strikes stopped dead, as all power left
their dying bodies. Gurgling on their own blood, both of Grath's
brothers collapsed on to the ground.

Raif spun in a quick circle as he deftly put away his bloodied
daggers and drew his sword.

Satisfied there were no more immediate threats, he stood still
once more.

'There is now more to share for all you lot!', he roared. 'Unless another one of you stinking goblins wants to try and take some before I have eaten!'

There was silence for a time, before one of the younger goblins walked over to a carcass and ripped off the entire front leg. Walking it over, he handed the bloodied stump to his village Chieftain.

A huge roar erupted as Raif tore a chunk off with his teeth, before raising it in the air in triumph.

The ones dragging the cart moved off, while the others went to get something to eat and tell those who had stayed behind how they individually were responsible for the death of all the monsters they had feared so much.

'Stay with them until I send someone else to do it,' Raif said, as the ones with the carts passed him. He could see the anger coming from them at having to stand guard while the others celebrated, but none were stupid enough to argue with him. 'And if any of you take anything else..' He left the rest unsaid. Letting a goblin imagine what might happen was sometimes more effective than actually telling it what would happen.

They stalked off slowly, as Raif turned to find something else to eat and drink.

It was going to be a long time before he got any rest.

It did not take long for the word of Raif's exploits and treasure hove to spread.

His village was only a few hours' ride from the main settlement, and the first of those curious goblins arrived early the following afternoon.

There were only about fifty of them in the first party, with their leader Prelch at the head of them. They came to see if the stories were true or whether some goblin had been knocked on the head a few too many times and made most of it up.

Prelch was one of the older goblins who had always coveted the main Chieftain title, but had never had enough support. He was cagey though, which was why he had lived so long.

Raif had never liked him much, and he was fairly sure Prelch felt the same about him. All goblins in these parts had known Prelch had not been favoured by Greeble, and Greeble had been Raif's brother.

'What do you want?' Raif asked, as he stood outside his hovel. Prelch had been brought into the centre of the village, while the fifty he came with had remained at the outskirts.

'Just wanted to see if the story was true,' Prelch replied. 'Looks like you have done well for yourself.'

Raif piled on as many jewels as he could before greeting Prelch, and had strapped on so many weapons it had been a little cumbersome just walking out to meet the other goblin.

'We get what we earn,' Raif said casually. 'And I have lots more.'

He could see little anger coming from the goblin standing in front of him. He assumed there would be more confusion and suspicion than there would be anger until he made sense of it all. Raif liked to keep his enemies guessing, and this goblin was definitely his enemy.

'It looks pretty, but how is the quality? Were there magical items found in the hoard?'

Raif was surprised how quickly Prelch got to the point, and that he assumed Raif would answer any of his questions.

'Are you wanting a demonstration,' Raif asked.

Prelch curled his lip. 'No,' he said.

'Then piss off!' Raif said. 'You've had your look, now you can scurry back and tell them all in that stinking cesspool what you saw.'

'Thought you were smarter than that Raif,' Prelch said. He didn't appear put off at all by Raif's words.

Raif didn't answer. He wanted the other goblin to talk now.

'If you want to be Chieftain you will need help to rule the Great Horde.'

This goblin was delusional, Raif thought.

There hadn't been a Great Horde for many hundreds of years.

It was a term used to describe the entire goblin population coming together to invade another realm. Any goblin with half a brain knew it was impossible to get them all together in one army without half of them trying to kill the other half.

Raif didn't bite though. He knew Prelch was trying to get him to talk to see what his intentions were.

He chuckled before responding. 'Any Chieftain probably would need help to rule the Great Horde. If he was stupid enough to try.'

'If what you've found is as great as I have heard, it could be done,' Prelch persisted.

'I didn't "*find*" it,' Raif said, getting a little angry now. 'I "*won*" it by killing the *louckrift*! No other goblin was able to do it. I killed them!'

He pointed at the heads of the blood-drainers, now planted outside his shack on huge spikes.

'You would have died with the rest of yours if you had tried,' Raif continued.

'Maybe,' Prelch said, sounding unimpressed. 'But I never got the chance to try.'

'You can challenge me if you like,' Raif said, his temper subsiding. He liked the thought of smashing in Prelch's skull.

'Challenge you for what?' Prelch exclaimed. 'This scummy village in the middle of nowhere.'

'No,' Raif said, smiling as he spoke now. 'Challenge for the treasures I have brought back, and the rest of it that is hidden further away.'

He didn't care that goblins would know there was more. They would come just for what he had now anyway. Let them come, he thought. None of them would be able to get enough goblins together to threaten him. They would be too busy fighting themselves on the way here.

Looking behind Prelch, he saw Shathez walking towards him, waving his arms to get his attention.

He didn't even hear what Prelch said next, waving Shathez forward.

'Qalz is here, with about as many as this one brought.'

'Bring him in then,' Raif said. Looking across at Prelch, he could see the anger bubbling out of him now.

Qalz was huge for a goblin, both in height and muscle. He had been Greeble's strongest enforcer before his death. His job had been to make sure any of those who opposed him were dealt with. Qalz had been very good at his job.

Apparently, he now saw himself as Chieftain material. Raif was curious to see what he had to say. He would not dismiss him as easily as he had Prelch, and he didn't plan on antagonising him.

Unless the goblin said stupid things. He was a tough one and quick to anger.

'Raif,' Qalz said, completely ignoring Prelch.

'Qalz,' Raif said. 'What do you want?'

'I wanted to see what you had found, and whether it was going to help me as Chieftain.' At least he didn't stuff around. Straight to the point.

'Help you how?' Raif said.

'If it is powerful like they say, I'll take back what I need.' Qalz had absolutely no fear. Raif guessed no fear came with stupid sometimes.

'Much of it is both magical and powerful,' Raif said. 'More than you will be able to take back with you.'

'Then your goblins will help,' Qalz said. 'Get them to pile it up and I'll have a look through it.'

Raif had quickly realised during his conversation with both Prelch and Qalz, that no goblins in the main settlement were ever going to take him seriously. They were going to keep coming, and he realised that he would need to keep killing them.

He wasn't overly worried about having to do that, but what now concerned him were Prelch's words about the Great Horde.

Eventually those in the main settlement and all of the other smaller villages around, would grow tired of Raif killing goblins.

Although none of them really got along, they were all from the same place and one of them might be lucky enough to get them together to form some kind of Great Horde. Raif had found a lot of treasure after all.

If that descended upon him, magic armour and weapons would not be enough to stop them.

The constant attacks would also deplete his village to the point where his own might turn on him.

Holding in a sigh, Raif came to the realisation he needed to think bigger.

He had shown off his wealth and power to them now, which meant they would not stop trying to get it from him.

Raif would have to do more than show them how powerful he was. He needed to get more than fear into them. But for now, it would have to do. With fear his power would grow.

He would also need those who would help his power grow, so that others would stop coming for him.

Although he had never previously coveted the title of Chieftain, he had learnt a little bit from when Greeble first took over. He needed allies and he needed to look after them.

That meant he would need to share more of the treasure, which made him a little sick in the stomach.

'Are you going to wait all day before you get the carts loaded?' Qalz asked. 'Get me some drink while I wait.'

Raif hadn't realised they were all waiting for him to say something. He had been lost in his thoughts.

Removing a few of the more cumbersome items from around his person, Raif placed them in a small pile behind him.

Qalz obviously thought he was beginning the pile he had demanded, as he stood silently watching.

'Prelch, step back,' he said, as he finished removing what he didn't need. He looked at the goblin, who narrowed his eyes before stepping away.

'Are you the new Chieftain already?' Raif asked Qalz.

'I have claimed it,' he said, 'and none have been stupid enough to challenge me.'

'Then call me stupid,' Raif said. 'This won't take long,' he said, looking over at Prelch. 'I have a Great Horde to organise.'

Prelch shook his head slowly. The look on his face left no doubt. He thought Raif insane.

'That will be hard when you are dead,' Prelch said, taking a few more steps back.

'You want to fight me?!' Qalz eventually said. It had taken a while for it to sink in. 'Just give me the treasure and I will leave this stink-hole.'

'Just draw your weapon Qalz so I can kill you, you stupid, stupid goblin. I will be shocked if you even have a brain when I cut your head open.'

The anger that burst forth from his opponent was intense.

Raif began drawing it in the moment he saw it, also drawing his sword as he did.

There wasn't time for him to draw enough energy to weaken Qalz however, as the hulking goblin lifted up the massive pole-arm he held and swung it. The head had a large axe-blade on one side, with a curved point on the reverse.

Raif underestimated the speed with which Qalz moved, and if it weren't for the full body chain-mail he now wore, he would have lost his arm, as the blade tried to bite deep into his bicep.

Raif gave a yelp of surprise and pain, but the armour stopped it from cutting him. Instead he was left with a numbness from his shoulder all the way down to his fingers. If it had been his sword arm, he would have been in a lot more trouble, but he recovered quickly and swung his sword in a wide arc at Qalz's torso. Qalz was quick and was able to swipe it aside with his weapon.

Raif would have pulled one of his daggers if his arm had worked properly, but it was still dangling uselessly at his side, completely numb.

He stepped back instead, hoping to move out of reach of his opponent, but the length of Qalz's weapon allowed the other goblin to step forward and drive it into Raif's stomach. He doubled-over, looking up just in time to see the axe-head come hammering down on to his helmet.

He expected to see stars and then the nothingness of death, but the blade simply slid off the helmet. He knew it had been a straight blow, and should have carved his head open.

The surprise on Qalz's face was clear to see, as he paused for a moment. It was all the time Raif needed to step forward and drive his sword up through the bottom of his opponent's chin, embedding itself in his skull.

The giant goblin fell limp, as Raif quickly drew his sword back, allowing Qalz's body to fall to the ground.

Like swinging an axe, he spliced open the dead goblin's head, before falling to his knees in front of his vanquished foe.

Although Raif was still reeling from the contest and had fallen because he was winded from the last blow to his stomach, he tried to make it look like he was casually inspecting the goblin's head. After a short rest, he looked up at the other goblins standing around.

'Seems he did have a brain,' Raif said. 'Although it looks on the small side.'

Roars of deep laughter broke out among those looking on, as Raif gingerly got to his feet.

'I don't like you Prelch, but you will probably be useful to me. Send word that there is a new Chieftain of your goblin settlement.

Yours will share in the spoils of that which I have hidden. Do what you do best and let them all know it is time the goblin's rode out in a Great Horde once more!'

The cheers continued for a while, none of them waiting to hear if Prelch had anything to say.

Eventually it died down and Raif spoke again.

'Shathez, take all the men you can muster with Prelch. Slaughter all of those that came with Qalz. We don't need any of them coming back for any stupid revenge killings.' He looked across at Prelch. 'Yours will help with the killing.'

Prelch nodded. 'I would like that,' he said, smiling.

'Until next time great Chieftain,' he said with a small bow, before turning and walking off.

'Get me something to drink,' Raif snarled at one of the younger goblins standing around. He ran off to do his Chieftain's bidding.

Taking off his helmet, Raif looked in wonder at it. Not a mark was left on it. Incredible, he thought, as the feeling slowly began coming back into his left arm.

After relieving his bladder on the fallen goblin, he turned around and went back into his shack.

He had some thinking to do, after deciding it might be smarter not to make so many rash, 'spur-of-the-moment' decisions in future.

CHAPTER 46

To Rule Is Hell

K ING DAYHEN RODE into High Fort, his army trailing not too
far behind him.
They had marched throughout the previous day and long
into the night before finally making camp.

The men of his realm had fought along this front for hundreds
of years and the tracks they walked and rode on were well known to
the older men within their ranks. Even through the forest they had
made good time, a well-worn roadway long ago designed to cater
for so many men moving at once.

It was early morning on the following day when reports reached
him that Kritch and his army had stopped on the plains before
the gate of the High Fort and had immediately moved into battle
formations.

He had been shocked when he heard it.

Why would any army choose to make their main assault at a
place such as this?

If their roles had been reversed, Dayhen would never dream of
such an act. He would be sending his men into a slaughter. It was as
simple as that.

He would need only a fraction of his army to defend the walls
of High Fort.

That report had come while his army was still a couple of hours away from where he now rode into.

His first call was to the northern fort, so he could see his enemy for himself and ensure they were still there.

Climbing the steps, he eventually reached the outside wall and looked down upon the waiting army of the Western Realm.

Even seeing it with his own eyes, he could hardly believe it.

Kritch had never shown himself to be a master strategist in past battles, but this was beyond stupid, and he knew even Kritch was not that foolish. Especially if he had joined forces with Mithrak.

The Dark-Mage was a lot smarter than his Ogre-Mage ally.

So why were they here?

'Why choose here?' Bilsont echoed in his ear.

'That is a question we need to answer very quickly,' Dayhen replied. 'It makes no sense.'

'It does if they choose not to attack,' Thaiden said, having also made the climb with his King and the head of the King's Shield.

'Why would he line his army up and ready them for battle, and then not attack?' Dayhen asked, realising the answer before Thaiden began to reply.

'To draw us away from Mithrak and his army,' his commander answered. 'And to draw us out from behind these walls to fight them on the plain below.'

Dayhen put his head forward and ran his hands through his hair, before standing straight up again and looking across at his friend.

'We have been played Thaiden, but in a way which gave us little option.'

He turned back to look out upon their foes.

'We will lose many, many lives here today, but we have no choice. We cannot delay. The elves will not be able to hold back all of Mithrak's army.'

Thaiden made no reply. He waited for his King to give his orders.

'Let them rest for a short time when they get here and then have them ready to march out through the gate. This will be a battle for the ages my friend,' he said, turning and clasping his commander on the shoulder. 'When it is over, I would like Kritch's head planted on a spike in this very spot.'

'It will be done my King,' Bilsont said, before turning and making his way back down the steps. Thaiden gave a curt bow and followed after.

Since arriving back with the body of Valdor, Bilsont had kept himself busy. When he was called upon by his King, his advice was short but sincere.

Dayhen liked it this way. He did not need too many voices in his ears. Especially not now.

He looked back one more time at the army awaiting them.

Too many lives, he thought, as he too made his way off the wall.

Linf had quickly grown bored, but was still pleased with the progress she was able to make. The potential her powers gave her; and the many ways she could see it being used; raised some hope within her that she might yet survive the coming battle.

'If that battle ever came' she said to no-one.

They had been standing in the same spot for hours and nothing had changed.

'Seriously, what are we waiting for?' she asked in a louder voice.

Rark continued to ignore her, but she had managed to draw from him the tiniest tendrils of anger the last couple of times she asked. Not enough to grasp hold of, but she was pleased to see something. There was at least the potential to push him far enough.

He was obviously growing tired of waiting also.

The rustle of armour of those to her right had grown louder the longer they waited. It had drawn a few curious looks from her Lava-Orc companion, but Linf thought nothing of it.

The day wasn't cold and there were no clouds in the sky, so it made sense they would be getting hot standing around in all that armour.

Linf chuckled to herself.

She had no fancy armour, so she was comfortable standing under the sun. Stupid creatures. They probably weren't even going to get a chance to fight. They would all just stand around for the rest of the day in their smelly armour, sweating and crapping on themselves.

Suddenly voices began to ring out amongst Kritch's army.

Those who had been sitting or slouching on their weapons all stood up straight again.

Linf looked out across the plains and saw what had drawn their attention.

The gates to the human walls had opened and men began marching out of it.

Linf's emotions swung from relief to nervousness, before settling on determination.

Whatever happened out there today, she would be walking out of here. No stinking man was going to end her life.

'Get in front of me,' Rark said to Linf, bringing her out of her thoughts.

Linf moved slowly to stand in front of the giant Lava-Orc, before being shoved hard in the back.

'When the Ve-Karn and their ogre-mage move forward, so do you,' he said.

'When who moves forward?' she asked. Was she supposed to know what a Ve-Karn was?

'The ones there in the dark armour are Ve-Karn,' he said, pointing to the smelly warriors on her right.

'Can they fight?' she asked.

'They are supposed to be Mithrak's finest,' Rark said, but there was something in his voice that gave her concern about their actual abilities. 'But like I told you before, none of them will look to help you goblin. You will die alone out there today.'

Linf looked back to the men filing out of the gate. First came the ones on horses, riding to the side as they exited. Then men on foot, who stood in front of the horses in several rows. When the gates finally closed behind them, the army of men stood facing them.

Linf could tell there were not as many in their army as Kritch had in his, but there was still a lot of them. At present, they were higher up than where she stood, but the ground soon levelled out. She hoped Kritch would wait for them to come down before attacking.

Amongst them would be those with magic, which didn't concern Linf as much as the others she knew would be with them. There would probably be many of the ones without emotion in their army.

They were the ones she needed to try and avoid if she hoped to get through this alive.

She remembered they didn't wear any of the fancy armour. Leather was all they had on. Remembering how they fought, it was probably all they needed.

Linf turned to look back at Rark. A couple of the chained orcs now stood before him, their faces blank and the blood seemingly gone from their faces. Linf had never seen such fear before.

'Where will the ones with no armour fight?' she asked the Lava-Orc.

'Ah,' he said smiling. 'You know of the humans King's Shield.'

'Do they stay with their King?' Linf asked. That would make it easy she thought. The King would be at the back, like Kritch was.

'They will most likely be sent against the Ve-Karn,' Rark said.

Linf turned around again. That was not good.

'Eyes in the back of your head goblin,' Rark said, taunting her one last time.

'Forward!' a different voice hollered from behind her. The Ve-Karn and Ogre-Mage began to walk in front of her and spread themselves across the front of the army.

Linf wasn't pushed forward this time. She was allowed to stand behind the row of Ve-Karn in front of her.

'You will move when they move,' Rark said. 'If you try to run or fall behind, I will take both of your legs out from under you.'

Linf turned and managed a short nod and a snarl, before turning back to the front.

'And when I say take them from under you, I mean I will chop them off from just below the knees.'

Linf didn't turn this time. She continued to look forward and bunch the energy in front of her. The time had come to see just how powerful she had become.

When they were finally lined up, another voice screamed out a command and the army of Kritch began to move forward.

The solitary goblin within that army moved off with them.

Dayhen stood up in his stirrups, surveying his army and the one now slowly moving towards them.

Their numbers were certainly greater than his own, but he knew his forces would prevail. His soldiers were better fighters than the ogres, orcs and other misbegotten creatures within Kritch's army.

He also had his full complement of King's Shield with him. It was something he had been loath to do, but his hand had been forced. He hoped beyond hope they would be the difference in limiting the number of deaths his army would sustain. Bilsont had asked his King if he could be at the front of them. Dayhen had been surprised at the request and had hesitated in his response, before allowing him to do it. He realised he did not need to fear for the welfare of the man. Losing Valdor had made him hesitate, but he knew he could not afford to try and protect anyone. Every man and woman would probably be needed to fight before this war was over.

Turning his attention back to the battle at hand, Dayhen knew the King's Shield needed to despatch the Ve-Karn horde as quickly as possible so they could assist in killing the rest of Kritch's army.

His magic-users were stronger than the Ogre-Mage, whose spells were limited to those of destruction.

On the open field, the Ogre-Mage will be dangerous and had the potential to kill many of his soldiers, but he had faith in Derekia and his order. Dayhen had seen his most powerful wizard fight Ogre-Mage before, and he had been devastating to watch.

They would use shields first to counter the arrows and fiery rocks thrown by the trolls, before the combat closed in and his wizards could unleash their own spells of destruction.

He was wary as to how Mithrak had convinced Kritch to separate their armies and face him without the support of the Dark-Mage.

Obviously the Ve-Karn had been one such sweetener, but he knew the Ogre-Mage would have wanted more.

Derekia had been made aware of his concerns, but had shrugged them off in his usual manner.

'My wizards will wipe their mage from the field of battle', he had said. 'They will have no tricks to help them here today.'

Dayhen had wanted to say more, but his wizard's arrogance was a great reason behind their strength in battle. Their belief in their own abilities limited their fear.

Until something went wrong, Dayhen thought.

He hoped today was not the day that happened.

Turning to his trusted friend he gave the order to advance.

Plans had been discussed and then discussed some more, until Dayhen was satisfied each of his leaders knew exactly what was expected of them.

Bilsont knew his role. He had been in more battles throughout his life than any other man present here today. Dayhen had no concerns in regards to his Shield. They would fight and kill as they had always done.

Thaiden was to lead those on foot, both soldier and archer, while he was in charge of the cavalry.

Despite protests from all of those in his war counsel, he would have it no other way. If his men were prepared to give their lives, he should be no different.

He had visualised the battle in his head too many times to count and felt that victory was assured. Yet there was always a constant nagging doubt in the back of his mind.

Why was Kritch so confident in battling them here of all places?

What did the Ogre-Mage have that he wasn't yet aware of?

Sighing deeply, Dayhen dug his heels gently into the belly of his horse, as he followed his army down on to the plain below.

If there was something, he would soon find out.

Kritch's army stopped well before the ground evened out. He would not give Dayhen the advantage of coming at them downhill.

As pleased as he had been to see the humans march from behind their walls, it was still going to be a massive effort to defeat them. He needed an even playing field if he was to win his victory here today.

Looking out at his army spread before him, he would find out shortly whether it was to pass.

He would have preferred Mithrak to have his army here with his own, but if he had been, they would never have marched out to meet him.

It had taken a great deal of convincing to let Kritch take his Ve-Karn, and even more persuading to get the few Lava-Orcs he had been given. In the end, he had gotten more from Mithrak than the stupid mage had wanted to give him.

Kritch smiled as he thought back on how he had out-smarted him.

Mithrak thought him foolish enough to sacrifice his own army so the dark-mage could wander through the forest of elves and out the back. Kritch had been the smart one though.

Not only did he get the Ve-Karn and Lava-Orcs, but each of his archers had been given a quiver of dwarven-wrought arrows from the Western Mountains. Mithrak had accidently let slip that the dwarves had been helping to supply his army. Kritch had demanded his share, and he had finally worn him down.

Now that the time was here and his army was lined up against those of the human realm, he was confident of victory. Dayhen wouldn't know what had hit him until it was too late.

Smiling, he waited until the other army reached the flat of the plain in front of him.

Raising his hand, he roared a command.

'Kill them all!'

Those in charge of his army turned from him the moment his arm swung down, and gave the order to advance.

'Finally,' Kritch said to those standing his guard. 'At last we will win through to the rich and fat lands beyond these stinking towers. Watch and enjoy,' he said, as the first volley of arrows arced towards his enemy.

Linf continued to walk behind those in front of her, as they marched steadily towards the forces coming against them.

She had expected a frantic charge at full speed, but as the arrows flew over her head, she saw why large-scale battles were fought differently to small skirmishes.

She watched on in disappointment as the arrows hit an invisible barrier above their opposing army and fell harmlessly to the ground below.

Surely these idiots knew that wasn't going to work.

As a return volley headed their way, she waited for them to hit a similar barrier. To her horror, there was no such barrier. Instead she heard the screams of pain, as many of the arrows found their mark.

The shield she had been practising saved her own skin from a couple of those arrows. She was extremely relieved to see them bounce off it, but it took valuable time away from building up her attacking balls of energy.

She then heard several loud calls behind her; above the cries of agony; and another volley of useless arrows flew out over her head.

To her surprise, many of these flew straight through the shields of the human wizards. She was able to see several of them hit their targets this time, much to the pleasure of those in front of her, who cheered their success.

Sneaky, Linf thought with a smile. She liked sneaky.

It was now the turn of the trolls to throw their own large, burning projectiles. They looked like rocks that were on fire, as they soared above her head.

Linf quickly turned her attention to the second round of arrows shot by the humans. Her shield again stopped any from striking her, although a few in front of her screamed out in agony again. Even with small shields, some of them were too stupid to stop an arrow from hitting them.

The trolls' first volley also bounced off the invisible shield, the same as the first lot of arrows. Dumb, stupid trolls, she thought, as she turned to look at them.

As she was shaking her head at them in disgust, her attention was drawn to where Rark stood.

One other Lava-Orc stood with him, next to a couple of trolls. The other Lava-Orcs must have moved further along the line.

The two Lava-Orcs had their hands wrapped around the head of a small child orc, the same ones who had been tied up. Linf could see the head begin to glow red, as Rark and the other one spoke quietly. She could see their lips moving but couldn't hear the words. It looked like they were chanting something. It didn't go for long, before each of the Lava-Orcs ripped the head from the child in front of them. Cupping the neck underneath as they continued to chant, each put their severed head on to the sling of a troll.

The troll didn't hesitate in flinging the glowing heads at the approaching army.

Following them as they flew through the air, Linf watched on as they shattered against the invisible barrier. But instead of falling harmlessly to the ground, whatever substance was inside the young orc's skulls, sprayed through the shield, landing on those standing behind it.

Linf could hear the screams of pain coming from the human army.

It was grotesque what they had done, but Linf was in awe. Rark had turned the head of that child orc into a ball of lava. His skin colour was not where he got the name from.

Those in front of her began to run now, as the armies closed in on each other.

Linf took the time to look back one more time at the giant Lava-Orc, who just happened to be looking in her direction.

He smiled at her, as he reached forward to grab hold of another orc child cowering in front of him.

Linf couldn't help but nod in respect, as she began pooling the energy in front of her. Turning back once more, she began to run in order to keep up with those in front of her.

She didn't want Rark firing one of those lava skulls in her direction.

CHAPTER 47

Make It Burn

'IS HE BACK yet?' Mithrak asked again.

'No,' Rastiss replied once more.

'He should have been back by now,' Mithrak said. His frustration was almost at breaking point. Jurg would have easily finished checking the readiness of his army. The only thing delaying him would be word of Kritch's position.

'Should we not go anyway,' Cordak said. 'The human army has followed him as you predicted. There will be nothing to stop us when we get through.'

'If I wanted to do that, don't you think I would have given the order already!' Mithrak snarled. Maybe he should have sent Cordak north. What an idiot!

The others remained silent, as Jurg was finally seen making his way up the rise to them.

'Here he comes King Mithrak,' Thrisc said, pointing in the direction of the Ve-Karn General.

'Are the Ve-Karn armoured again and ready?' Mithrak asked, as Jurg stopped in front of him.

'Of course, my King,' he said bowing. 'Word has reached us that Kritch has stopped in front of the High-Gates.'

'Excellent,' Mithrak said, a large smile on his face now.

The ogre-mage had been so easy to manipulate. Now his stupidity would be his undoing and at the same time, weaken the forces of King Dayhen.

Yet even Mithrak could not have hoped for the Ogre-Mage to be so easily fooled. Kritch's army now stood in front of the most formidable fortress along the entire border. How stupid could anyone be?!

Mithrak would not need to wait and hear what happened next. He knew already that Dayhen would not hide behind his walls. He would need to destroy Kritch's army so he could make his way back to defend his home against what was coming.

It was a shame he had to sacrifice a dozen of his Lava-Orc and the Ve-Karn who had accompanied them, but theirs was a sacrifice worth paying.

It would mean Kritch was no longer around to annoy him and it would ensure Dayhen received some heavy casualties. He wished he could be there when his Lava-Orc launched their first attack, but he was able to visualise it, so that would have to suffice.

If Kritch only knew how much more Mithrak had been prepared to offer him to send his army south, the Ogre-Mage would probably cry.

'Then we are ready,' he said.

He had thought about a speech, but it really wasn't necessary yet. He would wait until he was sitting on Dayhen's throne.

'It is time for the forest to burn,' Mithrak said, as he strode down the hill and walked in amongst his forward army.

The Ve-Karn moved aside to let their King and his other Dark-Mage through, until the only thing standing between the forest and himself was fifty paces of grass.

'Thrisc to the left, Rastiss right. Cordak, you are to remain with the rear army. When all is ready Thrisc, give the signal.' Both Dark-Mage nodded their heads and moved off to where they had been ordered.

Mithrak waited patiently for Thrisc to get into position.

A scorching fire-ball soared into the sky from the direction Thrisc had moved to, about two hundred paces away.

Looking up, the dark-mage couldn't help but smile.

When another fireball was seen in the distance, he turned back to face the forest.

Now it was his turn to wait.

Minutes past until Thrisc saw another fireball in the sky to the north. It was the signal he had been waiting for.

It meant those at the most Northern part of the forest had begun their attack into the trees. Led by Jeosh, the trees surrounding where they entered should be burning by now. He had been ordered not to enter until the smoke was thick enough for the elves to see.

Thrisc was hoping to be able to see it all the way from where they stood.

It was unlikely, but it was a clear day, so there was a chance.

Although Mithrak had not said why they were to wait, the reason seemed obvious to Thrisc.

They waited while Jeosh and his horde of orcs and half-goblins drew those elves who remained to his position. That would allow those that stood with Mithrak to move through the trees as quickly as possible and make their way behind the armies of Dayhen.

Thrisc disagreed with what they were about to do, but he was not in charge.

Why Mithrak had insisted, seemed to counteract what Jeosh was doing in the north. He suspected it was so Mithrak could kill some of the elves himself and may have something to do with his basic destructive nature.

Regardless of the true motive, they were going to burn the forest and kill anything they came across.

Thrisc hoped the elves had been decimated, as reported.

If not, this may be a very short trip.

Everyone knew what happened to those who ventured inside this forest without invitation.

He suspected the number of intruders would not really make much difference. The forest itself could very well be magic. None of them would know any different, not even Mithrak.

Even from this distance he could see nothing of what lay inside. It was unnatural, and despite Mithrak's confidence, his own had diminished somewhat now that he stood this close to it.

There was a reason why none ever came out alive.

Steeling himself, Thrisc decided the time had arrived. It was best if they just got this over and done with.

Moving even closer to the forest, Thrisc took out the amulet hanging around his neck. Pressing a small button, the dark gemstone clicked free.

He looked down at the obsidian in his palm, surrounded by an even darker metal. Even now he could not believe such a small object contained so much power.

Closing his hand over it and holding it out in front, he spoke a few words and a ray of intense heat burst forth from it.

Widening as it went, the blue fire tore into the trees before him, sending them bursting into flame the moment it struck.

The fire continued to pore forth from the amulet as the flame tore deeper and deeper into the forest. After less than a minute it stopped and he stepped back to look at the destruction it had caused.

Smoke billowed for a great distance inside, while the fires spread on either side of its trajectory. He looked across and saw the destruction Rastiss had created was just as devastating on his side.

They would not be surprised by any elves, if there had been any watching them from inside the trees.

He began walking back to where Mithrak stood at the front of his army, his hand held out toward the burning forest.

As he stood next to his King again, with Rastiss already stationary on his other side, Thrisc watched in awe as Mithrak unleashed the power of his amulet.

Unlike those he had given to his Dark-Mage, his had two gems contained within it.

It blazed out before them all, a light-blue beam that shone bright in the daytime sunlight.

It was cold enough to burn if it touched flesh, but he used it now to put out the flames between where Thrisc and Rastiss had set the forest on fire.

Aside from putting the flames out, it exploded all of those trees it came into contact with.

The sounds were deafening, as ancient trunks burst apart from the intense cold and the wood hissed where the fires were extinguished.

Once Mithrak had finished and let his hand fall to his side once more, there was a shattered path of sorts for them to enter. Although tree trunks and branches were scattered debris in their way, it was much preferable to walking under the trees.

Jurg went and stood behind his King, as Mithrak placed the amulet back around his neck.

Turning around, the hulking Ve-Karn gave the signal to move out, as his Ve-Karn soldiers began to stride past him, trailed by other dark-mage and the rest of Mithrak's army.

The conquest of Glorfiden and the realm of men had begun.

Taking up his position behind his King, Thrisc looked across at Rastiss as he stood next to him.

All animosity seemed to have been forgotten by his fellow Dark-Mage.

For now, he looked to be enjoying this as much as their King was.

Thrisc, however. was suddenly filled with a crushing dread, as he made his first step into the legendary Elven forest.

He felt genuine fear for the first time he could remember.

CHAPTER 48

Not Always For Glory

KABIR SAW THEM coming before those on guard duty did. Faggots of wood had been lit twenty paces out from where the wagons and carts had been set up as a token barrier, in case they were set upon. It was intended to give those inside some small amount of cover.

Whether he had a better view, or the guards were asleep, it was the Barbarian who sounded the alarm.

'We are beset upon!' he roared. None within the camp would have failed to hear him, but there was minimal movement.

The shadows that crept up to the flames now extinguished them, as they advanced on the wagons and carts. Fortunately, there were other fires lit around the camp, so they were not left in total darkness.

Quickly looking down, Kabir was surprised to see Ahlia had not yet awoken.

Looking back toward the oncoming threat, he grabbed her shoulder and shook it. There was no response.

Looking down at her again, his heart skipped a beat. For a moment, he thought she may have died in her sleep. Panicked, he shook her shoulder again, this time with more vigour.

He could see her chest moving, and this time her eyes slowly opened.

Relieved, he stood up again, trying to peer past the wagons in front of him.

He still couldn't make out what was out there in the darkness. So far all he had seen were small shadows, but just because they weren't large, it did not mean they were not dangerous.

Groggily, Ahlia lifted herself up on to her elbows.

'What is going on?' she asked, irritation in her voice.

'We are under attack,' Kabir said. Looking around, he saw that most of the camp had still not yet awoken. There was definitely magic at play here.

Atriol came into view as Ahlia eventually got to her feet. He was moving briskly through the camp, trying to wake those he went past, but with little success.

He saw Kabir and Ahlia and moved quickly to stand next to them.

'What is going on?' Kabir asked him. The King's Shield seemed to know a lot about a lot of things. He would certainly have a better idea than two strangers to his land.

'It is why we like to have wizards travelling with us,' Atriol said. Kabir thought the man was chastising him for not having wizards, but the King's Shield continued before he could say anything in reply. 'They are able to negate the sleeping spell of those surrounding our camp. On their own, *Vigglers* are no threat. Simple thieves and scavengers, they take only what they need. I am surprised they would attempt to put everyone to sleep, but it means they could have someone or something pushing them to do it.'

'How are we awake?' Kabir asked, still not sure if Atriol had been chastising him. He decided to let it go.

'There are always those who are less susceptible to their spell. We King's Shield are one type,' Atriol explained.

'I guess we Barbarians are the same,' Kabir said in reply. He now understood the lack of any real urgency from Atriol. 'What do they steal?' he asked.

'Food and small weapons mainly. However, if there is something else driving them out there tonight, then we need to get the camp woken.' Atriol said. 'They may be a good deal more dangerous than *Vigglers*.'

'And what might that be?' Kabir asked. His urgency had increased as Atriol talked. Just prior to seeing the King's Shield, he had been about to walk over and confiscate the old man's sword. He didn't think Atriol would appreciate him doing that, so he remained weaponless.

'You best go and get yourself a weapon Kabir,' Atriol said. 'That old man's sword over there should suffice. In case we need to fight them.'

Kabir hesitated for a moment, before quickly striding over and grabbing the sword. He had been right about the quality, as he drew it from its sheath.

Ahlia quickly got herself a weapon and jogged over to join them. She seemed to have shrugged off her lethargy.

'The ones driving them will probably be *Korn*. It will depend how many there are as to whether they will decide to risk a fight. They are capable enough, but we should have no fear of them. When we have killed enough, the rest will flee.'

Kabir liked the man's confidence.

Looking out at the approaching shadows, he noticed they moved very slowly, apparently in no hurry.

They were almost close enough for Kabir to make out features, when suddenly all the lights in the camp went out.

Everything was very dark all of a sudden, and Kabir was not as confident as he had been a moment before.

'Do they see in the dark?' Kabir asked the King's Shield.

'The *Vigglers* do,' Atriol replied in a soft voice. 'It is why they are so good at thievery. The *Korn* do not.'

Looking to their right, all three saw a light moving towards them from the centre of the makeshift camp.

Lord Marcus strode quickly into view, another of the King's Shield at his side.

Kabir knew straight away why his light had not been extinguished, as he looked at the sword grasped in his right hand. Even though it was designed to be held two-handed, its light weight meant it could still be wielded with one.

'We need to scatter them quickly,' Marcus said, looking at Atriol, before turning his look to Kabir and Ahlia.

He looked about to say something more, before he stopped and turned towards the oncoming threat.

Atriol moved to stand beside him, while Kabir and Ahlia stood to his left.

They would all need the light of Marcus' torch to see what they were fighting.

'If we run through the *Korn* and get to the *Vigglers*, then more of our people will awaken as we kill them.' He spoke quickly, but clearly.

None of those with them questioned his plan.

Kabir would be happy just to find something to attack.

He decided the *Vigglers* didn't have to die. Knocking them out should suffice. They meant only to steal, which to him was not something worthy of killing them over.

If the *Korn* attacked him, that would be a whole different story. He didn't much like the sound of them.

They hadn't made it to the first of the outlying carts, when several of the *Korn* walked past it, the surprise on their faces clear from the shining torchlight.

Not one of them hesitated in turning tail and sprinting back the way they had come. They certainly hadn't looked very threatening. Only half the height of a tall man, they looked like a cross between a man and some kind of lizard. But not a scary lizard. Their weapons were also small and not frightening. A short, curved blade, not much longer than a dagger.

Yet for their size and stature, they still moved rather quickly when threatened. On foot, Kabir knew he would not catch them.

'With me!' Marcus said, as he took off after them. He was on a horse, so he would be able to catch up to them.

Kabir wasn't sure that was the smartest thing to do, but he really had no choice. He needed to go where the light went.

Following close behind for a short distance, he saw a few of the *Vigglers* come into view as the fleeing *Korn* sprinted straight past them.

They were even shorter and thinner than the *Korn*, and much less threatening still. Haggard looking and extremely hairy, the *Vigglers* otherwise looked human, but unfortunately for them, they weren't as quick to react as the *Korn* and not as swift.

Marcus drove his sword into the first two of them before they could get far, the King's Shield by his side despatching a couple more, as his Lord continued to pursue the fleeing *Korn*.

'Is there a need to kill the little ones?' Kabir said out loud, as he followed behind the others. 'And why do we chase the others?'

Lord Marcus suddenly stopped and turned on him. He had not been galloping, else his protection would not be able to keep up with him.

'You should not be armed,' he said, turning to face Atriol. 'Take their weapons,' he said.

Kabir was taken aback by the ferocity in his voice, but he surrendered his weapon to Atriol without argument. He was confident he wouldn't need a weapon now anyway.

Those attacking their camp were no real threat.

'Shall Ahlia and I return and help those who are asleep and probably being attacked while you chase these others?' Kabir asked. He spoke evenly and with respect, but there was no mistaking the undertone in his words.

Marcus looked ready to explode, before he managed to calm himself.

'We will patrol the perimeter,' he said to Atriol and the other King's Shield. 'Keep an eye out for any that may have entered among us already, and try to take down as many *Vigglers* as you can,' he said, staring straight at Kabir as he said the last part.

Marcus then took off back toward the front of the camp, his two Shield trailing closely behind.

Kabir and Ahlia remained where they were, as they tried to adjust their sight to the darkness. Now that they had been in the darkness a short time, Kabir was able to make out shapes, both stationary and those moving.

Walking silently, they moved back to the first of the carts, before standing still. Their ears were more valuable to them than their sight at present.

Shutting out the screams of pain coming from the front of the camp, where Marcus was wreaking havoc with his sword, Kabir listened for movement within their area.

He heard nothing, so they made their way back into camp.

Shaking some of those that slept, they awoke more easily this time.

'There are *Korn* and *Vigglers* among us,' he said to each one he woke up. He assumed they would know what they were, so didn't elaborate.

As the camp came awake, and torches were lit once more, Kabir was able to make out the shadowy forms of both creatures that had attacked them, making their way back into the shadows.

Only a few of the men were unable to be woken, their throats cut where they slept and their weapons taken from their corpses.

He was gladdened and surprised there were so few, as the *Korn* would have had enough time to kill more. Kabir knew he and Ahlia had probably saved more lives this night, but he wasn't chasing accolades. He knew better than to expect any gratitude from Lord Marcus, having seen a different side to him this evening.

Kabir had seen in his eyes how displeased Marcus had been when forced to change his mind on Kabir's fate, after Ahlia's threat to bring plainsmen warriors against them.

He still had not asked her if she seriously thought they would come to avenge him, as he didn't want to risk insulting her again by asking such a stupid question. Best if he believed everything she said from now on. Better his pride be dented instead.

'Your turn to get some sleep,' Ahlia said to him, a large smile on her face. 'I think I have had enough for tonight.'

He smiled back at her, before nodding his head and walking back over to where they had been resting earlier.

Kabir was definitely tired. Hopefully they wouldn't be getting up too early in the morning.

They were up before the sun had risen above the horizon, with only a dim glow in the distance.

Stretching loudly, Kabir then stood, before walking a short distance away to relieve himself.

Returning to where Ahlia had been sleeping, he saw she was already up and ready to go. She did not even look tired.

'I am told we will be there this morning,' Ahlia said.

Kabir looked around at those also making themselves ready for the day's travel. Who had she had time to speak with?

'Okay,' he said, shrugging his shoulders.

It didn't take long for them to get moving. Despite how many were travelling in their group, and all of the provisions they had with them, it was extremely well organised.

Kabir and Ahlia kept to themselves for the remainder of their journey to Havern, not conversing with anyone the whole morning.

Kabir missed not having his sword with him, but he was comforted in the thought he would have it back again soon enough.

He was confident their trial in the Capital would be much different than the one held at Shadow Hill. He hoped so anyway. As much as Ahlia hated him calling her a Princess, it was exactly what she was. It would be what they would perceive her as here as well, which was what mattered.

Before they had reached the place called Havern, Kabir saw riders approaching. He and Ahlia had a great vantage point from where they sat on the back of Firth. They were able to see all around them.

As they came closer, Kabir was able to see there were men among them, as well as a number of wizards. The men looked to be regular soldiers. He saw none who resembled Atriol, which seemed odd, even to an outsider. He was accustomed to seeing their kind in this realm and had assumed they rode with all King's men.

Lord Marcus and his King's Shield rode out to meet with them.

They spoke with the riders for a few minutes, before one of the King's Shield turned in his saddle and gave the signal for everyone to move off again.

Within the hour, Havern came into view. It was quite a deal larger than Shadow Hill and by far larger than any town or village either Kabir or Ahlia had seen before.

Kabir watched as those riders who had spoken to Marcus rode back inside the large gates. He was surprised to see the gates close behind them and the people of Shadow Hill begin to make their way along the space below the walls.

'It looks as if they are setting their things up outside the wall,' Ahlia said. 'Why would they do that?' she asked.

'Perhaps there is no room within the town itself,' Kabir suggested.

Before Ahlia could say more, Atriol rode up to where they stood.

'You need to come with me,' he said to them, turning around without waiting to see if they followed.

He took them to where Marcus stood his own horse outside the large gates.

He was red in the face and looked as if he was about to explode.

Turning around when they got there, he glared at his two prisoners.

'It would have been better if I had killed you both back at Shadow Hill!' he said angrily.

Neither Kabir nor Ahlia responded.

'Get moving!' Marcus said to Atriol. 'There is no time to rest your horses.'

Atriol nodded his head, and beckoned for those men standing their horses a short distance away. Marcus' Captain Methan was among them.

They moved behind Firth.

'We are to continue on to Lakerth,' Atriol said. 'Without delay.'

Kabir couldn't help himself this time.

'My sword?' he asked. He was angry, but he still knew it was smarter to ask Atriol and not Marcus.

'Lord Marcus will be keeping your sword until after your trial,' he said. 'My apologies again barbarian, but there is nothing I can do unless you are released.'

Kabir nodded his head. He knew if he tried anything now, he would die in the attempt. Atriol's words gave him hope that he would be returned his sword once he was freed by their Princess, so he needed to continue waiting. As much as it pained him, he had no other choice.

'Lead on,' he said in response to the King's Shields' words.

Kabir nodded his head to Lord Marcus as he passed him, which was returned with a glare.

Kabir looked forward to seeing him again. Hopefully it was soon.

CHAPTER 49

Victory?

B ILSONT WAS AT the front of the charge, as he moved towards the ranks of Ve-Karn and Ogre-Mage.

He had just seen the balls of lava break through the wizard's shield and knew that haste was crucial. They needed to get amongst them, before more of those could be cast into Dayhen's army.

As he closed in on the first line of Ve-Karn, he noticed something straight away which sent a chill through him.

Not for his own safety, but for the defence of the Realm.

The Wizard's behind him shot forth their balls of energy at the Ogre-Mage, allowing his King's Shield opportunity to deal with the Ve-Karn.

It was only sheer luck that saved him, as the ranks of Ve-Karn before him opened up and an Ogre-Mage suddenly appeared, not ten paces away. The fireball was already leaving his fingers as Bilsont saw it before him. There was no time for him to move, yet somehow one of the Ve-Karn fell into the space before him and took the entire impact of the fireball. Its body exploded, the blood and guts spraying all over those around the Ogre-Mage and over Bilsont.

The old King's Shield was shocked to have seen one of the Ve-Karn push another out of his way, to enable him to flee the charging Shield.

One of the King' Shield to Bilsont's side was not so fortunate as he had been, as her chest exploded from the impact of a fireball. Another two or three of his Shield were also struck down as they made their way through Kritch's supposed elite fighters. At close range, it was almost impossible to dodge them. At close range, it was also difficult to survive the impact.

Bilsont struck out at one of the Ve-Karn, dropping his sword low, as he let his body move under and past the attack thrust. The King's Shield was able to drive his sword up and into the back of his opponent's neck as he moved past it. This one had not tried to flee, but he still made short work of him.

He was quickly joined by another three of his Shield, as they began to move further into the ranks of the Ve-Karn. They began to kill both Ve-Karn and Ogre-Mage, such was the speed with which they carved their way into the opposing army.

When Bilsont had first decided on speed, he didn't think he, or those who joined him, would survive. His intent had been to kill as many as they could, sending confusion and fear among the ranks of their enemies as they pushed further in.

But as he continued to kill his enemies and move further in, Bilsont realised quickly that not all of those wearing the armour of the Ve-Karn were what they portrayed themselves as. The one who was fleeing and had saved his life was a testament to that.

He had never before fought a Ve-Karn that had tried to flee.

His initial realisation was now clear to him. Bilsont could see by the way they stood and moved, and by the way they held their weapons that most of these were regular soldiers, dressed up as the vaunted Western warriors.

Realising this to be true of most of the Ve-Karn, Bilsont moved even faster, cutting a path through them with very little effort. His sword was a blur as the bodies stacked up around him and around those King's Shield who accompanied him.

He thought of returning so he could inform his King, but it would do nothing to change what had been done.

Bilsont decided it would be best if he instead continued on trying to wipe out every last one of Kritch's abominations from the field.

Now that all of his King Shield had joined the fray, it took them little time to complete the massacre Bilsont had begun.

Once all of the actual Ve-Karn had fallen, of which there was maybe fifty in total, the rest put up very little resistance. Those of them that stayed to fight at least. Many of them turned and ran, as they saw the tide of King's Shield heading toward them.

If watching from afar it would have looked like men fighting young children. Skilful, battle-hardened men and women, fighting children that had never even held a sword before.

The fear and confusion of those wearing the glossy armour of the Ve-Karn soon swept along the length of Kritch's army, as those closest to them saw the ease with which the King's Shield swept through them.

Even after their initial success at breaching the shields cast by Derekia and his order of wizards, the damage caused had not been enough to make any kind of dent in Dayhen's army. A few wizards had died from arrows and lava, but many more still remained to combat the fireballs of the Ogre-Mage.

Add to that almost two hundred King's Shield running rampant through Kritch's army, and it did more than turn the tide of battle.

It did not take long for all of those remaining, to turn and run for their lives. There was no order and no fight shown by any of those who turned and ran.

It was each orc, half-goblin, troll, ogre and ogre-mage for himself.

The slowest were quickly cut down by the swords of the King Shield, as the cavalry led by Dayhen joined what was left of the battle. The quicker ones were run down by those of Dayhen's men on horses as they fled.

The only ones who put up much of a fight were the giant, reddish-coloured orcs who had been responsible for the lava-rocks.

They killed many men before they fell, both with their lava and their giant swords, showing an incredible resistance to the magic of Dayhen's wizards.

It wasn't until the King's Shield joined the main part of the army, that the strongest and last of the Lava-Orcs fell.

Bilsont had finished that one himself. He had given a good account of himself, taking wounds that would have killed lesser creatures, but in the end the result was inevitable. Despite his size and strength, Bilsont was far too skilful.

When he was finally satisfied the day was won, Dayhen put away his sword and looked around for his commanders.

He quickly saw Bilsont making his way towards him, a grim expression on the face of his King's Shield. The man never looked happy, so Dayhen decided not to let him ruin his mood. This had been an amazing victory. The losses, although substantial, were far less than even his best hopes had been, and Kritch's army was all but destroyed.

'If I may have a word King Dayhen,' Bilsont said. It was not framed as a question.

Dayhen sighed, but got down from his horse and beckoned those nearest him to step away for a moment.

'Quickly Bilsont. We need to be away from here,' he said. 'The Shield fought remarkably today. I have never seen the like.' He didn't think Bilsont would care for compliments, but Dayhen wanted it said anyway.

'We do indeed need to make haste,' Bilsont said. 'but the shield fought only as well as they always do. There was nothing inspired about them today.'

Dayhen had become accustomed to his brash nature, but he was being pig-headed now.

'They were not Ve-Karn,' Bilsont said, before Dayhen could tell him what he thought of his last comment.

The words died on his lips.

'What do you mean not Ve-Karn?' he asked.

'A quarter of your Shield here today could have routed them quite easily,' Bilsont said, disgust clear in his voice. 'Kritch was fooled, as were we,' he finished.

Dayhen took a moment to let it sink in.

'So Mithrak has his full force of Ve-Karn with him,' Dayhen said, as much to himself as to the man in front of him.

'And they may well be marching through Glorfiden as we speak,' Bilsont said.

Dayhen knew too well what that would mean, if the Dark-Mage managed to get through the elven forest unscathed.

'Gather the King's Shield and get them back to Lakerth!' Dayhen said, turning to jump back on to his horse. 'As fast as you can!' he roared, but Bilsont had already left to execute his King's orders.

Thaiden pulled up his horse next to his King as Dayhen jumped backed on.

'We need to get back to Lakerth without delay,' Dayhen said, as he turned his horse back towards the High Gates.

'It shouldn't take long to finish off those that are left,' Thaiden said. 'Most of the cavalry and several of the King's Shield have been tasked to chase down..'

'Call them back,' Dayhen said, interrupting his commander. 'Get all of them back now!' he repeated, raising his voice.

Thaiden turned and bellowed the order to those nearest him.

'What happened?' he asked, riding to keep up with his King.

'Most of them were only dressed up as Ve-Karn,' Dayhen said, his voice losing a lot of its venom.

Thaiden didn't need to ask more.

That sneaky bastard, he thought to himself, as he reeled around to make sure his orders were carried out as quickly as possible.

CHAPTER 50

Expect The Unexpected

THEY FINALLY CRESTED the rise, the water either side of them gushing past and over. Mendina turned backed as she crested the top, and thought the view from the top of the waterfall to be just as majestic as when they had been at the bottom.

Until she turned around and looked at what was probably once a proud and beautiful forest.

Now it resembled a swampland, but without the bogs and horrible smells.

The branches and root systems of those trees that she could see, looked warped and struggling to survive. The pristine water coming out of the forest was in stark contrast to what she now looked at.

The swampland had felt wrong in many ways to her and she had feared going inside it.

This forest was something else entirely, and she didn't know how she felt about it.

'Will you be okay going in there?' Mort asked her, the dread clear in his voice.

'The deformity and poor health do not so much concern me,' Mendina said, continuing to look ahead as she spoke. 'What concerns me is walking past each tree knowing I can help them, but not taking the time to stop.' She did look at him this time. 'Is what we do more important, more urgent than that?'

Mort hated looking into her eyes and telling her no, but on this occasion, he could see she knew the answer before she even asked the question.

'I have a feeling we might find what is responsible for this before too long. Perhaps we can help them in a different way,' Mort said.

Mendina said nothing as she stepped forward, soon passing the first of the tangled trees. Mort followed behind her.

They walked for a time, neither of them saying anything.

The health of the trees and plants were not as bad as Mendina had first thought. As they moved further in, she realised it was simply different to what she was used to. The trees were not as majestic as those in Glorfiden, but they were still beautiful in their own fashion. The forest was thick with greenery where they walked, and was slow going even for an elf, but it was still a pleasant change to the lands they had walked through to get here.

The smaller trees battled for their share of the life-giving rays of sunshine, but most had found a way.

There was an abundance of colour, which pleased her senses, and the small animals were friendly and curious.

It was a surprise when the trees ahead began to thin out, and the first signs of destruction began to appear.

Mendina was certainly not prepared for what she came upon, as they made their way into a clearing that stretched for as far as she could see.

The ground here was worse than any swampland.

Cracks and craters littered the ground before them, with cesspools of some liquid she didn't recognise. It reminded her too closely of the destruction within Glorfiden after the storm had ripped through it. Her senses were repulsed by it. The damage done here was not natural.

As she took it all in, her gaze was drawn to a place a couple of hundred paces away, as the sleeping creature raised itself up on to its back legs.

Involuntarily, she reached across and grabbed hold of Mort's hand.

'What is that?' she asked softly.

Mort didn't answer her straight away.

Dragging her eyes away from the creature in front of them, Mendina looked across at him. Mort looked to be frozen where he stood, his eyes wide open.

Mendina looked back as the dragon spread its wings wide. It looked as if it were casually stretching.

Larger than anything she had seen before, Mendina could hardly believe her eyes. The dragon was a colossus, at least ten times larger than the one they had fought in Travis' valley.

Mendina remembered how difficult that one had been to kill. She could not begin to imagine how they would defeat a beast such as this.

Even with Mort's rod, it looked beyond them.

'Step forward,' it said to them. Mendina could see its mouth move, but wondered how its voice was so clear from such a distance. It didn't yell at them, but the words were spoken in such a way that it came to her as if the dragon were standing right before them. Mendina was stunned both by that ability and that it was able to speak to them at all.

Not only was it a creature born from the scariest of tales, it was intelligent as well.

She fervently hoped their task was not to fight it.

Already the fear within her had built to such a level she wasn't sure if she would be able to move any closer. Her legs almost buckled, as her feet involuntarily began taking her towards the waiting dragon.

Mort couldn't believe what he was seeing.

He felt Mendina take his hand and heard that she had spoken, but he was too entranced by the dragon in front of them to acknowledge her question.

The words 'step forward' were all he could think about.

As he stepped forward with Mendina, her next words somehow got through.

'Mort', he heard Mendina say.

He managed to look across at her this time, but it was a struggle.

'What do we do?' she asked. He could see she was scared, as was he. The dragon was bigger than any creature he had ever seen, yet it was the terror in her eyes that momentarily broke the spell and enabled him to hear the voice of *Iska*. That look of terror had somehow overshadowed the fear he was feeling towards the dragon.

He mouthed the words of the spell given to him by his fairie-dragon and the intense fear melted away.

Looking behind, he had not even realised they had walked ten paces forward.

'Mort. What do we do?' Mendina asked him again, the terror in her eyes this time sending a wave of intense anger through him.

'We will see what it wants,' Mort said, looking forward again. 'And if it seeks to harm us, we will fight it,' he continued, taking the rod from inside his jacket.

'Brave words,' the dragon said, folding its wings up, but still sitting upright. Even that pose was intimidating, such was its size, but Mort was no longer terrified by it.

It was an amazing beast, but it breathed, so he trusted it would also bleed.

'The little one will not help you further today,' it continued. Mort was confused for a moment, before he felt *Iska* take off from its perch on his shoulder. He looked on in shock as it flew back to the trees behind them, perching itself on the highest branch it could find.

Mort tried calling him back, but the fairie-dragon paid him no heed.

'If it attacks, stand behind me,' Mort said quietly to Mendina, as they continued walking towards the dragon.

Mendina nodded, but gave no answer. Mort looked to make sure she was okay. Apart from the fear on her face, she looked fine.

'That is close enough,' the dragon said, as they stood fifty paces away.

Up this close, Mort was entranced by the way its body looked as it spoke to him. The platinum scales were mesmerising in their movements, as they rippled along the whole length of its body in waves. Except for the tail, which moved separately to the rest of its body as it swung slowly left to right, sometimes pausing before rising into the air.

'What do you want?' Mort asked the dragon, as Mendina moved in closer to him, her shoulder touching his arm.

'I am your next task,' it said, looking down at them, its tail continuing to move from side to side. Mort had estimated the length of it and was satisfied they were far enough away if it tried to swing it at them.

'Which is?' Mort asked. The question referred to both this task and what it was they were being forced to do. He was hoping this dragon might be able to answer some of those questions for them.

'I am here to test both of you,' it said.

'To what end?' Mort asked.

'To see if you are worthy to walk away from here of course,' the dragon said, 'or whether your bones will join those of the others who are melted into this barren patch of ground.'

Mort readied himself, as he pushed Mendina behind him. She made no effort to stop him.

'What have you there?' the dragon asked. 'An Elven toy perhaps? Strange, considering you are not an elf.'

'He is an elf!' Mendina said. 'And that is no toy.'

Mort put his other hand up. 'I think it is trying to bait us Mendina. To distract us. Don't listen to its taunts. I will keep you safe.'

'I am satisfied with you protecting your companion, human-elf, but she will need to face her own test once yours is finished. So be warned little elf.' The dragon spoke in a softer voice now, almost as if it were saddened by what it had to do.

'Not if I finish you off first lizard,' Mort said.

How dare it threaten Mendina Mort thought, before realising he had only just told Mendina to ignore its taunts.

'I look forward to seeing you try,' the dragon said. 'I truly do.'

Mort decided they had talked long enough, as he began to call forth the powers of the rod.

As he did, the dragon raised itself up even higher and spewed forth its silver-coloured molten dragon breath. Mort was horrified to discover the rod did not work as quickly as he had hoped when calling forth a storm.

The sky above was clear, apart from the deadly substance hurtling towards them from the mouth of the dragon.

A week earlier and they both would have died in that moment.

However, Mort was no longer the same half-elf as the one who had frozen in panic and confusion before the dark-mage and blood wolves. He was still bitter that his father had been forced to save them, and so had worked hard to ensure it never happened again.

Although *Iska* was not able to help him, Mort still remembered those spells he had been shown so far. In particular, the beam of light.

He had no shortage of sunlight, as he gave up his attempts to use the rod and instead shot forth a burst of the concentrated light beams. They tore through the incoming dragon-breath, incinerating much of it, while the rest sprayed outwards, harmlessly impacting the ground either side of them.

'Is that all you have?' Mort yelled out, as he changed tact once more. Deciding to try the rod once more, he no longer attempted to summon a storm. This time he pulled to him that which was already in the air around them.

There really was no need for him to call forth a storm when there was wind all around them.

Although only a slight breeze blew, Mort was able to concentrate what there was and build it up quickly, just as the dragon physically launched itself at him.

Pushing the wind quickly at the dragon, Mort was able to slow it down, but not stop it. The mighty tail swung around, sweeping Mort's feet from under him as it impacted his left thigh.

Striking his head on the ground, Mort saw stars for a moment as tried to shake it off. Sitting up, he was able to focus on the tail this time, as the dragon raised it into the air above him.

He knew there was not time enough for him to cast another spell, as the tail begun its descent toward him. Mort saw his death coming for him in that moment and it made him angry. There was no time for any other thoughts, as a shadow suddenly moved above him.

'Mendina, no!' he cried, as the tail crashed down on to her. Mendina had flung herself between him and the tail of the dragon.

Mort had braced himself for the impact as it followed-through, but he felt nothing.

Lifting herself up, Mendina looked down at him, a shocked expression on her face.

'What did you do?' she asked quickly, before turning to face the dragon again.

Mort stood quickly, unable to respond straight away, as the dragon sat back and shot forth another breath weapon. This time it was more concentrated, aimed directly at Mendina.

It was the same kind of acidic breath as before, but it was thin and arced directly at her chest.

Mort was once again unable to act in time. Instead he was forced to watch on in horror as it struck her directly in the chest.

Mendina had futilely tried to gather the moisture around her and form a shield, but the dragon breath went through it like it was not even there.

Mort's own follow-up attempt to dispel it like he did the last time was too late.

Yet he need not have bothered.

His look of horror became an expression of awe, as the pendant around her neck absorbed the acid, leaving Mendina almost unscathed. Small drops slid off the side of the pendant, burning her skin, but such small hurts did not seem to bother her.

Mendina looked back at Mort again as she realised what had just happened.

Mort was able to smile quickly at her, before stepping forward and placing himself in front of her once more.

This time he put everything he had into the wind spell, drawing as much as he could from the storm rod.

The force of the wind began to push the dragon backwards, until it lost its feet and went sliding along the ground for a distance.

Mort cut the spell off as the dragon got back to its feet and stepped forward once more.

'I have more,' Mort said warningly, as he remembered their trick in killing the dragon they had fought in Travis' valley. He began to draw all of the moisture in the air to him. His belief was that the power the rod would give the projectiles would pierce the scales of even this beast.

'That will do,' the dragon said to them. 'This battle is over.'

'We have bested you,' Mortinan said to him, a defiant and proud look on his face. He continued to gather the moisture still, as Mendina walked up to stand by him as he spoke to the dragon.

The dragon made a sound which Mort took to be laughter.

'Bested me?' she chortled. 'You couldn't *best* me boy, but you have passed the challenge that is required.'

'Try again then,' Mortinan said. He believed the dragon was still trying to be boastful. He would be happy to teach her another lesson.

The dragon snapped her head forward, at a height equal to where Mort and Mendina stood.

'Oh, if it were permitted of me, I would have done so already.'

Mort took an involuntary step back and held his staff forward this time, sending another blast of wind at the dragon. Not as strong as the one using the rod, he thought it more than enough to get it out of his face.

The dragon nonchalantly grabbed the staff from his hands with its teeth and flung it aside, before putting both he and Mendina on the ground. She held them there, her huge claws doing them no harm, but they were helpless to move. The moisture Mort had been collecting was blown away and dispersed from the dragon's own wind spell.

'I am beholden to give those who come here a test of wills and strength. I am not however, required to listen to them brag about how easily they have bested me.' The voice of the dragon was not loud, but it seemed to roll over Mort, every word sinking into and latching on to his mind. He could not have ignored her if he tried.

'I am a Platinum Dragon little half-elf. I am magic, strength, wisdom and knowledge. If I want something dead, then it dies.'

Mort was beginning to see that perhaps he hadn't defeated it quite in the manner he believed.

'Okay,' Mort said, the cockiness gone from his voice. 'If you are not going to kill us, can you let us up again?'

'I will give you the message for succeeding in what was required. Then for your insolence, I will let you both up and give you until the count of ten to run from here, else I will make snacks of you. That twig of yours I will use to pick your flesh from out of my teeth afterwards.' This time she moved her head forward so that it was almost touching Mort's. 'You will have until ten.'

Mort stayed silent this time. He was helpless and he knew it. This beast was powerful. Far stronger than anything he had met before. He looked across at Mendina and saw she was okay. She looked startled, but appeared unharmed.

The dragon pulled its head away from Mort, but continued to keep both of them trapped underneath its huge feet and talons.

'Half-elf. You must go south from here. Your next clue will be found within your own home.'

'Another clue?' Mortinan bemoaned. 'Are these clues to go on forever?'

The dragon ignored him.

'You have to go straight home. No side-tracking, no deviating from the quickest path there. This is not allowed.'

Mort wasn't overly concerned about her last words. The quicker he got there the better.

'Fine,' he said. 'Let us go and we will be on our way. It will be our pleasure to leave you to your own beautiful home.'

Again, the dragon ignored him. It turned its gaze instead to Mendina.

'Little elf, you also need to go home. Back to the centre of Glorfiden, where your next clue will be found.'

'To which clue do we go first?' she asked. None of the arrogance of Mort was in her words. She both feared and respected this mighty creature. She spoke almost deferentially.

'Ah, you mistake my words little elfling.' She was not affronted by the dragon using the term elfling towards her. 'You must head straight home to find your clue. Your rude and insulting companion must go straight to his. You also may not deviate.'

Mort was about to say something as the dragon finished speaking with Mendina, when suddenly the giant claws withdrew and they were both free to stand.

Mortinan quickly got to his feet and held his hand out to help Mendina to hers.

He turned to the dragon and was again about to say something when he was interrupted by her.

'Ten...' was all she said.

Mort looked at her a moment, before succumbing to the arm tugging at his and turned with his elven companion. They began to walk away, before Mort looked across at where his staff had been tossed aside by the dragon.

'Nine,' the dragon roared, quickly following it with 'eight'.

Mort sprinted over to his staff and picked it up as the dragon counted six.

Mendina held her hand out to him as he ran towards her.

Although he continued to stare into his *eye*, Mortinan pushed himself forward, so he could lay back and rest his head on the cushion.

As quickly as that, the game had changed once more.

A new task had been set and his Champion was finally free of Mendina's tag-along Champion.

It would seem a simple enough task to those within the world of Dark Swell who now walked away from the Platinum Dragon. Mortinan knew better.

He knew what his Champion had to go through in order for him to find his way home again.

He had listened to the words of the Dragon very carefully.

There would be no deviation and haste was required.

As powerful as his Champion now was, he knew he would need to intervene before he reached the swamp. Exactly what words he would use to help him, he was not yet sure of, but the content of the message was already decided.

This could well be the final task within the game and he knew without question his Champion definitely had the advantage now.

Although Mendina was closer to Glorfiden than his Champion was to the home of Jarkene and Corein, Mortinan also knew what was waiting for her on the outskirts of the Elven Forest. Although she had somehow survived against the dragon, which still had him wondering how, she would not be so lucky a second time. Her time within the game was finally coming to an end.

He had two opportunities remaining to enter the world, and he intended on using them both very soon.

Once they were clear of the blasted area surrounding the dragon and back among the tangled mess of trees once more, they allowed themselves to slow to a walk.

Mort was furious, although the sight of his fairie-dragon fluttering toward him took some of the edge off it.

'How can....whatever it is pulling our strings, split us up?' he asked her. 'I have grown so tired of this game.'

Mendina clasped his hand and much of his anger dissipated. Her touch still amazed him. Since their first time together his only moods had been deliriously happy or angry. The thought of having to part ways with her was too hard for him to think about.

'It will only be for a short time Mort,' she said. 'I will get to the centre of the forest quickly and then meet you at your home.' She squeezed his hand and gently brushed his lips with hers.

Mort looked at her as they walked and he couldn't help but feel glad. She was almost skipping and had a smile on her face.

'We have just survived against a Platinum Dragon Mort!' Her eyes opened wide. 'We have survived and now we get to go home. We are not being sent to yet another distant corner of the land.'

Mort knew she was right. They were not only allowed to go home, they were being sent there.

Hopefully when they got home they would be able to stay a while, or at least have just one final clue to whatever task they have been set to accomplish.

He smiled back at her, happy at the joy he saw in her eyes.

Yet he also had a sinking feeling that even her smile could not shake.

Going home seemed a straightforward task. It was a much shorter journey and took them to a place they were intimately familiar with.

He should not be worried, but he was.

He was actually more than just worried, he was scared. He could not say exactly what it was he had seen in the eyes of the dragon when he looked at her that last time, but it had sent a chill through him and that chill had taken root.

The dragon had smiled at him before starting its count, and then quickly looked at Mendina with a sad, sorry look. That had been where the chill came from.

He did not want to leave her alone.

'I will stay with you for as long as I am able Mendina.' He kissed her more strongly on the lips this time. 'At least until you are into the forest again.'

'Okay,' she replied. 'But let us get out of here first. It smells.'

Mort nodded in agreement as they quickened their pace.

They journeyed together for a time, their destinations leading them on the same path.

Eventually they came to a spot south of the Ruined Forest where Mendina suddenly began to feel ill.

They stopped moving, but her stomach continued to churn.

'Is it something you have eaten?' Mort asked, concern in his voice and a silent dread in the pit of his stomach.

'No,' was all she said.

They looked at each other for a moment.

It was still such a long distance to both his home and to the Elven Forest. Mendina would not have to traverse the small mountain range, but she would need to journey north of it, through lands that were not friendly. And she would have to do it on her own.

Mort knew she could take care of herself against some beasts and monsters out there, but he knew there were also evil creatures against which she would have no chance.

'Take my staff.' Mort said. 'It may help you before you get to the forest. Once inside the trees you will be okay.' Then another thought occurred to him.

'Iska, go with Mendina,' he said.

Mendina looked shocked.

'Iska has bonded with you Mort. He will go with no other.'

Mort knew she was right, but still he hoped he would go with her.

Iska didn't move from where he perched nearby.

Mort frowned up at his fairie-dragon, before turning back to Mendina.

'Regardless, you will take my staff with you. We saw nothing in these lands when we left, so there is every likelihood it is still safe.'

Mendina nodded at his words, but they were not reassuring to her. It would be the first time she had ever been outside of the forest on her own, left to defend herself without the help of others. Without the help of Mort.

She knew his staff would help her. It would increase the potency of her magic and prolong her reserves, yet she was not powerful in attacking magic. It would be wasted on her.

'You will need your staff Mort,' she replied. 'The rod will need to recharge still.'

Mort smiled at her. He looked torn whether to chance giving her the rod also, even though she was almost certain she wouldn't be able to control it, maybe not even get it to work at all.

'The rod has plenty left within it Mendina. If I thought you would be able to use it, then it would be yours also.'

Mendina expected nothing less from him. His devotion to her made her happy, but it also made him act like a fool at times.

'Do you really think I would leave you defenceless Mort?' Mendina asked. She had taken one step in the direction of Glorfiden and the pain had disappeared immediately, confirming what they both already knew. 'Neither of us know what we will be walking into before we get home Mort, or what will be waiting for us when we get there.'

Mort nodded dumbly in agreement.

'I will have Jarkene there when I return, and the other elves,' she said. While you will have no-one, she thought, but did not speak the words.

Mort would be going home, to a place where there would be no welcome and no-one to offer help to him.

'I think I am more worried for you than you should be for me Mort.' She was glad he had the storm rod. She almost pitied anything that attacked him when he got home.

The pain started to slowly return to Mendina. Her stomach began cramping this time and her head began to hurt.

She looked across at Mort and could see the same thing was now happening to him. His face tried to hide it, but she knew.

'We need to go now,' Mendina said to him. His eyes were brimming with tears and she could feel her own doing the same.

They embraced each other and kissed briefly. The pain was quickly becoming unbearable, forcing them to let go of each other.

They held hands as each took a step towards their own destined paths.

The pain lessened enough for them to squeeze hands one last time as they stared into each other's eyes.

'I will see you soon,' Mort said, the tears running unchecked down his cheeks now.

Mendina could only nod, as their hands let go.

The directions they took were not vastly different, so they were able to look across at the other as their journey continued.

It was weird to Mendina to be so close and yet not be able to hold him or even walk with him. This game they were being forced to play was a cruel one.

Eventually, as the distance widened, all Mendina could do was watch as Mort walked slowly away, his fairie-dragon flying a short distance above him, her own legs involuntarily taking her back towards Glorfiden.

Neither of them waved.

Mendina passed over a rise and into a small ravine and Mort was no longer in sight.

He was gone from her and the world suddenly seemed a large and ever so dangerous place.

CHAPTER 51

Alone At Last

L INF CONTINUED TO ball the energy in front of her, even as she heard the first clash of swords and screams of agony from those at the front.

She could see a little of what was happening, but for the most part it was just a blur of swords and creatures dying.

She realised it may not take them long to find their way through to where she stood waiting.

Those in front of her stopped their advance as the two forces came together, and now began turning their heads to look at each other; the fear emanating from them intense. It was not what she had expected from warriors and certainly not what she had hoped for.

Before she even caught sight of the first human, several of those in front of Linf turned back towards her and began to run.

Linf couldn't believe it. They were fleeing already!

What was initially only a few running, quickly became a full-blown retreat, as the first of the humans with no fear or anger came into sight.

Those closest to them were quickly cut down before they had gotten far.

Linf suddenly knew this day was not going to end the way she had hoped. Firing off her ball of energy at the human nearest her, she turned and ran with the rest of them, not even looking to see if it struck anyone.

As she turned and began to run, she saw Rark standing with his giant weapon out now, hacking at those of his own army who were fleeing.

'Stand and fight!' he roared, as his attention turned back to the advancing humans.

Linf got close enough to say a few words, but still far enough away so his sword would not reach her.

'You were right!' she called out. 'They fight for themselves.' The Lava-Orc turned at the sound of her voice.

He snarled at her, before the gloriously disgusting smile returned to his face.

'Run little goblin, even eyes in the back of your head won't save you now,' he said, before turning back to face the coming onslaught.

As fast as she was, the fear driving those around her meant she only kept pace with them. Unable to overtake any of them, she knew her back was vulnerable to arrows or whatever else might come her way.

Spells of power began to impact those running with her, as the human wizards joined the rout, firing at them as they ran. Linf could not put her shield up as she sprinted, but there was no way she was going to turn around.

Another idea came to her instead, which might be just as effective.

Linf began draining those around her, intending to use them as a shield instead. Her idea was a simple one. As they weakened they would fall back. It would slow those chasing her, as they stopped to kill the slower ones.

It seemed to work for a time, as nothing had yet caught her, and the spells no longer smashed into those she ran with.

Ahead, far in the distance, she caught sight of Kritch and his guard galloping away on their horses. She had expected nothing less from the Ogre-Mage.

His army was beaten, that was obvious. There was no point hanging around.

As Linf ran, and the numbers with her began to drop off and dwindle, she thought she might be able to survive this after all.

Then she heard the thud of something galloping behind her. Daring to look behind for a quick glance, her hopes were quickly dashed, as she saw dozens of horses thundering towards them.

Even those she drained would not slow their charge.

With a deep sigh, she decided to turn and face them.

Firing off a quick ball of energy, she knocked the first one from his horse, the rider crashing to the ground. After her initial proud moment at the accuracy of her strike, Linf quickly focused and gathered as much energy as she could, forming it into a shield in front of her.

She hoped it might save her from a sword strike, but she knew that inevitably she could not hope to stop them all.

As the human rider leant to the side of his horse, Linf watched as his sword swung in an arc straight at her body.

The shield took most of the blow, but the follow-through still had enough force to knock her backwards on to the ground. As she hit the dirt, Linf felt pain in her back from the impact, but nothing from the sword blow.

It worked, she realised, as the other horses galloped past her.

Closing her eyes and leaving her arms out to the side, the goblin thought it a good time for her to act like she was dead.

It was all she had left.

Putting all of her energy into not moving, Linf lay where she was and hoped that none of those following would accidently ride over the top of her, or another drive a sword through her to make sure she was actually dead.

She didn't need her eyes to form a shield of energy above her. There was still plenty of fear to draw from, even from those who lay dying.

Linf had no idea how long she lay there for.

The noises of horses riding around her and the sounds of creatures dying was all she heard for what seemed like an eternity, but was probably nowhere near that long.

Her body remained tense the whole time, as she waited for the steel of a blade to slip through her shield and slide into her chest or face. As the sounds of horses and dying retreated, she warred with herself not to open her eyes and try to see what was going on around her.

She tried to convince her smarter self that it needed to be done, that it might help to save her if it were just one or two of them walking around stabbing all those lying on the ground. She may be able to save herself if she would only open her eyes.

Eventually, after the sounds of horses had completely disappeared and Linf could hear only the groans of those around her still dying, she decided it might be safe to have a look around.

Despite having no idea how long she had lain there trying not to move, Linf finally decided if there were men finishing off the injured, they would have done it by now.

Opening her eyes, she was able to look to both sides and in front of her without moving her head. Linf saw no-one moving. She was unable to see behind her however, not without moving her head.

She decided it worth the risk of moving her head slightly.

Ever so slowly, so as not to draw attention, she pushed her head back and looked behind.

There was no sign of any men close to her.

Eventually Linf built up the courage to lift her head off the ground. Looking towards the human fort, she could see the horses making their way towards the open gate.

It looked like all of the men were following behind. As far as she could tell, they had completely left the field of battle.

Sitting up, Linf looked around, bewildered by what she saw.

Bodies lay strewn all around her. Most of them belonged to Kritch's army, but a few men and horses lay dead among them. Standing up, she could see several of the fighting men with no fear and anger also lying dead. They were closer to where the two armies had first come together. There were none of them dead where she now stood.

Looking behind her, Linf could make out numerous small shapes in the far distance, getting even smaller as she looked on.

What remained of Kritch's mighty army.

Linf drew in some deep breaths as she stood alone among the dead. There were certainly those that still lived, but none of them were yet standing.

She had the unique gift of being able to tell exactly which creatures around her were still alive, as the wafts of fear rising up into the air gave away their position to the goblin.

Although she had received little hurt from the battle, Linf felt exhausted. She had been given little food in the last few days, and the effort to keep her shield strong while she lay motionless had taken a lot out of her.

Reaching out to those nearby who still lived, she began absorbing their life force. Some of them didn't have a lot to give and died quickly, while others appeared to have had the same idea as she. They took longer to die.

Eventually, she had all the energy she could absorb and left those further away to lie where they were. Either they would get up and walk off in their own time, or they would die where they now lay.

Either way, Linf did not care.

Her thoughts instead turned to what she would do now.

She was certainly not going to try and follow the men through their gate.

One option was to head north, following Kritch and the remnants of his army. Although she would enjoy killing the Ogre-Mage, he still had plenty of protection. His personal guards were similar in nature to the men with no emotions and Linf would rather not be his prisoner again.

She could head back toward where the army set up the first time. There was a town of men there, and she knew how to get around the wall near the forest. She shrugged and began walking in that direction, through the thousands of dead surrounding her.

Linf hadn't gone far, when she stopped.

Perhaps if she went in the other direction, there would be an easier way to get through, with less men and less wizards. Once she was in the realm of men, she could find a place to stay, like Brax had. She could then go hunting whenever she wanted to. Pick off men and other creatures at her leisure. She would certainly get the chance to feast on human children.

That sounded like a much better plan.

Changing her mind yet again, Linf turned and began walking back the way she had just come.

The goblin had not gone far past the last of the dead bodies, when the human witch suddenly appeared in front of her. It took her by surprise, which is why she didn't fire off a ball of energy the moment she saw her.

After the initial shock wore off, Linf decided she might try and talk with her this time. Maybe show some patience and get some information out of her.

'You are going the wrong way,' the woman said, before Linf could ask her anything.

'I don't see why,' Linf replied. 'Why don't you tell me why.'

'You need to go that way,' the woman said, ignoring her question and pointing with her finger in the direction Linf had just turned away from.

'I'm not going that way,' Linf said. 'Unless you think you can make me?' Linf smiled as she began balling the energy in front of her. Just in case the talking part didn't go so well.

Surprisingly to the goblin, Linf began to see small tendrils of fear flowing from the human witch. That was very interesting.

Grabbing on to the fear, Linf began to draw it in. It *tasted* different, unlike any life energy she had consumed before. It was amazing and Linf suddenly decided talking was very over-rated.

She was about to draw in more, when the woman vanished.

'I would love for you to teach me how to do that trick,' Linf said to the spot the woman had been standing in. 'Show me, and I will go where you want me to,' Linf said out loud.

She waited to see if the woman would return, but after a few moments she got bored of waiting and continued on her way.

'I guess she couldn't make me,' Linf said, chuckling at her own wit.

CHAPTER 52

Swamped

DRAUG WAS ALMOST into the northern caves when he heard the first sounds of battle ahead. It was sooner than he had dared hope and meant the hobgoblins had advanced a lot further than he believed they could.

What had happened to those defending it?

Turning a couple of more bends in the tunnel ahead, he entered a large cavern. It was the Northern Entry, where a lot of the northern tunnels funnelled into the one place. It made getting around much simpler.

It had obviously made it easier for the hobgoblins as well.

Draug was glad to see a large number of dwarves in front of him.

They were holding their position against several assaults.

The Dwarven King was able to sum up the situation rather quickly.

The hobgoblins had not yet been routed due to their numbers. He assumed there were a lot of them and they were attacking from what looked like four of the five tunnels leading into the Northern Hall.

There were obviously enough dwarves to defend the hall, but not enough to send into the tunnels. They may not know how many hobgoblins were in each. If they sent too many into one tunnel, those defending could be overrun by the other ones who were attacking.

Fortunately, Draug had another fifty dwarves following behind him.

One of the defending dwarves happened to turn around and see his King, quickly getting a message to the dwarf in charge of their defence.

Florgh jogged over to where Draug stood.

'Which one would you like us to enter?' his King asked.

'I think there are still dwarves trapped behind the stinking hobs' down that one,' he answered, turning and pointing to a tunnel second from his right.

The fighting looked to be fiercest there. Arrows were thick in the air, as the dwarves defending it were able to do nothing but stand their ground. Their shields looked like pin cushions.

Draug nodded his head.

'Follow me,' he said to his personal guards. The others behind followed without the need to be told. They would all be staying with their King.

Shields up, they kept low as they approached the defending dwarves.

As Draug got to the first of them, he grabbed him by his shoulder.

The dwarf spun his head around, the angry look on his face quickly gone.

'When I say, I will need you all to throw whatever weapons you have left at them and I will need you all to step left or right, so we can charge through the centre.' Draug spoke slowly and clearly. He hoped he hadn't made it too complicated for them.

The message was quickly passed along the ranks of dwarves.

'Stand ready!' Draug bellowed, as the arrows continued to rain down on them. Where were they getting so many arrows from? Draug wondered.

'Now,' he roared, as the dwarves in front all took a couple of steps either right or left. Standing straight, with their shields still held up, they threw whatever weapon they still possessed. Most had already dispensed their throwing weapons, so the large axes and hammers flew slowly through the air.

Yet they still had the desired effect. Even though most were very heavy, the dwarves lobbed them far enough to impact those standing at the opening to the passageway.

The number of arrows dwindled significantly for the moment, as Draug's personal guards led the charge, their King not far behind them.

They broke into the ranks of hobgoblins at full speed, knocking aside shields and weapons as they did.

The King's Personal Guard consisted of the finest dwarven warriors in the land. As a result, they also possessed some of the finest weapons and armour ever made within both Kingdoms.

Probably the greatest among them was Draaf.

The hobgoblins never stood a chance, as Draaf sliced open every hobgoblin that came within reach of his twin axes.

He did not bother with a shield, his chain mail armour covering him from head to foot. Although heavy, it was incredibly hardened and crafted with both skill and magic. Draaf personally doubted any other dwarf would be strong enough to walk around in it, let alone fight in it. His strength was legendary.

It didn't take long for the hobgoblins to try and make a hasty retreat, but they were doomed the moment they turned to run, the dwarves cutting them down without even slowing.

Eventually there were only a few surviving hobgoblins making their way back down the tunnel from where they came, loping ahead of the pursuing dwarves.

'Stop!' Draug bellowed. 'You ten go and kill what is left and find those dwarves who remain trapped back there.' He was confident in the ones he chose to get the job done right.

'The rest of you follow me. We have more tunnels to clear yet and a lot more hobgoblins to kill!' He hadn't enjoyed himself this much for as long as he could remember. Going by the looks on those dwarves surrounding him, he knew they felt the same.

'With me!' he roared, as he sped back down the tunnel.

Unlike the weary and sleep-deprived dwarves who had been frantically defending the northern caves for countless hours now, Draug and those accompanying him had only just warmed up.

And aside from the enjoyment they got from killing hobgoblins, they were also very angry. How dare hobgoblins attack them within their own home!

None of them would rest until every last hobgoblin lay dead with their skull crushed against the hard stone of these caves, or they were seen running for their lives outside of the Great Dwarven Mountains.

As tough as dwarves were and as fit as they were, there were no sprinters among them. Once the hobgoblins were out of the caves and running, they would not be chasing them.

'Try not to let any of them escape!' Draug bellowed, as they crashed into the panicked hobgoblins attacking down the next tunnel.

They hadn't even seen Draug and his fellow dwarves until it was too late for them.

CHAPTER 53

An Uneventful Journey

'WHAT WAS HAPPENING back there?' Kabir asked Atriol, after they had ridden a short distance.

'Nothing that concerns us,' the King's Shield answered.

'Is it normal to leave people seeking refuge outside of your walls?' he persisted.

'It is not for me to question,' Atriol said, his voice matching the expressionless look on his face.

Kabir wanted to ask more, but a sharp elbow to his mid-section stopped him.

'He doesn't want to tell you,' Ahlia said, turning her head around so she almost faced him. 'Leave it be.'

Kabir grunted, but let it be.

'Then what do you make of it?' Kabir asked.

She shook her head slightly before answering him.

'There could be many reasons,' she said.

Kabir waited for her to start telling him what they were.

Eventually she sighed.

'There could be disease within, they could be making room for them before entering or they might not want them there,' she finished abruptly.

Kabir sensed she also may not want to talk about it.

'I guess it really is none of our concern,' Kabir said. 'Except that he has my sword!'

'I am aware of that,' she replied. 'I saw him with it.'

Kabir was furious that Marcus had kept it and remained at Havern. It would make its return to him far more difficult.

It is one thing for a Princess to order its return while he is standing there with it. It is another thing entirely confronting the man in Havern and telling him to give his sword back. He had gotten the impression Marcus enjoyed having his sword and would not be keen on returning it. Even if ordered to from afar.

Kabir knew he would end up having to take it from him, which would probably land him in trouble again. He suspected killing one of their Lords might be even more serious than killing a wizard.

'What happens if Marcus refuses to give my sword back?' Kabir asked Atriol. Hopefully the man would be more comfortable answering that question.

'If you are given your freedom, then he is beholden to return it,' Atriol said. He did not elaborate.

'And if he still refuses?' Kabir asked.

'He is a Lord, Barbarian. He will not refuse.'

'Okay,' Kabir said. 'But if for some reason, even though he has to give it back, he refuses to give it back because he wants it for himself, what would happen?'

Atriol turned to look at him. Kabir felt the look he got was reserved for someone simple. Someone who had asked a stupid question and was having difficulty understanding the straight-forward answer he was given.

'If the sword is not his Kabir, then he will return it to its rightful owner. He only has it now because you are a prisoner.' Atriol looked at him for a short time longer, before turning back to surveying the surrounding countryside. He was forever vigilant.

Another elbow to the ribs stopped him trying to ask it in a different way again.

'Your elbows are very pointy,' Kabir said, rubbing his right side, as her left elbow struck him this time.

'What was that for?!' he exclaimed.

'For the next stupid question you are planning on asking him.'

'Trying not to get in trouble the next time I get my sword back is not stupid in my mind,' he replied, genuinely perplexed by her reaction.

'Why not wait and see what happens at our trial first,' she said. 'We are not free yet Kabir.'

He was painfully aware of that, and she was right to say it, but he also thought it important to be prepared if they were released. Hopefully their Princess has more sense than the Lord of Shadow Hill.

The rest of the journey to the capital was uneventful.

They came across nothing threatening and Ahlia had no more reason to thrust her elbows into Kabir's midriff.

As they neared the main gate, Kabir and Ahlia were both still wide-eyed at the sheer size of the place.

From the moment they had seen Lakerth come into view, neither of them had spoken a word.

When Kabir caught his first glimpse of the Dark Swell, his mouth matched the wideness of his eyes.

Ahlia had seen it before in her travels across the plains, but it was still a thrill for her to see it again.

'I will need your swords,' Atriol said, breaking them out of their stupor.

Once away from his Lord, Atriol had provided them both with a sword for the journey between the two cities.

Kabir and Ahlia handed over their swords to the King's Shield, and allowed him to bind their hands together. They were prisoners, and now they would need to be treated accordingly.

Once at the gate, the guards told them all to dismount, as they stared at Firth.

Their eyes moved quickly from his horse as Kabir dismounted and his true size was made clear to them.

'Prisoners to face the King's justice,' Methan said.

Now they were within Lakerth, he would take charge of them.

'What are the charges?' one of them asked. Kabir could tell these were not seasoned guards. The one who asked was old, the other one very young. Neither had the look of a soldier.

He was aware the King and his army had gone west to fight those armies of the Western Realm.

There might be no greater adventure within his lifetime, and he was stuck here in the Capital without his sword, awaiting his trial for killing a wizard. He hoped the war would not be all over by the time he was freed.

'They are charged with killing a wizard,' Methan said. 'But we are tired and would like nothing more than to drop these two off and return to my Lord.'

The guard asked another question, but Methan didn't wait to hear it, as he began leading his horse through the streets.

They eventually arrived at the main inner gate, where their horses were taken from them and their prisoners escorted down into the cells beneath the main hall.

Methan had dismissed his own men, but continued on with Kabir and Ahlia, until they had been placed in their respective cages.

'Why is Ahlia in a separate area to me?' Kabir asked.

Methan turned to the guard who had accompanied them.

'She is a Lady,' he said. 'Ladies are not put in cells within common thugs and thieves.'

Methan turned to Kabir and shrugged.

'She is better off than you barbarian,' he said. 'Nothing we can do about it.'

Kabir was not happy about it, but Methan was right. There was nothing he could do about it, nor about anything else while he was locked up here.

For the first time within his mind, he began to believe that perhaps he may not be getting out of here alive.

Sitting down on the hard, damp stone, he waited for someone to come and tell him what was going to happen next.

CHAPTER 54

Wrath of an Elven Lord

JARKENE WAS STILL reeling from the loss of yet another elf, as he slowed his walk before entering their new makeshift home.

Corein was inside, making a new outfit for her husband. She had shown herself to be quite talented at crafting such things, ever since he had known her.

Gently putting down the vest she was stitching, Corein stood up to greet her Lord.

Jarkene moved quickly to her, taking her in a strong embrace.

It was minutes before he let her go again, turning away to fetch a drink from the bench.

'They left safely?' she asked.

Jarkene nodded, without turning to face her.

'What has upset you then?' Corein asked.

He let out a long sigh, before turning to her again.

'I fought with dwarves along the north of Glorfiden,' he saw the shocked look on her face, but knew she would not interrupt, as he continued his story. 'Treille came to assist me and we killed many of them, before he lost his life in the battle.' He had assured himself over and over that he was not to blame for the loss of another life, but deep down he knew it was true. Had they needed to fight the dwarves? Probably not, he thought now. Yet his thirst for killing seemed to be insatiable.

Then Palir had come to speak with him before he arrived back.

Armies of the west were marching along the entire western border of Glorfiden. They were beginning to spread out, but did not look like they were intending on attacking the forest. Not yet anyway.

'And?' she asked, after he stopped talking. This human knew him far too well, even after they had been apart for so long.

'Armies from the West are moving on Glorfiden,' he said. 'I will need to leave again without delay.'

'Who will you take with you?' she asked.

'All of them,' Jarkene said, no emotion in his voice now.

'Then I will come too,' Corein said. 'I will not be left here alone!' she said, raising her voice, knowing full well what his response would be.

Jarkene didn't know what to say at first. He understood why she would not want to be left here alone. His heart pained him at the thought.

What if none of the elves ever came back? She would be left here for the foul beasts who over-ran the forest. That was not an option.

'You will head south, towards Mayfield. I will have Eltrik escort you there.'

She looked to say more, but he held up his hand.

'Please Corein. You will be a distraction for me if you are where the fighting is. I will need all of my wits about me if I am to defeat an entire army, one section at a time. I will need haste to cover such distances along the Western border.' He knew she would come around, because he was right this time.

Perhaps he did not know her as well as he thought he did.

'I will not have you leave my side again,' she said. 'I will come with you.'

Jarkene was shocked at her words. He knew she was headstrong, but he also knew she was intelligent. She must know what he said was true. Corein was not able to come with him.

'My love,' he said, taking her hands in his. 'If I were able to bring you with me, then I would do so. I never wish to be apart from you again. I simply have too much to do.'

'Then I will follow as best I can,' she said, looking into his eyes.

Had she gone mad?

'You cannot,' he said.

'And yet I will,' she replied.

Jarkene was at a loss. It would seem she had made up her mind. He knew it folly to try and change it now.

'Then you shall stay with Eltrik. I will not leave you without protection.'

Corein put her head down in acquiescence.

'Why?' he asked when she lifted her head again to look at him.

'Because I don't want to die alone,' she said simply. 'And if you die, I wish to be close to you so that I may lie where you do.'

He had no words to respond with, so he simply took her into his embrace again.

It wasn't long before each of the remaining elves returned to the new elven home.

Aside from Palir, Aimon and Thrinne, the rest had been close by.

'If you are not yet aware, the armies of the west are preparing to invade Glorfiden.' He spoke quietly, but without any hint of panic or alarm in his voice. 'It will be difficult to defend all of the forest, but we will do our best to remind them what happens to those who enter our home uninvited.'

'What can we few do?' Eltrik asked. 'Other than die defending Glorfiden.'

'We can live defending it,' Palir replied, with heat in his voice. 'If they cannot see us, then they cannot kill us. We have every advantage within Glorfiden.'

'Palir is right,' Jarkene said, trying to put more emotion into his voice as well. It didn't come naturally. 'If we put the fear of death back into them, they will undoubtedly panic and flee.'

'How do we do that Lord Jarkene?' Flynn asked. 'How will we kill so many of them that the others are cowered?'

'We do not need to kill great numbers,' Jarkene continued. 'We need to be selective in who we kill.' The passion in his voice was real now, as his plan was explained. 'Palir was right,' he continued, looking the other elf in the eye.

'We will remain hidden and kill only those who look most powerful amongst them. If we kill the strongest, then the weak will naturally lose heart.'

Palir nodded his head as he looked around at the other elves, trying to gauge what they were thinking.

Jarkene did the same. He wanted to know which of those standing here would be most valuable, and which would let the fear get to them.

Palir was strongest after himself and his heart was fierce.

Flynn would be smart and she would fight well. Of the others, he held concerns for both Thrinne and Aimon. Both were more suited to nurturing the forest rather than defending it with sword, bow and magic.

Those two he would leave with Corein. He knew they would do their best to protect her. In saying that, he knew they would hide her well within the forest. He preferred that scenario than leaving her with those who would fight back and risk leaving her vulnerable.

He would need to speak to them both alone before they all left. In a place where Corein could not hear him.

Already he felt better about the fight. If he was confident his beloved would be safe, he could give all of his concentration to killing the invaders from the west.

'Palir,' Jarkene said. The warrior elf looked back to him. 'You will take Eltrik to the edge of the forest near the Scourge Mountain. You will watch and wait, and when they enter you will kill off the strongest within their ranks. Questions?'

'Where do we meet when it is all done?' Palir asked with a grin.

Jarkene managed to smile back at him.

'We will meet within the fairie-dragon grove. If any of you are separated or injured, then go there. The grove will hide you until we have finished all of our tasks.'

'Flynn, you and Rhanc will go north to watch and wait there. Any questions?'

There were none this time.

'Aimon, you Thrinne and Corein will accompany me. We will go south and watch the border there. I may have to move ahead of you, but you will catch up as soon as you are able.' Jarkene tried not to look at Corein, but he couldn't help himself. He knew there would be no questions from her. She would wait until they were alone before telling him what she thought of his plan.

'Take the time you need to prepare, but you must hasten. We do not know how long they will wait. It would be better to choose your targets before they are among the trees of our home.' He was about to walk away to make his own preparations, but hesitated.

'Wait,' he said. All of the elves stopped and turned to look at their Lord.

'I need to make something clear to all of you.' He paused a moment to make sure they were all listening to him. 'The defence of this forest is important to us all. It has always been home to the elves and we are bound to it in blood and in magic. All of you here are bonded to Glorfiden in a special way, even you my wife.' He smiled at her, before looking around at each of them in turn.

'Yet I do not want any of you to take any unnecessary risks. We cannot lose any more elves. If, for any reason, it is too risky to attempt a return to the grove, then seek shelter and refuge wherever you may. Even if that means leaving the forest.' He had expected the look of shock on all their faces.

'I will never abandon Glorfiden,' Palir said, glaring at his Lord.

'I am not asking you to abandon it!' Jarkene said back to him, raising his own voice. 'I am telling you all that you must live. Above all else, you must survive whatever it is coming for our home.' He continued to focus his attention on Palir. 'If fleeing today means you can fight for our home another day, then that is what you will do.'

Palir did not look convinced.

'And what if there is nothing left of our home when we come skulking back?' he asked, contempt heavy in his voice.

'Then we will grow it again,' Corein said.

All eyes turned to her.

'Without any of you, there is no Glorfiden. But so long as one of you lives, then there is always hope.' She looked solely at Jarkene as she spoke, the love in her eyes humbling to him as always. 'These monsters may destroy your home, but they cannot touch the real heart of this forest. The magic within and below. I was told once the magic belongs only to the elves and no other can call it forth.' Jarkene looked across at Palir as she spoke. 'If no elves remain,' she finished, 'then what will happen to the magic?'

Jarkene saw the wrath on Palir's face slowly fade, as Corein's words sunk in. To hear a human woman speak such truth to an elf would be hard for him to hear. It seemed the elves were not the only ones able to weave magic within Glorfiden.

'Time to get ready,' Jarkene said quietly, when the silence began to stretch out. Taking Corein by the hand, he walked with her back to their new home.

Once inside she turned to look up at him.

'Your words struck a chord,' he said, smiling down at her. 'I thank you for that.'

'You need thank me for nothing Jarkene,' she said. 'Instead you can tell me what you think to achieve by sending me off with Aimon and Thrinne.'

'I have chosen the strongest elves to accompany those with less prowess. It seemed logical to have the weakest elves with me.' He knew she would see right through him, but he intended to stand his ground this time.

'I agree with you,' she said, putting her arms around him and leaning her head into his chest.

Jarkene furrowed his brow. What game was she playing?

Corein looked up at him, a wisp of hair falling across her face. She had never looked more beautiful.

'I understand that you mean to hide me,' she said. 'However, I will at least be near you if something were to happen. The others will show me where you lie when it is safe.'

Jarkene did not think she was being totally honest with him.

'My beautiful lady. I fear that if I were to fall, there would be nought left for you to find.' He felt horrible saying it and it probably did not help his argument, but it was the truth. Their enemies would not leave his body unmolested if he were killed in battle.

'I do not believe you will fall so easily,' she replied, smiling at him still.

Jarkene laughed at her. 'I have no intention of falling at all. But if it comes to pass that I do, the piles of dead creatures from the Western Realm will show you where I fell.'

It was a morbid conversation they held, yet it somehow made Jarkene feel better. After all of the death and destruction he had dispensed recently, he knew his was a life that deserved to be extinguished. It would be selfish to believe he deserved happiness after all he had done.

These thoughts allowed him not to dwell on his own mortality. He had lived a long life, found a woman to love and had a child with her. A child who had now grown into an adult. He regretted not telling Mortinan how proud he was to have him as his son. It would not have been a hard thing to do, but his pride and fears did not allow it.

'I have been thinking about Mortinan,' he said. 'I should have done more to help him.' He paused. 'I should have told him how I felt about him.'

'You gave him your rod. You gave him your staff. He will know,' she replied.

'Can you tell..' he began.

'You will tell him when he returns,' Corein said, talking over the top of him. 'It will need to come from you.'

Jarkene slowly nodded.

'When he returns,' he said, before leaning down and kissing her.

Less than an hour later, the elves were ready to leave.

Jarkene had spoken with Aimon and Thrinne alone for a time. They were both more than pleased to have Corein's safety as their primary task.

Jarkene knew neither of them would want to fight against the armies of the West.

Even were there hundreds of elves alive, including his father and brothers, still both of them would have been loath to fight. It was not in their nature.

Jarkene was not bothered by it. He was well aware of the importance to their home of those like Aimon and Thrinne. Those elves who nurtured the forest. It was a great part of what made Glorfiden the home it was.

'You both need to survive what comes,' he said. 'Without you and Mendina, there will be no re-birth for Glorfiden.'

'We will take care of the Lady Corein,' Thrinne said. 'I know of places in the south where they will not find us. There are powerful charms there. Old magic Lord Jarkene.'

'Good,' he said. 'I am relieved.' Indeed he was. Jarkene did not know where this place was that she spoke of, which concerned him only a little. So long as they kept her safe.

'Lord Jarkene,' Aimon said. 'How bad do you think it will get? How much of the forest will they try and ruin?'

Jarkene turned to look at the young elf. The future of the forest was in good hands, but he feared for the future of the elves if these were the only ones to survive. They would no longer be feared. It would be a constant challenge for them just to survive.

He didn't answer straight away, as his thoughts drifted.

'Lord Jarkene,' Aimon asked again.

Jarkene focused his vision, looking directly into Aimon's eyes as he answered.

'All of it,' he said. 'They will try to burn the entire forest to the ground and kill everything that lives within it.'

'Then you must stop them Lord Jarkene,' Aimon said, not cowered by his Lord's words.

Jarkene did not think to hear such words from the young elf, but it put a smile on his face. Perhaps they were not doomed yet.

'I will do more than stop them,' Jarkene said. 'I will make it so no others will dare set foot within Glorfiden again.' He paused once more as he stared at nothing. 'They will all die,' he said quietly. 'All of them.'

CHAPTER 55

Answers Revealed

'Yes!' Mendina exclaimed, jumping up from her cushion and punching the air with a fist.

It was an uncharacteristic outburst, and Brindel couldn't help smiling at her.

He liked Mendina and was genuinely pleased for her Champion. He still didn't quite know how she had done it, but he knew it would upset Mortinan, so he was extra happy.

Somehow her Champion had prevailed against the dragon.

Against all odds, she had survived and was still in the game.

Brindel continued to watch her, as Mendina sat back down hurriedly in front of her *eye*. He then turned back to his own *eye* as the Dragon began to speak.

None within the clearing stirred, as they sat transfixed by each word the dragon spoke. It was like the Creator himself was speaking.

As the Champions of Mortinan and Mendina began their journeys out of the ruined forest, Brindel began to think about what it meant for the game and for his own Champion.

In a way, he was pleased. If Mendina and Mortinan had survived against it, his Champion was just as likely to do the same.

What concerned him though, was the fact Mortinan and Mendina's next quest was much less of a journey than his own Champion's would be.

They had only to return to their home. That was it.

Mortinan lived within the Western Realm, and Mendina's Elven Forest was even closer!

Yet that was nowhere near the worst of it. The direct route to his Champion's home would take him through the heart of Glorfiden. His Champion would certainly be killed. It was a quest he could never hope to survive.

Where was the fairness in any of that?

Yet he wasn't panicking just yet. He did not believe the Creator would make his Champion walk through Glorfiden. If he did, then so too would Kabir and Linf's Champions. If either of them even made it to the dragon.

If they did and survived, then not only would Kabir need to walk through Glorfiden, he would also need to walk through the Dwarven Mountains. Brindel doubted even his Champion would survive such a journey.

As he sat back, wondering again how Mendina's champion had survived, he put the next hypothetical stage of his Champion's journey to the back of his mind. Before he needed to worry about what the Creator would come up with, he needed to be sure his Champion would survive against the dragon.

Kabir had been partly right.

Although Mortinan and Mendina had a good head start on their next quest, he now knew what his Champion could expect. And he could plan for ways in which he might be able to help him.

The advantage was definitely his and he now had plenty of time to think about it before Brindel the Dwarven Smith commenced his battle with the mightiest dragon on Dark Swell.

Once more he ran through the list of spells contained in his scroll, and began estimating their effectiveness against each attack the dragon had used against Mortinan and Mendina. She would undoubtedly have more, but Brindel could not afford to guess.

Most of the spells he discounted straight away, but some he put aside for more thought. If he decided to intervene in the battle, he needed to make certain he was safe from the dragon. That obviously had to be his highest priority.

He knew the mighty beast would be able to see him and he had no idea what she would do against someone interfering in the test.

Even if that someone was a gamer, Brindel did not think she would be pleased.

Linf was more than a little shaken this time, as she stepped back through her *eye*.

She had known the risk she took in entering and speaking with her Champion, but to have her goblin begin to drain energy from her had been quite frightening.

It made it far too risky to enter in future, which was going to make it very difficult to relay any advice to her.

Linf knew she would need to try something different. A completely new tactic to get her Champion turned around. Her current tactic did not seem to be working too well.

Already both Mortinan and Mendina had faced off with the Dragon, and were making for their next destination, while her Champion was walking away in the complete opposite direction.

The more she thought about it, the more she knew there was little she could do.

The goblin thought it humorous now when she appeared. It no longer annoyed nor angered her. She had also become considerably more confident in the use of her powers, which made any excursion on to Dark Swell to speak with her Champion, considerably more dangerous.

The next time Linf entered, the goblin may fire one of her energy balls straight at her.

Although able to see the energy as easily as her Champion could, Linf had also been able to see how quickly the goblin was able to ball and fire it now.

There was a very real risk she may not be quick enough to react, and being struck by one would almost certainly kill her.

Winning this game and receiving the reward that awaited the victor was incredibly important to her, but it was secondary to her surviving. Linf was not about to sacrifice her life in order to try and win.

Mortinan had shown in the cave that not even he was prepared to do that, and she held no doubt he would do anything he could in order to win.

CHAPTER 56

Time to Make Ready

'STILL NOTHING AHEAD of us,' Kagen said, in answer to Granwith's question. 'I have told you already, I will let you know if Feng sees anything.'

Granwith just grunted in response.

They were coming to the end of the forest to their right, for which he was extremely grateful.

He would be glad if he never had to come this close to the Elven Forest again.

Not that he was afraid, he simply didn't like being in such a vulnerable place. Especially knowing how important it was they returned home as quickly as possible.

Granwith hoped the old smith was okay. Brindel was without question the most stubborn dwarf he had ever met, which was part of the reason he liked him so much. He was stupidly brave and would never give up in a fight.

He was still annoyed he had been forced to turn around and come back. The thought of fighting something as powerful as that which the old dwarf was searching for, sounded like something he would always regret not doing.

'Feng has returned,' Kagen said, breaking Granwith out of his thoughts. 'There is something up ahead.'

'What is it?' Granwith asked.

'Hobgoblins I think,' Kagen said.

'You think?' Granwith asked. 'Can you do better?'

'Feng has no name for them, so he had to describe them to me. I think they are hobgoblins.' Kagen sounded annoyed, so Granwith let it be. There was never any point arguing with the young dwarf. It got you nowhere.

'How many?' he asked instead.

'A lot,' Kagen said, 'but they are travelling north of us. He says they look to be going above the swamp.'

'If they are no threat to us, then why is he telling us?' Granwith asked, annoyed that he wouldn't get to kill any hobgoblins.

'You asked to be told if he saw anything up ahead!' Kagen said, sounding just as annoyed as Granwith. 'Will I ask him not to tell us from now on?' the young dwarf asked.

Granwith was about to bite this time, but stopped what he was going to say.

'Tell your friend thank you for letting us know,' Granwith said.

'That it?' Kagen asked.

'That is all,' Granwith said, as he increased his speed to a slow jog. 'We should move faster though,' he added, 'unless you are tired.'

Kagen didn't answer as he increased his speed to match that of Granwith.

They continued to make good time and arrived at the dwarven entrance not long after darkness had descended upon them.

Granwith was a little surprised to see that still no works had started on securing it. He knew that would change quickly once he informed King Draug of what was heading their way.

He didn't recognise the dwarf at the entrance, but he obviously knew who Granwith was.

'Granwith,' he said in greeting. 'I bet you haven't heard the news of the Northern tunnels.'

'Of course I haven't,' Granwith replied, but tempered his tone a little. The guard was probably bored and simply happy to talk to someone.

He was going to be very busy soon enough.

'What has happened?' he asked.

'A huge army of hobgoblins has attacked. The King and his guard have gone themselves to try and stop them getting into the central parts. There is still no word come from them.' He sounded excited. 'Will you be heading that way?'

'There were hobgoblins running back home earlier this afternoon,' Granwith said. 'I doubt they are still a threat to us.'

The dwarf nodded his head in a sagely manner.

'That is good then. There has been too much happening under this mountain of late. Too many good dwarves losing their lives.'

'There has,' Granwith agreed. 'But you need to be on your guard. I fear there is worse yet to come, and it could be headed straight for this entrance you guard.'

The dwarves' eyes opened wide.

'Here? What is it? How far away is it?' He sounded concerned.

Granwith held up one hand and put the other on the dwarf's shoulder. 'I need to speak with King Draug first, but I'm sure he will send dwarves to strengthen the door here. Until that happens, you need to remain vigilant. Let the others know.'

He stared into the eyes of the dwarf so that his message would be believed.

He didn't know if the Dwarven army from the West had sent scouts out ahead of the main army. It would make sense if he had.

'Do not presume any dwarf you see to be a friend. Be on your guard,' he said again before moving off.

They didn't stop to speak with any of the other dwarves staggered back from the entrance. A quick nod was all he had time for now. He needed to speak with Draug.

But if Draug was delayed in getting back, he needed to convince others of the urgency in securing the Western entrance, otherwise the dwarven army from the west would be left to just walk inside unchallenged.

Granwith knew they would be a whole lot harder to get out than a band of hobgoblins.

Who knew what surprises they had in store for their eastern cousins.

They were dwarves after all.

Granwith finally reached the main hall and told Kagen to go and get something to eat. Granwith was hungry for a hot meal also, but he needed to speak with someone who could get things moving on the western entrance.

'Branwen!' He hollered across the hall. A few dwarves looked up briefly, but then went back to their food. That any bothered to look up at all told Granwith how on edge things were within the great Northern Mountains.

The old steward looked over at Granwith but made no move to stand.

With a sigh, Granwith walked over to where he sat.

Grabbing a seat opposite him, the warrior dwarf grabbed a piece of flatbread off the old dwarf's plate.

'Any news from the west?' Branwen asked, but with little conviction.

Granwith knew things were bad when Branwen was too tired to show any real interest in anything.

'When did you last sleep?' Granwith asked.

Branwen waved away his question like he was swatting away a cave pest.

'No-one has time to sleep,' he answered. 'Too much to do.'

Granwith sighed before continuing.

'Then you really aren't going to like what I have to tell you.'

Branwen looked up from his plate this time, his deadpan eyes boring themselves into Granwith.

'An army of dwarves from the west are approaching. They shouldn't be far off by now.'

Branwen said nothing for a time. He just continued to stare.

Not the response Granwith had been expecting, or hoping for.

Eventually an answer did come.

'I told Draug to fix that western entrance ages ago!' he said, real anger in his voice. 'Now it will be the death of us all.'

'Surely you can do something?' Granwith asked.

'Yes, we can do *something*', he said. 'We can patch up a wall to cover the entrance, but do you really think something done in such haste is going to fool a dwarf?!'

'No,' Granwith said. 'But it may be enough they do not notice it from a distance.'

'Perhaps,' Branwen said. 'But then you must ask yourself how careful you were in covering your tracks when you returned, and how careful every other dwarf who has used that entrance was. Would a dwarven tracker be able to follow your steps right to the door?'

Granwith cursed out loud.

He had done what he could to minimise his tracks, but he knew any tracker worth his name would be able to follow where he and Kagen had been.

'Put the door there nevertheless,' Granwith said. 'The entrance is narrow. It was designed that way to make it hard for anything to come at us in numbers. We can hold off anything that tries to get in there.'

Branwen didn't look convinced, but then shrugged his shoulders.

'If nothing else, it will alert us if they decide to come in that way.'

Granwith nodded in reply.

'I will get some dwarves to head that way as soon as I have finished here,' the old steward said.

Granwith was going to say something, but held his tongue.

There would be time for a makeshift door to be made before they arrived.

While that happened, he needed to help sort the rest of the realm.

First of all his King needed to be told. Then he would no doubt sit down with the rest of Draug's counsel and work out how they would best defeat the advancing army of dwarves.

Whatever happened, it was going to be a fight the likes of which they had never seen before.

He tried to contain himself, but Granwith was more than a little excited at the prospect.

The closer he got, the more impressed Zuroth was with the size of the Northern Mountains. They would make for a fantastic kingdom.

He was sure there were many, many parts that remained untouched, their treasures waiting to be found.

He was also sure there would be places and things found that the current occupants had no idea about. That their true purpose was something that needed a western dwarf to bring forth its greatness.

The great forges in the south he had heard tell of, would make it the perfect realm for his new kingdom. That none of those dwarves

within the southern mountains could fight meant he only needed
to worry about conquering one Kingdom. If those tales were true,
then once he had taken the Northern Mountains, the rest would
probably just give up.

He wasn't sure he wanted such cowardly dwarves to serve him,
but there was bound to be a few that were of use to him. Those few
he would allow to live.

The rest would be sport for his warriors.

'Two of your scouts return,' Kroff said to him, breaking him
from his thoughts.

'Bring them here,' Zuroth said.

He waited while the dwarves came to him.

The first one was an older dwarf. He knew him well.

'There has been a great number of hobgoblins fleeing the
mountains from the north,' Lirth said. 'They are many less than
when they went into the mountains.'

'How long ago?' Zuroth asked.

'Less than a day,' he replied. 'They fled north of the swamp.'

Zuroth didn't respond straight away.

The entrance was obviously a large one, with so many hobgoblins
attacking. It was obviously not very well defended either, if that
stinking vermin were brave enough to try their luck.

His respect for his eastern cousins just dropped even further.

With no other options, it seemed to be the best way in. There
would be a myriad of tunnels, so once inside they would be almost
impossible to stop.

He knew caves and he knew what his army was capable of.

'Go back and find out all you can about the entrance there,'
Zuroth said.

'Others have already gone ahead,' Lirth said. 'I returned to tell
you about the hobgoblins.'

'Good,' Zuroth said. 'That is good.'

He nodded and Lirth left to find some food.

'You said scouts,' Zuroth said, turning to Kroff.

Kroff nodded and indicated in front again with a flick of his head.

Zuroth turned and saw another dwarf approaching. This one was
younger and he couldn't remember her name.

'Where have you been?' Zuroth asked.

'I went along the western side of the mountains Zuroth,' she replied. 'Followed some dwarf tracks all the way to a small opening in the side of the mountain.' She was a cocky little dwarf, Zuroth thought. Her news better be good.

'How well is it hidden?' Zuroth asked. 'Did you try to get in?'

'Hidden?' his scout said. 'There is no door. Just a single dwarf guarding it, sitting behind a bit of rock.'

'Are you kidding?' Zuroth asked.

'No,' the dwarf said, a big smile on her face. 'You can pretty much just walk straight in.'

Zuroth laughed and signalled for the scout to leave.

'Walk straight in she said,' Zuroth said, turning to Kroff and laughing. 'I think that is what we will do.'

Kroff smiled and nodded.

'I think we will still send most to the northern entrance, but my best and most fearless will go in through that little door and cause untold damage when they are inside.'

Zuroth couldn't believe how arrogant and stupid these dwarves were. He was embarrassed to even call them dwarves. They had obviously lived a sheltered life.

Well that was all about to change, he thought, as his leaders began the task of choosing who would get to go through the side of the mountain.

Many of them would probably be killed, but they would have a lot of fun before they died. A true warrior's death. It would be an honour to be chosen, and he regretted that he wouldn't be able to join them.

'Give whoever you choose to lead them the javelin,' Zuroth said, as Kroff and the others went to move off.

'Are you sure?' Kroff asked. 'That should be wielded by you.'

'Don't you think I should be able to decide who gets to use it?' Zuroth asked.

Kroff walked back over to his King.

'If they are all killed, the weakling eastern dwarves will have it.' Kroff spoke softly, so the others wouldn't hear. It was never a good idea to question the King, let alone in front of others.

'Then choose well,' Zuroth said, even softer, 'because you will be leading them.'

Kroff looked stunned for a moment, before nodding his head to the King.

'I am honoured,' he said. 'I will not let you down.'

'I expect you to meet us in the middle,' Zuroth said.

'I will be there,' Kroff said, turning away this time and striding off.

Zuroth was pleased with his choice.

Although Kroff could sometimes speak out of turn, he was an exceptional warrior and a fine leader of dwarves. He was always going to be his choice, but his insolence made it easier.

He did not hope death on any of them, but if Kroff died so the rest could prevail, then so be it.

He would get a hero's burial and have his name sung in the halls of Zuroth's new kingdom.

Kroff walked away knowing he had been given a fantastic opportunity. Most were scared to stand up to Zuroth, but he had always tried to speak his mind, and now it had given him the greatest of honours.

Not only leading a small, but fierce band of warriors against a kingdom of dwarves, but carrying with him the King's Javelin.

Kroff had assisted with the pendants they had made for Mithrak and his dark-mage and knew the power they possessed. Unlike Mithrak however, the dwarves had no magic within them to take their weapons to the next level and augment that which they imbued.

Nevertheless, they were still able to put magic into the weapons they made, and there was none greater than the King's Javelin.

Never before had a ruling King allowed any other to use it, let alone relinquish it for another to use in battle.

Although he knew the King meant for it to be used by Brishner; the best of their elite warriors and the first he would choose; he would be loath to let any other use it once they were away from Zuroth. If he was leading these dwarves into battle, then he would be the one wielding the Javelin.

CHAPTER 57

A Surprise Visit

F LEK-NIHT STOOD HIGH in the stirrups of her mount as she looked down at the Barbarian village below.

Night still blanketed the land and the fires burning throughout the village made those inside easily visible.

Looking around at her army of dark-elves, Flek-Niht knew none of them would be seen until it was too late for the Barbarians.

The orders were simple this time. There would be no capturing of their young ones. That could be done at a later time when all of her expectations were met. Resources were required to keep prisoners, and for now she needed all of her warriors to fight.

For their confidence, this first attack should be a complete slaughter with no dark-elves losing their lives this night.

Flek-Niht knew it was inevitable some would probably die tonight, but she could still hope.

It was a monumental time for those dark-elves who had chosen to accompany her, and she wanted them all to be able to enjoy their victory.

The loss of her own son still burnt within her. She did not wish that upon any other who had pledged to come on this journey with her and her clan.

There was no fear within her, but it had been decided earlier who would have the honour of entering the village first. It was their task to kill off as many Barbarians as they were able before the alarm was raised.

There were those among the dark-elf ranks who were perfectly suited for this task. Her son had been one of those, but hopefully those about to enter now had learnt from the mistakes of those before. Perhaps her son had not died in vain!

A shallow whistle was the signal for them to move forward.

If Flek-Niht wasn't searching the night for them and hadn't grown up living in the dark, she would not have been able to see any of them as they moved down the rise toward the village.

Even with her skilful night vision, it was difficult to keep track of them.

The night was cloudy and the moon was currently covered.

The walls of the village weren't high, but scouts reported there was some kind of substance splashed over them. Those she had sent would not have difficulty getting over them. Once inside the walls, they knew what had to be done.

Others had been tasked to open the main gate the moment the alarm was given. When that time came and the gate was open, the remainder of her army would descend upon them.

Small watch-towers were spread out along the walls. Each had one barbarian keeping watch. They were easily visible by torchlight and neither of the two Flek-Niht could see from her vantage point looked particularly vigilant.

An arrow or spear would see to them. So long as it went through the head.

It had been reported to her from the first assault how difficult it had been to kill the Barbarians. The same battle where her son had been taken from her. Some had told her the large warriors kept fighting even after they had died. As preposterous as that sounded to her in the beginning, Flek-Niht was not one to ever dismiss anything because it sounded far-fetched.

She had learnt many things throughout her long life. One of the most important lessons was that strange things happened, and when you think you have seen them all, there were still stranger things out there waiting to surprise you.

Flek-Niht had been given the opportunity to test what those dark-elves had told her when the Barbarians were seen climbing the mountain towards their army.

Those she had sent to dispatch them had been ordered to kill a couple of them in the conventional manner. Through the heart.

Others were instructed to kill theirs by impaling the head.

She had been astonished to hear that the Barbarians ability to continue fighting even after being dealt mortal blows had been true. Except for those struck fatal blows in the head. Those ones had died as quickly as any other creature did.

Every dark-elf had now been given this knowledge. It may help many to avoid the same fate as her son.

The Barbarian named Devon looked out into the night, his visibility not going far past what the torches along the wall allowed him to see. Which wasn't much. He was tired, he was bored and he was angry at Scraff for making him stand guard here for a second night in a row.

Devon had argued with Scraff for not letting him take men into the mountains to look for those who were still missing.

He knew Dougal would have sent the entire village out to look for them, but Scraff was different to his father. He was no coward, but he thought too much. He believed they may all be at risk and that the village was their best chance to survive whatever was coming.

Devon had thought him delusional and may have told him as much.

So it was that the village's finest warrior was stuck doing watch-duty, as the dark-elves fired off their first shots into the village. Each arrow and spear was loosed at the same time and at each of the five guard-towers.

Four Barbarians were killed instantly. One saw a blur in the night and moved his head enough for the arrow to glance from his helmet.

Although not as powerful an artefact as those owned by others in his village, Devon's helmet was still powerful and did enough to save his life. The spear that followed struck the side and penetrated the steel, but fortunately it did not penetrate far and the wound was not deep enough to kill him.

Devon was dizzy, but had enough wits about him to fall down behind the lower defence of the tower. Looking across and behind the side of the tower he was in, he was able to see shadows scaling the wall not far from where he lay.

He knew he needed to sound the alarm or many more within the village of Horned Peak would die tonight.

Moving slowly so he didn't attract attention, Devon reached to his belt and unclipped the horn. Raising it to his lips he began to blow into it with all he had.

The sound rang out loud and true throughout the village, and he soon heard voices begin to shout their own alarms. Moving his head from side to side in an attempt to shake off the pain and numbness in his skull, Devon put his hands underneath him and pushed himself up to stand. The spear that impaled his chest and dug into the wood underneath him pushed him straight back down again.

Turning his head to the side in an attempt to look behind him, the last thing the Barbarian saw was a second spear coming toward his face, and the grimacing face of the dark-elf thrusting it forward.

Flek-Niht was surprised the alarm had been sounded so early in their assault, but she knew it would not alter the end result.

Already she could see dark-elves swarming over the fence next to the main gate. Whatever was rubbed all over the walls was not intended to make it slippery or difficult to climb. Her forces went over with ease.

She surmised it was probably something to prevent it burning easily.

How unfortunate for them that this enemy had no intention of burning their little village to the ground.

It was going to be the first trophy of many more to come.

Flek-Niht began to move forward now, as the gates swung open and the dark-elf army swarmed inside the walls.

She knew the fighting wouldn't last long and once it was over it would be over. One of the Barbarian's greatest strengths was their courage and willingness to run headlong into a fight. This night it would be the reason for their downfall.

None of them would flee and none would hide.

They would all be killed within these walls and none of the other villages would be any the wiser. They would be able to move from one village to the next, slaughtering them all as they went.

Flek-Niht didn't know how long it would take to completely wipe out the Barbarians that inhabited these mountains, but that day would soon be one night closer.

The only thing she was unsure of tonight was how many of her own dark-elves would be left dead after the rout was complete and finding out what happened to enable one of them to give the alarm so early on.

Soon enough these questions would be answered, but for now she sat back on her Telquin as he trotted in through the gates. She could see and hear pockets of fighting continuing around her, as the army of dark-elves finished off the last of those alive within the walls.

Eventually she was approached by one of those leading the main fighting-force, the one selected to represent her family.

'It is done,' Glim-Stad said to her. He was breathing heavily and had blood-stains on his clothing, but the smile on his face told her the blood was not his.

Flek-Niht nodded her head to him, indicating she had heard him.

'What next?' he asked. Their immediate actions after the battle had not been discussed. Flek-Niht thought it bad luck to discuss them before they had won.

The overall invasion was a different matter entirely. That needed to be discussed in order to get the other families to fight with hers.

'Remove all clothing, armours, weapons and trinkets before we harvest the bodies. Ensure they are all bled as soon as possible. They might be meat for our pets, but I don't want them stinking up the place.' Flek-Niht waved him away after she stopped speaking. He would be able to work out the rest without her. He was not stupid, or else she would not have chosen him for the honour.

'Where is the home of their leader?' she asked one of her personal guards.

He turned to another, who pointed south.

'This way,' he said, leading the way.

Flek–Niht was not overly impressed with how their leader lived. It was very primitive and rather dirty. The skins and wall-hangings smelled funny and the mattress felt lumpy.

Yet she was aware they were on a campaign and her usual luxuries had been deemed unnecessary until the conquest was complete.

'Lay my things over the top,' she said to a guard, before sitting down in a large chair.

Scouts continued to come and go throughout the night, updating her on conditions both east and west of where they were.

Only one village lay to their east. Near to the black waters themselves, it would be their next target.

Almost half would remain here to defend the village they had just taken, although all reports indicated no movements between any of the villages in the last couple of days.

The rest of her army would travel east and slaughter all of those Barbarians living near the dark waters.

That village could then be left vacant until the rest had been taken.

Their losses had been acceptable. More dark-elves than she had hoped or expected had lost their lives to the Barbarians, but not enough to make her re-think her plans.

Flek–Niht would do it without the help of the other families, safely hidden away in their ancient home. They did not deserve to share in her glory, so she would not be calling on them, no matter what happened.

'Bring me their valuables,' she said.

It would be light soon, but she was not tired.

Flek–Niht did not expect to need sleep for many days yet. There was still so much to do.

CHAPTER 58

Cold Hearted

THE LAND AROUND the swamp was not difficult terrain and for a dwarf it was not taxing at all.

However, for Brindel it was mind-numbingly boring.

There appeared to be nothing else alive in this part of the land. All morning while he trudged along, he had not even seen a single bird in the sky. What kind of land was this? How could there be no signs of life? It was ridiculous.

Even the caves where he lived housed far more than this.

At least he had slept well the night before, finding himself a small niche to squeeze into among a pile of boulders. It wasn't comfortable, but at least he was warm and dry.

Thankfully he now found himself approaching an area thicker with trees. It was a positive sign that he was nearing the ruined forest that he sought. Or so he believed.

At least the stinking swamplands had been left behind.

Brindel dreaded the walk back through them, but for now he was thankful he could breathe in fresh air again.

He had almost become accustomed to the lack of sounds around him, so he quickly became aware of movement and voices ahead. Although he couldn't understand what they were saying, he was thankful at least that something else was alive around here.

Even if those voices sounded like orcs, it was still comforting to him. Brindel had always been a bit of a loner, but he still sometimes enjoyed the company of others and the sounds animals in the wild made. He didn't know just how much until recent times.

As he walked closer he found himself a large tree to stand behind, so he could cautiously look around the large trunk. Before him he saw a small village.

There were numerous pale skinned orcs walking around, while others sat around doing not much. As he looked more intently, he could see this village contained only the elderly and the very young.

It would seem all those of fighting age had been summoned elsewhere.

That was probably a good thing for him.

It meant he wouldn't need to walk all the way around the village. He had nothing to fear from a bunch of decrepit old orcs and their great-offspring.

If he had to kill a few of them, so be it.

Brindel just wanted to finish the task that had been given to him and be on his way home again.

Hopefully they had not all been killed by the Western Dwarves and his home usurped, because he had some serious armour he needed to put together.

Although the words and pictures were burnt into his mind, he also still wanted his journal back.

It only just now occurred to him what might happen if those stinking invading dwarves got their hands on it.

They could go south and just take the diamond from Elenda.

If the Northern Dwarves were unable to stop them, then the cowardly Southern Dwarves would be no match. They would crumble as swiftly as these orcs he was about to confront.

With a sudden, renewed urgency, Brindel stepped out from behind the tree and began jogging toward the orc village.

The first to see him was one of the younger orcs.

It had obviously never seen a dwarf before, as it just stood there, staring at Brindel as he approached.

As others saw him and voices began to ring out within the village, other young ones began picking up whatever they had close by to use as a weapon.

The first one he came across had picked up a curved blade, probably used to cut fruits from the trees. It ran at Brindel, swinging the weapon as it ran.

Brindel knew it was important to set a good example early on. He wanted to try and deter as many as he could from throwing their lives away.

For although he despised orcs and had enjoyed killing them in the past, these were only children. He would get no satisfaction from killing their younglings.

The first one he allowed to strike him, the blade bouncing harmlessly off his shoulder plate. The orc swung again and this time Brindel caught it in his gauntlet. Pulling the orc closer to him, he swung his axe upwards, driving the blade deep into the orc child's face.

It did not have the desired effect on the others. Instead of them standing down or running away, it drove them all into a frenzy. There were at least eight of them that swarmed him all at once.

Brindel began swinging his axe above his head in an arc, severing limbs and imbedding it into chests, as he moved around in a circle.

It didn't take long before all eight of them lay dead on the ground around him.

Turning in a circle as he looked around, Brindel saw many of the old orcs holding on to other young ones, preventing them from charging at him also.

He nodded his head towards them. They may well have seen dwarves fight during their lifetimes and knew better than to attack this one.

Brindel was able to casually stroll through the centre of their village and out the other side. No more of them tried to stop him.

Without looking back once, he continued on towards the ruined forest.

The next part of his journey was no harder than the previous part. Although the land was thicker with trees and sloped up and down in places, Brindel made his way without further incident.

The undergrowth was not thick and there were no more creatures wanting to cross paths with him.

He was also able to follow beside a fast-running stream. He had heard the waterfall ahead, and surmised it would be a good place to catch some food.

It didn't take him long to arrive.

As he moved up to drink from the water, he noticed he was not the only one to have been here recently.

Two others had sat here. Looking around some more, he saw the remains of a small fire and the bones of a good-sized fish. That was encouraging.

The footprints were not large enough to be orc and he was aware they didn't bother cooking their meals.

They were also not big enough to be those of a man.

Maybe the right size for a half-man and a small elf though.

'Well, well, well,' he said out loud to the trees. 'My friends are back, only this time they are in front of me.'

Brindel had not forgotten he had a score to settle with these two. Especially the half-elf.

Now it looked like he would get his chance.

After he had caught himself some fish.

Checking their fire up close, he found the embers were already cold. They still had a good lead on him, but he was confident they would cross paths again.

Maybe on their way back from the ruined forest.

At least he knew he was on the right path.

After another loud burp, Brindel threw down the fish bones and stood up to take another drink from the pool of water.

It was cold, but extremely refreshing. The two fish he had just eaten were also delicious. He was tempted to lay here for a time and maybe even have a nap, but there was still an urgency for him to get home.

Although he would never get back in time to influence what was happening there, he still saw no reason to delay.

Following the footprints of the elf and her half-breed, he saw they had climbed the cliff face by grabbing hold of the vines that fed out of the stones.

Looking up, he could see it would not be an easy climb. Not for a dwarf anyway. There were no vines that grew from the top all the way down.

He would need to jump from vine to vine, not knowing if the next one he jumped to would be able sustain his weight.

Cursing, he decided to try and find another way up.

It took him almost an hour before he came upon a place where the cliff was not sheer, and he was confident of being able to climb his way up using both vines and hand and footholds.

Climbing to the top, the view was starkly different to that down below. Although there were trees up here as well, they didn't look right. Something was definitely off about them.

He had finally found the ruined forest.

Walking through the tangled mess of trees was not easy for Brindel. It took the better part of the day for him to weave his way through the root systems, thick undergrowth and the myriad of small, fast flowing streams.

The smell was not toxic like that in the swamps, but there was something wrong about it. He could taste whatever was in the air on his tongue and he didn't like it. Strangely though, the water still looked and tasted pure.

The trees were a completely different story, but he wasn't too concerned about it. Unless they came to life and attacked him, he wouldn't give their plight another thought.

What was really concerning though, even to a dwarf, was the lack of any sign of life within this forest.

He had come across no animal tracks, seen no nests or hollows in the trees and heard no sounds other than the trickle of water.

The forest was alive, but it hosted no life within it.

As he wondered again how far this forest stretched, the trees suddenly stopped and Brindel stepped out in to a barren landscape.

There were no more trees in front of him. It was a broken land ahead of him now, with ground that bubbled.

It would be easier to walk over, but as he looked across into the distance, Brindel was in two minds on whether he should.

He had seen the dragon, even from this distance.

It was huge and there was no way he would ever be able to defeat such a creature.

If the dragon wanted him dead, then the march across this bare patch of ground would be his final trek.

'Welcome dwarf,' a voice said within his mind. It was loud and all other sounds were closed off. 'Your next task is almost complete.'

Brindel froze where he was.

Not only was it huge, but it was intelligent. Perhaps it wasn't here to kill him?

After all, what sort of a suicide challenge would that be?

'You do however need to keep walking,' it said to him.

Brindel began to step involuntarily forward towards the waiting dragon.

He had never been so in awe of anything before in his life. The closer he got, the larger it kept getting, until at one point he stopped moving.

'Not yet,' it said to him. 'I can't get at you from that far away.' He thought he heard it laugh softly. It laughed? It was enough for Brindel to question what was happening, and time enough for him to reach into his vest and grasp hold of the stone he had 'forgotten' to return to the Southern Dwarves.

The moment he touched it, the confusion and fear within his mind dissipated, as he looked at the dragon standing two hundred paces in front of him. It was still massive, and he still believed he was no chance of defeating it, but he was no longer afraid and daunted by it.

The old Brindel had returned, as he took his axe into his right hand.

'You can still try to get at me my pretty little dragon,' Brindel replied, 'but you may get stung.'

This time there was no mistaking the laughter, and it was no longer within his mind.

'Very good dwarf,' the dragon said. 'I do like a battle of wits as much as I like a fight.'

It was to be a battle of wits then. Brindel liked his odds there more than if it were a fight.

'You think you are smarter than me?' Brindel asked.

'I do,' the dragon replied casually, 'but that is not why you are here and it is not why I am here.'

'Oh,' Brindel said. 'Then why are you here?' he asked.

'I am here for one purpose only dwarf. I am here to kill you.' It still spoke in a casual voice and with little emotion.

Brindel sighed deeply.

'That's a shame,' the dwarf replied. 'I'm not quite ready to die yet. I have things to do you see.'

Rearing up on to its hind legs, the dragon began to spew forth its breath weapon, as Brindel watched on in awe.

CHAPTER 59

Judgement

AREANA STRETCHED WHILE she waited for the next case. The chair she was forced to sit in was not a comfortable one. Despite her protestations, Heridah insisted she use it. Something about reflecting her position and showing she was interested in those before her.

So far today, it had been boring petition after boring petition.

Why someone else could not look after it she had no idea. Heridah had left her a short time ago with 'pressing duties'. He was probably relaxing somewhere right now.

'The next one is a very serious matter Princess,' Mellor said softly to her. 'An Eastern Barbarian is charged with the killing of a wizard.'

Areana sat up straight. This sounded more like it.

It would obviously be an easy decision, but a lot more interesting nevertheless.

The great doors opened as the persons she had just dealt with left. They remained open, as several of the King's Shield walked in, followed behind by a huge man and a tall female. Two more King's Shield brought up the rear, as the doors were closed once more.

The King's Shield in front took up their spots on the steps in front of the Princess, turning to look at the Barbarian and his woman. The others remained standing behind them.

Princess Areana had a clear view of the two before her, and their appearance shocked her.

She had heard tales of the ferocious and lawless Barbarians who lived in mountains far to the east of her father's realm.

The man before her was indeed a monster; in that he was larger and more muscular than anyone she had ever seen; but he did not look how her imagination had portrayed him to be. He was rather attractive and looked at her without a nasty expression on his face.

The woman by his side also looked nothing like she had imagined their women to appear. She was elegant and beautiful and at the same time had a dangerous feel about her, much like that of Catlin. A confidence that bespoke strength.

'Before you stand Kabir of the village Deerstep and his companion, the Lady Ahlia of the Plains People.' Areana saw the woman flinch as her name was called out. She had no idea why.

'Kabir is charged with killing a wizard in the lands east of Shadow Hill,' Mellor continued. 'The Lady Ahlia fought by his side, taking up a sword against one of the King's Shield. She is therefore guilty of the same crime committed by her companion.'

This was certainly so much more interesting than anything she had heard today, or any other day so far.

Areana had already decided to give this one her full attention.

Mellor turned away from his Princess and looked to Kabir and Ahlia.

'Before you is the Princess Areana, daughter to King Dayhen of The Storm and ruler of Lakerth in his absence. She will be deciding your fates this day. Do not speak to her unless invited and do not attempt to approach or you will be killed without hesitation. Do you understand?'

They both nodded, neither taking their eyes off the Princess.

'Kabir of Deerstep,' Areana said, in a voice she thought resonated with command and royalty, 'you have heard the charge against you. Are you guilty of the said crime?'

'I am guilty of killing the wizard Princess, but I am guilty of no crime.' He spoke without anger or fear, but what Areana noted most, was that he spoke without remorse. The man admitted to killing a wizard and declared it not a crime!

She turned to look at the woman by his side.

'You have been introduced as Lady Ahlia,' Areana said. 'What is your relation to the Chieftain of the Plains?' She had been schooled in the social aspects of all realms within the land. She knew there was a single Chieftain within the plains, but had never been told of any other known titles. She was intrigued.

'I am no Lady,' Ahlia replied. 'Crenshen is my father, but the women of the plains have no want or need of titles, Princess.'

Although her words were polite, the way she said Princess was like a barb to Areana. Was she saying she didn't recognise Areana's own title as legitimate? Because she was a woman? If this daughter of their Chieftain thought of herself as just another warrior, then she would treat her as such.

'Very well plainswoman Ahlia, you have also heard the charge against you. Are you guilty of taking up a sword against one of the King's Shield?'

She heard the tone of her own voice change, and schooled herself against it as soon as she finished speaking. She needed to be better than that.

'I used a sword to defend myself,' Ahlia said. 'If that is a crime, then I am guilty of it.'

'What was the name of the wizard who was killed?' Areana asked.

'His name was Ethan, Princess. A wizard from Shadow Hill.'

'Thank you,' she said, looking around for Heridah. It suddenly occurred to her how strange it was her mentor was not here for a trial about the killing of a fellow wizard.

She quickly turned her attention back to Mellor.

'You may continue with the reading of the events that took place. I will need to hear them before I can give my sentence.'

'You give sentence without even hearing from us?' Kabir asked.

'You will remain silent,' Mellor said, before a wave of Areana's hand stopped him saying more.

'The both of you have already admitted to the crime,' she said. 'Therefore, I need not hear from either of you again.'

'What crime?' Kabir asked. 'We have admitted to no crime. A wizard attacks me without cause or ill-intent on my part, so I killed him. What crime is there?'

Areana was not enjoying this as much as she had first anticipated.

It may not be as simple as she had hoped.

'I ask you again then, are you guilty of killing the wizard?'

'I killed the wizard Princess, but I am not guilty of a crime. I defended myself. Are you not permitted to defend yourself in this realm if someone is trying to kill you?' The barbarian sounded genuinely confused, but still there was no anger or disrespect in his voice. It was the only reason she was permitting him to speak. However, Areana knew she would need to take control. The barbarian could not have free rein to speak whenever he chose.

Kabir was obviously ignorant of their laws, but such ignorance did not nullify them.

'Mellor, I will hear from one who was witness to what happened.'

The Chamberlain nodded in obedience, before signalling to someone further down the room near the door.

A man strode forward to stand on the far left of where the two prisoners stood.

'Your name and position,' Areana said.

'My name is Methan, Princess and I am Captain at Shadow Hill. Was Captain at Shadow Hill', he corrected.

'Tell me what happened,' she said.

As Methan relayed his version of events, Areana looked to the two standing in front of her, trying to gauge any reaction they may have to what Methan was saying.

Both of them were stone-faced during the entire re-telling of it. Neither gave away anything to her.

When he had finished, Methan remained standing where he was.

'Do you accept this version of what happened?' Areana asked the two standing in front of her.

'It is a fair account,' Kabir said.

'And you?' she asked Ahlia.

'It is how I also remember it,' she said.

'Thank you, Captain,' Ahlia said, indicating for him to return to the back of the great hall.

'If you have nothing else to add, then I will hand down my sentence now,' Areana said.

'Your sentence?' Ahlia asked. 'So you think we are guilty, despite what the Captain said.'

'You were given the opportunity to relinquish your weapons,' Areana said. 'It was a reasonable request of two strangers to our lands. If you had done so, then Ethan would not have attacked you. The fault is your own, and you will both be sentenced accordingly.' She had heard enough. Nothing they said now would sway her decision.

Kabir grabbed Ahlia by the wrist, causing her to turn and face him. Scowling at him, she eventually turned back to the Princess and said no more.

'Kabir of the village Deerstep, for the crime of killing Ethan, wizard to the Realm and loyal subject to King Dayhen of the Storm, I sentence you to be hung until you are dead. The execution will be carried out on the morrow.'

'You cannot!' Ahlia said, shrugging his hand off this time. 'My father will hear of this!'

'And why would the Chieftain of the Plains deem it necessary to interfere with the laws of our realm?' Areana asked. 'Would he put up with such transgressions if the situation were reversed?'

'You cannot kill this man,' Ahlia said. Areana did not fail to notice that she had no answer to her question. Just an empty plea.

'As for yourself,' she continued. 'Because of your standing within your realm, and the fact you had no part in the killing of Ethan, I am banishing you from these lands. You will return home to the Eastern Plains and you will not return here again.'

'I cannot return home yet,' Ahlia said.

'I am not giving you a choice!' Areana said, standing from her chair. This plainswoman had finally gotten under her skin. 'You will return home or you will share the same punishment as the Barbarian.'

'His name is Kabir,' Ahlia continued, undaunted. 'And his journey here was endorsed by my father. My father and all who live under his command owe this man a blood debt. And until his quest is complete, neither of us will be returning to our home.'

'A blood debt?' Areana asked. Although she was angry at this woman's defiance, she was now also curious why they were here. 'What is this quest you speak of?'

'It is something I cannot explain and it sounds like a fool's dream,' Kabir said, breaking his silence. Unlike Ahlia and the Princess, his voice was still calm. 'Someone or something has appeared to me more than once and set me upon a vague, unknown task. I do not know what it means or where I must go.'

'It sounds exactly like a fool's story to me,' Areana said, sitting back down. She had quickly lost interest in his ridiculous quest. Did he think her a fool? Yet she was still curious and concerned about this 'blood debt', so did not dismiss them both just yet. Her father did not need further enemies crossing their borders from the east.

She looked again at the plains woman.

'What is this blood debt you speak of?' she asked.

Before Ahlia could answer, Areana's attention moved to someone who had just entered from behind where she stood. Turning, she saw Heridah striding towards her, an alarmed look on his face.

'I am almost finished,' she said to him.

'If I may ask the barbarian a question?' Heridah asked, as he stopped next to her. He directed his attention to the barbarian before Areana even had a chance to say yes.

'Were you given a quest before this one you now speak of?' the wizard asked.

Kabir nodded.

'To where and what for?'

'I was not successful in obtaining it,' he answered.

'What was it you were sent to look for?' Heridah asked again.

Areana was taken aback by the wizard's question. She did not like that he had usurped her trial in this way.

'I think this can wait until later,' she interjected.

'My Princess,' Catlin said to her from the other side.

Areana was surprised to hear her speak, as she turned to look at her Shield.

'I would like to hear what the barbarian has to say also,' she said. Areana wasn't sure if she detected some emotion in her voice. That she had asked was shocking enough.

Kabir stood patiently waiting for the Princess to decide.

'What were you unable to find?' Areana asked.

'I was sent to find an idol of mud Princess,' he answered. 'I was told it would be found in the plains.'

'What else?' Heridah asked, with passion still in his voice.

'Nothing else,' Kabir said. 'As I said, I was unable to locate it before the compulsion driving me disappeared.'

Heridah audibly gasped and looked passed his Princess to Catlin.

'Take the prisoners away!' Areana said loudly. The King's Shield surrounding them sprang into action.

'I would like to speak with him some more,' Heridah said to her.

'Now,' she exclaimed.

It wasn't necessary for her to repeat it to the King's Shield. It was for the benefit of Heridah only.

'Clear the hall,' she ordered.

Mellor bowed low to her and began ushering everyone else out behind the King's Shield.

When they had all gone, Areana stood and turned to face Heridah.

'You will tell me what is going on!' she ordered.

'You cannot kill the barbarian,' he said. 'Ask Catlin.'

Areana turned to face her Shield.

Catlin looked her directly in the eye.

'Well?' Areana asked.

'I believe also that the Barbarian should be spared my Princess, but that is not my decision to make. There is more we need to learn from him. That much I know.'

'Tell me why,' she said to her friend.

'He shares..' Heridah began, before Areana turned on him.

'I asked Catlin to tell me, not you,' she said, turning back again to face Catlin.

'The quest he speaks of was the same quest Valdor was given,' she said.

'Given by whom?' Areana asked.

'He did not know Princess, but he believed within his heart it was a deity of some form.'

Areana felt her mouth fall open.

'Why does that spare the Barbarian from his fate?' she asked, no less confused.

'He speaks of another quest,' Heridah said, moving to stand next to Catlin. 'We need to speak more with him about this and about who spoke to him. It could be more important than anything else we do.' He spoke quickly, probably so she wouldn't interrupt him again.

'It could be the reason why Valdor was killed,' Catlin said.

That was enough to get through to Areana.

'We will speak to him about it, but nothing else changes. My sentence stands.'

'Thank you Princess,' Heridah said, breathing a sigh of relief. 'I apologise for the interruption. My emotions sometimes get the better of me.'

'Be careful where they may get you in future,' she said. 'I am going for a walk now. We will speak with the barbarian in the morning.'

'I fear we cannot delay,' Heridah began.

'The morning!' Areana repeated, 'or you can spend the night with him in an adjoining cell.'

She signalled for Catlin to follow her, as she walked down the steps of the dais.

Heridah said nothing as she left.

She was becoming more like her father every day, for which he was thankful. It was also why he said nothing else to her. Her father was famous for always carrying through on any threat he had ever made.

The influence Catlin was having was also immeasurable.

As she and Catlin left the hall, his thoughts quickly turned back to the barbarian.

He had been watching his Princess throughout the trial, assessing her performance in secret. He had been very pleased with how she conducted herself. Her decision making had been sound, along with the questions she asked.

Yet when Kabir had mentioned his quest he hadn't been able to stop himself. It haunted him still that Valdor had died so soon after failing the quest set for him.

That another had been sent on the same quest and failed raised so many questions.

Questions which he refused to wait until morning to ask.

Although his Princess had said they were to wait, she had not actually forbidden him to speak with the barbarian today. He knew she would not see it that way, but he believed time was critical and it helped him justify his actions within his own mind.

Valdor had run out of time. They may never know how that may impact upon the realm, if it hadn't already, but Heridah had a chance now to possibly rectify things.

He was especially intrigued by the fact a Barbarian had been chosen to compete in the first quest.

He knew there was at least one other who had been chosen, because neither Valdor nor Kabir had reached the idol first.

More importantly, he needed to know what the second quest now was.

Kabir didn't seem overly distressed, so perhaps the compulsion that had driven Valdor was less this time around.

Heridah was aware he could continue to think about it as much as he wanted, but what he actually needed to do was speak with the barbarian, so he could give this wizard the answers he craved.

Once he had that information, Heridah knew the Princess' ire would be reduced somewhat.

It is what he was hoping anyway, as he made his way down into the dungeon.

CHAPTER 60

Do Not Stop Running

'WE NEED TO bolster the defences at Mayfield,' Dayhen said as they rode. 'Then the rest of us will ride east.'

Neither of the two men riding on either side of him said anything in reply.

They all knew what was at stake, and none of them had anything further to add.

'All of the Shield will accompany us,' Dayhen said, looking across at Bilsont.

'Is that wise?' he asked. 'We do not know where they may come through. They may yet come through Mayfield itself.'

'He has spread out along Glorfiden,' Dayhen said. 'The elves are his first target. Why would he suddenly send them all south?'

'If they are repelled by the Elven Lord, they will certainly funnel down towards Mayfield,' Bilsont said. 'If they are able to breach there, then the Realm is open to them.'

Although a similar conversation had been held already, Dayhen still acknowledged that Bilsont might be right. Yet it didn't sway him from his decision.

If they did attack Mayfield and were able to breach, he was confident he could manoeuvre his army to cut off any that got through.

Yet if they managed to get through Glorfiden, he needed an army to face them before they got to Lakerth.

The centre of the capital could be defended, but the outer battlements were not enough to repel Mithrak's army and his Dark Mage. Thousands of innocent lives would be slaughtered on his arrival. As their King, Dayhen would not allow that to happen.

'Lakerth needs to be the priority,' Dayhen said. 'Mithrak is cunning. I would not under-estimate him. If I did, I would be no smarter than the cowardly ogre-mage Kritch.'

'The Shield are yours to command,' Bilsont said.

Of course they were, Dayhen thought. Why would he need to say such a thing? Letting it go, they continued their gallop towards Mayfield.

Dayhen knew his men and horses were fatigued. They had worked tirelessly since leaving the Capital.

First off, they had helped to build further defences at Mayfield and fortify the existing ones. They were then forced to ride hard to High Fort and fight the battle against Kritch's horde.

Now, without respite, he was forcing them to ride at speed back to Mayfield.

He knew they would need to rest at some point.

Dayhen would not let his army face that of Mithrak if they were too tired to swing their swords properly, or concentrate enough to protect the soldier at their side.

Even with huge hearts and the motivation to fight and give everything they had, a fatigued army was at a huge disadvantage.

'We will rest at Mayfield,' Dayhen said. 'Regardless of the news, the army will need to sleep and regain their strength.'

'There may not be time for that,' Thaiden said. 'The men will fight. With or without sleep, they will die defending your Realm Dayhen.'

'I know that,' Dayhen said. 'I would prefer they lived defending it.'

'You could send the wizards and Shield forward,' Bilsont suggested. 'The wizards have the best horses.' He didn't need to sing the praises of the Shield. Their constitution was legendary. Far beyond that of any other human.

Dayhen did not answer straight away.

He saw the logic in it, but was loathe to split his forces. Each of those within his army played a crucial role.

Although his wizards and Shield were obviously the most powerful, they needed the support of his infantry, cavalry and archers to maximize their effectiveness. Mithrak still had his full contingent of Ve-Karn, as well as his own personal guard. Add to that his most powerful dark-mage and the two armies were evenly matched. If Dayhen faced them without the main part of his army, those extra orcs and other misbegotten creatures Mithrak had fighting for him would go unchecked. They would swing the balance well and truly in favour of the Western Realm's army.

And who knew what else Mithrak had in store for him. The giant orcs who tossed lava were creatures made of nightmare. He dreaded to think Mithrak had more like them.

'The army stays together,' he eventually said. 'We need to face him whole and rested. We can make up ground if we need to, but we cannot replace the loss of so many King's Shield and wizards.'

Bilsont said nothing more.

There was nothing else for him to say.

Their future was simple enough.

Ride, rest and then ride some more. Eventually they would fight.

Then you either won or lost. Lived or died.

At the end of the day, that is all it came down to.

They rode through the night again and arrived at Mayfield early the next day.

The reports were as Dayhen had feared.

While he was away, his scouts had seen Mithrak burn a swathe through the trees of Glorfiden. He had made no efforts to try and kill or capture Dayhen's scouts. He did not appear to care enough about being watched.

Those scouts were able to get a good look at what he and his mage did, as they burnt their way into Glorfiden with weapons of incredible power.

If he were able to go unchecked through the Elven forest; and dependent on where he exited; then Dayhen estimated Mithrak would almost be through the forest already and into the Realm of men.

'Three hours,' he said to Thaiden, once the news was delivered. 'Three hours sleep and then we march.'

'Can we wait that long?' Thaiden asked. 'The men are strong.'

'I made the decision when my mind was clear Thaiden. I would be remiss to change it now, even knowing what we do.'

Thaiden looked to say more, but instead just nodded his head.

'We will get to them before they reach the Capital,' Dayhen said. He tried to sound convincing, but found it difficult to try and fool himself into believing it.

They would need a miracle to stop Mithrak now.

CHAPTER 61

Tell Me The Truth

'MARCUS AND HIS entire town approach,' Porthon said. 'Are you going to meet him my Lord?'

'That is Lord Marcus to your mouth,' Jaron said to his new steward.

'Apologies my Lord,' Porthon said, bowing low. 'Are you to meet with Lord Marcus?'

'You don't need to ask me questions,' Jaron said. 'I will tell you when I want something done. Is that clear?'

'Yes, My Lord,' Porthon said, still in the bowing position.

'Tell Gareth to come and speak with me,' Jaron said, waving the man away.

Another fool, he thought, but this one seemed sufficiently frightened of him. He shouldn't pose any risk to him and his confidences.

It didn't take long for Gareth to attend his audience room.

'I want you to go down and speak with Marcus and tell him that none may enter. They can rest outside the walls, where we will give them provisions for their journey on to Lakerth.'

'He will not want to hear it from me,' Gareth said. Jaron knew him to be a loyal hound, but he did throw out his own opinion far too often.

'I don't care what he wants,' Jaron said. 'Not he; nor any of his people; will step one foot inside my walls. They will speak to no-one from inside the walls either. The supplies will be lowered over the walls and you will make sure all of my King's Shield are busy with tasks in other parts of Havern. Is that clear?' he asked. 'Do I need to repeat it all to you Gareth?'

Gareth drew in a deep breath before answering.

'I can remember all of that,' he replied.

'Good. Then go and do it,' Jaron said, sweeping his arms forward in a motion to have his wizard leave.

The sooner Marcus and his horde from Shadow Hill had gone, the happier he would be. They would also be able to pass on to those in Lakerth why Jaron had not sent any of his wizards or King's Shield.

An added bonus in not having them stay here, but it would only help him in the short term.

In the long term, Dayhen would eventually discover what he had done and he would without doubt look to punish him for it. Jaron knew quite well what the sentence for treachery was.

Yet he still believed he was doing the right thing, and time would show that he was right in what he did. Dayhen would still see it as treachery, but Jaron knew the people of Havern would support him. They would see how he had saved them at a time when their King wanted to leave them to the mercy of the monsters surrounding their walls. He would need to get them to support him in numbers when Dayhen sent his guard to take him.

Or perhaps something might happen to Dayhen while he was away fighting in the West. Perhaps it already had. That would be such a tragedy, leaving Areana in charge. She was but a girl, and a weak one as well. He did not fear the wrath of Areana.

Sitting back down in his chair, Jaron continued to think about all of the different ways this could still play out.

It helped to lessen his stress and relax him.

So much could happen before he ever need worry about losing his head to the king's executioner.

Marcus watched as Atriol and his least weary men, escorted the barbarian and his woman back to Lakerth.

He didn't like playing the unreasonable, rude and unbending leader, but his people needed to see that he was still in command and was strong enough to lead them through the trials that were to come. He actually respected both Kabir and Ahlia, and in different circumstances would have welcomed them in to his town and to his table.

But the man had killed one of his wizards. He could not be seen to befriend them in any way as a result. The girl's threat had nearly forced his hand, but he felt he had handled the situation quite well.

However, being left waiting outside the gates of Havern like animals, was more than he could stand. His patience had run out.

The next one to come outside of those gates was going to get it.

'Why don't you try the helmet?' Mikael suggested. The old King's Shield still did not look upset by the situation.

'Do you think it strange that no-one was at the gate to meet us, other than a couple of old guards?' Marcus had never trusted Jaron, and right now he was certain the Lord of Havern was up to something.

'If there is pestilence, it can decimate a town even the size of Havern,' Mikael said.

'I am aware of that,' Marcus replied. 'Did those two old guards strike you as being fearful and on edge?'

'Not really,' Mikael replied. 'Should they have been?'

'Most people are when their town is struck down by a sickness. Those two did not appear to be. And when I asked where their Shield were, they told me they were elsewhere, keeping those who had been struck down isolated.'

'I was with you when he said it Lord Marcus.' Mikael did seem at all concerned by Marcus' theory, which served only in adding to his frustration.

As Mikael finished speaking, the gate opened again, and a wizard strode out. The gate was quickly closed behind him.

'Greetings Lord Marcus,' Gareth said to him. He tried to sound pleasant, but again Marcus wasn't buying it.

'This is a disgrace Gareth!' Marcus had warmed up talking to Mikael and was now ready to go. 'You will let us inside those walls right now and give us lodging and food. The King's laws demand it and so do I!'

Marcus deliberately got close into Gareth's personal space, forcing the wizard to step back a couple of paces.

'I am but the messenger Lord Marcus. It is not in my power...'
he began, before Marcus yelled over the top of him.

'Then get Jaron out here so he can tell me himself! I won't hear
it from his wizard.'

'Lord, the pestilence is only in its infancy. We are unable to say
for certain who has it and who does not. There may still be those
who have yet to show symptoms, yet could still be infectious. I don't
know what else I can say. Would you put yourself and your people
in harm's way?'

Marcus had dealt with Gareth on a few occasions in the past. He
knew the man was clever and he also knew he had a silver tongue.

He could not dispute what he said, but he still suspected he was
being lied to.

Maybe Mikael was correct about the helmet.

Reaching to his side, Marcus removed it from his belt and placed
it on his head.

Gareth looked at him sceptically, as well he should. Why would
the Lord of Shadow Hill put a helmet on his head mid-discussion,
unless he was planning on fighting him? Gareth knew Marcus would
not attack him, which is why he continued to look questioningly
at him.

'What is actually going on within Havern?' Lord Marcus asked.
It was only a small risk he took. If Gareth was being truthful then
he will simply repeat what he has already said and will be none the
wiser that Marcus had used magic against him.

'My Lord Marcus. Lord Jaron has bid me have you leave Havern
and make for Lakerth. With all of your people.' Gareth looked
confused.

Marcus was surprised. The man looked to be fighting against it.

He was aware that wizards went to some lengths to protect their
minds against intrusion or persuasion. Perhaps Gareth had set up
protections within his mind, unlike Ethan, who he had been able
to easily manipulate when he first tested the helmet back in Shadow
Hill.

'I need you to tell me why Jaron does not want us inside the
walls.' He decided to begin with an order this time. It might increase
the power of the relic he wore on his head.

Gareth did not answer straight away, and the strain showed on his face. He looked to be fighting within himself.

'You must tell me!' Marcus said, raising his voice this time.

'He does not wish you to speak with anyone, else word reaches the King's Shield and several of his wizards that Dayhen has ordered their departure for Lakerth.' Gareth spoke slowly, and with effort. His eyes revealed to Marcus that he knew what was happening and would stop him if he were able.

'Tell me why he has disobeyed the King's order,' Marcus said.

'Without them, the city and its people are at too great a risk from the evils moving through the lands surrounding Havern. With the goblin threat on top of that, he believes our King would doom Havern in order to try and save Lakerth.'

'We must stop him,' Mikael said from behind Marcus. 'This cannot be allowed.'

'No more,' Gareth managed to say between deep breaths. 'No more!' he said again, this time louder and with more authority.

'You will bid your men at the gate open it now and allow our entry,' Marcus said.

Gareth turned and walked over to the main gate, before knocking on the small door within the main part. A man opened the latch to speak with the wizard, before he closed it again and quickly opened the door. Gareth snuck in before they could prevent him and the door was quickly closed.

'It seems he has managed to fight off the helmet's influence,' Mikael said. 'That is a shame.'

'No matter,' Marcus said, 'but we must now make haste. Quickly tell the others what you now know, while I have the gate opened.'

'The wizard will not let you enter,' Mikael said.

'I am counting on the wizard returning to his master to gather more forces to try and stop us. I doubt he is waiting inside the gate.'

Mikael gave a quick nod, before moving back amongst the folk of Shadow Hill, passing word of what the Lord of Havern had done.

Marcus walked up to the gate and knocked on the same door Gareth had gone through.

Instead of the latch opening, the whole door was quickly opened and to Marcus' surprise, Gareth stood there waiting for him.

'I cannot allow you to control the minds of those here at the gate. Forgive me my Lord,' he said, as he shot a bolt of energy into the chest of the Lord of Shadow Hill. Marcus had not expected an attack and so did not have hold of the grip on Kabir's sword. It would have saved his life.

Instead his chest exploded. Leaning down, Gareth grabbed hold of his shoulders and dragged his lifeless body in through the gate.

Mikael raced back toward his Lord, but by the time he got there, Gareth and his Lord's body were both safely behind the closed door.

'Coward wizard, you will hang for what you have done.' Mikael remained calm as he spoke.

'You will all now leave for Lakerth Shield. If you do not, then I will order my men to begin showering the good folk of Shadow Hill with arrows. You and your fellow King's Shield I will take care of personally.' Mikael knew the wizard meant what he said. He would have nothing further to lose. His life was forfeit already.

'I will return wizard and I will personally take your head from your shoulders,' Mikael said, before walking away from the gate to give the order for them to move on.

He said nothing more to those behind the gate.

Their time would come, but it was not this day.

CHAPTER 62

A Simple Request

L INF CONTINUED WALKING for the rest of the day, hardly seeing another living creature.

The land was sparse where she travelled and was incredibly boring.

A few trees, numerous small hills and a several shallow streams were the only things that broke the monotony of the short, dry grasslands in which she walked.

Perhaps she should have gone the other way.

Maybe the human witch was trying to help her?

Linf quickly dismissed that idea. Everyone and everything in these lands was interested in helping only one thing. Themselves. She could think of no reason why the witch would be doing anything to help a solitary goblin.

Then what was it that made her so special to this witch?

Linf knew herself that she was special, but what would a wizard hope to get from her. Other than drained and then killed, she thought, chuckling to herself again.

She remembered clearly the look of shock and fear in the witch's eyes before she disappeared.

The witch hadn't showed itself for the rest of the day and Linf didn't expect to see her again any time soon.

Looking again to her left, she still didn't see anywhere that looked safe to change direction.

Perhaps that is why Kritch had chosen such a stupid spot to fight the human army. Maybe there was no other way to get across into the land of men.

So far there had been nothing but high cliffs, very steep hills with lots of cliffs within them and thick, dark forests.

Although forests did not scare her, in these lands she would prefer to be able to see what was around her. If she could see it, then she was confident she could kill it. Who knew what kind of creatures dwelt within these forests? She wasn't prepared to take that chance until all other options had been exhausted.

Just how long she would keep walking and looking for those options was questionable, but for now she was looking for somewhere relatively safe-looking to sleep for the night.

In the morning she could decide whether she kept going or turned around.

Crawling out of the shallow cave, Linf stood up and stretched. The sun had not been out too long, but it was already beginning to warm up. It looked like it would be another cloudless day today, not that the goblin particularly cared about the weather.

Looking forward in the direction she had been walking last night, she saw nothing in the landscape that made her think it was going to change any time soon, other than some mountains in the distance. That certainly did not interest her. Perhaps it was time to cut her losses and turn back.

Linf was also feeling quite hungry again and would at least be able to scavenge for some food when she got back to the battle field. Not feeling fatigued when she left yesterday, Linf had neglected to take any food with her.

At times the energy she absorbed was enough to sustain her, but when she went an extended period of time without either, it began to drain her of strength rather quickly.

Letting out a loud curse, she decided she would definitely have to head back the way she had come.

As she was about to turn around, the witch again appeared before her.

'Why do you keep coming back?' Linf asked. She was too tired and weak to be too angry, but still she wasn't pleased to see her. The stinking scab had better not say I told you so.

'Because you need to go the way I have told you,' the witch said. Linf could see the fear coming from her. She was right to be nervous still.

'Okay,' Linf said, 'but you need to come closer and tell me why.'

'Are you not hungry?' the witch asked her. She made no move to come any closer.

That nearly set Linf off. Of course she was hungry! She had been walking all this time without any food and without drawing in any life energy.

'I am hungry,' Linf said. 'Do you have food?' That would help her mood.

'I do not have food. I can only tell you where you need to go.'

'Come closer,' Linf said. 'If you want me to trust you, then you need to trust me.'

She could see the witch was hesitant, but surprisingly to the goblin, she could also see the witch was considering it. Was she that stupid? Trying her hardest to hide the grin, Linf asked her again. 'Come closer, I want to look into your eyes and see if you are telling me the truth.'

She obviously couldn't tell by looking into someone's eyes, but this human still looked to be considering it. She really was stupid.

'If I come closer, you will go in that direction?' she asked, pointing again in the direction where the battle had been fought.

'I will,' Linf said, trying to sound genuine.

To Linf's surprise, the human witch took several steps in her direction.

With a quick lunge, Linf thought she might be able to grab hold of her.

'Not a lot of trust,' Linf said.

The woman looked confused.

'That is not very close,' Linf said. Although she knew the witch would not come any closer, it was still humouring her to try.

To her shock, the witch took another couple of short steps.

Linf had only to lean forward now and reach out and she could grab her around the throat.

The goblin wondered whether the witch would be able to disappear if she had hold of her. Would that stop the magic from working?

She decided to try talking first, and if that didn't work, she would grab her.

'Now you need to go in that direction,' the witch said. The fear had increased with each step she took and it was pouring from her now.

It was so hard for Linf not to grab it, but she didn't want to risk her disappearing again. Not yet.

'I will go in that direction,' Linf conceded, 'but can you tell me what is there? Why is it so important, that you would be dumb enough to get this close to a goblin?'

The fear spiked again, and Linf feared she would vanish, but once again the witch waited and the fear slowly lessened a little.

'I cannot tell you why Linf, only that you need to go there and search for that which you have been tasked.'

Linf thought for a moment about her next question, but quickly realised this witch was not going to tell her anything more. She just kept repeating the same boring message.

Like a striking snake, Linf whipped out an arm and dug her sharpened nails into the arm of the witch. She saw blood squirt from the wounds, before the human vanished.

Putting her fingers to her lips, she licked the blood off her nails. The taste was something else again. It was intoxicating.

Sitting down, Linf savoured the taste as she licked her nails clean.

She knew now that she had to work out a plan on how to draw energy from the human witch, so she could feed on her properly. Like the time when she and Brax had those farmers.

Once she finally caught her, she needed to work out how to stop the witch from disappearing. She would want to keep this one alive as long as she was able to.

Standing up and turning back towards the direction of the battlefield, Linf began running ideas through her mind on how she might achieve it.

Linf made good time back to where she had started. For some reason, time always seemed to go quicker when you knew where your destination was.

The battlefield had changed quite dramatically in just one day.

All kinds of scavengers had descended upon it, from birds of numerous description to four-legged beasts. Even several creatures that were once part of Kritch's army. They would be those who had pretended to be killed, as Linf had done.

As she approached and looked on, Linf was initially confused at the lack of fighting among those that walked and fluttered among the corpses. As she approached closer, Linf realised it was because there were so many dead scattered throughout. There was no need to fight when they all had more than enough to keep them satisfied.

They would not find Linf to be so kind-hearted. If there was something within the piles of corpses that she wanted, she would be taking it.

It took a while for a group of orcs moving through the field of battle to notice her approach. At first, they didn't show a lot of interest. As she got closer, a couple of them spoke among themselves, before all four turned to face her.

'What are you?' one of them asked.

'Some kind of skinny hobgoblin,' another of them said.

Linf wasn't in any hurry, so she figured a bit of fun was warranted. It had been a while since she had enjoyed herself.

'I am a goblin,' she answered. 'What is a hobgoblin? Are they stupider than orcs?'

A couple of them grunted in displeasure.

'Best you go somewhere else,' another of them said. 'Or else we will add you to the dead lying around here.'

'Why let it go?' said one of those who had grunted. 'It is scrawny, but I have never eaten goblin before.'

'Not enough for you here?' Linf asked, truly surprised by his words. 'I would rather your friend there ate me,' she said to him. 'He is not as ugly or as puny as you are. I would rather be killed by an average orc than a weakling one.'

The angry one started running at her before Linf even finished her sentence. He held a curved sword in his right hand, which he held up as he ran.

Linf had plenty of time to squeeze together a small ball of power.

As he got close she released it, aiming straight for his face. The orc collapsed at her feet as the back of his head exploded.

Linf immediately began to absorb the fear of the other three. None of them moved straight away, stunned by what had happened to their companion.

'You are a user of magic,' one of them said. It sounded to her like an apology, but she was having none of it. Linf continued to drain all of them.

When they were all nothing but empty husks lying on the ground, Linf looked around again at her surroundings once more. She noticed straight away that the remaining scavengers had given her a very wide berth. They continued to do so even as she moved through the decaying corpses.

It was curious to her to watch. Although none of them were looking directly at her, they still moved away from her as she got closer.

Linf liked it.

She was the apex predator now and the feeling it gave her was something she had not felt before. It was amazing. The more she creatures she killed, the stronger she felt, but it wasn't until this moment that she truly understood what real power was and what it felt like.

Uncompromising fear and respect.

Nothing wanted to come near her, because if it did, it was aware there was a good chance she would kill it. And they were all correct in their thinking.

Linf crossed the remainder of the battlefield without being disturbed, and continued on walking in the same direction.

She had checked many of the corpses she walked past for anything of value, but there was nothing that took her fancy. Before long she realised it was because she didn't really need anything.

Her true powers were not in using a sword or spear. She had never been trained to use any weapons, so most creatures she faced who had a sword or an axe or a spear, would probably be able to best her.

Linf also didn't wish for any of their fancy armour. A helmet would make it harder for her to see her surroundings. She remembered well Rark's words, telling her she needed to grow eyes in the back of her head. A helmet would make that even more difficult.

As for armour, she was simply not interested. She had felt the weight of armour before and refused to walk anywhere with something so heavy. It also made it hard to move quickly. There may still come a time when she needed to run. As unlikely as that seemed to her now, Linf was still smart enough to know she wasn't the most powerful thing in these lands. Not yet anyway.

And if her skills couldn't save her, she doubted armour would be able to.

Linf had taken whatever morsels she could find to eat as she walked through the field of dead, but there hadn't been much there.

Not many of those who died had carried food with them.

Most of the meals in this army had been made at camp, from slaughtering animals or deserters. Those animals had either already been killed or had fled the battle field.

Although goblins were not fussy eaters, she had never been one to eat her own, nor anything related to her kind. The Ve-Karn would have sufficed, but she preferred her meat fresh. This amount of time lying in that armour with nothing to shade them from the sun, meant they had already started to go bad.

Linf had left the battle grounds well behind her as the sun began to sink below the ground to her left. The land here was still rocky and so she had no trouble finding another small cave to spend the night in.

When she awoke the next morning, Linf knew she would have a decision to make.

Should she try to find her way into the human realm, or should she choose to go in the direction the witch wanted her to go.

The fact she had told the human she would go in that direction had no bearing on her decision. It didn't matter what was said, a goblin could always change its mind if it wanted to. Linf had never understood why lying and deceiving were frowned upon by some that she knew.

Whatever it took to make her healthy and happy was what she would do.

Linf stepped back through her *eye* and took a deep breath.

Turning around to look into Dark Swell, she wasn't surprised to see her Champion licking the blood from her nails. She had never trusted the goblin, but she needed her to start moving north, so she was prepared to risk herself in order to achieve it.

She never truly feared Linf would try and kill her. She wasn't at that stage yet, but she had still been taken by surprise at how fast Linf had struck.

Looking down at her arm, she was surprised to see the blood trickling from the four puncture wounds on her forearm.

Although the Creator had told them they could die within the world of Dark Swell, she had not truly believed they were vulnerable.

The pain she felt in her arm re-assured her they were all most certainly vulnerable.

Looking back to her *eye* in order to gauge her Champion's reaction, Linf was pleased to see her begin walking in the right direction. At least for now there was hope she might still make it to the dragon before the game had finished.

'That looks painful,' Brindel said. She had not noticed him walking up to stand next to her. Taking her arm, Brindel brought it closer to his face so he could see it better.

'It hurts only a little,' Linf said, pulling her arm gently away from him.

'You will still need a bandage,' he said, not taking his eyes from her hurts.

'You are certainly not afraid to risk yourself,' he continued. 'I am super impressed with your bravery.' He smiled at her, before walking back to sit in front of his *eye*.

Thanks for the bandage, she thought, as she watched him sit down.

Linf did not think of herself as brave.

Being able to disappear at a moment's thought did not lend itself to much bravery in her opinion. Desperate was a word she believed to be closer to how she felt about herself.

Desperate to get her Champion into the ruined forest and face-to-face with the most powerful creature within the world of Dark Swell.

She almost laughed out loud at the lunacy of it all.

Did she believe her Champion was strong enough to face the dragon and survive?

Yes, was her honest answer.

The goblin continued to grow in strength and confidence.

By the time she reached the ruined forest, there would be no stopping her.

Moving off to find herself a bandage, Linf was more confident now than she had ever been during this game. She had a worthy Champion with devastating powers, who would continue to get stronger.

If only she would listen to her advice and get to the dragon, then she could turn this game upside-down.

Linf still had surprises in store for her Champion, which in turn would surprise those she played this game against. Those same people who continued to underestimate her Champion.

She knew the others would be wondering why she didn't use her second opportunity to enter the world and convince her Champion to make for the ruined forest with all haste.

It was because Linf knew her Champion better than the others and she knew the goblin race as intimately as anyone could.

As frustrating as they were, she had a plan for her third visit into the world. A plan which she was convinced would win her the game.

None would be able to match her Champion once Linf returned home and claimed her God's final contribution.

CHAPTER 63

Attack, Defend Or Do Nothing

RINDEL STARED INTO his *eye* as his Champion finally made it through the ruined forest and into the dragon's clearing.

His mind had been racing ever since he made it through the orc village and there remained nothing left between him and the mighty platinum dragon that awaited his dwarf.

Should he enter and help his Champion, or should he hold on to his opportunities to enter.

To be honest he didn't much care about holding on to them. He was still desperate to enter Dark Swell and speak with his Champion.

The only thing holding him back at the moment was the risk it posed to his own welfare.

His Champion had extraordinary armour that would protect him against most of the dragon's attacks, whereas he would be vulnerable against every attack made by the most powerful creature on Dark Swell.

Brindel continued to look for a way that he could be protected, while at the same time offering his Champion assistance in fighting the dragon.

As he arrived at the clearing, he still had nothing which had satisfied him.

'Are we finally going to see you within Dark Swell,' Mortinan asked. 'Your Champion will need all the help he can get.'

Brindel refused to allow Mortinan to disturb his thoughts at such a time.

'Smug little turd,' Brindel said to himself. 'His Champion got lucky.'

'Fortunate that your dwarf did not come across my Champion on his way out. Such a wind from the rod would have blown him all the way back to where Linf's Champion is.' Mortinan chuckled at his own humour.

Brindel tried again to ignore his fellow gamer, as his Champion battled against the fear spell the dragon put forward.

'You could enter and dispel the fear right now if you wanted,' Mortinan said helpfully.

'Only warning Mortinan. If you say another word before this battle is over, I will come over there and hurt you. This I promise.' Brindel spoke without taking his eyes off his Champion.

Whether Mortinan believed him or not, he decided to remain quiet after he laughed for a short time.

Brindel was pleased when his Champion eventually pulled out the stone and the fear was dispelled.

Despite Mortinan's taunts, he had thought briefly about going into the world and telling him to take the stone out. He was glad he had refrained, but if Brindel had walked much closer he probably would have done it.

Yet he still had a decision to make.

Should he enter and cast his powerful spell at the dragon, in the hope he would then ignore him for the remainder of the battle, or should he enter with a defensive spell that might keep both himself and his Champion safe.

As the dragon lifted itself on to its back legs and began to spew out its dragon breath, Brindel had finally made his decision.

Mortinan hoped the dwarf would finally die at the feet of the dragon.

Brindel was a bully and thought far too highly of himself and of his Champion. He needed to be taught a lesson, and who better to do it than this dragon.

He knew the dwarf was no longer in the same league as his own Champion. Mort had finally come into his power and now that he possessed the rod, there would be no stopping him.

All of his plans had come to fruition, including being separated from Mendina.

Hopefully she would not make it back to the Elven Forest, but even if she did, her time was short. Soon enough all of the elves would be dead, making his Champion all the more formidable.

A pity he could not have learned more from Jarkene, but his fairie-dragon still had much to show him. Along with his own opportunity to enter Dark Swell and provide his Champion with key pieces of information and direction.

As the dwarf entered the clearing, he couldn't help himself. It was the perfect time to stir Brindel up. Pay back for all the times he had stuck his nose into the conversation of others.

'Are we finally going to see you within Dark Swell,' he said. 'Your Champion will need all the help he can get.'

Sometimes it was fun to taunt the others, but only because they deserved it.

Then would come the threats, as they always did.

It was no surprise to him when the conversation once again ended with Brindel threatening violence against him.

One day he would take him up on the offer. Unbeknownst to them all, he had been trained since he could walk in various weapons and hand-to-hand combat. Yet another surprise for Brindel, if he ever tried anything.

Mortinan simply chuckled at his latest threat, as he sat back to watch the dragon tear his fellow gamer's Champion into pieces.

He was going to enjoy this very much.

Kabir barely heard the exchange between Brindel and Mortinan. He had learnt over the years to switch off from their many arguments and verbal jousting. At times it was entertaining, but right now he was in no mood for it.

Yet another Champion had arrived at the ruined forest, while his awaited the hangman in Lakerth.

Even if he were somehow able to get free, he was still a great distance from the dragon. Adding to his woe was the fact his Champion still did not know where the damned dragon was!

If the dwarf were to survive, then he would also be heading back home.

Not as close as both the elf and half-elf, but still considerably closer than his barbarian.

If Kabir were to win his freedom and find his way to the dragon, he would then still need to survive against it without his sword. He knew his Champion had no chance without his sword.

So if he were somehow set free and then somehow able to get his sword back, he would not only need to make it to the dragon and survive against it, he would then need to make the journey back to Deerstep, through both Glorfiden and the Dwarven Mountains.

Kabir was of the firm belief that even if the Barbarian managed to achieve all of that against all odds, the game would already be long finished and the victor named.

Was it any wonder he was not interested in what Mortinan and Brindel had to say to each other?

His best and only hope was for misfortune to befall each of those who had already succeeded against the dragon and for Brindel's Champion to fall trying.

Looking intently into his *eye*, Kabir watched on in anticipation as the mighty dragon reared up in front of Brindel's Champion.

Unlike Kabir, Linf was still optimistic when it came to her Champion despite her being so far behind the others.

She was at least further advanced than the barbarian and no longer anyone's prisoner.

And she still enjoyed the comradery that came with jesting and poking fun at other gamers. For although they had invested almost half of their lives into this pursuit, it was still a life she enjoyed living. The game was paramount, but it was not all-consuming to her, as it appeared to be for Mortinan and even Kabir to some degree.

Brindel often amused her, even when he was acting as he was now.

He made no effort to hide his nervousness and difficulty at choosing a course of action. For someone like Mortinan, who was guarded with almost everything he said and did, it was easy for him to goad Brindel.

Linf sometimes found herself putting the hat of another gamer on, metaphorically speaking.

Right now she was thinking about what she would do in Brindel's stead.

Should he enter and help his Champion? It would be extremely dangerous. There was no other creature on Dark Swell more powerful than the Platinum Dragon. She was a sight to behold, even looking on from the safety of her *eye*. Linf could only imagine how breathtaking she would be standing on the ground and looking up at her.

An attack spell was out of the question. None of them could survive against her for any period of time, and there were no spells that could vanquish the dragon quickly.

A defensive spell might work for a time, or it may shatter against the power of the dragon.

Linf knew what she would do if it were her.

She would have faith in her Champion and if they failed, then she would live to fight another day.

Her eyes widened at the sight of the dragon lifting herself up and shooting forth her breath weapon, as she glanced across at Brindel standing in front of his *eye*.

CHAPTER 64

Homecoming

MORT HAD NEVER felt so alone.

It had been hours since his last glimpse of Mendina, but it seemed like a lifetime since she walked away from him and back towards Glorfiden.

It gave him a good reason to increase his speed, as he alternated between walking and running. He had never felt such determination, as he needed nothing more than to be back with her as soon as he was able.

Mort had no idea what would be awaiting him when he arrived back at his old home, but he was under no illusions it would be a happy homecoming.

Nothing had been easy since the old man first appeared and he expected things would probably get worse before they ever got better.

Taking the rod from his robe, Mort looked at it as he walked. He had almost drained it while fighting the dragon and even that had barely been enough for them to prevail. He hated to think what might have happened if his father had not given it to him, although he had a fairly good idea.

Now the rod was regenerating, as his father told him it would. Mort could feel a tiny breeze coming from it, but it was barely there. He had no idea how long it would take to be powerful again, but

he doubted it would be anywhere near its full capacity before he
arrived home.

No longer possessing the staff he had given to Mendina, Mort
knew he was vulnerable. He had his own reserves; which were
strong; but he had a sinking feeling he would need much more by
the time he had to face whatever was waiting for him. He fervently
hoped what he had now would be enough, because he needed to get
back to Mendina.

She consumed his thoughts, as he broke into a run again. He
needed to try and cover as much ground as he could before he found
somewhere suitable to rest for the night.

Whatever compulsion controlled him now, he hoped it would
allow him to rest at night.

Mort did not want to be walking these lands at night, although
so far he had met no creature with evil purpose since leaving the
ruined forest.

He knew he should have been buoyed by this turn of events, but
it rested heavy on his heart instead. He knew this land was untamed;
that there were countless beings of power and ill intent that made it
their home; yet he had come across nothing.

He wondered where they had all gone, but he got no answer to
that question for the remainder of that day.

Mort managed to find somewhere sheltered to rest for the night
and to his relief, the cramps did not come upon him during the night.
The old man had some compassion and sense of fair play after all.

He was up and about early the next day and the first thing he
did when he woke was check the rod. He could sense the power
within it had grown, but not by much. It still had a long way to go
before he would be able to use it for any extended period of time
and have enough power to overcome anything with real strength he
may come across.

In the mid-morning he came to a shallow river. It was probably
more of a stream in depth and current, but it was as wide as a river.
He located a couple of deep pools nearby and managed to coax some
fish on to the bank using the currents and a small amount of wind.

He felt a little better from the fresh food as he continued on his way.

Mort did not know exactly how far he needed to go to reach his home.

He was unfamiliar with this land, having never ventured west of the land surrounding his home in all the time he had lived there. His mother had warned him against doing it and there had never been any need.

The town of Mayfield lay to the east and the forest to their north. It had provided everything they had needed and more than enough to satisfy a young boys curiosity.

The only things that came from the east had come with ill-intent.

For some reason they had never approached his house, but he had sometimes seen them in the distance or on their journeys to Mayfield and the surrounding areas. The birds and other small animals always warned him of their approach and he had always been able to flee from them.

Looking back now, he realised it was probably the glamour Glendrond had put on their home that had kept them away. The very thing that kept their father away had done the same for the evils that lurked on their western border. That and their proximity to Glorfiden. Not many of the monsters that lived in the east saw any point in travelling too close to the Elven forest.

A few hours later, as Mort made his way through some marshland, a figure appeared in front of him.

Mort removed the rod from his robe and held it out in front. He was confident it would have enough power within it to overcome one solitary man, although he knew of only one creature who appeared in front of him out of nowhere. He did not think he was a threat, but he was in a strange land and he could not be sure.

'Mortinan, believe me when I say that causing you harm is the last thing I would ever wish for.' He stared at Mort in such a way that he believed what the young man said, yet it still made him very uncomfortable. He knew he should no longer be surprised at strange men appearing out of nowhere and knowing who he was, but it was something he did not think he would ever get used to.

'What do you want?' Mort asked, still far from at ease. How did he know his name? This was not the same old man.

'You still have so much potential in you Mortinan, however what you are about to face is the hardest test put before you yet.' He spoke with a passion that had been absent in the old man.

'Are you here to finally tell me what these tests are all about, or are you also here to spin riddles and waste my time?' Mort was not in a good mood.

'I would tell you all Mortinan, if it were permitted of me.'

Mort shook his head in disgust.

'Then just tell me what it is you are allowed to say and let me be on my way. I am in sore need of haste.'

The man smiled at him. A genuine smile.

'I am so pleased to be given this opportunity to speak with you Mortinan. It sounds peculiar hearing my voice say your name.' The smile remained.

'Who are you?' Mort asked, suddenly curious as to what hid the reason for his smile. 'Can you at least tell me that?'

The man's face grew serious for a moment and then he smiled again.

'My name is Mortinan,' he said.

Mort was taken aback. He did not know how to respond.

'But now,' the man with his own name continued, 'I must get to the reason why I am here.'

Mort was still thinking about the meaning behind them having the same name, as he tried to also focus on what he was saying. The female in Glorfiden had Mendina's name also.

'As I said, what you are headed towards now is the greatest test you have faced so far. Your task now is to make it back to your home, of that you are already aware.' He paused and drew a deep breath. 'I am sure you have noticed the lack of anything inhabiting these lands since you left the ruined forest?'

Mort nodded. Was he finally going to get an answer to at least one of his questions?

'This is because they have all been called to another place. They have been summoned to your home and await you there.' He spoke in a voice full of dread.

Mort's heart sunk. All of them?!

'You need to get through all of the misbegotten creatures put into this realm and make your way to your house. Stepping inside your home will end the task and free you to return to Mendina.'

Mort was stunned as he looked at his namesake. He was struck mute as he waited for the man to either continue talking or disappear.

'I am permitted to give you one piece of information, which I have just done.

I am also permitted to give you one piece of advice, which you need to listen to.' The last part he spoke in a louder voice and it drew Mort out of his stupor.

'How can I?' Mort said, still reeling at the thought of having to face the entirety of the Western Realm before he arrived home. 'If the rod were at full strength I may have a chance, but it contains little of the power for which I would need.'

'You have days of travel before you reach your home Mortinan. In that time, you need to feed the rod with your own power. Feed it with that which is ingrained within you. Which is a part of your being.'

'I wasn't aware I could do that.' Mort replied. 'Jarkene never mentioned it.'

'There were no instructions given to your father when I...when it was given to him Mortinan.'

Mort wasn't sure if it was a deliberate slip, but he certainly picked up on it. He had given the rod to his father. Why?

'How do I do it?' Mort asked. 'How do I power the rod?'

'Each morning when you wake, you need to feed it your magic. This will give you time during the day to recharge your own strength. Then at night before you sleep you must do the same.'

Mort nodded. 'So how do I do it?' he asked.

'You feel the breeze coming from the rod. So far both you and Jarkene have only used it to send forth the storm. Instead of pushing the storm out, you need to reverse the breeze. It will take time to achieve, but as it pulls in the wind, you must direct your magic towards it.' He stopped and stared at Mort before continuing. 'It will weaken you Mortinan, so hold on to some of your strength. You will need it to travel.'

Mort looked at the rod in his hand and felt the breeze. He concentrated on reversing the wind, to have the rod draw it into itself. To his surprise and relief, it worked. He sent strands of his magic towards it and watched in fascination as the rod sucked them into itself.

'I must leave you now,' Mortinan said, once again drawing Mort's focus back to him. 'It has been a joy to see you, of that you can be assured.'

Mort stared at his face, at his eyes of pure white.

'Who…what are you?' Mort asked, studying him intently now that he was more relaxed. The answer to some of his questions had been answered and although they sprouted many more questions, he was content in at least knowing what it was he now faced.

Mortinan smiled at him again and clasped his Champion on the shoulder.

'I do hope we meet again,' was all he said before disappearing.

There was no fading away. One moment he was there, the next he was not.

Mort stood there for a time after he had gone, just staring out at nothing.

His eyes were not focused on the landscape. He stood there thinking about all he had just been told and of the man who had appeared before him.

His mother had spoken to him of beings, those that the humans believed were responsible for creating the world they lived in and the creatures that inhabited it. He was not sure if this man had been one of those, but he could think of no other explanation.

He and Mendina had discussed in length the old man, of who or what he was. This man was like him in some ways, but so much more unlike him in others.

The fact he had admitted to restrictions on what he could and could not say, led Mort to conclude he was not the same as the old man. It may mean that he probably answered to him in some way. The old man seemed to be the one who set the rules for whatever it was they were doing.

Mortinan, his namesake, was probably a minion of his. He had no idea what his purpose was, but the fact he had the same name must be significant.

He turned his mind back to the rod in his hand, sat down on the grass and began feeding his magic into it.

He had been going for about half an hour, slowly letting his magic seep into it, before the cramps began.

He stopped the flow, stood up and began his journey again. He was weakened as he set off, but he had a purpose and a goal now. His strength would hold out long enough to accomplish that end.

The rest of that day was uneventful. Traversing rocky ground, interspersed with wooded areas, he found himself a small cave in a rocky output to rest for the night. Before sleeping he put as much into the rod as he was able before fatigue took him into a nightmare of ghoulish creatures and dragons that spewed acid.

Mort was still tired when he awoke, but he managed to feed the rod again for a short time before the cramps began.

After an hour or so of mindless walking, Mort came to the edge of a rise, the last of the high ground in this part of the land. In the distance to his left he could just make out the great forest of Glorfiden. It was a sea of green beyond the land he now walked in and seemed to go on forever. It pulled to him now and he yearned to be back under the peaceful swaying of the trees branches.

He turned his vision forward. Away in the distance, although he couldn't make it out, was his home and every monster within the empty realm lying in wait.

Lowering his view, he looked at what now lay between him and his destination.

There was a vast swampland, which he had not even known was there before now. Looking at it made him realise the journey he had taken so far would feel like an afternoon stroll compared to what he would have to go through in there. The stench of it wafted up to him already and he could see the water bubbling in parts even from this distance.

It stretched on for a way further east towards the forest, but Mort knew he would not be able to go around it.

To the west it stretched for as far as he could see. He wondered what kind of monstrous beasts would make their home in such a place and would have now joined the others around his home.

As he looked out over the swamp, he thought it fortunate that those who lay in wait for him to return home were not able to attack him within their own environment. It was a small blessing, but a blessing nonetheless.

A low-lying fog covered many parts of the swamp that he could see, which would have otherwise hidden a myriad of foul beasts.

His strength was still low as he made his way down the slope. He sighed as the stench grew worse, let out a big breath of air and urged himself to get through it before he had to camp again tonight.

He did not want to have to sleep in such a place as this.

CHAPTER 65

The Realm of Men

T HEY MADE GOOD speed, despite the size of his force and the terrain they moved through.

After his initial burst of destruction, Mithrak had not used his pendant again. That first ball of power had been a show of strength to his enemies and a burst of inspiration to his army. He did not intend using it again until he faced a living opponent, of which there had been none so far.

Mithrak was genuinely surprised he had yet to see a single elf.

He had hoped they had been decimated by the storm; his plans had depended on it; but there was no real way for any of his scouts to discover just how severe their losses had been.

Half a day of steady marching through the forest told him there were none left with any kind of power within the Elven forest. Not enough to challenge his army at least.

As disappointing as it was to Mithrak that he would not be able to kill any elves, he was still pleased that none of his army would be killed before they entered Dayhen's realm.

To have them all alive, healthy and strong would make the journey to the Capital that much easier. To have walked unscathed through the forest of the elves would give them all incredible confidence for the challenge ahead.

For although he did not envisage much resistance as they traversed the land, or even when they arrived at Lakerth, he knew Dayhen's army would be marching to try and stop them before they reached the Capital.

Their defeat would still prove to be a challenge, but if he had the advantage of a large wall between them, his chances increased immeasurably.

'We need to start angling toward Dayhen's realm now,' Mithrak said to Thrisc.

'Have them change direction.'

Thrisc nodded, but hesitated before passing on the order.

'We have followed the path of least resistance so far my King, but the new path is thick with entanglements and large boughs.'

'You think I am unaware of that?' Mithrak asked, anger stirring within him. He calmed himself quickly though. He would not let anyone ruin this for him. He was enjoying it too much.

'Of course not,' Thrisc said quickly. 'I merely wanted to ask if you would permit me to make a path through.'

Mithrak thought about it for a moment. They were almost through the forest and nothing had tried to attack them. Having one of his mage use up a bit more of his own power should not matter. Thrisc would have time to replenish it before the real fighting began.

'As you wish,' he said, 'but concentrate it this time. I do not need it as wide as last time. The elves are cowards and we will be out of their forest soon enough.'

Thrisc smiled, before moving off to the front of the advancing army. Word had already spread for them to stop, so it did not take the dark-mage long before he was standing at the front.

He turned to face those behind him.

'You are ordered to change direction and begin the march into the lands of the coward Dayhen.' A loud roar broke out from those at the front. They were mainly orcs and trolls, responsible for clearing a path for the rest of them to follow more comfortably. It was slow going at times, but they still moved forward. Hopefully the next part of the journey would be much quicker now.

'Now watch, as I make the path a little easier for you.' Thrisc spoke loudly, before turning to face right of where they had been marching.

Grasping hold of the pendant in his hand, the dark-mage pulled the obsidian stone out from it and held it out in front.

He was confident with the control he had over it and would make the flame narrow as ordered, but it would allow him to make it more intense also. If his King wanted a path, he would give him one.

Speaking the words to unleash the fire, Thrisc sent it forth at the trees in front of him.

The first few bushes and trees disintegrated, such was the intensity of the flame. Then it was extinguished.

Thrisc was in shock as he looked around.

He could see nothing and nothing attacked them, yet he knew something or someone had been responsible for his flame going out.

Speaking the words again, he fired off another shot into the trees before him. As before, the flame was extinguished prior to it impacting any more of the undergrowth.

Perhaps it was some kind of defence these particular trees had, although they looked no different than all of the others inside this cursed forest.

Turning slightly, he looked to make the next blast a short distance away from his previous attempt.

This time it was extinguished as soon as it left the black gemstone.

Something was definitely out there and for the first time since they had entered, Thrisc felt a genuine pang of fear within his body.

Scouring the trees, he looked for anything that moved or appeared out of the ordinary. There was nothing.

Suddenly a shot of lightning arced toward him from out of the trees where he just now looked. He only just had time to shoot his own projectile at it. They struck one another a short distance in front of Thrisc, sending sparks into the air.

The dark mage readied himself for the next attack, which followed soon after.

A burst of what looked like pure energy shot towards him. Once more he fired from his gemstone, but this time it did little to impact what was coming at him.

The bright ball of energy impacted the chest of Thrisc, causing his body to explode. Parts of his body fell on and around those who had been standing behind him.

The orcs and trolls took out their weapons and stood ready to fight, or run. Some had already tried the latter, before they were pulled up by those behind them.

Mithrak looked on as his dark-mage's body exploded. It seemed he was wrong about there being any powerful elves left within Glorfiden.

He waited to see what it would do next, as did the rest of his army.

When a minute had passed and no more attacks were forthcoming, he turned to Jurg.

'Have them move off,' he said quietly. Perhaps the elf was looking to cut off the head of the beast, he thought to himself. Best not to give it reason to suspect it had not already succeeded.

Jurg grunted the command to march and those at the front eventually did so, after some whippings were quickly dispensed. Despite their added caution, they all moved with a renewed urgency.

The army of Mithrak and even the great Dark-Mage himself, were suddenly very keen to leave this forest behind them.

Mithrak wanted to take out his gemstone, but he feared doing so may attract the eyes of those hidden within the trees.

He was surprised there had been no further attacks after Thrisc was so effortlessly dispatched.

Whatever had killed him had been powerful. He had seen Thrisc use the gem and it had no effect on the spell at his second attempt.

He suspected the elves were few in number around him and this part of his army. There may in fact be as few as only one or two of them.

If they were as decimated as he believed to be the case, then the elves would have needed to spread themselves out along the borders of their forest in response to his armies lined outside of it.

If it was the case that only a couple watched his army in this part of the forest, it would make sense why they had only attacked Thrisc and then stopped. They would not want to put themselves at too great a risk.

Not yet and especially not now that his army was headed outside of their forest and towards the land of men.

If he were an elf stalking this army, he would either leave now to help his fellow elves further north, or else he would wait until most of the army was out and then kill as many within the tail as he could.

Mithrak wanted to believe that for now his army was safe, but he did not like the thought of having a large chunk of his army decimated before they made it out of the forest.

Yet if he spread out before exiting, it may leave them even more vulnerable at both ends. When the edge of the forest came into sight, there was no doubt in his mind that most of those under his command would try to get out of the forest as quickly as their legs could carry them.

Mithrak needed another plan to ensure the survival of his army in its entirety. Losing one of his strongest Dark-Mage was already one loss too many. He would have sacrificed a hundred orcs in place of Thrisc.

'Jurg,' he said in a hushed voice, calling his general back close to him.

The large Orc walked back over to his master.

'When we are nearing the edge of the forest, I want everyone to spread out.' It was the plan he would go with unless he came up with a better one in the near future. 'I do not want large groups together. Is that clear?'

'Yes,' Jurg said, bowing his head.

'Stop that,' Mithrak hissed at him. 'No bowing until we are clear of the forest.'

His general looked confused, but he would do as ordered.

'You will remain close to me and when I give the order, they are all to run. Run as fast as their legs will carry them. All those scouting ahead are not to leave the sight of those following.'

'It will be done,' Jurg said.

Now all that he needed to do was wait.

Hopefully the elves had left already. If that were so, he had nothing to worry about.

Mithrak feared it wasn't the case however and whatever was out there had another surprise awaiting him. He hoped he would be ready.

CHAPTER 66

A Dwarf And A Dragon

BRINDEL LIMPED AWAY from the dragon and collapsed on to the ground. He was beaten, bloodied and exhausted.

He took off his helmet and let it fall into the dirt next to him.

Looking up at the blue sky above, he wondered how he was still breathing.

The dragon was certainly not beaten. Brindel had barely hurt it, when all of a sudden it just stopped attacking.

He did not understand what happened, but he was glad it was over.

Suddenly the sky was blocked from his view. Re-focusing, he looked up and into the eyes of the beast he had just battled.

'Impressive performance young dwarf.' The words coming from the dragon were softly spoken. 'You have a strong heart and marvellous resilience. I am oddly impressed.'

Brindel had no energy left to think of a response. He continued to lay still, his arms spread out and his chest heaving. He sucked in deeply, filling his deprived lungs with air.

'I will give you some more time,' he heard the dragon say, as the sky was once again visible above him.

After several minutes, Brindel finally found the strength to push himself up into a sitting position. The dragon was still there, staring in his direction with unblinking eyes.

'Welcome back dwarf,' the dragon said.

Brindel felt the hurts covering almost every part of his body, but his armour had protected him from those attacks that would have otherwise killed him.

'Why did you stop?' Brindel asked. Perhaps it was due to his fatigue that he had accepted so quickly the words of the dragon when she said they were done fighting.

Now that he was slightly rested, he was no longer so sure it was over.

'I have been tasked to test each of those that come to me. I only kill if the one I battle is not up to the challenge.'

Brindel could feel his temper rising again, but he kept it under control.

'Another test? This was just another test? What is this game I am being forced to play dragon and why have I have been chosen?'

'I cannot give you the answers you seek dwarf,' the dragon replied. Brindel did not detect any arrogance or satisfaction in its response. He decided that perhaps the dragon was not the one deserving of his sharp tongue.

It was the old man he wanted to vent against.

'So this was simply another test with no answers and no reward?' Brindel half asked it as a question and half spoke out loud to himself.

'Perhaps what I have to tell you is more to your liking.' The dragon continued to speak in a soft, but polite voice.

'Very good,' Brindel said in a voice resigned to his fate. 'Where to now?'

'Now you need to go home, but this time you are not permitted to deviate from the path set for you. There can be no detours. You must head straight home.' The dragon spoke seriously now and the dwarf knew the words he spoke were truth.

'Then I am to die in the Elven Forest,' Brindel said and sighed.

'The one responsible for setting these tasks has allowed me to grant you one boon in regard to that situation. It has been conceded that for you to travel through Glorfiden would indeed mean your death and that is not what this task requires.'

'Are you giving me wings?' Brindel asked, his humour slowly returning. 'I can assure you that dwarves were not meant to fly. I can vouch for it first-hand.'

The dragon chuckled at him. It actually laughed.

Brindel himself laughed softly at hearing it.

'No dwarf..' the dragon began.

'Brindel,' the dwarf interrupted. 'My name is Brindel.'

'No Brindel,' the dragon began again. 'You will be shielded as you walk between the boundaries of the Elven Forest. None that reside in there will be able to harm you.'

Brindel smiled as the dragon finished.

'However, I caution you,' the dragon continued. 'If you attack anyone or anything within the forest, the shield will fall and you will be as vulnerable as you are standing before me now.'

Brindel's smile was replaced by a frown, but he was satisfied that what was offered was reasonable. He would love to be able to attack his enemies risk free. Chopping up elves in their own forest would be such joy he almost giggled out loud just thinking about it. What a shame.

'You must leave now Brindel and make haste. This task will not suffer delays.'

Brindel nodded. He wanted to ask more questions of the dragon, but he realised if there was anything more it knew that could help him, it probably would have told him already.

There also wasn't much more he needed to know.

All he had to do was travel back home. Sounded like a far more pleasant task.

Yet he wondered why he was feeling nervous about it.

It was probably because nothing about the tasks he had been set so far had been easy. He somehow suspected this next task would not end with hugs and kisses.

Nodding his head in thanks to the creature that had almost beaten and burned him to death only a short time ago, Brindel limped away.

'To the Elven Forest,' he said out loud, as he trundled away from the dragon. He looked over his shoulder as he spoke one last time to the mighty beast.

'I may not be able to fight any elves in their forest, but I am sure going to make them angry when they realise I'm untouchable.'

He smiled and turned his head away from the dragon. 'This is going to be so much fun!'

CHAPTER 67

Freedom or Death

KABIR WAS COMFORTABLE enough in his cell, but he was growing tired of being caged.

Never before had he been so restricted in his movements. For a Barbarian who had never been locked up before, it was difficult for him to remain calm. But he knew he had to. It was just another consequence of his need for adventure.

Thinking of Ahlia in her own cell was more difficult for him to accept. Her lack of freedom would be harder on a horsewoman from the plains.

Yet he had been given a renewed hope. From another death sentence, the intervention of the wizard had changed things again.

It was therefore no real surprise to Kabir to look up from where he was seated and see the wizard standing on the other side of his barred cage.

'We need to talk,' the wizard said, a real urgency in his voice. 'I need you to tell me all you can about the man who came to you and what your current quest is for.' The words were not a request. They sounded to Kabir like an order.

Despite his predicament, the barbarian still expected more from the man.

'I have been treated with very little respect since I arrived in these lands,' Kabir said, 'except from a select few. These men I would happily share my tales with.' He stopped talking and waited to see what the wizard would say next.

The wizard paused, before finally responding.

'I begin to see why you are where you are,' Heridah said. 'Wizards can be...very focused at times. It seems to grate against your own ideals.'

Kabir remained silent. There was no question and no attempt to speak to him differently. He was not even sure the wizard was speaking to him at all.

'We need a common ground,' Heridah finally said into the silence. 'I wish to hear your tale barbarian, but you need to understand where it is you are and why you came to be in captivity.'

'I know why I am here,' Kabir replied. 'I defended myself against one of yours.'

'Why did you not put away your weapons when it was requested of you?' he asked.

'It was no request,' Kabir said. 'He spoke down to me and would not listen to what I had to say.'

'Would you expect someone entering your lands to abide by your customs and laws?'

They had covered off on this during his trial. If he had somewhere else to go, he would have left about now. As it was, he decided to humour the only person that could probably save his life.

'I would wizard, but I would not speak to them how I was spoken to by your wizard friend.'

'What if it were during a time of war?' Heridah persisted. 'Would it be any different?'

'There was no war,' Kabir said.

'How do you know that?' Heridah asked him. 'Is the slaughter of farm folk and those walking the tracks and roads of Dayhen's Realm not a form of war? The displacement of homes due to attacks and the abandonment of Shadow Hill. Does war make a difference? Have you experienced it within your own lands?'

Kabir didn't see what this had to do with killing the wizard. It seemed to be a pointless conversation.

'You like to talk a lot, yet you have never given me your name,' Kabir said. 'My point from the very beginning.'

The wizard paused again, as he continued to stare at Kabir.

'Why did you come to our realm?' the wizard asked.

Kabir clenched his jaw, but tried not to let another insult annoy him too much. These wizards were different to other men.

'I came for adventure,' Kabir answered. He would give him nothing more.

'A friend of mine, and probably the greatest warrior who has ever lived, was sent on an adventure,' Heridah said. 'That adventure took his life.'

Kabir didn't respond. It was not much of a story.

'Would you like to hear about his adventure?' Heridah asked.

Kabir didn't want to be rude, but he had put up with the other's rudeness long enough.

'Your name?' Kabir asked. He would not ask again.

'I am Heridah,' the wizard said, as if he had just given Kabir a gift of some sort. 'Would you like to hear it?'

'I am tired,' Kabir said. 'Tales of old do not particularly interest me right now.'

'Oh, but this is not an old tale,' Heridah said. 'It is a new tale and it continues still to this day.'

Kabir was a little more interested, but he didn't intend to tell the wizard that. He did admit to himself that the part about the man being the greatest warrior ever had him intrigued.

'Go on then,' Kabir said. 'But keep it brief if you could.'

The wizard smiled, before pulling up a nearby stool and taking a seat.

'Where to begin,' he said to himself. 'Perhaps near the end,' he decided.

Kabir thought it odd to start a tale near its end, but he wasn't about to say anything. This wizard seemed to choose his words carefully. He had no doubt this was no exception.

'His name was Valdor, and he was the greatest of the King's Shield.' That certainly got Kabir's attention.

'His devotion was to his King, his Deity and to the Realm. He lived his life to protect those weaker than himself and to keep those within the Realm safe from monsters, both without and within.'

Kabir liked the way the old man told a story. His voice was strong and he made the listener believe what he was hearing.

'Which is why it was such a shock to his King, when Valdor told him he had been visited by a man he believed to be his deity and was told he must set out on a quest. He told his King the quest was all important and any delay could prove his downfall.'

He definitely had Kabir's attention now, and as the barbarian looked at the wizard Heridah, he could see the wizard knew it.

'The King forbade it of course. At such a time as this; as he called together every able-bodied man in the Kingdom to fight against the coming evil; why would he let his greatest warrior ride east on a fool's quest to try and seek out some idol?'

'Did he find it,' Kabir asked. It was a simple question, but it changed the look on Heridah's face completely.

'Ah, so you are not the one who found it either,' Heridah replied.

'I did not,' Kabir conceded. 'I was close to it when first given the task, but I was unable to get to it in time.' The time for word games seemed to be over. The wizard had brought them back around to where he had begun the conversation. Kabir was aware of it, but no longer cared. That another had been chosen peaked his curiosity.

'Was there not a compulsion upon you?' Heridah asked. He looked confused.

'There was,' Kabir said, 'but I was honour-bound not to seek it, and then physically unable to. It was not easy.'

The wizard nodded.

'I have another question of you Kabir, if I may?' he added.

His sudden politeness almost brought a smile to Kabir's face.

Kabir just nodded in response.

'Were you well thought of where you come from?'

Kabir thought it an odd question.

'I hope I still am well thought of,' he replied. 'I plan on returning there again one day.'

'That is not what I meant,' Heridah said, sounding a little annoyed. 'Were you.... I mean, are you a great warrior there?'

'I am best with the sword in my village of Deerstep,' he answered, 'which is the largest of all villages in the highlands.' He tried not to sound boastful.

'Anything else?' Heridah asked. 'I mean, is there anything else which makes you special?'

Kabir wasn't sure if the wizard was trying to insult him or not. In a short time speaking with this one, he had begun to learn how differently they looked at the world and interacted with others. Perhaps it wasn't rudeness or arrogance. Perhaps they just thought differently. He decided not to be insulted. Yet.

'Nothing more,' he said, 'other than the sword my father gave to me before I left. You have probably already heard about my sword.'

'I heard talk of it, now that you mention it, but nothing more. What is so special about your sword?'

'It is lighter than any other metal I have held. It heals mortal wounds and protects against magic. I am yet to see what else it does, as it has been stolen from me.' He again had to make an effort to rein back his temper.

The wizard looked to be thinking now, as he looked away from Kabir.

'One final question if I may?' Heridah asked, looking back at Kabir again. This time he had a seriously intense look on his face and he didn't wait for Kabir to give his acceptance.

'What is the new quest you have been set?'

Kabir didn't answer straight away, but decided to ask a question of his own instead.

'What happened to Valdor?'

It was obviously not the answer Heridah was expecting, but the look of anger quickly disappeared.

'He was set upon by creatures able to control his mind. They took him back to their lair and slaughtered him.' Kabir could see it still hurt Heridah to speak of it.

'You were not there to support him with your magic?'

This time the look of anger remained longer on his face.

'I was not,' he eventually answered.

'I am to find a spoiled forest,' Kabir said. 'Somewhere in the west, only this time there is nothing compelling me to go there. Once I find it, I am supposed to locate the one who does not belong there.'

'Where in the west?' Heridah asked. 'How long ago did he appear and tell you to find it?'

'I don't know where. I was hoping someone in this realm would know which forest,' Kabir said. The look on the face of the wizard told the barbarian he knew of such a place. 'You look like you do,' he added.

'I know of a forest which was recently attacked and much damage caused, but if that is your destination, then you will not survive if you go in there.'

'If you return my sword to me, I might surprise you,' Kabir said. 'Do you think it the place I seek?'

'Perhaps,' Heridah said. 'Perhaps not. It is west of where you started, but it is not part of the Western Realm. There is almost certainly a spoiled forest somewhere within those forsaken lands.'

'Where is the forest you know of?' Kabir asked.

'It is north of here. It is the forest of the elves.' Heridah said. 'None who enter uninvited survive.'

'Why is it spoilt?' Kabir asked, not perturbed by the wizard's warning.

'The elves were attacked by a storm unlike any before seen anywhere in these lands,' Heridah said. 'Many, many elves would have perished.'

'Then it is no longer so dangerous,' Kabir said. 'Who would not belong there?'

'There was a Lord banished from the forest many years ago,' Heridah said. 'He dwelt in the lands to the west for many years. It is reported he has now returned. There is no-one alive who would stand a chance against an Elven Lord within his own forest,' Heridah said. 'Magic sword or no magic sword.'

Kabir still wasn't convinced the forest would mean his certain death, but he now believed it was probably the place he needed to go.

Both spoiled and one who didn't belong there. It sounded right.

'If I help you Kabir, we will not be going into Glorfiden,' Heridah said. 'That is my condition for convincing the Princess to allow you to live and my accompanying you.'

'Do we stand at the border and yell until someone comes out?' Kabir asked. It sounded like cowardice to him and he never shied away from something because it was dangerous. As much as Ahlia may have tempered him a little, he still knew when action was required.

'I am not convinced it is where we must go,' Heridah said, no longer looking at Kabir. Once more Kabir tried his best not to be offended. The wizards were a strange breed and he now realised he needed to treat them as such. 'There must be something in the west and Jarkene is an elf. He certainly belongs in Glorfiden.'

Kabir could tell he was definitely talking to himself now.

'Who is Jarkene?' Kabir asked, trying to keep up.

'He is the Elven Lord,' Heridah said, looking back at Kabir as if he were some kind of distraction. 'There will be those within the Western Realm who we will be able to speak with. They are not all evil savages.'

'I haven't agreed to let you accompany us yet,' Kabir said, as soon as Heridah stopped talking.

'Then you will be going nowhere,' Heridah said. 'You will die here.'

'You would want me dead rather than to go without you?' Kabir asked, a little bewildered. 'What is to stop me cutting your head off the moment we are out of sight from this place?'

'You are honourable, that is why,' Heridah said with a smile. 'And there will be some of the King's Shield accompanying us. As many as can be spared.'

'Very well,' Kabir eventually said. 'We will try for a forest in the West. But you are not in charge.'

'Someone has to be in charge,' Heridah said.

'I will be,' Kabir said in reply.

The wizard took his time answering.

'You seem to make rash decisions,' Heridah said. 'I will decide where we go. You will guide us only.'

Kabir was about to respond, when the wizard held up his hand.

'This is going nowhere Kabir. Let us see if I can convince the Princess to spare your life first and perhaps she can decide for us.'

Kabir knew whose side she would be on, but he didn't press the issue. Time to worry about that if and when he was released.

'I will wait until then,' Kabir said and smiled. As if he had anywhere else to go.

'I will speak to you again in the morning,' Heridah said, before turning and making his way out of the cell complex.

Kabir decided he should probably get some rest.

He would either die tomorrow, or they would begin his search for the ruined forest again.

He hoped for the latter. It would be such a waste of time sleeping if they were to execute him when he awoke.

CHAPTER 68

It Is What It Is

THE CREATOR WATCHED as the remaining gamers sat looking into their eyes. He was able to take in what they did, as well as what continued to happen within the world of Dark Swell. He required no special *eye*.

Hovering a short distance above the clearing, he remained invisible to them all.

This part of the game had always been his favourite time within the worlds he created. That time in the game when so much was happening and the nerves of his gamers were at breaking point as it drew closer to its finale.

Each of those seated around the clearing had invested so much of their young lives towards this contest. Many years of study and many more years creating and building their realms.

A great number of those in previous games had been hugely disappointed when the contest had ended so soon after their Champions were selected. Yet he would not have it any other way.

It made the events so much more enjoyable for him to watch, and it generally meant the weaker ones were not victorious.

Although it was quick, his challenges were designed to weed out those not worthy. This was looking to be the case again this time.

He had already admitted this was building towards being one of his most enjoyable games ever.

Each of the remaining champions still had an excellent chance of winning the contest, which was generally not the case.

Although some seemed to be lagging well behind the others, there would be opportunity for them to catch up.

He knew some of those Gamers below him might not agree with decisions he would make moving forward, but as the game neared its conclusion, their feelings were not his concern. He knew what he did was fair and didn't feel obligated to explain everything to them, yet a few words now would not hurt.

He was not bothered if any of them felt aggrieved, but he still wanted them to give their all.

Their feelings had never truly been a concern to him, but he needed to have them believe the game was equal for each. It was important they felt that way so each gamer would give their best effort. It was one of the criteria for being chosen in the first place. The competitive spirit, but also their sense of fairness.

What actually mattered most to the Creator was how exciting the end of this game was going to be. And as the finale neared, none of the gamer's grievances would affect how they played the game.

This late in the game, each would be consumed with winning. Not much else mattered to them any longer.

He smiled thinking about it.

To have so many Champions still alive was going to make for an epic finish. But to ensure such a finale, he needed to give them all the opportunity to be there at the end, while still maintaining his distance. Allowing the game to run its natural course was important to him, or else why have them in the first place?

A pre-determined ending was boring, which is why he always needed to minimise his influence, while still maximising the final impact of having so many Champions still alive at the end.

As always, he was confident that what he did would make for a lot of excitement.

Floating gracefully down into the clearing, the Creator stood proudly in the centre as he dispelled the mask of invisibility surrounding him.

Each of their *eyes* went blank the moment he appeared and time stood still on the world of Dark Swell.

He looked around at the surprised looks, which never grew old. He always enjoyed how shocked and excited they got.

'You have seen the assistance I provided Brindel's Champion. Do any of you have any thoughts or objections?'

He knew there would be none, but it humoured him to ask anyway. You never know, one of them might surprise him.

When he had looked at each in turn, the Creator looked down at the ground next to his feet, as if he were deep in thought.

'To those of you who think the challenge is now too great for their Champion, tell me what I can do to help. After all, this game is nearing its conclusion.' He softened his tone as he spoke, before once more looking around at the stunned faces circling him.

He was sure at least one of them would speak this time.

'With respect,' Linf said, 'my Champion has furthest to travel if she survives against the dragon.'

'Yes, she does,' the Creator answered. 'If she even makes it that far.'

He knew those words would sound ominous coming from him, but he had not truly intended to offer them help here. It was merely to gauge their responses.

'Can you help?' she asked.

'Would it be fair to the others if I was to give your Champion special treatment?' he asked. 'Would that not diminish the efforts their own Champions have made already.'

He could see the confusion on her face. She warred with what she wanted to say to him, with that she did not dare to say.

Of course it would be fair, the Creator thought. The Champions who had already faced the dragon had nowhere near as far to travel as her Champion did, and they had not faced the same dangers Linf had.

The Creator watched as Linf steeled herself.

'It would be fair,' she said. 'My Champion had furthest to travel.' He could see she wanted to say more, but decided to try her luck with this first.

'Your Champion also got captured and went in the wrong direction,' Mortinan said, cutting off the Creator, who looked sternly at Mortinan.

The Creator almost laughed at Mortinan's lack of contrition.

'She deserves nothing,' Mortinan added.

'What about my Champion?' Kabir asked.

'What about him?' Mortinan asked in response.

'I was not talking to you,' Kabir said.

This time Mortinan appeared a little abashed, as he looked across briefly at the Creator, before looking down at his feet.

'What can I do to help your Champion Kabir?' the Creator asked.

'You could bring the Dragon to him,' Kabir answered. He obviously had more time to think about what he needed. 'Once he is free of his bonds.'

Mortinan made a noise of disbelief, which Kabir ignored. His focus remained on the Creator.

'Was the first challenge brought closer to the Elven forest because they were furthest away?' The Creator asked him.

Kabir shook his head and said no more.

'Anyone else?' The Creator asked.

The clearing remained silent this time.

'As I said before,' he continued. 'Although this game is nearing its conclusion, there is still time for those who are yet to challenge the dragon to catch up.'

None of those surrounding him stirred now.

'Once you arrive safely home, just one more task will be set for your Champion. A task that will send them to a place within the world of Dark Swell that is very special to me. A place where your Champions will face the ultimate test of survival. If they are the first to survive this test, the reward will be yours.... and theirs,' he added cryptically.

He could see they all wanted to hear more. To be given an insight, or at least a clue to what they would have to fight.

They should know better by now, the Creator thought, as he disappeared from their view.

CHAPTER 69

Closing In

'STOP WHERE YOU are!' Stuart hollered, holding his halberd up and out in front of him. The giant horse coming towards the gate was not slowing.

Stepping to the side, Stuart readied himself to strike, but at the last moment the rider dug in his heels and pulled back hard on the reins. The horse stopped quickly, sending mud up into the air. Some of the small pieces struck the guard. Although it did him no harm, it annoyed him nevertheless.

'I am in a hurry,' the man on the horse said. Although he was the size of a large man, he sounded like a boy and looked like one sitting on such a large mount.

'Get down from your horse right now!' Stuart snarled, his halberd still pointing up at the rider. He indicated for the other two guards to come and join him. The man had an accent. He was not from around these parts.

'What have I done?' he asked, making no move to get down from his horse.

'Last chance boy. Get down now or I will knock you from that horse.'

Cursing quietly to himself, the young man jumped from his horse.

'Now what?' he asked, spreading his arms out wide.

'Now you will tell me what your business is here. Don't try to be smart. Not the time or the place,' Stuart said. He was tired from all the double shifts he had to do since the army left. Also, the whole place was on edge waiting for news.

'I am looking for my brother. That is it,' the young man said. 'When I find him, I will likely return home with him.'

'And where is home?' Stuart asked. 'Are you from down south?'

The man chuckled at him. 'I am from a long way north, above the eastern plains. A highlander from the village of Deerstep.'

'Ah,' Stuart said. 'You are looking for the one who killed the wizard.'

'That I am,' Wilhelm said. 'Can you point me in his direction?'

'That would be in the King's dungeon,' Stuart said. 'You probably don't want to go in there. Perhaps you can wait like the rest of us. We'll all be seeing him soon enough. He is to be hung at sun's high today.'

'Then you better point me to the King, so I can discuss his release,' Wilhelm said.

Cocky young sprout, Stuart thought.

'No King here at the moment. He's off fighting the Western hordes. The Princess is the one who gives sentences while he's gone.'

'Then point the way to the Princess,' Wilhelm said. 'Is she pretty?'

'Watch your mouth,' Stuart said, genuinely insulted. 'Talk like that will have you sharing a cell with your brother.'

'Apologies,' Wilhelm said. 'I forget myself sometimes. Where can I find the Princess?'

'She won't be seeing the likes of you. Especially not this morning. There are no audiences listed for today. Not with the hangings.'

The highlander sighed. 'Can you please tell me where I need to go to plead for an audience?'

Stuart thought a moment and then shrugged his shoulders.

'That way,' he said, pointing down the main street. 'Follow that one all the way and you'll come to the next big gate. They may let you in, they may not.'

Wilhelm turned and got back on to his horse. Walking his way through the small crowds of people, he soon arrived at the main gate.

The guards here were not the same as those at the other gate. These ones appeared far more dangerous, and looked to take their job seriously.

Wilhelm decided there would be no fooling with these two.

One put up a hand as he approached and Wilhelm stopped and dismounted.

He took another two steps forward, before the man again put his hand up.

'State your business,' was all he said.

'I am here for an audience with the Princess,' he said with a small bow.

The man's expression did not change.

'The Princess Areana is seeing no-one today. Come back tomorrow and you may try again.'

'That will be too late,' Wilhelm said. 'My brother is due to be hanged today.'

The guard looked back at him.

'Wait here,' the guard said, as he turned and walked inside the gate. Wilhelm watched as he entered the large doors a hundred paces away and disappeared from view.

'Where has he gone?' Wilhelm asked the other guard.

'Family of the condemned are usually allowed in to say good-bye. He is checking to see if you are permitted.' This guard showed exactly the same level of emotion as the one who had left; which was none.

After a short time, the other guard returned.

'You are to come with me,' the guard said. 'You will leave all of your weapons here at the gate.'

Wilhelm was about to protest, before remembering where he was and why he was here. He did not need to get into an argument with these men.

Handing over his sword and daggers, Wilhelm followed behind as the man led him through the halls of the great palace, before heading down into the cell area.

They walked through a long tunnel and passed several more guards, before finally coming to a small cell with wide open bars on the door.

Sitting down in the middle of the room was his brother, looking very unimpressed with his situation.

When he caught sight of his latest visitor he jumped to his feet and strode over to the door.

The guard stepped aside, allowing Wilhelm to walk over to the door and clasp arms with his brother.

'It is good to see you brother,' Wilhelm said with a smile.

Kabir couldn't get the shocked look from his face. He was speechless, until finally he was able to replace it with one of anger.

'What in the god's names are you doing here?!' he said loudly. 'None would have let you leave, so you must have run away.'

Wilhelm continued to smile. He had expected a lecture from his brother.

'Meghan and I left Deerstep to come and find you. Grogan came to Deerstep saying all of the villages needed to come together. An evil is spreading throughout the land Kabir. You are needed at home.' He was glad he had been able to get it all out without interruption.

'Where is Meghan?' Wilhelm asked. 'Did she have the good sense to return home?'

Wilhelm paused before answering this time. He knew his brother had been fond of her.

'She was captured near the goblin lands,' Wilhelm said. 'I am sorry Kabir, but I fear the worst. Denizen and some of his plainsmen took off to find her, but I doubt they will get there in time.'

'You know Denizen?' Kabir asked. 'Taken by what?'

'Taken by giant cats,' Wilhelm said. 'They only left me because they thought me dead.'

Kabir looked confused.

'Giant cats? Are you sure?' he asked. 'Why did they not feed on you if they thought you dead?' Kabir asked.

Wilhelm could only shrug his shoulders. He had thought the same thing when he awoke.

'But we need to talk about how to get you out of here,' Wilhelm said. 'Will I be able to speak with the Princess?'

'You will not,' a voice said from behind him, further along the corridor through which he had arrived.

It was a female voice, and had the same emotionless tone as the men who guarded the inner gate.

'You will step aside from the door,' she said, as she came closer.

Wilhelm sized her up and could see she was just as dangerous as the two guards he had already met, possibly even more dangerous.

He bowed to her and moved away from the door.

She stood on the same side of it as he did, staring at him from about three paces away.

'You will remain where you are and not speak,' she said.

Wilhelm put his hands up in a gesture of peaceful intentions.

'Of course,' he said, as he looked past the woman guard at the two persons walking behind her.

One was a tall man with a beard. He looked to be a teacher of sorts, or else he was a wizard. Probably a wizard, Wilhelm thought.

The girl in front of him had to be the Princess Areana. She was breathtakingly pretty. Wilhelm had never seen anyone that came close to being as beautiful as she was. Meghan, he was sorry to say, was almost plain in comparison.

'Princess,' Kabir said, bowing his head to her.

'Heridah has informed me that you may be able to assist with a matter I have some interest in.' Her words were melodic as well, Wilhelm thought.

'If I can help you I will,' Kabir said. 'Despite you sentencing me to death.'

'You killed a wizard in the King's Guard. I had no choice,' she replied.

'We do not need to go over the events of yesterday again do we?' the old man asked.

Wilhelm saw the Princess shoot the old man an angry look, before she turned back to his brother.

'Tell me of this quest you were given,' she asked him.

'A man came to me Princess, who I believe is not of these lands. He bid me find something in the east, something to which I was pushed towards. Unfortunately another found it first. I did not get there in time,' he finished.

'How do you know someone else got there first?' she asked.

Wilhelm was having difficulty following exactly what it was they were talking about. A man from another land came to his brother and told him to fetch something? The woman guard staring at him also made it difficult to fully concentrate on what was happening.

'The compulsion that was driving me suddenly disappeared,' Kabir replied. 'I only now assume that another found it first after speaking with your wizard last night and hearing of the same task being given to one of your King's Shield.'

Wilhelm didn't miss the small groan and look of horror on the face of the old man, as the Princess turned on him.

'You came down here and spoke with him despite what I said?!' she said in a soft voice.

Wilhelm decided he would not want to upset this one.

'My Princess, I could see the urgency in speaking with him so I quickly came down for a brief conversation. I apologise.' Wilhelm thought he sounded sincere, but he also knew what leaders were like when their orders were ignored. He had suffered beneath his father's hand many a time in the past. Most of them well deserved.

'You will leave now Heridah. I will call on you later,' she said, turning to look at the back of the female guard staring at him. 'Catlin, if he does not leave this instant I would have you escort him out.'

The female guard named Catlin turned immediately and took two steps towards the wizard. He turned without a word and left along the corridor.

As Wilhelm turned back from watching the wizard leave, he saw the Princess was now staring at him.

'Who are you?' she asked. 'What are you doing here? I know the barbarian knows no-one else in my city, other than his woman from the plains.'

'I am Wilhelm,' he said, bowing low. 'And this giant of a man is my big brother. I have been sent by our father, the Chieftain of our village Deerstep, to have my brother return. He is needed to help fight the evils that now run through the highlands of our home.' He turned to his brother. 'He would also like his sword back.'

Catlin stepped forward again.

'You will not speak to another when you are being addressed by the Princess,' she said sternly.

'My apologies Princess Areana, but if I am to look upon you too long, I fear for my sight,' he said. 'Your beauty is blinding, and unsurpassed within all the lands.'

She furrowed her brow.

'Your brother is sentenced to die; my Shield Catlin has just berated you and you think it appropriate to say something like that? Are you stupid Wilhelm of Deerstep?'

It was an effort for him not to smile. Instead he tried to look suitably remorseful.

'I apologise Princess. I am a simple highland warrior and ignorant to your ways. In my life when I have seen a pretty girl I have told her as much. Seeing someone who surpasses every other woman I have ever seen made it difficult for me to remain silent. But again, I apologise.'

Her brow again furrowed, and her eyes squinted a little as she looked to work out what he had just said.

In the end, she appeared to give up and turned back to his brother.

Catlin continued to glare at him, so Wilhelm tried not to look at her.

'Is there more you need to tell me?' Areana asked him.

'A second task has been given to me Princess,' he said. 'Only this time there is no compulsion for me to find it.'

'Why is that?' she asked.

'I know not,' he said, 'but the one who set me this second task said that I should not delay. That I need to find the ruined forest and seek the one who doesn't belong there.'

'That is it?' Areana asked. 'A ruined forest? Does he speak of the Elven Forest?'

'I do not know,' Kabir said. 'He said nothing else before he disappeared in front of my eyes.'

There was a silence for a short time, as the Princess looked to be thinking on what his brother had said.

'The one of your Shield who was given the same task, I was told he died,' Kabir said.

'He was killed by monsters born of nightmares,' Princess Areana said, 'but he was the best and strongest of us all. Your story sounds contrived. Did Heridah tell you what to say?'

'My condolences,' Kabir said, 'and my story is how it happened. I do not lie.'

'Kabir is our best and strongest warrior,' Wilhelm said.

'You were told not to speak,' Catlin said, taking a step toward him again. The look on her face had grown even harder if that were possible. She did not look happy.

Wilhelm again put his hands up in front showing that he meant no harm.

'Why do you tell me this?' Areana asked, turning back to Wilhelm.

'Do you think it a coincidence that your strongest and best was chosen, as was ours? I am only just hearing this tale, but already I see there is something going on none of us can explain. I think we need to see this adventure through to its end.' Wilhelm was getting excited.

'I think you are forgetting that your brother killed a wizard Wilhelm. I have already passed sentence. He is to be hung today.' Wilhelm could see she wasn't happy about having to pass such a sentence. He needed to convince her to change her mind. 'Such fanciful talk of men from other lands selecting our finest warriors and sending them on secret tasks is to be honest, quite ludicrous.'

'Or else it is not,' Wilhelm persisted. 'What if it is something that could help our realms fight off the evils spreading through the land.'

'He sounds like Valdor did,' Catlin said.

'Valdor sounds like a man I would have liked to have met,' Wilhelm said. 'And he had first-hand experience with who gave the task. Was he someone prone to fanciful talk?' Wilhelm asked. He suspected he was not, having met others of his order.

'He was not,' Catlin said.

'No, he was not,' Areana echoed. 'He deserved better.'

'My brother is also not one for fanciful talk Princess,' Wilhelm said. 'He was the serious one, needing to constantly keep his brother out of trouble after our mother was killed when we were only young. My mouth sometimes got me into fights. It sounds very strange to me hearing about mystical quests come from my brother's mouth.'

'I need time to think,' Areana said. 'I cannot just go back on my sentence. It was a fair decision and I will look weak and indecisive if I were to change it.'

'You are the future Queen of this realm,' Wilhelm said. 'You can change it if you wish. If it is best for your realm. The highlanders and plains people would make for powerful allies.'

She looked at Wilhelm for a time before beckoning to Catlin and turning to leave.

When they had gone, Wilhelm walked back over to the cell door.

'You didn't say much,' Wilhelm said.

'I missed hearing you talk,' Kabir said, 'and I forgot how good you are at it, when you are not trying to goad someone into a fight.'

Wilhelm smiled and grabbed his brother's forearms again.

'I missed you too Kabir,' he said.

When the Princess got back to her room, she bid Catlin head to her practice.

Her Shield nodded, as her replacements stood outside the door.

Areana sat down on her bed and went over in her mind once again what had just happened.

Was she seriously considering changing her decision? Based purely on the words of a barbarian boy?

She had to admit that he spoke well, despite his lack of culture and respect, and that he was respectful in other ways.

What was wrong with her? She was seriously considering it and she knew the real reason. He was very, very handsome and looked to be a strong warrior, despite his age.

Yet she was currently the ruler of Lakerth and would one day rule all of the Realm. She was not in a position to be influenced by a boy with a nice smile and a strong build, and one who said such charming things to her.

How dare he! she thought, but then perhaps he had been genuine in what he said. What if he was genuine?

So what if he was? He was a barbarian! A highlander with a smooth tongue, who had probably used it to charm every girl in his village.

No, she would not be changing her decision.

The sentence would be carried out when the sun was at its highest today.

Calling in her servants, she began to prepare herself for the execution.

CHAPTER 70

Another Village Burns

THEY COVERED A lot of ground during the day, their scouts reporting no movements ahead.

Their travels had actually been quite leisurely, considering where they went. The land between these two Barbarian villages was reasonably flat, and as they got closer, the trees also thinned out, replaced with small bushes and clumps of long spindly grasses.

The smells in the air changed as well.

None of the dark elves had been this close to the vast dark waters before and the smell of it was foreign to them.

They had been able to glimpse them from afar; high up in their mountain realm; but none had ever ventured down to the great cliffs, which were told to them in fables. There had been no need for them to go there, so it had been forbidden.

Flek-Niht had to admit to herself that she was looking forward to seeing it up close. In truth, it had been part of why she wanted to come south and take over the lands of the Barbarians. The freedom for her people to go wherever they wanted and to walk along the shore of the dark waters, was a dream she had held since she was only young.

Not even an hour had passed since one of her spies had told her there were no cliffs where the barbarians lived. They moved freely along the edge of the water, and he had even seen some of them pulling strange looking fish from the waters!

It was a glorious thing she was doing. A pity not all of the families had shared her vision and bravery.

A new world was hers for the taking and her people would chant about what she now did for many, many lifetimes to come.

The name of Flek-Niht would not be forgotten.

When the sun disappeared from the sky the main force was still an hour away.

Flek-Niht had decided to camp away from the village, spreading her scouts throughout the lands between them and the Barbarian village.

There would be less risk making their plans here, while still plenty of night left for them to travel the last part of the journey and kill all of those within and surrounding the village.

Most of the scouts she had sent to report back on the defences the barbarians had and where they slept had returned, however those who were ordered to wait and see where they moved once night fell, had obviously not made their way back yet.

Some of those would stay until the main force joined them, in case there were further movements. The others would return and allow Flek-Niht to plan their next onslaught against the barbarians.

She did not want to lose so many dark-elves this time.

There were still more villages to take after this one, and she knew high casualties would make it a lot harder.

Flek-Niht's tent was set up first and she had eaten and bathed by the time the first of the evening scouts returned.

'Nearly all of them have returned to the main village before last light,' he said. Flek-Niht could hear the fatigue in his voice, but there was also excitement. 'The others remain near the water, gutting and preparing what they have caught. They will return when it is done.'

'You are sure of this?' she asked.

'There is no reason for them to stay,' he replied.

She bid him leave with a flick of her hand. That was all she needed to know. How the village was set up and defended had been reported to her as she travelled here.

Now all that she needed to do was brief her leaders and have them all move into position.

Everyone within the army who had come with her would be entering the village tonight. Even herself.

She enjoyed battle as much as any dark-elf and none had ever dared question her abilities.

Flek-Niht smiled as they strode into her tent, the large table in front of her already adorned with a crude map drawn on it of the barbarian village.

Wooden symbols with a marking to identify each dark-elf attacking force had been spaced around the map.

'Study well where you will each be attacking from. Next to your marker, I have also put the name of the scout who reported on that area. When we are done here, you may speak to them and ask what you need. They are waiting outside.'

There was silence as each scrutinised the table in front of them.

'Any dwellings outside the village?' Glin-Peln asked.

'There are a few,' Flek-Niht said, 'but I have dispatched some to take care of them. They await only the signal to attack.'

Glin-Peln nodded and smiled at her.

'Thank you again for the honour of helping to lead this attack,' he said.

Flek-Niht nodded her head in return. She had known Glin-Peln since he was born to her sister. She knew he did not say it to gain favour. It was genuine, as were all of those within her own family and those others who had ridden with her.

Although she would have preferred all of the houses to have joined her, she was still pleased with those who had chosen to come. They had done so of their own free will, which made them more valuable to her than five dark-elves who would have been forced.

'All of you here have earned the honour,' Flek-Niht said. 'I do not doubt you will each again show yourself more than worthy of it.' She looked around the room, each of them looking at her now.

'Are we ready?' she asked.

They each nodded in reply and put a hand to their weapons, a sign they were ready to fight.

'Then it is time to go,' she said. 'Speak with the scouts and then ready your soldiers. This night we are one step closer to our dream, and in the morning we will dine on the edge of the dark waters!'

Each of them turned and left the tent, as Flek–Niht took out her own weapon.

'Tonight you will taste barbarian blood,' she said to it, as if she were speaking to a child. She smiled as she left her tent.

The moon hid itself momentarily behind some drifting clouds, as the last of the dark-elves moved into position. All was now exactly as it had been planned. Visibility was still good to each of those waiting outside the walls of the barbarian village.

There was no signal given. Those around Flek–Niht simply moved forward when given the word, and those within sight of them mirrored their movements. So it went, all the way around to the other side of the village.

Those who moved first waited for the ones beside them, so by the time they reached the walls, all of the dark-elf warriors arrived at almost the same time.

The plan was to enter the village and kill them all in a swarming attack.

Flek–Niht was excited as she grabbed the thin rope dangling from the wooden wall above her. Looking to those beside her, she smiled as she pulled herself upwards.

As she stood on the walkway behind the wall and looked down, she was surprised to see no guards and no-one moving around.

It was late and it was to be expected that most would be asleep, but the village looked almost deserted.

Only the wisps of smoke coming from several rooftops showed there was any life at all within the village.

A chill went up her back and she froze where she stood.

They knew her army was coming and they were ready for them.

Flek–Niht knew it was too late to call off the attack, so she needed to think fast to minimise her losses. Should she call those nearest to her and fortify their position, or should she have them hold where they stood.

Their current position gave them the advantage of attacking the barbarians from above. It was still a good a place to attack from, and considering the barbarians had yet to show themselves, they were obviously waiting for them to keep moving.

'Stay,' she hissed into the night.

The order was passed on quickly, but not before those further around the village had already made their way on to the ground.

Most of them turned around as they saw the ones next to them hesitate and hold their position, so none moved in among the houses and halls yet.

The dark-elves all just waited, looking around and waiting for something to happen. Waiting for their leader to make another decision.

Which is exactly what Flek-Niht was trying to do, but she wanted to first see what would come next. Where would the attack come from?

What would she have done if forewarned of an invading army?

Despite the night remaining eerily quiet, she sensed a quick decision was still needed. She felt it in the cold breeze running inland off the dark waters. Something was about to happen.

If she saw an army coming, the size of the one she had, Flek-Niht would know she could not hold out hope of stopping them from getting into the village.

The next best thing would be to have them enter and then surround them from outside.

Yet that would still leave them horribly outnumbered against a foe which could be at least as powerful as their own warriors.

She would need to devise of a way to inflict maximum casualties with the least amount of risk. They did not possess the ability to use real magic, other than in the weapons they wielded and the armour they wore, so she need not worry about that. They appeared to live a simple life and used simple means to defend themselves.

The liquid on the walls to make it difficult to climb was a simple ploy. Higher and stronger walls would have been smarter.

Surveying the village, Flek-Niht saw the same liquid smeared on the side of their houses closest to her. Was it to stop them climbing on the roof and shooting at them from high? That made little sense.

What is it they were waiting for? Then a thought came to her and her heart skipped a beat.

'Get everyone out,' she said to those next to her. 'Full retreat back over the walls as quickly as they can!' She tried to keep her voice low, but the urgency was enough to get them passing on the message. Flek-Niht quickly leapt back over the wall.

As soon as the first few started jumping back over the wall, Flek-Niht saw movement all around from outside the village.

Small fires began to appear, which were quickly fired into the air towards them.

Flek-Niht managed to hit the ground before the first of the burning arrows struck the wall.

She didn't need to turn around to see the wall erupt in flame.

The brightness that lit up the Barbarians before her and the screams of pain behind her, made it clear what had happened.

They had set their own village on fire. Both along the walls and inside.

Flek-Niht and her army of dark-elves, in their arrogance, had walked right over the top of their enemies as they hid under the ground.

'To me,' she roared, as those quick enough to evade the flames on the walls, moved toward where she stood.

There would be no killing anyone in their sleep tonight.

The barbarians facing them across the short clearing were wide awake and ready for a fight.

Roaring a war chant, they began sprinting at the dark-elves.

Flek-Niht gripped her weapons tight and roared her own battle-cry in defiance, as the barbarians charged into their ranks.

CHAPTER 71

Untouchable

B RINDEL HAD MIXED feelings as he strode out of the spoiled forest and back towards his home.

He was ecstatic that he had survived against the platinum dragon. What a beast she was! It was a real pity no other dwarf would ever believe he had fought her and survived. Just a couple of witnesses and his stocks as a smith would have soared above those even in the Southern Kingdom. He would tell Granwith and Kagen about it, but that would be all. The others would simply call him a liar and ridicule him some more. Granwith would just be angry that he missed out on fighting the dragon with him.

Which brought his thoughts back to his home.

The Western Dwarves would be there by now. He hoped they had been foiled in their attempts to access the mountain, but he was definitely nervous about it. There were just too many ways to get in, especially for a dwarf!

He did not know what to expect when he got back there.

As he began to walk south and avoid the swamplands to his left, his stomach began to cramp. It hit him much sooner and was a lot worse than the compulsion during his first task.

Turning himself to face the direction of his home, he took two steps towards the swamp and the pain disappeared.

As quickly as that and the pain was no longer there.

He walked through the same part of the forest as when he entered, but after he had exited, his path would need to take him in a direction a little further south this time.

Cursing as he stepped into the bog, the water immediately moved up level with his calf. It was almost as irritating as the thousands of bugs that began to hover around him, and the hundred or so that were brave enough to land and try to make their way under his armour.

It was going to be an itchy walk back to the forest.

The swamp ended before night arrived, for which he was thankful and Brindel was able to lie down on dry ground. Stripping off most of his armour he spent the first twenty minutes scratching at the bites scattered all over his body and scraping them off the inside of his armour and undergarments.

Once he was satisfied he had most of them, he put his armour back on.

He had yet to see anything threatening since he left the spoiled forest, so he was not too concerned about lying down to get some sleep, but he would not do it without protection.

Despite how uncomfortable it was pressed up against all of his bites, Brindel no longer had Kagen's companion to keep watch for him. He instead curled up in such a way that his face and neck were protected. He was confident his armour would keep him safe from any sneak attack while he slept.

At least long enough for him to wake up and defend himself properly with his axe.

Brindel awoke before the sun came up, stiff and sore from another night sleeping on the ground in his armour, but he was unharmed and ready to continue.

It was just after midday when he crested a rise and the forest of the elves came into sight, spread out before him. At the same time, the silhouette of his mountain home became visible in the distance.

It spurred him to increase his speed.

Brindel surprised himself at how quickly he covered the ground. Before the afternoon was gone, he was close enough to the forest to see the new devastation that had been caused to it.

There were no longer flames and only a little smoke, but a giant swathe of trees had been burnt and then shattered. It looked as if a dragon twice the size of the one he had just fought, had flown over the forest and razed it with its fiery breath.

As he approached closer, he could see the trees had not been flattened, but rather shattered and burnt.

The path he was being driven to by the compulsion was south of the damage, so he would not have to walk through it. He was happy with that. It would be much easier walking on flat ground than trying to make his way through that.

As Brindel entered the forest he felt no different. He hadn't been sure what to expect, but the fact there was no visible shield buzzing around him was a little disappointing.

As a result, a sinking feeling suddenly struck him. Maybe the dragon had lied to him and there was nothing to protect him as he walked confidently into the forest of the elves. That would be hilarious, he thought, as he slowly began to walk backward and out from under the trees.

He had not walked far, when the pain took hold of him again.

Brindel had no choice but to trust the dragon had been true with him.

He had walked for a couple of hours when the trail of destruction he had seen when he first walked into the forest, again crossed his path.

The devastation to the trees was no different this far in. Whatever had caused it had not lost any of its momentum or destructive power. It made Brindel think that perhaps the Western Dwarves had in fact killed the Elven Lord.

If he were alive still, he would not have let anything kill so many trees. Certainly not for such a great distance into the forest. All dwarves knew the elves loved their trees and did all sorts of weird rituals with them. He had heard it said they even liked to hug them while they were naked. He suspected that story had come from a dwarven warrior ridiculing elves, but it may still be true. Who was he to say it wasn't?

Crossing over the mangled trees, he looked further along and was surprised to see the destruction end. Perhaps another hundred paces further along, the mangled trees stopped and were surrounded by tall and healthy ones.

He was able to make out the bodies of many humans, half-goblins, orcs and other miscreants in that area. The dead started only a few paces in front of him and ended a further fifty paces along.

He had been wrong about the Elven Lord's demise. It had simply taken him a while to get here.

And by the look of the smouldering trees, it may have all happened only a short time ago.

Brindel was in awe at the sight before him.

The mangled bodies all looked to have died in excruciating pain. They were bloodied and twisted, some with their limbs ripped off.

He was mesmerised for a time, but quickly taken from his stupor by the pain returning, which propelled him forward again.

'I was hoping I would see you again dwarf,' a voice said from behind him.

Brindel turned and looked into the eyes of the Elven Lord, not ten paces away from him. They burned a bright orange, as if they were consumed by flames.

Although he was fairly confident he would be safe, there was still an involuntary part of the old dwarf that felt a sharp pang of panic in the pit of his stomach.

'Just passing through,' Brindel said, trying to sound jovial.

'Although I have much left to do, I still have time to cause you the suffering you deserve. Are there no creatures remaining who still fear to walk inside Glorfiden? I believed of all the creatures in these lands, a dwarf would be the last to dare trespass beneath these branches.' He paused. 'That will change again soon.'

Brindel could hear the madness in his voice. The Elven Lord was not the same elf as when Brindel had seen him last time. Something inside of him seemed to have snapped.

'I am sorry to see your forest looking a bit sad,' Brindel said. He couldn't help himself. Either he was about to die painfully, or else he was going to have some fun with the elf. 'Maybe you should not let so many orcs and humans in to play. Gives the rest of us way too much confidence.'

Brindel saw him lift his right arm and point it in his direction, but nothing happened.

He did the same movement again, and still nothing.

Another movement and this time Brindel saw the lightning shoot forth, coming straight at him.

The moment it was about to strike him, the magic disappeared and Brindel felt nothing. He couldn't help but close his eyes and flinch, before opening them again and checking to make sure he was still in one piece.

Smiling, he turned to continue on his way. He had stopped too long and the pain was returning.

He was still able to look over his shoulder though and see the elf casting spell after spell. Laughing out loud, Brindel turned back to face the way he was going. He realised ignoring the elf would probably make him even angrier.

Even knowing he was protected, Brindel couldn't help but stop as the elf dropped from a tree and landed only a few paces in front of him.

He had his sword out now and swung it at the dwarf's shoulder. Brindel flinched a little, suddenly unsure if the protection worked only against magic. When the Elven Lord's sword bounced harmlessly away from him, he knew it extended to weapons also.

He had almost pulled his axe out to defend the blow, before he remembered the dragon's warning. If he attacked anything, the protection would be gone. Defending himself would keep him safe, but he could reflexively move from defence to attack without even thinking about what he did. If that happened, he would die soon after.

'I am sorry elf, but you cannot harm me. My magic is stronger than yours.' Brindel walked around the elf in front of him, ignoring the look he gave him.

'It is not dwarven magic keeping you safe from me,' the elf said. His voice seemed calmer now, as he walked only a short distance behind Brindel.

'It is dwarven magic,' Brindel said. 'Strong magic. Stronger than elf magic.' He laughed at the absurdity of it all, and at the frustration he knew the elf would be feeling.

'It is something beyond what you yourself understand dwarf,' the elf said.

'Explain it to me then?' Brindel said. 'If you are able.'

There was no response and Brindel wasn't sure if the elf was still there.

'Perhaps whatever it is will wear off before you leave this forest,' the elf said, closer now.

'Unlikely,' Brindel said in a jovial voice. 'Dwarven magic is long lasting, just like a dwarf.'

'Or perhaps it is only protective while you are in Glorfiden,' the elf continued, still close behind Brindel. 'I wonder if you would be so confident if I escort you to the edge of the forest. You did not seem to have the same protection last time.'

Brindel realised it was too late for him to stop mocking the elf now. He knew if the elf followed him to the edge of the forest, he would not get very far. Perhaps one pace or maybe two.

This was an Elven Lord after all. An Elven Lord who had lost his mind and was in a killing frenzy.

'If you have nothing better to do, then I would enjoy your company,' Brindel said. 'What would you like to talk about? Did you see that amazing storm that came this way not even two weeks past?

'Good bye for now dwarf,' the elf said, almost whispering it in his ear this time. 'I will see you again soon. The trees will keep me updated with your progress through my forest. You will need a proper farewell before you leave.'

Brindel turned his head this time, but the elf was gone.

'He is bluffing,' Brindel said quietly to himself, as he picked up the pace a little.

That was not as much fun as he had hoped it would be.

CHAPTER 72

The Long Way Around

THE NEXT PART of her journey was relatively easy, although Linf remained hungry and had found nothing to absorb the life energy she craved.

She also had no further visits from the witch since her direction had changed.

'The cow probably thinks I am going this way for her,' Linf said out loud.

Maybe it was true, but she would never admit it. Perhaps she was listening to what Linf said, so letting her know the truth was important. 'Not doing this for you, you stinking pile of filth,' Linf yelled into the sky.

There was a large part of her that was curious about why the human witch wanted her to go in this direction. She risked her life each time she appeared, so it was definitely important to her.

But was it important to Linf? She knew it would continue to annoy her until she found out.

So long as the trip was not too draining or risky, then she would keep going this way. Although so far it had been boring and she was getting hungrier by the minute.

If she did not find something to feed on soon, Linf decided she would be changing direction again.

Then, just as she was about to stop and walk in a completely different direction, a movement to her right caught her attention.

At first she had no idea what it was.

There were very few trees in the immediate landscape, but it was also hilly in parts with long grasses and large bushes.

What she saw moving was coming in her direction from a flat stretch of ground.

As it came closer, she realised it was flying through the air, but only a short distance off the ground. It was why she had difficulty recognising it at first. Of course she had seen birds before; they were everywhere throughout the lands she had been through; but this one was larger than the others she had seen and none of those had hands at the end of their wings.

When it was almost upon her, Linf was able to make out the small dagger it held in each hand. She also got a look at the second one flying directly behind the first. That was a surprise, as she reached out her senses to them. As expected, there was no anger and no fear. They were intent on their prey and had full confidence in their abilities to take it down.

Moments before it struck, Linf fired off a ball of energy, striking the first one directly on the beak. It spiralled to her left and crashed in a heap on to the ground. The one behind it immediately turned right, before shooting off into the sky above. Linf watched it for a few moments longer to be sure it fled, before turning her attention to the fallen bird on the ground.

Walking over to it, she was fascinated with the hands on its wings and the daggers still firmly grasped within each. Although still alive, it looked to be in a lot of pain as it squawked loudly and thrashed around.

This time Linf was able to effortlessly draw the pain from it.

In less than half a minute its struggling ceased.

Reaching down, Linf grabbed a dagger from its lifeless hand. Remaining stooped over, she ran it through the chest of the large bird, cutting it open.

Putting her hand inside the wound, Linf was able to pull chunks of flesh from her victim without the mess of feathers getting in her way. Sitting down next to it, she kept eating until she was no longer hungry.

Stretching out beside it, she decided now was a good time to rest.

Trying hard to stay awake, Linf eventually stood up again. This was not a safe place to sleep and she was finding it very difficult not to close her eyes.

The direction the bird came from seemed like a better direction for her to take. She took it as a sign there would be more food that way and it was a different direction to the one the witch wanted her to take.

Although no longer hungry, she was getting bored. Perhaps a visit from her friend might cheer her up a little.

Despite walking for a couple of hours, the human did not show herself again. Linf assumed she was too afraid. Being drained once and then having her arm punctured by her claws had been too much for the weakling to handle.

The goblin would have been disappointed if not for the sight that now confronted her.

Looking down from the rise she stood on, Linf looked to her left. There was nothing but a giant swampland for as far as she could see. Rank ground bubbled and festered, with spindly trees, thick patches of long grass and sharp-looking bushes. Not somewhere she was keen to venture, but through which she would need to travel if she wanted to go in the direction the witch directed her.

Even if it were just the swamp, she would not go through it.

The fact there was a myriad of creatures spread out within it, just re-confirmed her decision. There were things out there she could only have imagined previously in her worst nightmares. Large tentacled monsters which looked like they were attached to the ground itself, their appendages swinging around looking for prey. She could see other things moving about, trying to stay clear of the large monsters while still looking to find their own prey. Most of those looked scary enough on their own.

There looked to be a lot going on down there and Linf was not interested in being part of it.

Straight ahead was no better though.

A large grassland that stretched for a distance, before it became a huge forest. Between where she now stood and the forest were thousands of creatures, as various as those in the swamp. Watching them for a time, Linf got no closer to working out what they were doing here. Yet they weren't all there for a friendly feast. It looked to her like they were here for a purpose and did not look to be going anywhere in a hurry.

'Are they waiting for me?' she asked aloud. 'Are you waiting for me?' she yelled into the distance.

Several creatures turned and looked in her direction, but none made any immediate move to approach her. She had suspected as much, which is why it was a surprise when a small group of animals shaped like *Krett* broke away and started bounding towards her.

'That might have been a dumb thing to do,' Linf said to herself.

As they got closer she counted eight of them.

A good-sized number, but she was still confident in defeating them. Even though simple animals were stupid and possessed no anger, they almost always had some degree of fear. These no longer looked like *Krett*. They ran on four legs and had large jaws designed for biting and rending flesh, but that is where the similarities ended. These things had spikes on their shoulders, which bristled as they ran, while the tail sat upright and curved up above it's back, pointed in the same direction it ran. There looked to be something pointed at the end of these tails. They had a thin dark-grey skin that shimmered a little in the sun, making it difficult to look directly at them for too long. Yet for all their differences, Linf knew they were of the same kind of animal as the *Krett* from her home lands.

Within each group of *Krett*, there was always a leader of their pack. One that the others all showed a deferential fear towards.

Reaching out with her powers, Linf discovered that the one in front showed absolutely no fear, but she was able to pick up small amounts coming from the others. There was just enough for her to grab hold of and draw out from them.

By the time the leader had crested the rise and was almost upon her, the rest of his pack were lying on the ground further back. Panting in distress, each of them had been drained to the point where they could no longer run, however Linf had not killed them.

As they ran toward her and she surmised what they were, Linf had devised a plan of sorts.

She remembered the lesson Brax had shown her in relation to his two horses. Drain them enough so they fear death, and then nurse them back to health so they think you saved them.

Linf thought it might work with these animals, but not in the same way as it did with a horse. These were obviously hunters, and so followed only the strongest.

As Linf prepared to shoot her ball of energy into their leader, a multitude of small projectiles were released into the air from its shoulders.

The goblin had only enough time to send her ball of energy at it. She had no time to try and do anything about the spikes, as several of the small projectiles embedded themselves into her chest and stomach.

They were extraordinarily sharp, and pierced her body almost through to her back.

Fortunately, her ball of energy had blasted her attacker into a mess of blood and shattered bones. It was no longer recognisable where it lay. Linf had intended to send the rest of the pack a message and she had.

Unfortunately, she was in no position to take advantage of it. Although none of the spikes had penetrated any of her vital organs, she was still hurting and losing a considerable amount of blood. The bone around the heart and lungs of a goblin were hardened. The two spikes that struck her there had bounced off.

It was some small consolation to Linf, as she groaned in pain each time she pulled one of the spikes from her body.

When it was all done, she stood gingerly and checked all of her wounds again, before walking down the rise to where the last of them had fallen.

It looked up and growled, but Linf knew it was too weak to make a move against her. She also saw the same deferential fear seeping from its body as before.

She had succeeded in the first part of her quickly formulated plan.

Linf had shown them who was strongest by easily killing their leader. Next, she needed to communicate to them that they needed to go with her now. She wanted them to accept her as their new leader.

Her plan was to have them follow and protect her. Perhaps even hunt for her.

'Why hadn't I thought of this earlier,' she said. Her goblin-kind had always had pets who they used for many different purposes.

Why should she not have her own pack?

Her only real obstacle was how she would communicate to them that she was now their leader and they must follow her. That was going to be the hard part.

Linf figured she may as well start with the first one. If it didn't work, she may have to set another example.

'Get up,' she said to it, indicating with her hands for it to rise.

It made no move. The blades on its tail remained on the ground, sweeping from side to side. Linf had no idea what that meant, but the level of fear had not changed.

Leaning down, she grabbed it by the skin at the back of its neck and lifted it off the ground.

This time the blades on its shoulders shuddered in response and its tail shot out like a dart, striking at her from over its head.

Linf was fast enough to grab the tail just below the blade and shove it down into the back of the beast. While it howled in pain, Linf sucked the remaining life energy from it. Kicking it to the side, she moved on to the next one.

This one peered at her from the corner of its eyes, its head on the ground and its tail motionless behind it. It's level of fear was greater than the last had been. Looking down at the others lying on the slope further down, their levels of fear had also gone up marginally.

'Now we are getting somewhere,' Linf said to them. 'Perhaps the rest of you may not have to die.'

Then a thought occurred to her. They had all been struck down by her and rendered too exhausted to get up. How could she expect them to suddenly regain their strength and follow after her?

Perhaps she had expected too much too soon of the one she had just killed.

Patience was not something she possessed, but Linf realised if she wanted her own pack of *Vleyk*, she may need to give them the chance to get their strength back. Vleyk was the goblin word for blades and she thought it an appropriate name for them. If they regained their strength, she would be able to use that as a punishment and reward to get them to understand her.

'You can rest for a little while,' she said to them, looking out over the land between her and the forest again. Despite what was down there, no others had decided to chance their luck against the goblin.

Whether they were scared because of what she had done to the Vleyk, or whether they simply were not interested, it didn't concern Linf. So long as they stayed down there.

When her new pack of Vleyk were well enough to follow her, she decided she would go back the way she had just come.

She would need to go around the swampland if she wanted to go where the witch wanted her to.

Unless something more interesting came along, that was her new intention.

And now she would have others to do her hunting for her.

Things were looking up for the runt, and Linf was finally pleased with her situation.

Things might have finally started going her way.

CHAPTER 73

Mind Games

'WHAT IS SHE doing?' Kabir asked Linf, looking across at her from where he sat in front of his own *eye*.

None of them had said much since the Creator's last visit. It had been a shock to all of them and not what any of them had come to expect from him.

Linf looked across at him.

'I think she is starting to listen to me,' she said to him. 'I was confident she would eventually.'

'Are you looking at something different to the rest of us?' Mortinan asked her.

She chose to ignore his words. Linf was confident one of the others would answer for her. Probably Brindel, considering he had not said anything for a while.

'A pity she is unlikely to go through the swamp,' Brindel said, on cue. 'I believe your Champion Mortinan, has enough fear and anger for her to see him from a great distance. Linf's Champion is one creature that would get the better of your half-elf,' he finished.

'Unlike your dwarf,' he retorted. 'How do you think he will fare once he is out of the forest? I believe he will get only what he deserves,' Mort said.

'I agree with you there Mortinan. Perhaps I will be able to assist him in some small way with that,' Brindel said. 'It would seem his sharp tongue may have landed him into a little bit of trouble.'

'He will die or you will die,' Mortinan said. 'Either way you are out of this contest. It will be sad to see you go.'

'Thank you Mortinan,' Brindel said. 'I will also miss our chats.'

He turned to look at Linf.

'I must admit though, I am also confused at your comment Linf. Why do you think your Champion is now listening to you? She looks to be simply going in the direction of least resistance.'

'I know my Champion Brindel. She is starting to come around.' It didn't really matter to her what they thought, but it was nice to converse again. There was too much silence within this clearing.

'I meant no insult,' Brindel replied. 'To you,' he added.

'Thank you Brindel,' Linf said. 'I know you didn't.'

She turned back to her *eye*. It was enjoyable watching her Champion's efforts in training the pack of *Vleyk*. Although it would probably take some time and effort to have them understand what she wanted, in the short term she believed Linf might be able to get them to follow without trying to kill her.

They might come in handy finding food for her.

Once she made her way around the great swampland, it was a fairly easy run to the Dragon's Forest. Most creatures within the realm were either fighting in the armies of Mithrak, had fled the battle at High Fort, or were waiting for Mortinan to return home. Her Champion should have a fairly comfortable trek, all going well.

But of course, things never seemed to just 'go well' in this game.

The *Vleyk* would at least provide her with companionship and give her the skills to try and lead others. Both were attributes and abilities she needed to get better at. Companions was something she had never had before, not counting Brax. She had a taste of it with him, but that had ended badly. Animals such as these, that could eventually show her loyalty, may be invaluable for what was to come.

Once back home amongst her own kind, she would need to try and find friends and allies. If not, she would be consumed by them. She was an outcast before and had barely escaped with her life.

Even with her new powers, she could not fight them all.

First things first however. She needed to get to the dragon and then she needed to survive against it.

Linf had one more opportunity to enter the world of Dark Swell and she had already decided when she would do it.

Before her Champion reached the dragon, she would need to pass on her last remaining piece of advice. She smiled as she thought about what she would say. Mortinan thought himself so clever, but he would never be able to foresee what she intended to do.

'How does your Champion fare now Mortinan?' she asked him, looking over at where he sat looking into his *eye*.

He looked surprised by her question, as he shifted his head to look over at her. The look of surprise quickly turned to one of disdain.

'He is obviously still the best placed of all of us,' he said, looking away from Linf before he had even finished his sentence.

She continued smiling as she looked at him.

'Even with all that is waiting for him at the edge of the swamp?' she continued. Despite his arrogant dismissal of her first question, she was feeling a little playful. 'There are some creatures of tremendous power within the swamp,' she said. 'Not an ideal battle ground for a half-elf.'

Mortinan took a deep sigh, before looking across at her again.

'Why are you annoying me?' he asked. 'It is bad enough Brindel thinks of it as a sport, I would expect better from you Linf.'

'You began by questioning my own Champion,' she replied. 'Am I not permitted to do the same?'

'Your questions are obvious ones, where the answers are clear for all to see. They don't require an answer from me. My question was a reasonable one.' He continued to look at her this time.

'Fine,' she conceded. 'I was just wanting to have a conversation with you, but only because they are always enlightening.'

'I would think you had more important things to do,' he suggested. 'Such as your final entry into the world.'

'Oh that,' she said, acting as if she wasn't really concerned with it. 'I already know when I am going to enter and exactly what I intend to say.'

'Things can change,' Mortinan said. 'You should not be so sure of what you are going to do.'

'It will not matter,' she said. 'It is what I most need to do to ensure my Champion will win this game.'

Mortinan chuckled.

'That will not happen,' he said.

'We will see,' Linf said with a smile. 'You will see.'

CHAPTER 74

Race To The Forest

THE JOURNEY FROM when she left Mort and the moment she caught sight of the mighty forest that was her home, was uneventful. Mendina was surprised at just how deserted the land was that she travelled through.

A few small animals and larger grazing ones were the only signs of life anywhere in the land she traversed.

There was no sign of intelligent life, no scouting parties from those that lived further north and south and no settlements.

Mendina found places to stay along the way and slept surprisingly well. She knew it was because she was so tired, both mentally and physically.

She missed Mort's companionship. It was not just because of the fear she felt travelling alone, it was not knowing what it was they were each travelling towards.

After days of walking she finally came to a spot where she could clearly see the forest before her once more and Mendina's heart missed a beat.

The last part of her journey had been skirting the northern end of a small mountain range.

She had been able to see parts of Glorfiden spread out before her early the day before, but it was only as she topped the last rise before the forest that she could make out a sea of forms that moved outside the border of Glorfiden.

There were both men and beast milling about, spread out for hundreds of paces along the edge of the trees. Mendina did not yet know what their purpose was, but there would have been at least a thousand of them.

She ducked back over the ridge, not wanting to risk being seen by any of them.

Crawling back to where she could sneak another look at them, Mendina assessed her next move.

From what she could see, none of them were entering the forest. She saw no movement amongst the trees and none were closer than one hundred paces to the forest itself.

Taking a longer look, she saw that some camps had been set up even further away from the forest. There were none of the frantic movements she would expect from a force ready to attack, but she had not had any experience with armies before now. Perhaps she was completely mistaken, however it looked more like they were settling in to where they were or else waiting for something to happen.

Mendina looked to her right and was horrified to see a similar number of creatures away in the distance. They were further away than the ones she saw first and she was unable to make out individuals, but there looked to be just as many lined up along there.

She wondered how many more gatherings there were along the border of her home.

Looking at the space between them, Mendina tried to guess the time it would take her to make it to the forest, from the time when they would likely first spy her.

If she managed to work her away along behind this ridge line to the point in between the two forces, then she knew she would make the forest in plenty of time.

Walking back down a small distance to be sure she wouldn't be seen, the small elven girl began walking further south.

As soon as Mendina had walked about fifty steps the cramps began in her stomach. She knew she had to keep going, but she managed only another ten steps before the pain doubled her over in agony and she fell to her knees.

Mendina crawled towards the rise and the pain disappeared. She stood again and carefully made her way between trees, so she would be able to see the forest again.

She would have to move towards the forest from here and she was horrified at the thought of it.

Mendina knew once she was inside the forest, none of the men or creatures milling outside would catch her. Even if they dared enter Glorfiden, they would never find her within.

If they did enter, she knew Jarkene would sense them. Maybe some of the elves were just inside the border of the forest now, watching those that swarmed outside. Perhaps they were simply waiting to see when and where they would enter. She knew these creatures had not come all this way in such large numbers to simply stand outside and look at the trees.

As she looked again at those to her left, she saw several figures further along on horseback. They were approaching the main force from the rear. The same direction she had travelled from. As they got close, Mendina saw the creatures they rode may not be horses.

Their riders were shaped like men, but had thick, dark cloaks disguising their appearance. Activity amongst those waiting suddenly increased and Mendina quickly surmised that she needed to move now.

It was still only the middle of the day and Mendina knew she would not be able to wait for night to make her move. The compulsion within her would not let her wait that long. Already she could feel it stirring within her as she lay there on her stomach contemplating.

Taking a deep breath, she began to snake her way along the ground, moving slowly, but without pause.

Mendina tried to keep her focus in front, but she could not stop herself looking to her left regularly as she pulled herself forward.

She could hear them now. They were making no effort to be quiet. They were probably aware that once they entered the forest there would be no hiding for them anyway.

Mendina continued to move, slowly slithering forward and then stopping. The less frequently she moved, the greater were her chances of not being seen.

Still some distance away from the forest and not even to the flat ground yet, Mendina froze when all sound at the gathering stopped.

Just prior to the noises sharply ceasing she had heard a loud, guttural yell.

Looking across, Mendina could just make out one of those on horseback standing high in his stirrups. He was speaking loudly and facing her from the other side of the main host. Although she could hear him clearly, Mendina could not understand any of the words he was saying. But from what he was doing, she guessed he was rallying them for an attack on her home. Slowing her breathing once more, Mendina continued to slide along the ground. For a terrifying moment, she thought they had seen her.

The fear and hopelessness of the situation nearly overcame her as she began moving again. She felt a tightening in her chest as she thought about how unfair this all was and how hopeless her own situation and that of her home was.

Most of her people had been slain by the one who now protected what was left. Given the time to heal, Glorfiden and the elves would have thrived again, she just knew it.

Yet now there were enemies at her boundaries numbering in the hundreds; quite possibly thousands. Even with all of his powers, Jarkene could not hope to slaughter every last one of them.

And he had given the storm rod to Mortinan.

She came out of her self-pity for a moment and looked back at the horde. The one on horseback had stopped talking and the sudden quiet drew her attention once more.

Looking across, it appeared he was pointing in her direction. All of the hopelessness she had felt only moments before was washed away, as a primal fear totally overcame her.

Jumping to her feet Mendina started to sprint for the safety of the forest as every creature within the gathering started sprinting towards her.

Coming down off the slope, Mendina almost stumbled as she hit the flat ground, but somehow managed to keep her feet under her. She continued to sprint for all she was worth.

She thought about tossing Jarkene's staff to give her more speed, but Mendina knew she would need it if they came upon her before she made it to the trees.

Looking across as she ran, Mendina saw a small group of them break away towards the forest to try and cut her off. They had obviously seen how fast she moved. They were on horseback and she realised they were the ones who had only recently joined the others within the gathering.

There were blood wolves too, which she watched streak out in front of the main force.

Although they were closing in fast, Mendina believed she might still get to the forest before they reached her.

Turning her attention back to the trees and the ground in front of her, there was nothing to it now but to run as fast as her legs could carry her. They would either catch her, kill her or she would make it in time.

As her confidence began to grow a little, a fireball scorched through the air in front of her, missing her face by only a few paces. She felt the heat of it as it passed and couldn't help but look across again.

Those on the horses were closer now, their hoods blown back by the wind in their faces. Dark-Mage! Mendina thought momentarily of stopping and confronting them, but she knew if she did the other abominations running behind would be upon her in no time. Even with Jarkene's staff and the amulet, she would be no match for them.

Looking back to the forest again, she saw an elf step out from behind a tree and shoot a fire arrow from his bow. It crackled through the air and struck one of those on horseback, sending him and his steed crashing into the turf.

Palir stepped back behind the cover of the tree as two fireballs tore into the forest, hitting only the air where he had been standing moments before.

'Run!' he called out to Mendina, as he pulled another arrow from his quiver and set it alight using his magic. 'You need to run faster!' he roared, as he cocked it to his bow.

She could hear the panic in his voice as he stepped out again from behind the tree and fired off the arrow.

A second rider fell, as the last one sent another fireball at Palir, this time impacting the tree he again stood behind.

'Watch out!' she heard him cry, as he stepped once more from behind the tree. She turned from him and looked to her left. The fireball struck her front on as she turned her body to look at it. The impact scorched her clothes surrounding the amulet, while the rest of the fireball was absorbed. The shock slowed her run to a jog, as she looked down at the flames flickering on the outside of the amulet. That should not have happened Mendina thought, as she patted out the small flames on her jacket. When fighting the dragon, the amulet had absorbed all of the damage.

A frightening thought struck her and she nearly tripped. What if it was full?

With renewed fear, she began sprinting again. Her adrenaline pushed her to go even faster.

She was still only half way to full speed however, when the fireball left the hand of the last Dark-Mage and streamed straight at her. She knew this time it would not miss and she had no time to jump out of the way.

Wide-eyed, she watched as one of Palir's arrows struck the ball of fire ten paces in front of her, exploding it prematurely mid-air.

Mendina was stunned for a moment and her sprint slowed once more, before Palir brought her out of her stupor.

'Run!' he screamed at her, as she turned to look at him again. 'Don't stop Mendina!' Her feet once more began moving her involuntarily towards the trees.

Mendina saw Palir behind the tree, holding out his hand as she closed the gap to him.

'What are you doing?!' she had time to yell.

Why didn't he kill the last one?

It was her final thought as a fireball impacted the side of her head, mere paces from the edge of her home.

Mendina was dead before her body even hit the ground.

CHAPTER 75

One More Gone

ORTINAN LOOKED INTO his *eye* again at the fallen elf on the ground, just to make sure she was actually dead. The horrific wounds inflicted by the fireball left him in no doubt. It was difficult to recognise her.

He looked away from his *eye* and across at Mendina. She sat there with a stunned look on her face, still staring into her own *eye*. As he would have expected.

Then she furrowed her brow and looked across at Mortinan with a more relaxed look on her face. That he had not expected.

If it were he who had just been removed from the game, he would be feeling all sorts of emotions. Contemplation would not be one of them.

He assumed she had simply accepted her fate. After all, her Champion was never going to be victorious. She had survived far longer than he thought she would.

As the Creator appeared, Mortinan began to move his head in his direction, but stopped himself.

The look of horror and surprise on her face at his appearance made Mortinan wonder what was truly going on in her mind. It had apparently not been a look of acceptance.

Then he shrugged and turned away from her to see if the Creator had anything important to say.

Mendina's frame of mind no longer concerned him.

She would shortly step through her *eye*.

Her game was over.

END OF BOOK 3

GLOSSARY OF DARK SWELL

<u>MORTINAN & MENDINA</u>

JARKENE –	MORT'S FATHER
COREIN -	MORT'S MOTHER
TIMYN –	MENDINA'S FATHER
ENTINE –	MENDINA'S MOTHER
GLENDROND –	JARKENE'S FATHER
PERILLIAN –	JARKENE'S BROTHER
QUANEILLAN –	JARKENE'S BROTHER
PALIR -	SURVIVING MALE ELF
FLYNN -	SURVIVING FEMALE ELF
TREILLE -	SURVIVING MALE ELF
ELTRIK -	SURVIVING MALE ELF
AIMON -	SURVIVING ELF - FRIEND OF MENDINA
THRINNE -	SURVIVING FEMALE ELF
RHANC -	SURVIVING MALE ELF
TRAVIS –	VALLEY OF ROCK CATS
LORD HATHAM -	LORD OF MAYFIELD

KABIR

WILHELM –	KABIR'S BROTHER
RONDIG –	KABIR's FATHER – DEERSTEP CHIEFTAIN
DENIZEN –	PLAINSMAN - CAPTAIN
TREMILL –	PLAINSMAN WARRIOR
CRENSHEN –	PLAINSMAN - CHIEFTAIN
FIRTH –	KABIR'S HORSE
GRISTENN –	SON OF GRINSOM – OWNED FIRTH
HALLOR –	PLAINSMAN SCOUT
FENTIN –	PLAINSMAN SCOUT
KRITHEL –	PLAINSMAN - KILLED BY INSECT
PETEIR –	PLAINSMAN - FRIEND OF KRITHEL
FESTEN –	PLAINSMAN - AROUND CAMPFIRE
GREGG –	PLAINSMAN - AROUND CAMPFIRE
ARTON –	PLAINSMAN - KILLED BY TREE
GROGAN –	HIGHLAND CHIEFTAIN – WOLFSBANE
MEGHAN –	WILHELM'S FRIEND
FASTERN –	MEGHAN's HORSE

HENGRAT –	BOY WHOSE BODY TAKEN FROM INSECT
GINDRED -	FATHER OF HENGRAT – WITH TREMILL
MITCHALL -	PLAINSMAN – CARRIED HENGRAT
BAGHAN -	SWORDSMITH
ARTER -	BAGHAN'S SON
AHLIA -	DAUGHTER OF CRENSHEN
ETHAN -	WIZARD – SHADOW HILL
YANDOW -	WIZARD – SHADOW HILL
METHAN -	SOLDIER – SHADOW HILL
FARGESH -	EASTERN BARBARIAN
HERID -	EASTERN BARBARIAN
DOUGAL -	CHIEFTAIN – HORNED PEAK
KRITH -	BARBARIAN SLAIN BY DARK ELVES
BRINN -	EASTERN BARBARIAN – SENT FOR HELP
FRETA -	EASTERN BARBARIAN
SCRAFF -	SON OF DOUGAL
DEVON -	EASTERN BARBARIAN – HORNED PEAK

LINF

BRAX –	LINF'S COMPANION/MENTOR/CAPTOR
HORSES	- STORM CLOUD
	- DARK STAR
GREEBLE –	CHIEFTAIN – FATHER OF LINF
MERTHIC -	GREEBLE'S 2ND IN COMMAND – INJURED
MORKIN –	FARMER/WIZARD
MELKOR –	MORKIN'S SON
HARRIET –	MORKIN'S WIFE
ETHAN -	WIZARD – SHADOW HILL
HELBOT -	GUARD – SHADOW HILL
ATRIOL -	KINGS SHIELD – SHADOW HILL
LORD MARCUS -	LORD AT SHADOW HILL
FLORREK –	GOBLIN CHIEFTAIN AFTER GREEBLE
DALMORX -	2ND IN COMMAND TO FLORREK
LORRICH -	ONE OF FLORREK'S GUARDS
MURCHEN -	FLORREK'S COUSIN / GUARD
RAIF -	LEADER OF GOBLIN VILLAGE
SHATHEZ -	RAIF'S VILLAGE
GURTH -	RAIF'S VILLAGE – CRINTIN HANDLER

GORTH -   LINF'S BROTHER

VITCH -   WESTERN ORC
FLORKE -   WESTERN ORC
GORT -   WESTERN ORC – GUARD/GUIDE

RARK -   LAVA ORC

PRELCH -   CHIEFTAIN CONTENDER
QALZ -   CHIEFTAIN CONTENDER

GRATH -   KILLED BY RAIF

VALDOR

CATLIN –	KING'S SHIELD – VALDOR'S FRIEND
HERIDAH –	WIZARD / AREANA'S PROTECTOR HORSE IS 'ARROW'
AREANA –	PRINCESS – DAYHEN'S DAUGHTER
KING DAYHEN –	KING OF HUMAN REALM
DEREKIA –	DAYHEN'S LEAD WIZARD
DUKE OF LETHERIS –	AREANA'S BETROTHED
LORD THAIDEN –	COMMANDER OF DAYHEN'S ARMIES
MELLOR –	DAYHEN'S CHAMBERLAIN/ COREIN'S FATHER
MILLON –	KINGS SHIELD – FIGHTS SQUARGRIN
WERKITH –	KINGS SHIELD – FIGHTS SQUARGRIN
VICTOR –	KINGS SHIELD – FIGHTS SQUARGRIN
GRENTHEM –	KINGS SHIELD – FIGHTS SQUARGRIN
MARKEL –	STABLE BOY – CAPITAL

BRENTON -	GUARD POST – HAVERN
TALOR -	KINGS SHIELD – HAVERN
GARETH -	WIZARD – HAVERN
FLETCHER -	WIZARD – HAVERN
CLADEN -	OLD MAN – KING'S SHIELD HOME
BILSONT -	KING'S SHIELD – FORMER LEADER
CAPTAIN RANKIN -	GUARD CAPTAIN - LAKERTH
BRAND -	GUARD – LAKERTH
THATCH -	WIZARD - LAKERTH
LORD JARON -	LORD OF HAVERN – BRAX'S FATHER
PORTHON -	JARON'S STEWARD
TRINTE -	HANDMAIDEN TO AREANA
LORD BANTAN -	CHIEF OF THE WEST
LORD KYLLE -	CHIEF OF THE EAST
CLERON -	HIGH RANKING KING'S SHIELD - LAKERTH
FLOUTH -	DWARVEN MASON
PRUKIN -	FLOUTH'S WORKER
BRADIC -	SOLDIER – MESSENGER IN LAKERTH

LORD MARCUS - LORD OF SHADOW HILL

ATRIOL - KING'S SHIELD – SHADOW HILL

ETHAN - WIZARD – SHADOW HILL

YANDOW - WIZARD – SHADOW HILL

METHAN - CAPTAIN – SHADOW HILL

MIKAEL - KING'S SHIELD – SHADOW HILL

BRYCEN - WIZARD – SHADOW HILL

PALINDA - WIZARD – SHADOW HILL

PATRIC - KING'S SHIELD – SHADOW HILL

DARID - KING'S SHIELD –
LAKERTH - ARCHER

BRINDEL

KAGEN –	CHILD - FRIEND OF BRINDEL
FENG -	KAGEN'S PET
BRANWEN –	STEWARD AT NORTHERN KINGDOM
KING DRAUG -	NORTHERN DWARVEN KING
CAPTAIN FORSYTHE –	KILLED BY BRINDEL AT WAY STATION
GRANWITH -	GREATEST DWARVEN WARRIOR
GRANWEN -	BROTHER OF GRANWITH
ELENDA -	1ST APPRENTICE TO MASTER SMITH
KEGAN -	MERCHANT - SOUTHERN DWARF
BRANGOLD -	MASTER SMITH – SOUTHERN KINGDOM
BLEYNT -	GUARD – SOUTHERN DWARF - SOUTH
DENITH -	GUARD – SOUTHERN DWARF - WEST
THADIS -	GUARD – SOUTHERN DWARF – WEST
TREYNITH -	GUARD – NORTHERN DWARF

QUIRREL –	GUARD – NORTHERN DWARF
TREGIN –	WARRIOR – NORTHERN DWARF
WENDAL –	OLD WARRIOR – NORTHERN DWARF
BURGETT –	KING'S GUARD – NORTHERN DWARF
BRAYDEN –	ASSASSIN – SOUTHERN DWARF
JORWEN –	SMITH – SOUTHERN DWARF
DRAAF –	WARRIOR – NORTHERN DWARF
CRANDLE –	WARRIOR – NORTHERN DWARF
FLORGH –	LEADER – NORTHERN DWARF

WESTERN REALM

MITHRAK –   KING – DARK-MAGE

KRITCH –   KING – OGRE MAGE

RASTISS –   DARK-MAGE
CORDAK –   DARK-MAGE
JEOSH –   DARK-MAGE
THRISC –   DARK-MAGE
FLITCH –   DARK-MAGE

JURG –   MITHRAK'S GENERAL – VE-KARN

ZUROTH –   KING OF THE WESTERN DWARVES
KROFF –   WESTERN DWARF
LIRTH –   WESTERN DWARF SCOUT
BRISHNER –   WESTERN DWARF WARRIOR

DARK-ELVES

DOTH-LINQ –	DARK-ELF WARRIOR
MIRT-KRIL –	SON of FLEK-NIHT
PARZ-MELD –	DARK-ELF WARRIOR
FLEK-NIHT –	DARK-ELF 1st ELDER
HELV-PLIR –	DARK-ELF ELDER
LORN-QUOD –	DARK-ELF ELDER
CLEN-JONT –	DARK-ELF ELDER
GLIM-STAD –	A LEADER OF DALK-ELF ARMY
GLIN-PELN –	A LEADER IN DARK-ELF ARMY

CREATURES

SQUARGRIN -	TREE-SWINGING CREATURES
BLOOD-WOLVES -	WOLVES – DARK-MAGE PETS
HALF-GOBLINS -	LIVING NORTH OF GLORFIDEN
BLACK OOZE -	IN DWARVEN TUNNELS
DEATH SPIKE -	PLAINS TREE
SCRITHON -	GIANT CAT OF THE EAST PLAINS
HOBGOBLINS -	NORTHERN DWARF MOUNTAINS
GOBLIN WIGHT -	UNDEAD GOBLINS
KRICKSHEN -	DWARVEN MONSTER OF LEGEND
CRINTIN -	GOBLIN TRACKING HOUNDS
KRETT -	GOBLIN REPTILES
MURTIIN -	PSIONIC CREATURES
FREEGOL -	LARGE-TUSKED PRIMATE
ORCS -	WESTERN REALM ARMY
OGRES -	WESTERN REALM ARMY

TROLLS –	WESTERN REALM ARMY
CRELCH –	TORTURE CREATURE
LOKAAN –	CAVE DWELLING GOLEM
FETCHLING –	TUNNEL CREATURES
TELQUIN –	DARK-ELF MOUNTS
VIGGLERS –	SMALL SLEEP-INDUCING CREATURES
KORN –	LEADING VIGGLERS
VLEYK –	WESTERN REALM BLADED CANINES
LOUCKRIFT –	BLOOD-SUCKING MONSTERS

PLANTS AND TREES

CACHAN BERRIES –   LOCATED IN GLORFIDEN
FEATHERLEAF TEA –   LOCATED IN GLORFIDEN

GINSENG –   LOCATED IN PLAINS

FAIRIE-DRAGONS

LINN –	JARKENE
YORN –	TREILLE
EBO –	MENDINA
KILAT - silver	MORTINAN
ISKA – plain/multi–coloured	MORTINAN

BARBARIAN VILLAGES

DEERSTEP -   FURTHEST WEST
                 LARGEST SETTLEMENT
                 CHIEFTAIN – RONDIG

WOLFSBANE -   CENTRAL VILLAGE
                 BETWEEN HORNED PEAK AND
                 THE FORGE
                 SECOND LARGEST
                 CHIEFTAIN – GROGAN

LAND'S END -   FURTHEST EAST
                 OVERLOOKS THE DARK SWELL
                 CHIEFTAIN – FIOR

HORNED PEAK -   BETWEEN LAND'S END AND
                 WOLFSBANE
                 CHEIFTAIN – DOUGAL

CLEAR WATER -   BETWEEN DEERSTEP AND THE
                 FORGE
                 SITS ON A LARGE LAKE
                 CHIEFTAIN – GUSTUS

THE FORGE -   BETWEEN CLEAR WATER AND
                 WOLFSBANE
                 MINERS OF IRON AND STONE
                 CHIEFTAIN - KASTOR

ABOUT THE AUTHOR

DAVID DOWELL WORKS full-time in Emergency Services in country Victoria, Australia. Inspired by a deep love of fantasy adventure, and an active participant of role-playing games when he was younger, Dowell has now penned the first three novels in his fantasy series `The Gods of Dark Swell'.

"I have often imagined my own work propped up on my book shelf - right next to some epic fantasy series. I understand the need for a captivating and adventurous story, but in addition to that I wanted to create characters with real personalities that readers will grow to love or despise.

The Gods of Dark Swell is as character driven as it is story driven, taking place in a world and concept unique in many ways to the fantasy genre."

CPSIA information can be obtained
at www.ICGtesting.com
Printed in the USA
BVHW032112071119
563198BV00011B/7/P